After the Thaw

Therese Heckenkamp

Ivory Tower Press

www.ivorytowerpress.com

Fleuron by Foglihten DecoH02

Cover design by Elena Karoumpali (L1graphics)

Published by
Ivory Tower Press
www.ivorytowerpress.com

Printed in the United States of America

Also by Therese Heckenkamp:

Frozen Footprints

Past Suspicion

*For everyone who wanted a sequel
to Frozen Footprints.*

*And in loving memory of my brother.
Jerome, you are missed more deeply
than words can describe.*

*"Eternal rest grant unto him, O Lord,
and may perpetual light shine upon him."*

"For though I should walk in the midst of the shadow of death, I will fear no evils, for thou art with me."

— Psalms 22:4

Prologue

She was dying. No matter how she danced around it in her letter, Clay Morrow knew his ma well enough to read between the lines. The cancer was consuming her.

But how much longer did she have? Months? Weeks? Days?

He squeezed the paper, crumpling it in his fist, regretting it instantly because this might be her last letter, her last words to him.

"Move it," barked a voice behind him.

He tried not to flinch at the jab in his back.

My own fault.

He knew better than to drift into thought out here, knew he had to be alert if he didn't want to be an easy target. He picked up his pace and followed the orange-suited men into the yard—the razor-wire-topped, metal-fenced, cement yard. Guard towers punctuated the corners, and correctional officers patrolled the prison perimeter, on alert for any unruly action.

Clay gladly turned from the sight of his reality to glance at the sky. It was smeared with soggy gray clouds, but the fresh air felt good, smelled good. Man, it even tasted good. And look at that, the first snow of the season. Or at least, he amended, the first snow that he was aware of.

A shiver of something—a pathetic remnant of childhood fascination, maybe—came over him as he watched the flakes sift down. Dear God, for all it reminded him of, he wanted to hate the snow, but he couldn't.

"Hey, Cissy!"

Clay clenched his teeth. Company. Great, just what he never wanted here. And that name, that lamest of nicknames. He'd like to know who first leaked the fact that Tarcisius was his middle name. If any con tried spelling it, he wondered if they'd be smart enough to use the "C." Probably not.

However the name had been discovered, it didn't much matter now. His first week here, he'd backed down from a fight, ending up with a broken nose anyway. Didn't exactly create a tough reputation.

Yeah, he'd been known to walk away from potential fights, but he didn't care. By his way of thinking, not much was worth getting busted up over and then thrown in the hole for. His plan was to finish his time quietly, with as little trouble as possible, and be out in two months.

Surprisingly, time was passing. Reading helped. So did the gym. He'd even found some satisfaction working in the woodshop. Just thinking about it, he flexed his hands, not minding that his skin was worn rough, his palms calloused and cracked. The physical labor and the smell of lumber brought him a little closer to the outdoors that he missed so much. The real outdoors, not this nature-bereft, concrete yard.

"Cissy!" the voice yelled again.

His fingers tightened on the letter. Not being free to see his ma, be with her when she needed him most—that was the real punishment here.

"Ya deaf, Cissy?" An inmate of wiry proportions and greasy sparse brown hair stepped in front of him. Weasel had earned his nickname for obvious reasons. He was an offensive, slick, agile side-kick to a con called Nails.

Rumor had it Nails had pulled off twenty-plus armed-robberies before being busted. His charge had been small, though, and his sentence light. Woe to the world when he was released.

Clay had been fortunate to avoid coming under his radar.

Till now.

Nails, his big chin cocked loftily, stood looking down on him with an expression Clay didn't care to read. He glanced instead at the guy's powerful forearms, bare in the chill air and sporting tattoos of scattered nails.

Not ordinary round nails, either. Long angular ones. The kind the ancient Romans pounded through people.

Clay resumed walking, distinctly disliking the foreboding swelling his gut.

Both cons fell in step alongside him, one on either side, stealing the fresh air. Replacing it with prison stench.

Weasel turned to face him. "Nails's got something to say to you, Cissy, so listen up."

"Here's the deal," Nails said pleasantly, walking with an easy swagger and aiming a predatory smile and nod at a female CO on the perimeter. The foolish woman actually acknowledged him with something close to a smile and a slight dip of her head.

"I think we need to come to an understanding," Nails continued, focusing again on Clay. "You and me, our bids are almost up. We'll be out within a year. It'll be time to get back to work. One last big job, a job to end all jobs. And you're the ticket." He smacked his fist into his palm. "I know you've got connections with a certain Perigard." He paused, as if waiting for Clay to fill in details.

"You know who I'm talking about." Nails's tone lost some friendliness. "That Charlene girl with the Perigard fortune. She's the key into her billionaire grandfather's mansion, and the way I figure it, you're the key to her. I got connections and I hear how it was with you two. You kidnap her, torture her, and she still defends you on the stand." Something like leering admiration surfaced in his voice. "What won't she do for you?"

Weasel chuckled in the background.

Clay was still struggling to think past hot anger at hearing Charlene's name on Nails's foul lips. His first instinct was to curse him out, but he bit back the urge. "Your connections are wrong."

"Don't be modest." Nails grinned. "I wanna hear all about her. Does she write to you? Visit you? Is she waiting for you to get out?"

Clay clamped his tongue and kept walking.

Patience left Nails's voice. "You make this happen, man, and I can promise you an easy time in your last months here, and enough dough to take care of you once you're out. They say the old Perigard scrooge doesn't trust banks. He's got a fortune stashed away in a safe. Once we're in, it'll be an easy job. What do you say?"

Nothing. Clay picked up his pace, but he knew the discussion wasn't going to end that simply.

"You don't make this happen, kid, and I can promise you a very unpleasant time in your last months here. Your choice."

Clay half-realized his ma's letter was growing moist in his fist. "It would never work. Perigard and I aren't ever gonna see each other again, and anyway, I heard she was disowned by her grandfather. She's got no money." He knew he should add, *She's worthless,* but he couldn't bring himself to say it. "She'd be no help."

"I'll be the judge of that." Nails sent him a mocking glance. "What do you know? You're what, barely twenty?"

Twenty-two.

"You in?"

"Nope."

"Afraid? You're even more of a coward than everyone says," Weasel sneered, letting loose a string of scathing insults.

Clay let the tirade roll over him with relative ease. Funny how he used to care what others said about him. He rotated his shoulder, stretching a muscle, and kept walking.

When the verbal lashing failed to provoke a reaction, Nails interrupted Weasel. "Fine, Cissy, have it your way. You won't work on her, I will. I've seen pictures of her, that sweet little nineteen-year-old body. It would be my pleasure to work that—"

Right hand seizing into a fist, Clay swung. His knuckles smashed into Nails's jaw, with all his body weight thrown in behind. Through the rage buzzing in Clay's ears, he heard the smack of flesh and an instantaneous crush of bone as Nails's jaw snapped. For one second, Clay felt a rush of pure jubilation.

The next second, painful retaliation.

Nails and Weasel slammed him to the pavement. Cement chewed his cheek. Powerful kicks struck him in the stomach, the ribs, thrusting air from his lungs. Gasping, he heaved himself over, started to rise, but the blows bashed him back down. Pummeled him from every direction. Sharp pain became a deep, blending blur.

He was vaguely aware of a cheering roar. Even if he'd been able, he didn't have to look to know the inmates were circled around, watching his pounding like prime entertainment.

Gun blasts from the guard tower silenced the crowd, the shots a welcome sound. An alarm blared and COs ran in, bellowing, "Get on the ground!"

Not a problem, Clay thought with a groan. *Already there.*

But as soon as the COs ripped his attackers off, he heaved himself up in time to catch an evil, smug sneer on Nails's busted face. Despite the damaged jaw, Clay was sure he saw Nails mouth the word "Charlene," and he couldn't help going for him again with a wild swing of his fist.

Before he could make the satisfactory connection, a CO's club cracked his knuckles. "Down, con!" The burst of pain shot his fingers open, and something dropped out. The letter, his ma's letter.

He tried to grab for it, but the COs tackled him, rammed him back to the pavement. Stars flickered in his vision. His teeth cut his tongue, and he tasted blood. A knee crushed into his back. As he struggled for breath, his arms were yanked behind him and his wrists cuffed, the metal clamping sharply. Then he was hauled up and dragged, stumbling, away. He caught a last glance of the crumpled paper, squashed underfoot in the snow.

It's just a piece of paper.

Swallowing blood, he hustled his steps to keep up with the COs' angry pace. They lugged him past the other cons who, following policy, were still on the ground. The whole prison would be in lockdown now.

Teeth gritting and eyes smarting, he looked up and blinked against the natural light, memorizing the sky, knowing it would be artificial glare and claustrophobia where he was going. He'd pay with time in the hole for this one. A month, maybe longer. Fine. He'd handle it. He was getting good at letting his mind take him elsewhere.

It had all been worth it, anyhow. It had felt good to defend Charlene, and he'd do it again, even though she'd never know. A penance for all those times he'd failed her in the past. Not that there was much honor in the world, but she had it at least, and he'd fight for that.

A sick, hooting laugh caught his ears. A weaselly laugh. *If weasels could laugh, that is.*

"You're in for it now, Cissy!" Weasel's voice erupted with glee, despite the CO marching him away. "Nails don't forget. You're a dead man, Cissy, ya hear? A dead man!"

Clay's lip curled and he strained in Weasel's direction, but the COs wrenched him back. He sucked in one last breath of the clean outside air, knowing it would be his last for a while.

But things would get better, he told himself as he landed in solitary. He drew his knees to his throbbing chest and clutched his head. Dear God, it had to get better than this . . .

Chapter One

Over three years later . . .

"How much farther?" Charlene tried not to sound impatient as she followed Ben Jorgensen up the steep rocky path that narrowed and twisted like a labyrinth. They would have walked side by side, hand in hand, if the trail allowed it.

"Almost there," Ben promised, turning to flash an encouraging smile.

Just the spark she needed. Pulling in a breath, she held the image of his grin and trudged on carefully. The treacherous paths of Sunset Lookout Park had, on occasion, been known to lose hikers over the cliffs, or so Ben had told her.

She wished he hadn't.

Despite the cool April evening, sweat trickled down her neck and under her sweatshirt, wet and itchy, and she felt like a mess. Her jeans sported dirt at the hem and, even though she'd done her best to confine her hair in a ponytail, her maple-brown curls kept springing free and snagging on branches.

Ben, in contrast, appeared clean and cool as always. His smooth dark hair, his crisp khakis, his forest green sweater—all perfect. His easy stride was much longer than her short, anxious one. Even toting a backpack, he didn't seem winded. But then, this hike was nothing compared to his grueling firefighter training with a heavy SCBA strapped to his back.

"This way." Ben ducked under pine boughs and moved off the path onto a thread of a trail that, on second thought, Charlene didn't think deserved to be called a trail. The ground under her feet became slippery with old rust-colored pine needles.

Ben squeezed through a mossy outcropping, and as she followed, she wondered if he really knew where he was going. She picked her way down a jumble of boulders, and in the next instant, she gasped.

Before her, endless sky glowed with sunset colors that blended and melted into the rolling horizon. And below her lay a lake, a shimmering jade jewel set in the green expanse of new spring foliage.

She breathed in the sight. "It's beautiful."

"Yep, it sure is. Thought you'd like it." Ben sounded almost smug, but there was a humorous sparkle in his eyes as he took her hand. "Come on, I reserved balcony seats."

He led her around a rock wall to a sandstone ledge, so confidently that she didn't pause to question the nearness of the drop off. Following his lead, she sat down on the bluff, propping her back against rock while her heels rested only a foot from the edge.

Holding hands, the two of them watched the impressive show of purples, pinks, and golds. The panoramic sunset subtly shifted and changed. Eventually her gaze wavered from the sky and fell to the lake far below, which seemed to have darkened.

Distracted now, she tossed tentative glances down and around at the huge gray and purplish rock slabs, which looked like weird blocks that had been balanced precariously by a child. Branches and sparse vegetation clung to random crevices. Her perch offered a remarkable vantage point, but her body tensed with nervous energy, the view losing its appeal.

As if sensing her apprehension, Ben's arm came around her, snuggling her securely. His nearness comforted her, and she caught a whiff of his spicy cologne.

She met his eyes, and then her gaze slid to the curve of his lips. Calming, she nestled closer. Two years of dating had proved that with Ben, she would always be safe.

"Are you happy?" he asked as dull clouds began blotting out the sunset.

"Yes, so happy. It was worth the long hike. This moment couldn't get any better."

A strange look crossed Ben's face, a sort of knowing half smile as he countered, "I think it could."

Before she had time to wonder, he released her and dropped to one knee on the pine needle covered rock. "Charlene Elizabeth Perigard . . ."

As he said something about loving her forever, her pulse raced and her ears hummed.

Here it came—the moment she'd been longing for . . .

Nails stepped off the bus and cracked his knuckles as he surveyed the town in the evening light. Nothin' like comin' home. Ha, what a stinkin' load of bull. No such thing as home to him. The longest he'd ever stayed in any place had been the one he'd just come from.

He strode forward, noting things had changed in the years he'd been gone. New roads. New signs. More buildings. Shops and a parking lot stood where a field used to.

And look at that. On the corner. A welcome back gift. A new, shiny-windowed bank. Advertising money. Flaunting it.

His fingers twitched, aching for a gun. Adrenaline surged. He eyed the exits, scanned for security, felt a pull to move closer, his mind spinning a plan. Pure instinct. It would be so easy—

But no, not yet. He stilled his fingers.

Not yet.

He already had a plan. Tearing his gaze from the bank, he headed for the older part of town. He had a stash he could live on for now. There was something he had to do before replenishing his cash. A score that needed settling.

He cracked his jaw from side to side.

Some people thought they were better than him.

He poked his tongue into the spot where he was missing a molar.

Some people needed to be taught a lesson.

He clenched a fist. Some people thought they could hide, but he'd find 'em. He grinned.

He'd find him.

And when he did, this time there'd be no COs to save him.

⌐

Charlene remained unblinking while Ben produced a diamond ring, a bright angular orb in a yellow-gold band. The diamond caught the dying rays of the sun and threw them into a blinding, sparkling display.

He spoke the words that had to come next. "Will you marry me?"

Emotion rippled through her. She looked into his eyes, eyes so earnest, reflecting devotion and love. *Everything I need. Everything I want.*

"Charlene?" His gaze flickered concern.

"Yes, Ben, of course I'll marry you."

Joy flooded his face. In one fluid motion, he lifted her to her feet and slipped the ring over her finger. A perfect fit. Perfect, like him.

Mesmerized by the diamond's fiery play of light, time stood still. "Aren't you going to kiss me?" he teased, and she blushed and smiled, and then the smile was lost in a warm kiss. She clung to him as her heart thrummed. *I'll marry him and finally live happily ever after.*

Finally.

"So you like the ring?"

"I love it." She lifted her hand. The gold band branched into tendrils, caressing the low-set diamond in intricate scrolls. *It's like a fairytale princess ring.* "Where did you find it?"

"In my pocket. How lucky was that?"

"Ben." She smiled and shook her head. "You know what I mean."

"Sure." His fingertips brushed her arm. "Let's just say, there's not another ring exactly like it. It's unique, like you."

"I'll never take it off."

He chuckled. "I'll be happy to hold you to that, but first, go ahead. Just this once. I want you to see what's inscribed in the band."

An inscription, too? But that was Ben, always above and beyond. She eased the ring from her finger, all set to peek in the band, when instead her traitorous eyes fell on the scar encircling her ring finger.

In a flashback, she saw blood beading up, forming a cruel crimson wedding band.

No!

Her insides coiled, binding with fear. Her teeth clenched. *Don't think. Don't remember.*

She'd had the thin white scar for years. She was used to seeing it, though she did her best to avoid it. So why now, at this crucial moment, did the sight of it bring the hideous memories squirming back?

The cold earthen room.

Burning black candles.

Evil Abner slicing first her finger, then Clay's, with a snake-handled knife. Their blood mingled in a twisted ceremony. Scarring more than just her finger.

She shuddered. The slight tremor of her hand, combined with slick sweat, was all it took.

The engagement ring popped free from her fingertips and went sailing through the air.

She let out a little gasp and, unthinkingly, lunged forward to save

9

the ring from falling off the cliff. But at that same moment, Ben swiped for it, and instead of saving the ring, she bumped into him. He teetered. His feet, already too close to the rocky edge, scrambled for footing as he flailed for balance.

She should have reached for him, but she remained rooted to the spot, horrified. Though the moment happened in a flash, it was as if she had time to comprehend that if she tried to save him, she would fall too. So she didn't move. She let him go. Wide eyed, she processed every split-second change in his expression: shock, panic, terrible realization.

He fell from sight, his awful yell ripping the air. Then, *thunk.* Silence.

Dreadful, meaningful, deathly silence.

A scream scraped her throat but didn't make it out. *Ben!* She fell to her knees. Her forehead dropped to the cold stone.

God, no!

In desperate disbelief, she crawled forward, her nails scraping the stone. When she reached the edge, she gripped the slab, craned her neck, and looked down.

Her heart leaped when she spotted him. He lay on another ledge, only about fifteen feet down. He hadn't fallen countless feet to the jagged rocks lining the lake, thank God.

But still, his lifeless form was frightening, his body splayed at an awkward angle. That dark spot near his head—was it a shadow, or blood seeping out from under him?

"Ben!" She willed him to answer, to move, but there was no response.

"Ben! Can you hear me?" Her voice echoed, unnatural and frantic. "Are you all right?" She waited several painful heartbeats. *"Ben!"*

When her scream died, she thought she heard a groan float up from where he lay. If she stared at him long enough, hard enough, maybe he would move. Suddenly, there it was, a sign of life, a slight lift of his elbow. A fleeting movement, but something. Hope kindled in her chest.

"Hang on, Ben! I'll get help. Just hang on!" Her brain fired her muscles to action. She scrambled her way back to the main path and, though she already knew what she'd find, she yanked out her phone. Sure enough, no service. Always no service when you needed it the most.

Alone in this forsaken wilderness, how would she ever find her way back down the bluffs? And if she did, it would surely be too late to do Ben any good.

No, she couldn't think like that.

Ben needs me. Just follow the path. I can do this. She had to think of something besides his broken, bleeding body and this rapidly darkening, steep terrain.

It was as if once she acknowledged the impending night, a gauzy black curtain dropped over the world. Nocturnal noises erupted— hoots and howls, scurrying and swooping sounds, underbrush rustling and branches snapping—and her mind whirled with terrible thoughts. What was out here? Wolves? Bears? She'd never been fond of the dark, but after her kidnapping experience, being lost and alone in a shadowed network of trees was not what she needed.

So what, she thought, stomping down her emotions. *This isn't about me. I'll do whatever it takes, Ben, I promise.*

Navigating the path took much longer than it would have with Ben guiding her. So many roots and rocks and branches. Her heart's rapid pulsing reminded her of a ticking clock.

Time's running out.

As she picked her way down loose slopes and a narrow set of natural rock steps, she imagined Ben's heart beating slower and slower, until—

Think positive. Think of the future, all we have to look forward to.

But deep down, she knew she was kidding herself. There would be no wedding now.

I've destroyed us.

Guilt gnawed at her soul. She gulped deep breaths to calm her nerves. Her parched mouth tasted sour. At last she emerged from the overgrown trail into the parking lot. A slight sense of relief touched her, but a quick glimpse of her phone still showed no service. She'd have to drive closer to civilization before she could call for help.

Pushing past exhaustion, she ran for Ben's car, the only vehicle in the lot. Despite moonlight giving off a halfhearted glow, the darkness felt heavy, smothering.

She halted at Ben's car, realizing she didn't have his key.

Swallowing frustration, she pulled at the door, begging it to open. No good. She slumped against the car, but only for a second.

Ben's counting on me.

She clenched her hands and glanced back at the towering bluffs,

11

the monstrous silhouette. Her mind flashed a picture of Ben sprawled in a pool of blood on the rock, waiting, dying . . .

She sprinted down the road, her hiking boots beating a lonely rhythm. Every few moments, she checked her phone, but no service still taunted her. She jogged past the cheery "Thank you for visiting Sunset Lookout Park" sign, and emotion clogged her throat. When at last her phone signal kicked in, she had to fight down breathless panting so she could talk to the 911 dispatcher. Her words tumbled out, urgent, pleading, but somehow intelligible.

The dispatcher assured her help was on the way.

"Hurry," Charlene begged. "It's already been so long."

Dear God, don't let it be too late.

―――

Sirens shrieking and lights whirling, emergency vehicles careened into the lot. Charlene ran to meet them so she could guide the rescue to Ben.

The time she'd spent waiting and praying had allowed her to recharge slightly, and she soldiered back up the bluff path, this time illuminated by numerous flashlights and surrounded by capable firefighters and EMTs hauling a stretcher with metal sides. She began to hope that things might actually turn out okay.

Radio dispatch voices crackled to life, died, then crackled again in a distracting, erratic rhythm. She watched the bobbing letters on the backs of the firefighters' jackets and thought of Ben. For some reason, her lips moved and she rambled. "Ben's a firefighter for Woodfield. He was part time for so long, and he finally got a fulltime position. He was so excited . . . he was going to start this week . . ."

And now he won't. He can't. There's no way. If he survived, this fact alone would devastate him.

She stilled her lips and saved her strength for climbing.

The firefighter hiking directly in front of her turned briefly, and their eyes connected as she gave Charlene a look of . . . what? Sympathy? Pity? Encouragement? As her head turned back, Charlene noticed for the first time the woman's long, thick dark ponytail.

Charlene found the hidden turnoff to the cliff easily, surprising herself. Swallowing, she pointed. "There. He fell off there." She wilted onto a rock, not wanting to get in the way as the experts worked their rescue. Her ears tuned in to catch any indication, good or bad, of Ben's situation.

The firefighters lowered the stretcher, which she heard called a "basket," over the side of the bluff. Two of them—a muscular young man and the ponytailed woman—harnessed themselves to ropes which they secured around thick tree trunks before rappelling down the bluff.

Eventually, at their signal, the others pulled, carefully lugging Ben, in the basket, up and over the side.

Charlene sprang to her feet, dizzy at the sight of him. "Ben." She tried to make her way over, then realized he needed the professionals much more than he needed her.

The tone of their voices told her his condition was serious. Her fingers grappled together and twisted, but she stayed back, determined not to do anything more to hurt him than she already had.

Chapter Two

*I*t wasn't right that he should be so still. Not Ben, so full of life. From her chair, Charlene gazed at him in the hospital bed while his mom, dad, and younger sister clustered near, murmuring prayers.

They'd believed her so readily.

Too readily.

Her explanation echoed in her mind, a scourge to her conscience. *"We were too close to the edge. He lost his balance."* It was the truth, but not the whole truth.

She would tell them the rest, but not now, with him unconscious and wrapped in bandages, hooked up to IVs and monitors. The bruises, the abrasions, they would heal. But the spinal damage . . .

No. Hold on to hope.

Her lashes lowered. Almost as if to torture her, her thoughts strayed to a happier time . . .

"Seriously, you've never been on a rollercoaster?" Ben's incredulity had been tangible—as had her apprehension when he insisted on taking her to Six Flags and she saw the monster tracks looping hundreds of feet in the air.

"Come on, you'll be fine," he promised after they climbed aboard their first ride. *"Live a little."*

"That's just it." She laughed nervously as she sat beside him in the metal car, dreading takeoff. *"I want to live."*

Before he could answer, they surged forward. The fierce speed rammed her against her seat. Her hands clutched a death grip on the lap bar, which didn't seem tight enough. What if she flew out from under it? They zoomed, the wild motion flinging her worries and hair in all directions.

Her heart pounded as the car slowed and, clacking and creaking ominously, climbed a practically vertical track. They crested the top, paused, and whoosh, *they fell.*

Her stomach dropped. She screamed.

"Yeah!" Ben hollered.

They wove up, down, around, flashing, flying. It was reckless exhilaration, careless abandon unlike anything she'd ever experienced, and when the ride stopped, her eyes stayed wide, her heart racing. The expression "throwing caution to the wind" took on a whole new meaning.

Ben turned to her. "Well?"

Her lips twitched. "Let's ride it again."

Ben's smile deepened, a dimple appearing. He grabbed her hand and they dashed for the line.

Near the end of the day, as they strolled along deciding which ride to make their last, he bought them cotton candy. He pulled off a piece, and she did the same, saying, "I've never had cotton candy before."

"What?" He stopped in his tracks to gape. "How's that even possible?" He nudged her. "Weirdo."

She smiled. Only Ben could make an insult sound endearing. She plucked more cotton candy, fascinated by how the sticky sugary fluff dissolved almost instantly on her tongue.

He watched her, clearly amused. "You've got some stuck on your lip. Right there." He touched her mouth, and her lips tingled.

His fingers slid to her cheek and lingered, warm and expressive. "Never been on a rollercoaster, never had cotton candy . . . You've been missing out." He looked into her eyes, his gaze turning deep. Perceptive. Knowing there was so much she'd never done.

Her heart fluttered. He leaned in, his lips landing soft on hers, sweet with cotton candy. Taking her breath away. More thrilling than the rollercoaster.

Now, pulling in a ragged breath and returning to the present, her eyes traced Ben's lips. So dry, so inert. She wanted to kiss him, but didn't know if that would be okay. She was so afraid of hurting him now. Despite his muscular physique, he looked fragile, lying silent and still, eyes closed.

She bit her lip. *I love you, Ben. Come back to me.*

"Charlene, how were your days off?" Julie, the children's librarian, asked brightly. Her hair, though blond, was almost as curly as Charlene's. Julie seemed better able to control hers, though, often using fancy clips and pins to create strategic styles Charlene could never figure out.

Julie's question was inevitable, innocent, yet it released a flood of pain. The room's colorful storybook themed walls seemed to close in on Charlene. She braced herself against the librarian's desk and filled her in on Ben.

Julie blinked. Her thickly lashed eyes went wide as she expressed sympathy and concern. "Are you sure you're up for working today?"

Charlene nodded. "It's better to keep busy." Besides, Ben's parents had insisted she take a break from her vigil at the hospital, assuring her they would call the second he woke up.

Julie's brow puckered. "Why don't I take over storytime? You could shelve instead. Have some peace and quiet."

More silence? "No way. Don't worry, I can do this. I love storytime." Charlene grabbed the waiting books and stuffed animals and hurried into the connecting room before Julie could protest.

Parents and kids were already gathering, claiming seats. Moms with toddlers and babies sat in chairs near the back, while preschoolers clustered on a round alphabet rug, their legs crossed and eyes expectant.

At precisely nine, Charlene began, digging deep to find her carefree, happy voice and a big smile. After welcoming everyone, she introduced herself, for the benefit of those who weren't regulars, as Miss Charlene. Then she started with a customary get-all-the-wiggles-out rhyming and action song. Here, in this role, she didn't mind being silly, and most of the adults joined in, looking as goofy as her as they used their arms as elephant trunks.

When the giggles subsided, everyone sat and she read, "*Stand Back," Said the Elephant, "I'm Going to Sneeze!"*

While children practiced elephant sneezes, she passed around the stuffed elephants for them to cuddle. After the last story, everyone stomped like elephants.

As Charlene encouraged each child to pick up a coloring page on the way out, she noticed a short man standing against a wall and holding a sheet of paper. He didn't seem to belong with any child. Stout and balding, he wore little glasses and an oversized tan jacket. She glanced at him repeatedly, uncomfortable as she tidied the room under his shifting eyes.

Sensing him heading her way, she looked up and he was already beside her. She tried to hide her startled expression.

"Excuse me, Miss Charlene, since you're a librarian, I have kind of an odd research question for you." His stubby finger touched the thin mustache on his upper lip.

"Well, I'm not officially a librarian, not yet, but I'm working toward it. I take classes part time, so another few years—"

"Yes, well, that's very nice, but I'm sure you can still help me."

"I'll try. What do you need?"

He moved closer, and she noticed an odor, as if he needed a shower. She struggled to keep a pleasant look on her face and willed herself not to step back.

"I deal in rare and antique pieces," he said, "and at the moment I'm trying to gather information on this particular piece."

He held a paper out to her, and she took a sharp intake of breath. Her hand stopped halfway to her throat and trembled as she stared at the photo of an all too familiar snake-handled knife.

Knowing first-hand the damage that wicked knife could do, she clenched her fingers and tried not to shiver as she was hit with a jolting memory. The current of pain. The debilitating fear.

"Everything okay, miss?" The man watched her too intently, like a boy studying a butterfly before plucking off its wings.

She wanted to tell the ill-smelling man to go away, but she caught a glimpse of Geraldine, the library director, observing from a distance. Charlene took a deep breath and, rewarded with a lungful of stench, immediately regretted it.

"I'm fine," she said with forced pleasantness. She dropped into a red plastic chair and pushed her fingertips against her forehead.

He slid the paper under her gaze. "Take a real good look."

That was the last thing she wanted to do—stare at that horrid thing, the hunched snake body handle, the slivered eyes, the sharp protruding, hissing tongue, the tail curling over the silver blade.

"Very interesting," she managed at last.

Why do you have this? And why are you asking me about it?

This couldn't be coincidence. As far as she knew, this knife was one of a kind. "Where did you get this picture?"

"A colleague."

Abner?

She pushed the paper away, hoping he'd remove it from sight. "All I can suggest is researching online or in a rare weapons or antique weapons book." She stood, trying to ignore her squeamish stomach, which roiled like a pile of twisting serpents. "I can show you where those are."

"That would be something, I suppose. You're sure you don't

have anything more to offer?" Very slowly, the man reclaimed the picture. "Any idea where I could locate one of these treasures in person, perhaps?"

Waves of trepidation rolled over her. She forced a short laugh and began walking. "I'm afraid not. Why would you think I would?" He followed her to the nonfiction stacks and took his time answering, suddenly choosing to speak in a whisper, although no other people were near. "Because I believe you've seen that knife in person."

Her hand froze near the spine of a book.

"Come now, your kidnapping is common knowledge."

She squirmed when she felt his breath warm on her ear.

"And I happen to know that Abner Morrow owned that knife. It's not a stretch to imagine he used it in your presence."

Clamping her tongue, she neither agreed nor disagreed.

His gaze prodded. "What happened to it?"

"I don't know." A fiber of anger worked itself into her voice. "And even if I did, I don't think an evil knife like that is something anyone needs to have."

"Needs aren't subjective."

In that case . . . "I need you to leave."

His eyes narrowed.

She narrowed hers right back.

"You might change your mind." He held out a business card. When she didn't reach for it, he stuck it between her fingers. The sharp cardboard edge nicked her skin. "The name's Horace Cain. Call me if you remember anything about the knife and where it might be now. It's extremely valuable and I'm willing to pay generously for it. Very generously."

He smiled a flubber-lipped, gap-toothed smile, then turned and retreated, whistling tunelessly.

Coming to her senses, she flicked the card from her fingers and walked in the opposite direction, pulling in untainted breaths and rubbing her scarred finger so furiously, it stung.

The weird encounter weighed on her mind the rest of her shift, and when she turned out of the library parking lot, it lingered still, consuming her thoughts. She drove by habit, her mind disconnected from the road.

She was barely a block from the library when flashing lights and a siren kicked into her consciousness. Seized by concern, she pulled over. The police car didn't sail past, but stopped behind her.

Great.

She shifted to park and rolled her window down, then pulled out her driver's license. She'd been distracted, but didn't think she'd been speeding. Maybe one of her indicator lights was out or something.

Trying not to worry, she tapped her foot as she waited with her hands at the top of the steering wheel, tension mounting.

Eyes on her side mirror, she saw a thin officer emerge from the squad car. Gravel crunched as he strode her way. His calm demeanor and blank expression met her at her window. She waited for him to speak as she handed him her license.

Studying it, he said, "Perigard."

She swallowed dryness.

The officer tapped her license and assessed her with cool gray eyes. "Do you know why I pulled you over?"

"No, sir, I don't."

"You rolled the stop sign back there." He motioned with his head.

She frowned. She didn't think he was right, but then, she'd been preoccupied, her mind whirling with thoughts of the strange man in the library. She'd also been eager to get to the hospital to see Ben.

The officer straightened. "I need you to step out of the car, please."

Really? Shouldn't he return to his car and write her a ticket? Trying not to appear hesitant, she obligingly slipped out.

The officer put his hand on her door before she could close it. "You don't mind if I search your vehicle real quick, do you?"

"No, go ahead." *I've got nothing to hide.* Still, she hovered near, feeling uncomfortable, knowing she'd agreed too readily.

She pictured Max, her twin, shaking his head. *"No cop's got a right to search your car or house without a warrant."*

I've got nothing to hide, she repeated to herself. *And if I cooperate, maybe I won't get a ticket.*

She folded her arms against her churning stomach and watched the officer as he ran his hand over and under the seats, searched the console, then opened the glove box. He leaned closer, interested in the contents.

After a moment, he pulled out several plastic baggies. She didn't recognize them, nor the small grayish cubes they contained. All she knew was, they shouldn't be there.

A wave of nausea rolled over her, followed by a dreadful pang.

The officer emerged.

Charlene willed his stern lips to reassure her, to squelch her mounting fear, but instead he went for his handcuffs.

"Ms. Perigard, you're under arrest."

Chapter Three

*D*rugs? *In my car? How?* Charlene's head pounded, trying to make sense of it. Impossible. It was all a huge, terrible mistake. She tried to detach herself from the arrest process and pretend it wasn't really happening.

Didn't work.

She was acutely aware of her hands tugged behind her back and metal clamped to her wrists.

"You have the right to remain silent . . ." The familiar words took on a new meaning now that they were directed at her. Each word struck her like a physical blow.

She tensed as she was patted down, then ushered into the back of the squad car. The plastic seats were hard, unyielding. She eyed the clear solid partition that divided the car: the front, for the cops; the back, for criminals. And here she sat.

During the drive, she kept her neck stiff, her face expressionless, not wanting anyone—even strangers—catching sight of her. She watched the familiar town pass by, yet it felt unfamiliar, somehow, from this degrading position.

There was the church, the cemetery. She thought she saw a man standing just about where Margaret Morrow's grave was. Who . . . ? She craned for a better view. Could it be . . . ?

No, the man was too large. Couldn't be Clay.

Her head swimming, the cemetery flashed by, but she closed her eyes and returned to it, escaping the cop car the only way she could, into memory. And to the last time she had seen Clay. Over three years ago, at his mother's funeral . . .

Plodding through the snow in St. Paul's Cemetery, Charlene trailed along at the end of the short procession, her eyes at the front of the line, on Clay's rigid back.

He hadn't looked at her once.

Does he even know I'm here?

Of course, she realized he had the weight of his mother's death on his mind, and she couldn't blame him for his tunnel vision. Still, she couldn't help yearning for one glimpse of his eyes. Just one, to know he was okay.

He wore a black suit and no winter coat—nowhere near warm enough for this January day. What was he thinking? He had to be freezing.

He stopped at the mouth of the gaping rectangular pit, a rough blight in the soft white snow. Artificial turf, too green for the dead of winter, draped the opening.

He stood stiffly, but his head bent slightly as he looked down into the depths, and her heart ached. Please, God, let this year be a better one for him.

Indeed, her thoughts were more for him than his mother. She, Charlene was sure, was at peace now, while Clay . . .

She blinked at the hole in the earth, which summoned too many horrid memories to count, memories that she shared with Clay and her brother Max. Memories of evil, torture, blackness, and near-death.

Shivering, she forced the images away and tugged her wool hat tighter over her hair and ears. Inside the soft lining of her right mitten, she moved her fingers to brush gently over the cross-shaped scar in her palm. Stroking the scar had become a habit over the past year, and she couldn't quite decide if it was a nervous or a comforting gesture. Perhaps some of both.

Once the plain wooden casket was gently deposited by the pallbearers onto the supports spanning the open grave, Father Villateshire began the graveside service. The sky pressed down like a slab of gray ice, threatening fresh snow. Meanwhile, arctic winds scraped flakes from the ground and tossed them about with spiteful abandon.

She felt a touch on her shoulder before someone whispered, "Hey, Charlene."

Turning slightly, she saw Ben standing beside her, gentle concern clouding his blue eyes, and she offered a small smile. It was so like him to make a point of coming to the service. He must have been in church, too, and she just hadn't noticed.

Tall and attractive, with shiny hair so dark brown it looked practically black, Ben was surely at the top of the church ladies' eligible bachelor list. Guys these days just didn't come this perfect. Charlene knew she should be happy that he showed such patient interest in her, but today she only felt sad.

"How are you doing?" he whispered.

For lack of sufficient words, she merely gave a little shrug. He continued standing close beside her, a warm pillar blocking the wind.

She shifted slightly and glanced heavenward, imagining Margaret free of earthly pain and suffering, her soul joyous in the radiance of God's love.

Then her gaze returned to earth. To Clay. She saw no tears, but she suspected he was fighting them. She resisted the urge to go to his side.

Father Villateshire finished the prayers and blessing, then moved to say something to Clay before grasping his shoulder in a way that said, "Stay strong," and departing.

The funeral director stepped forward and announced formally, "This concludes the service."

As people dispersed and moved away, she noticed one man, thin and dressed in black, far beyond the headstones, lingering near a cluster of trees. Watching. She didn't think she'd ever seen him at St. Paul's before, but then he wasn't close enough for her to see him well. She couldn't tell if he was young or old.

Her train of thought broke as a sudden swarm of cameramen and microphone-wielding news-reporters descended on the cemetery. Her heart lurched as the crew barreled toward Clay.

"Mr. Morrow . . ." They addressed him respectfully, but their questions were invasive.

"Were you released from prison in time to speak with your mother before she died?"

"What can you tell us about your time in prison?"

"Do you think that you got a fair sentence?"

Her eyes squeezed shut briefly. Why hadn't anyone foreseen and prevented this? The obituary had been in the paper, the funeral wasn't private, and of course the sensation-hungry media would seize this opportunity to revive and expand on the famous Perigard kidnapping case.

Before Clay had a chance to respond, the vultures spotted her and swooped her way.

"Charlene Perigard, do you still maintain that Mr. Morrow was innocent of all charges?"

Instead of dignifying the news crew with a reply, she pressed her lips together.

Undeterred, they continued. "Has your grandfather welcomed

23

you back yet, or are you still disinherited?"

"Are you and Mr. Morrow on friendly terms now that he's been released from prison? Do you have any plans to—"

"That's enough." Ben stepped in front of her and spoke gruffly. "You're all way out of line. This is a funeral service, people. A funeral! Where's your respect?"

Clay, reacting belatedly because he'd likely been stunned speechless by the rude intrusion, suddenly charged forward, pushing microphones away and shoving a cameraman.

Stumbling, the cameraman cursed.

Clay brandished a fist. "Get out of here."

The guy took a hasty step back. "Man, they should've kept you locked up. You'd better watch it unless you want another assault charge thrown at you."

The charge was *Accessory* to Assault, *Charlene silently and indignantly clarified, as if the technical distinction would make a difference in anyone's opinion. The conviction had been very light, considering all the charges Clay had been facing—but not light enough considering the fact that he should have walked free.*

"Like I said," Ben repeated, stepping in front of Clay and facing the cameraman, "this is a funeral. You're not welcome here."

"We got what we needed." *The cameraman thrust his chin in Clay's direction. Looking smug, he and the rest of the crew departed to the sidewalk and disappeared past the church.*

Clay's ears burned red as he glared after them. She studied his face, which seemed too thin; his eyes, too shadowed; and his nose still had that slightly off-kilter look. Her gaze moved to his russet hair, which was longer and more disheveled than the last time she'd seen him. That was at the sentencing back in early September, when he'd been slapped with a year and a day in prison. Since he'd already served eight months while waiting for trial and sentencing, he'd only had to finish out the remaining four.

Only, *her mind scoffed.*

Even one day was too long.

He'd been released a week ago—just in time to plan his mother's funeral. God knew Margaret had hung in as long as she could in hopes of seeing her son free, but it wasn't quite long enough. In a cruel twist of irony, she'd died the day before Clay's release.

Charlene had wanted to visit him in prison, but he'd been adamant in his letters to his mother that he didn't want any visitors, particularly her, and she wasn't quite sure how to take that. She had tried to write him, but no matter how she worded the letters, they seemed so far from sufficient that she never could bring herself to send them . . .

But what did all that matter now?

She opened her eyes as the police car pulled to a stop at the station, halting her morose trip down memory lane. Her wrists shifted, clinking the handcuffs.

Lord help me, it's not the past I need to worry about.

―――

Nails had easily found the old obituary online, then clomped through the cemetery and found the headstone.

On the road past the church, a cop car drove by, and he smiled because he wasn't in it. Never would be again. He'd make certain.

He grinned at the shiny headstone and pictured the kid standing here at his mother's burial, probably crying like a baby. The image gave him some satisfaction, but not enough. Not near enough.

And that church behind him. His back muscles tightened. Catholic. The thought dredged up twenty-two years ago, life with the Callaghans. An angelic, smiling face framed in copper curls intruded into his bitter thoughts, but he severed the vision and forced his gaze to the ground.

Wrinkly brown flowers lay on the plot. Old, but not very. Figured the kid still visited like a dutiful son. Sickening.

Beloved Mother, read the stone. More sickening.

His own mother had been a screaming manic witch who ended up plunging a needle into herself to escape life. A weak woman. The only thing she'd ever cared about was finding a vein to shoot herself up. He hadn't visited her grave since they'd forced him to the funeral.

With the heel of his boot, he ground the dead flowers into the earth, then stomped away.

―――

The black receiver felt slick in Charlene's hand. She stared at the silver-corded jail phone, the numbers on the dirty keypad, and willed her brother to answer her collect call.

I need you, Max.

When he didn't answer, she willed him to sense her need, but she knew it was useless. He'd never really bought into her twin-

25

intuition claim, despite the fact that it had helped her come to his aid in the past.

Payback time, brother.

Not that he could do much from where he was, California, countless states away. Even if he was a professional magician. She cracked a smile. That would be quite the trick, relocating from some fancy stage to this dingy jail to perform a Houdini escape. At least he was living his dream, anyway. Good for him.

She clunked the useless phone down and wished for hand sanitizer. Then she dropped into a seat as far away from the other inmates as possible.

With Ben in the hospital, Max was the only person she could call for help. Her sheltered upbringing and introvert ways had left her rather bereft of friends. Yes, she had acquaintances, particularly from school, church, and the library, but not one person she'd be willing to call from jail.

Her gaze roved the large lounge, called a "day room," afraid to meet the other inmates' eyes. Everything about the room was depressing—the wall of phones, hard plastic chairs, and a TV mounted on a cinderblock wall. Doors to cells surrounded the perimeter of the room. The overhead fluorescent light hurt her eyes, and she averted her gaze.

Out of nowhere, her thoughts turned to Clay, how he had been through this, much worse than this, and she wished . . .

What?

She wished she wouldn't think about him. Ever. She was sure he didn't waste time thinking about her. Frustrated, she tried to grind her socked heels into the floor. All they did was slip.

If only her parents were still alive. Calling Ben's parents crossed her mind, but she recoiled at the thought. They had enough to deal with. Calling them right now would be nothing but selfish.

Nope, it had to be Max. If she could just get ahold of him.

With a raging sigh, she dropped her throbbing head in her hands and drove her elbows into her knees. The fear and indignity of the past hours ate at her, and she choked back the urge to cry. She wouldn't show weakness. Not here.

She stared at a scuff mark on the beige floor and rubbed her neck. She'd wait ten minutes, then try Max again. She had till ten-thirty before lockdown. The only nice surprise in this entire ordeal was that she was allowed, contrary to popular belief, more than one phone call.

And why not? It's not like the police station paid for collect calls. No, the hilarious part was that while she could call freely, she simply had no one to call.

Ten minutes later, she picked up the germ-infested receiver once again, then paused when she heard footsteps approaching. Turning, she met an officer.

She swallowed past the dryness in her throat and replaced the receiver with a shaky hand. They'd already booked her, complete with mug shot, fingerprinting, and a strip search, after which they'd issued her an ugly jail jumpsuit. She was told she'd see a judge in the morning and bail would be set. *So what now?*

"You've got a visitor." The officer showed her to a seat in front of a black encased monitor. Apparently, "visit" did not mean in-person. As she picked up the phone receiver, an old man's face appeared onscreen.

"Hello, Charlene."

Her spine stiffened. Even without the screen, she'd know that tone anywhere. "Grandfather."

His gaze assessed her, so she returned the favor. Never a slender man, he had really packed on some pounds since the last time she'd seen him; at the same time, he looked as though he'd shed quite a lot of hair. He'd changed on the outside, but not on the inside, she wagered.

His nose tilted upward. "You've been managing to do very well with your life, I see. Luxurious accommodations, splendid views, excellent room service—"

"I get it, Grandfather. Life's really working out for me."

"Indeed. See where your headstrong independence has gotten you? All because you chose to turn your back on me years ago."

I turned my back on you? She remembered it a little differently. Although she had refused to answer his recent calls and even the door when he showed up unexpectedly at her condo, it was his own fault. After how he'd treated her and Max, she had nothing good left to say to him.

"You've been corrupted by bad influences," Grandfather went on. "If it weren't for that worthless convict, you wouldn't be here now. He's the one who started you down your dark path . . ."

As it usually did in Grandfather's presence, irritation bubbled within her.

"You need me," he continued, "and if you are finally ready to admit that and apologize for the way you treated me, I might—I just

might—" he paused to dust the shoulder of his expensive suit—
"consider taking you back. And with the power you know I have, I
can make this—all this trouble you're in—disappear. You can
return to the life you had, the wealth, the luxury, the life that others
only dream of."

Knowing him too well, she eyed him suspiciously. "Why would
you help me now? You disowned me, remember?"

"I'm feeling particularly benevolent, so humor me."

She shifted on her seat. Had he been waiting for an opportunity
like this all along? For her to slip up in some way? So he could lord
it over her, then take her back, saving face by requiring a humble
apology—perhaps even a public one—for her refusal to side with
him during Clay's trial? But why did he want her back? He had
everything. Everything material, that is.

Her stepsister Gwen had married a very wealthy man the year
before, thus breaking away from dependence on Grandfather's
money and any need to toe his line. When Gwen left the mansion
he'd provided, she'd brought her mother with her. Charlene doubted
they'd cared to visit him since.

Could he be lonely?

She peered closer at the screen. He held his jaw stiff while
waiting for her answer, as if her response didn't matter. But it must.
He'd gone to the trouble of coming to this unpleasant place. She
noticed more wrinkles and liver spots on his skin.

"How did you even know I was here?"

He made an impatient sound. "I have my connections. Anything
that comes up involving the Perigard name will always be reported
to me."

She nodded. Sure, the news of her arrest would have traveled
easily. In fact, it was probably splashed all over the internet by now,
and she guessed she'd soon grace a few tabloids as well.

"And I must say, you are once again doing an exceptional job of
smearing the family name. I do believe you've now topped
Maxwell."

Ignoring the dig, she adjusted her grip on the phone. "You could
really get me out of this mess?"

"I can pay your bail and have you out in an instant." He snapped
his fingers. "I can provide the best lawyer there is and get the
charges dropped so fast it'll make your head spin."

Tempting indeed.

"Then you'll be free to come and work for me and live in style again."

Her quickening heartbeat fell to a plodding pace. She'd had that life, and grand as it was, she didn't miss it. "We can reconcile, Grandfather, but I can't go back to living under your rule. And I won't say I was wrong to defend Clay. I wasn't. I'd do it again."

His throat rumbled, wrinkles tightened around his mouth, bushy eyebrows dove down, eyes sparked. "That worthless convict deserves no name. He should be in prison for life."

"He helped save my life. Maybe that doesn't mean anything to you, but it does to me." Her lips compressed as she wondered briefly what Clay's life was like now. But she'd never know. *Can't go down that road.*

She took a deep breath. "I already have a nice place to live. And I like working at the library. I'm studying for my library science degree. I'm already doing storytimes and—"

"You'll never make your fortune that way."

"It's not all about money."

"So says the one who wants me to pay her bail."

She shook her head. "Then don't." *I won't beg.* "You don't owe me."

"I most certainly don't." The words sputtered from his mouth. "You're nothing but stubborn and uncooperative."

"Learned from the best, I guess." She found herself briefly wishing that he could have been a kind man like a grandfather was supposed to be. He was nothing like his son, her father.

"Look," she attempted, "I'm sorry that things ended so badly between us back when the trial was going on, but it's over now."

Grandfather *harrumph*ed. "A weak apology is worse than none at all."

She met his gaze. "Then I guess we have nothing more to say."

"So you'd rather sit in jail?"

"If the alternative is being forced to say I shouldn't have defended Clay, and I have to go live with your tyranny, then yes. I guess we can't reach an agreement."

Grandfather scrutinized her, his eyes granite. "You look terrible."

And gaining twenty pounds hasn't exactly done wonders for you. She shrugged.

Silence ensued.

At last he said, "Don't apologize, then. My offer still stands. All I ask is you come back to the mansion with me. Where you'll be safe and provided for." He shifted his gaze. "I only want what's best for you."

The words stunned her. Had he ever told her that before? She studied his image on the screen and wished she could see him in person, to read him better. The grandfather she knew was an unyielding man of ambitious ulterior motives. How could she trust him?

"Well?" Something like hope came through in his voice.

She pinched the bridge of her nose and felt the vein pulsating under her fingertips. "I need to talk to Max first."

—〜—

Her last chance before lockdown.

Charlene lifted the phone and punched in the numbers. Moments later, Max's voice burst onto the line.

"Are you kidding me? Char, what the heck are you doing in jail? Tell me you're joking." He groaned. "Never mind, I know you don't joke."

The semi-insult slid over her. She gave him the summary, as best she could, of how she'd ended up here.

"What, are they blind?" Max fumed. "Any idiot can see you wouldn't touch drugs—not even if someone paid you. You wouldn't even know drugs if you saw them."

She gave him a few seconds to vent, appreciating it, then cut him off. "Max, I'm going to need a lawyer, and bail money. Grandfather said he would—"

"No." Max sounded horrified. "Don't trust him. Just hang tight. I've got you covered. I'll be there as soon as I can and I'll get you out of this, I promise."

She hung the weight of her worry on his words, and the load lightened. "Thanks, but you don't have to come here. I know with your schedule and your shows—"

"Char, are you crazy? Of course I'm coming. I'll be there by morning."

After saying goodbye, she hung up and slunk back to a cold bench to await lockup.

Morning couldn't come soon enough.

—〜—

The woman laid her purchases on the conveyer belt, attempting to camouflage the only item that mattered by burying it under unnecessary food items.

Even so, the cashier recognized her and glanced twice at the item as she scanned it—the little box with the little stick that would give the verdict.

The cashier finished the transaction, bagged the items, and handed them over with no comment. Good thing, because if the cashier had spouted any stupid remark, the woman would have made her regret it.

The plastic bag twisting and crinkling in her sweaty grip, she stalked out of the store.

Chapter Four

"*H*ere, you'll want to put these on." Max handed Charlene a pair of Hollywood sunglasses. "We're about to go through the media mob."

How well he knew her. She slipped the shades on, glad to hide behind the huge concealing lenses, but much more relieved to be free of the jail and the courthouse, despite the crowd awaiting her. The arraignment before the judge had been brief and relatively painless, her pride notwithstanding. Max had come through with a promising lawyer and generous bail money. True, another court date loomed before her, but it was weeks away. She wouldn't think about that right now.

Right now, she stepped out into sunshine. She pulled in a deep lungful of fresh spring air as Max hustled her down the concrete steps.

Cameras, microphones, and questions bombarded her. Reporters obviously craved any comment on her arrest, but Max plowed through, parting the crowd. She remained silent. Behind her dark glasses, she rolled her eyes when she heard a reporter broadcast, "Unable to cope with her traumatic past, did the formerly affluent Charlene Perigard turn to drugs for an easy escape from reality?"

"Much too longwinded to make a good headline," Charlene mumbled.

Max unlocked his rental car. He and Charlene ducked inside, slammed the doors, and let out their breath simultaneously. With a jaunty, mocking wave at everyone pressing in and attempting pictures through the windows, Max tore out of the lot as fast as he could without risking a ticket.

She removed her sunglasses and carefully ran a hand through her snarly curls. The past day was a lot to process, and the charge she faced echoed ominously in her head: *possession of heroin with the intent to distribute.* If convicted, she'd get anywhere from thirty to ninety days in jail. Not an extreme length of time, but the thought of serving it sent panic through her.

"It's like Vivian said," Max spoke up, referring to the lawyer he'd provided, Vivian Fenwick. "You have no drug history, and all your tests came back negative. She's already digging into this, and she'll get the charges dismissed, don't worry."

Charlene nibbled the edge of her lip, dry and ragged from lip balm deprivation. She grabbed her purse and dove a hand inside, fingers scrambling. She seized a red tube, then slicked on strawberry ChapStick, savoring the soothing smoothness.

Max shot her a glance. "The only thing you're addicted to is that stuff."

She capped the tube and dropped it back in her bag. "Dry lips are uncomfortable."

Max signaled a turn, indicator ticking. "The things you worry about."

But the little things were so much easier to worry about than the big ones. No matter how she tried, she couldn't fathom why anyone would target her and plant drugs in her car. Perhaps back when she was in the limelight—but why now, when she'd gladly faded from the short attention span of the public eye, was she under attack? She could think of no motive besides pure hatefulness. Not comforting. She forked fingers through her oily hair and longed for a hot shower.

Fifteen minutes later, Max parked in front of her condo, a beautiful eight-unit structure that was both modern and comfortable. It had never looked so good to her tired eyes.

"Thanks for driving, Max." She let them into the narrow entryway, then slipped her feet out of her shoes and flexed her toes. "Thanks for everything."

"No problem, Char. You got any food in this place?"

"Help yourself." As she watched him head through her tidy living room and into the pristine kitchen, she hoped he wouldn't leave anytime soon. It had been too long since they'd spent time together. "I don't know how long you're planning on staying, but you're welcome as long as you want."

Bags crinkled in the cupboard. "Sounds good. I could use a vacation from the magic scene, anyway."

That surprised her. Maybe he was just saying it to make her feel better. Either way, she wouldn't argue. "I'll be in the shower," she called as she trotted up the carpeted stairs.

She wanted nothing more than to savor the steaming water pelting her skin, but she made sure not to take a second longer than necessary. She didn't deserve the luxury, not with Ben still in the hospital.

She toweled her hair, well aware that it would turn into a mane of fluffy out-of-control curls, but she had no time for tedious styling. She tossed on her clothes and grabbed her purse.

Resisting the urge to remind Max not to drop potato chips all over her carpet, she left him with his feet on the coffee table, watching Nascar races on TV. He grunted something like a goodbye as she left, and it warmed her, reminding her of old times.

On the drive to the hospital, she flicked the radio on and off repeatedly, barely realizing it. Her scattered thoughts were as nervous as her fingers. She hadn't taken time to eat, and her empty stomach twisted in on itself, churning and grumbling queasily.

Once in the hospital, she stood outside Ben's door, her heart pounding. She tucked her hair behind her ears, but it immediately sprang free. Hearing voices inside the room, she gave a light knock.

"Come in," called a soft voice. Ben's mom, Mrs. Jorgensen.

Charlene eased open the door to see Ben's family still gathered around his bed. From the selective glimpses she managed, he still didn't look good. He lay immobile, bandaged, and hooked up to IVs. Still not awake. She stepped inside and closed the door gently. "How is he?"

Mrs. Jorgensen descended on her with a hug. The woman's thin, tall frame draped her heavily as she wept.

Mr. Jorgensen watched. He looked like a shorter, more time-weary version of Ben, but his voice was much gruffer. "If he doesn't wake up soon . . ." He cleared his throat, like there was more to say, but he didn't want to.

Lucy, Ben's twelve-year-old sister, stepped forward, her pixie-like face grave. "He might never wake up. And if he does, he might never walk again." Her mouth crushed into an angry knot.

Mrs. Jorgenson shed a few more tears on Charlene's shoulder, then led her to Ben's side. "We're not giving up," she quavered. "We have him on the prayer list; the whole church is praying for him. We've been praying Rosaries by his side, nonstop. It's good for him to hear our voices." She sniffed, straightened her posture, and wiped her eyes. "Thanks for coming, Charlene."

Still trying to process the terrible news, Charlene heard herself say, "I'm sorry I couldn't come yesterday—"

"No, we knew you couldn't. We heard about what happened."

Of course. Charlene frowned. "Someone set me up."

Silence stretched until Mr. Jorgensen said, "Why in the world would anyone do that to you? You're such a nice person. I can't believe it."

Well, it was believe that, or believe her guilty.

"We'll pray for you," Mr. Jorgensen assured her. "And we can't thank you enough for all you've done."

All I've done? If they only knew.

Charlene swallowed, forcing down a huge lump. She owed Ben's family the full story—the fact that she was responsible for his fall. Guilt settled on her. Guilt, and dread at the thought of confessing. It would only be worse the longer she waited. The Jorgensens had always been unconditionally welcoming to her, and this was how she repaid them?

"I haven't done enough," she whispered, trying to work up her courage.

"Talk to him, Charlene," Mrs. Jorgensen urged. "I'm sure he's just waiting to hear your voice."

She's hoping he'll magically wake up, like in a fairytale. Charlene faced him.

"Talk to him, please," Mrs. Jorgensen repeated, clasping her hands to her breast.

Charlene knew it shouldn't matter, but she felt put on the spot, unnerved by everyone listening. She didn't know what to say, yet she had so much to say. She lowered herself slowly into a bedside chair, to buy a moment.

Taking a deep breath, she leaned in. "I'm sorry, Ben." Could he really hear her? "This shouldn't have happened. But you're strong, you'll get through this. We're here for you, and we're all praying for you, and . . ." Her mind fished for more.

"Tell him you love him, sweetie."

A hot flush swept Charlene's face. "I love you, Ben." *I love you. Don't you remember . . .*

And everyone faded away except for him. In her mind, she saw him as he had been. Strong and unbreakable. A firefighter. Her hero . . .

He opened the door to her at the small number two Woodfield Fire Station. Since he was the only member of the paid-on-call crew who didn't live within a couple blocks of the station, he was alone as usual on his twelve hour shift. He'd asked her to stop by, promising a tour and pizza.

She felt incredibly special to have the attention of this handsome firefighter all to herself as he took her through the small lounge, kitchen, office, then into the garage, which he explained was called a bay. It housed the engine and ambulance and smelled slightly of rubber and mop water. Yellow exhaust hoses hung from the ceiling like long tubular accordions. Open lockers lined one wall, turnout gear hanging ready. Boots stood encased in bulky bunker pants so the firefighters could jump into them quickly—anything to improve response time, when seconds made the difference between life and death.

Ben took her through the ambulance and engine, describing everything, then he showed her the screen of a black-handled device.

"It's a thermal imaging camera. We use this to see in dense smoke or darkness. It picks up images by sensing temperature. So if a kid's hiding in a corner, we can see that on the screen."

The timer buzzed from the kitchen. "Could you pull the pizza out?" Ben didn't look up from fiddling with the camera. "Then I have one more thing to show you."

When she returned, he handed her the device. "I thought you'd like to see it work. Go ahead, point it at that wall."

Curious, she aimed the tool at the cinderblock wall, wondering what it could possibly pick up. Then, in reddish orange hues, a message appeared. Her brows knitted. "How . . ."

Ben grinned. "While you were in the kitchen, I pressed my hands on the wall and wrote that. The camera's sensing the heat left by my hands."

She stared at the message again. The letter "I" was followed by a heart, then the letter "U." I love you. Her heart swelled as she looked at Ben shyly. "You—you do?"

"Of course I do." He took her in his arms and nuzzled her neck. "I would have told you months ago, but I didn't want to scare you away."

That was Ben, always putting her and her ridiculously delicate heart first. Always. It was impossible not to love him in return.

Now, she clung to the memory and embraced him in her mind. Her eyes settled on his lips, lips that were usually always smiling, now listless and pale. She remembered his soft, gentle kisses, and her throat tightened. "Please, wake up. Come back to us."

The *tick, tick, tick* of a clock filled the silence. She became aware again of the Jorgensens as everyone waited and watched Ben for the flicker of an eyelid, the twitch of a muscle. Any kind of response. Any.

When none came, Mrs. Jorgensen pulled her seat beside Charlene with a sigh. "He was so excited to take you to that sunset place. He's been there so many times before, I don't know why this time . . . " She shook her head, the ends of her brown hair sweeping her neck. "He was so eager to propose, even silly enough to be nervous that you'd say no." She glanced with shimmery eyes at Charlene's hand, as if to prove a point, and her mouth dropped open at the sight of Charlene's bare finger. "You—you aren't wearing the ring. You didn't say no, did you?"

Charlene rushed to cancel the incredulity in her eyes. "No, of course not. I said yes!"

"But then, why . . . why aren't you wearing the ring? Didn't it fit? I know some girls these days like to pick out their own, but Ben didn't think that was very romantic. He's kind of old-fashioned. It had to be a diamond, and he wanted to surprise you. He—"

"No, truly, I love the ring. The fit was perfect. I wanted to wear it, it's just—" she ducked sheepishly and forced out the words—"it slipped, and I dropped it, and it fell. Over the cliff."

After a stunned silence, Mrs. Jorgensen found enough voice to rasp, "What?"

But Charlene knew she didn't need to repeat it. Besides, loss of the ring was not nearly as terrible as her cowardice to admit the whole truth of what had happened to Ben.

Her gaze spotted a crucifix resting beside a prayer book on the side table. *Please, Jesus, make Ben better. I'll be such a good wife, I promise.* She touched his hand, the skin neither warm nor cold, but a disturbing blend of the two.

"So tell us again. How exactly did Ben fall?" Lucy's direct question, spoken in a voice dead of emotion, hit Charlene like an arrow in the heart. Her hand shrank from Ben's as she stood and turned to face his family.

She wanted to whisper, but she made herself speak up. "It was my fault." She closed her eyes, unable to watch their faces. "We were near the edge when he proposed. The ring slipped, and we both grabbed for it, but I—I bumped into him. I knocked him over."

Mrs. Jorgensen gasped, and Charlene's eyes popped open in time to see Mr. Jorgensen steady her shoulders.

Lucy stood ramrod straight, staring at Charlene as if she'd grown horns.

Charlene's lips trembled. "I'm so sorry."

After a moment, Mr. Jorgensen said, "It was an accident. It's not your fault."

"Yes," agreed his wife, though the word sounded forced. "Don't blame yourself."

Tears trickled from Charlene's eyes. The Jorgensens were good, forgiving people. They wanted to forgive her, they had said the words they needed to, but she knew at that moment that they couldn't stand looking at her. She didn't blame them.

And Lucy said nothing.

"I'll go now." As Charlene edged past them, a dainty tap sounded at the door. A moment later, a pretty young woman slipped into the room.

"Hey, I just finished another call and thought I'd check in. How are you all holding up? How's Ben doing?"

Charlene watched as the woman spoke with Ben's family. She heard someone call her "Kate," and she noted her firefighter shirt and long ponytail of chocolate-brown hair.

Kate didn't look at her, but Charlene suddenly remembered her from that horrible night. She had been part of the rescue, had gone over the cliffside, and was right there beside Ben after they pulled him up. But shouldn't her job be over? Was it normal to check in like this?

Kate stood beside Ben now, and for some reason, Charlene's chest seized.

Even in his dismal condition, it was still obvious he was very attractive; his five o'clock shadow even enhanced the effect. Charlene hovered, watching, until she realized she was being petty. What did it matter if another girl visited him? He wasn't even conscious. That was the only thing she should be concerned about.

Mentally, she gave him a hug. *Bye, Ben. Wake up soon.*

She left the hospital and wandered the town for a good portion of the afternoon, feeling aimless, but needing the sun and the breeze on her skin, the golden rays and the caress of warm air acting as a kind of therapy.

But through her contemplation came an uncomfortable awareness. As if she was being watched, or whispered about. But then, after her arrest, she realized she should have expected that. She tucked her head down, returned to her car, and drove home.

Woodfield. A stupid name for a stupid town.

Nails chomped on cold leftover pizza, chewed the rubbery cheese, and stared at the weak watercolor print on the motel wall. Figured the kid would have ties to a stupid town.

His girl, though, that Charlene, she was something. Nails pulled out her picture and raked it with his eyes. She was even more of a looker in person, and the years had been kind to her. She'd gone from a teen to a real woman.

His lip curled. What was her problem? Despite killer looks, she dressed like a prude and walked with timid hesitance, eyes downcast, as if she could hide herself from the world.

But she couldn't hide from him.

He barked a laugh. He might scare the life right out of her. Then again, those quiet ones could be tigers. He'd enjoy finding out. Like he had with Raquel. That she-cat wasn't a keeper, but she'd been fun while he needed her.

His stomach full, he tossed the last piece of pizza at the cheap framed watercolor. It bounced off the glass, leaving a greasy smear. An improvement.

Crossing his arms behind his head, he leaned back against the pillow. The motel room was lousy, but it beat a rank cell any day. He zapped on the TV and flicked through channels till his thumb paused on the remote.

There she was, on the news, wearing sunglasses like a celebrity. Her protective brother stuck to her side, leading her down the courthouse steps. Her cheeks burned red. Her hair flew wild. He grinned as he wondered how she'd liked the taste of jail. Now that was one jail he would have liked to have been in.

Drugs, they said? Who'd have thought? Such a sweet little innocent girl like that. Just went to show, no one's perfect. No one.

He chuckled and hoped the charges would stick.

The kid wouldn't like that. No, not one bit.

Chapter Five

*T*hat night, sleep came at last, but at a price. Charlene dreamed, and it changed into a nightmare. She awoke to a splitting pain in her head, and a scream, not her own, still shrieked on. After a moment, she realized it came from outside her window—the whistle of a passing train.

She rubbed her forehead and then her temples while letting her racing heart recede to a normal pace.

She'd dealt with enough nightmares in her life to know not to attempt to analyze them. Tonight's dream was nothing more than the result of an overactive imagination and her visit to the hospital.

Though why Clay was in it, she didn't know. He did that, intruding unexpectedly every once in a while. Quite annoying. And what was with him being surrounded by light? Her heart skipped a beat. *Maybe he's dead.*

Or maybe I shouldn't have eaten chocolate ice cream right before bed.

At least it hadn't been an Abner dream. Those ones, about Clay's evil, vengeful brother who had kidnapped and tortured her and Max, were the worst. But she hadn't had that kind of nightmare in over a year now.

What kind of nightmares would she have if she went to jail?

Don't think about it. She shuddered and pushed her hair out of her face.

Deep inside, she knew she was still tired and should plop her head back down on her pillow, but instead, she flicked on her bedside light. Moving quicker than any censoring thoughts, her hand reached into her nightstand drawer and snatched out a wrinkled envelope. She held it, and that was all it took for the memory to come flooding back. She was there once more, in the cemetery . . .

Clay's eyes, a rich brown, finally found hers for the briefest second before turning back to his mother's grave. Despite the fact that it was well past the customary time to leave the cemetery, Charlene lingered. At Margaret's request, there was no funeral luncheon to attend.

Charlene's eyes watered in the cold, and then grief tore a hot tear from her eye as she watched the casket being lowered down, down, until, too soon, it was out of sight forever.

Watch over her, Dear Lord. Goodbye, Margaret. I pray we'll meet again in heaven . . .

Charlene flinched as Clay watched what he really wasn't meant to: the abrupt dropping of a load of earth into the open grave, from a truck bed, onto his mother's vault. Nothing gentle or subtle about that. But efficient. Very efficient.

"Charlene?" Ben's voice. How easily she'd forgotten him. She turned almost guiltily.

"You okay?" he asked.

She nodded.

"What do you say we go grab ourselves a cup of coffee and warm up?"

"Oh, no thanks. I actually think I'll stay just a bit longer." She couldn't imagine leaving Clay yet. Besides, she had an important letter to give him, one that his mother had entrusted her to deliver if she wasn't able to speak with him before she died. Margaret's one stipulation was that Charlene had to give him the letter in private. "It's a sad letter," *was all the explanation Margaret had provided.*

"But please, Ben, you go ahead," Charlene urged. "Don't stay because of me."

"That's all right. I don't mind, really."

She lowered her gaze as they fell into silence, waiting. She couldn't bring herself to intrude on Clay's solitude, and yet she couldn't bring herself to leave.

The cemetery workers finished spreading the mounded dirt, and at that moment, white crystalline flakes began fluttering from the sky. The workers left, and still Clay stood at the foot of the grave. So stiff. Not even shivering.

She heard Ben clear his throat softly, and she knew he was wondering what she was waiting for.

And suddenly, she knew.

She was afraid. Afraid to talk to Clay. It was what she had wanted for so long, and yet now the thought terrified her. How much had his time in prison affected him? What if he still didn't want to see her? After all, what was she to him but a reminder of a horrible time best forgotten?

Go to him.

She heard the words as something like a whisper in her head, and she was reminded of Margaret's gentle, guiding voice.

Praying that she could be more of a comfort than a curse, Charlene took a deep breath and moved forward.

Just as she was about to open her mouth, Clay, his eyes still on the grave, spoke. "Thanks for coming, Charlene. And thanks for looking after her all those months. I know it meant the world to her."

She shook her head. "You meant the world to her, Clay."

He was silent for a long time as he watched the snow sprinkling the fresh grave, covering it flake by flake and weaving a heavenly white blanket.

"No headstone, no flowers." He spoke the words without emotion.

She remembered how Margaret had specifically requested, with all the strength of a dying woman, that, in lieu of flowers, all money be used for Masses. "Masses for the repose of my soul. That's all I'll want. Plant flowers later, for your own sake, if you wish, but I won't need them."

"She doesn't care," Charlene assured him. "There will be plenty of time for that later. When the ground's thawed and summer comes, we can plant some of her favorite flowers . . ." She tapered off, hoping she hadn't been presumptuous in saying "we."

With something like a nod, he picked up a nearby stick. Slowly, he traced one long line in the snow down the middle of his mother's plot. He followed this with another line, forming a cross. He drew a letter under the left arm of the cross, an "M." Under the right arm, he wrote an "A."

MA.

He set the stick down and stared at the simple markings. He swallowed a few times. At last he cleared his throat and said, "I'm gonna miss her."

"Me too," she whispered.

In her pocket, she clasped Margaret's letter and wondered, Is this the right time?

Her ears detected the scrunching sound of footsteps in the snow, and Ben appeared by her side.

Clay looked up.

"I'm sorry about your loss," Ben said with deep sincerity.

"Thanks."

Ben offered his hand. "My name's Ben, by the way. Ben Jorgensen." He glanced at her. "I'm a friend of Charlene's."

Clay shook Ben's hand but remained silent, obviously feeling no need to say his own name. He knew, of course, that Ben was already familiar with it from the news and from her.

Her hand released the letter in her pocket.

Now was not the time.

"Max wanted to be here, too," she told Clay, suddenly feeling the need to fill the silence, "but his flight got canceled because of the weather. He's very sorry, too."

"Tell him I appreciate it."

After another few moments of awkwardness, Ben spoke up. "Well, Charlene, what do you say we let Clay say his goodbyes in private?"

She nodded. Yes, of course, how inconsiderate of me . . . *But still, there was the matter of the letter. "Will we see you around?"*

Clay's dark brows pulled together and he eyed her directly, as if trying to decipher just exactly what she was asking. For some reason, she couldn't hold his gaze, and she moved on to a new question. "Are you staying in town?"

"For now," he said vaguely, still not answering her first question.

She didn't want to beg for a meeting with him, but the letter weighed on her.

Ben began moving to the sidewalk. She glanced again at Clay with a strange feeling close to urgency, as if she had to convince him of something. She decided to be honest. "I'm glad you're finally free, and I hope I'll see you again. You know you have a fresh start now, right?"

He gave a wry smile. "Do I?"

"Of course."

He rubbed his forehead wearily before gazing past her. Then, with a sad attempt at a smile, he said, "Ben's waiting for you."

She was being dismissed. With a nod, she walked away to join Ben, who lingered patiently on the sidewalk. "It's slippery," he warned, and he took her arm.

They walked a few steps. Then, unable to resist, she glanced back over her shoulder to see Clay still at his mother's grave, his head bowed.

Beyond him, beyond the headstones, she caught a glimpse of a thin man lurking near the trees. Was it the same man she had noticed earlier, right after the service? He slipped from sight back into the shadows, as if he had been a mere extension of the darkness, and she shivered.

"Come on, Charlene," Ben said, "let's go get you that cup of coffee."

She let him lead her away while all the while there was only one thought on her mind. When and how would she see Clay next?

Two days later, a letter came for her in the mail. She recognized Clay's handwriting from all the letters he'd sent to his mother, though there was something terribly messy and careless about the writing on this one. With a sense of foreboding, Charlene removed the letter and read the badly scrawled words.

Now, sitting on her rumpled bed, with the memories pressing in, she pulled out that letter again. If one could call two short sentences a letter.

She ran her fingers over the ragged edge where the blue-lined, thin white page had been torn from a spiral notebook. The paper was even more wrinkled than the envelope. She'd tugged it out and read it way too many times, especially in those first weeks after receiving it, always looking for more, hoping that somehow, it didn't really say what it did, didn't really mean what it did. His letters to his mom had always been so kind.

But this one, to her . . . she gave in and glanced at it.

Charlene,
I'm leaving town. You won't see me again.
Clay

The words, short and clipped, still stung.

So why did she keep it?

It was the mystery, she supposed, the unanswered questions. Why had he left so suddenly, without even a goodbye?

Maybe she'd simply expected too much.

She sighed and turned the note over and over in her hand, examining the paper as she knew she'd done before. Only this time, she noticed something.

Nothing much. A tiny spot along the paper's edge. Had it always been there? Or had she soiled the letter at some point? She'd certainly handled it enough.

She brought it closer to her eyes. The mark was a brownish rust color, reminding her of dried blood. From a paper cut, perhaps? *Like it matters.*

Disgusted at her obsessiveness, she shoved the paper back in its envelope and banished it once more to the drawer.

The only other envelope in the drawer still remained sealed.

"My Dear Son" was written on the front.

Slowly, Charlene reached for it. Maybe she would never really be able to truly forget Clay and put him completely out of her mind until she'd done her duty and delivered this letter as promised. After all, she'd made the promise to a dying woman. A deathbed promise. That was serious.

She set the letter on her dresser as a reminder. She'd make one last effort to find Clay's address and mail it. After that, she was done. Even though she'd promised to deliver the letter in person, she couldn't do the impossible.

Completely awake and restless now, she doubted sleep would come anytime soon, so she stepped into slippers, wrapped herself in her fleece robe, and padded downstairs to the kitchen.

She grabbed a mug, then gathered milk, sugar, and cocoa to make hot chocolate. As if she hadn't had enough chocolate tonight.

While she microwaved her drink, she pulled out a bag of mini marshmallows and a spoon. She removed the hot mug and was stirring rather crankily when she heard footsteps above.

Max's head appeared around the wall at the top of the stairs, confounding her. He usually slept through anything.

"Hey, Char, why're you up?" He scratched his scalp, his hair too short to make bedhead possible. He kept his hair practically shaved because heaven forbid a curl should appear on his macho head.

"Just having some hot chocolate." She settled into a wooden chair at the table. "Want some?"

He gave a gaping yawn, and she expected a no, but he said, "Sure, why not?" So she began preparing another cup.

When they were both seated at the table, he asked, "So you do this a lot? Get up in the middle of the night to drink? Sounds like a dangerous habit to me." He grinned, grabbed a handful of marshmallows, and dropped them in his mug.

She bounced her own marshmallows with the back of her spoon, dunking them and watching them melt in the hot liquid. "No. Hardly ever."

"So why tonight?"

"I had a bad dream."

"Oh." The way he said it, drawn out and pumped with too much understanding, made her shake her head.

"No, not like that. Not an Abner dream." She forced a smile. "I think I've got enough new stuff to worry about that it kind of cancels out the old nightmares."

"So there's a plus." Max paused. "Or was this dream worse?"

She blew lightly on the surface of her drink, creating ripples against the marshmallows.

"No, not worse, I guess." She wrapped her fingers around the mug. "Clay was in it."

Another expressive "Oh."

"What?"

Max cocked an eyebrow. "So Clay was in it. That good or bad?"

"Well, it was . . . neither. I mean, he was trying to help me, but— it was just a dream." She shrugged.

Max swallowed a gulp of hot chocolate. "Uh-huh."

She stiffened. "What do you mean, 'uh-huh'?"

"Who else was in your dream?"

"A bunch of mummies, and Ben and his mom. Why?"

"Funny that you didn't mention them."

"Oh, please, you didn't give me a chance."

"You'd rather talk about Clay."

She rolled her eyes. "Don't get all psychoanalyst on me."

"I'm not. It's called mindreading." He tapped his temple and smirked. "Magician, remember?"

She took a dainty sip and ignored him, glancing at the clock. *I should be sleeping.*

"You don't have to pretend with me, Char. I've known for a long time that you had a crush on Clay."

"What?!" She sputtered her drink. "I do not. And I *did* not!"

"And your face is red from the hot chocolate?"

"That's right." She grabbed a napkin. "Sure, I liked him. After he helped save my life, I'd better—but just as a friend." She folded her arms and wrinkled her nose. "But then he had to go and be all 'you can't visit me in prison.' It would have been nice if things could have been—different—after it was all over. But he didn't give anything a chance."

"You mean he didn't give you a chance."

"No, I mean *anything*. He didn't stay around, just took off."

"Aw, Char, don't take it so personally. He went through a lot,

46

and then his mom died. You can't blame the guy for wanting a new start, just because it didn't include you."

"Obviously." She huffed. "He can do what he wants. But why did he bother writing at all, if he was just going to make the letter so nasty?"

"Refresh my memory. What did it say again?"

She recited it word-for-word.

"You kept it, didn't you?"

Dang, caught.

"So what if I did? It's a reminder that he wasn't a friend worth having, after all."

"Didn't sound like he was trying to be insulting." Max shrugged. "How could he know you were going to be all sensitive over it? Wow, just like a girl."

She crumpled her napkin.

Max leaned back in his chair. "Come back to California with me. We could do all the touristy stuff you like. Walk the Golden Gate, visit the beach."

She released the napkin and her eyelids closed slightly. She imagined the sound of the waves, imagined watching their rhythmic ebb and flow. "Sounds nice." She grimaced. "But I can't do that. I'm not free to leave while I'm out on bond. Besides, I can't leave Ben. He's going to wake up any time. I need to be with him."

"Right. Then what if while I'm here, we try to fit in a visit to Lake Michigan? We haven't been there since we were kids. You used to love it there."

She was touched that he remembered. "Yeah, I did . . ."

"So what do you say?"

"We should. I'd really like that." Good, something to look forward to.

Max tossed a marshmallow at her forehead, and it bounced off. "But for what it's worth, Char, I always thought Clay liked you too."

"Whatever." She downed the last of her hot chocolate, now cool, and banged it on the table. She scraped back her chair and stood. "I need to get some sleep. I have to be up in three hours for class."

Max nodded and winked. "Sweet dreams."

―――

Sealed in the bathroom, the woman waited with her back turned, facing the shower but staring at the clock on her phone. The plastic stick lay on the countertop behind her.

47

The three minutes were up. She could turn any moment and learn her fate.

Don't be a coward, her mind rebuked. *Turn and look!*

Shoulders set, she pivoted.

She didn't even need to squint. She could see it clearly. The pink plus sign, made of two thin lines crossed in the middle, was vivid. Undeniable and inescapable.

Like the crosshairs of a gun.

Chapter Six

*C*harlene was late for class. Very unlike her, but Vivian's call had thrown her.

"I got the surveillance tapes from the library parking lot. If they show someone planting the drugs in your car—which I think is very likely—your case will have to be dismissed."

Dismissed. A wonderful word.

"I think you're the victim of a classic setup," Vivian went on in her mile-a-minute manner. "Someone called to conveniently 'tip off' the police, which is the real reason they pulled you over when you left the library."

After the heartening call, Charlene picked up her pace, weaving through students as she hurried down the hall. Rounding a corner sharply, she smacked into what felt like a solid, unyielding wall.

Looking up, she met a pair of very dark blue eyes. The "wall" was actually a tower of a man. His hair was cropped short, almost nonexistent. His face, somewhat attractive in an older, unrefined athletic way, made her picture him as a football player, plowing into players with no fear. His long-sleeved striped shirt and worn jeans fit him well, yet made it clear he wasn't lacking muscle.

"Sorry," they said at the same time, and as she stood there, momentarily forgetting her urgency to get to class, she realized he was handing over her bag, which must have dropped during their collision.

"Thanks," she said, accepting the bag.

"No problem."

They'd only exchanged a few words, and yet, as she snapped back to reality and hurried away, she couldn't shake the feeling that there was something very non-ordinary about the guy. She didn't think she'd seen him around campus before, which, even at this relatively small college, was no surprise. Maybe he was part time, like her.

After an hour-long lecture, her stomach pleaded for lunch. In the cafeteria, she chose a chicken salad sub, then stepped slowly around backpacks and made her way to a newly vacated table. She sat, then ran strawberry lip balm over her dry lips.

"Hey. This seat free?"

She pocketed the lip balm, looked up, and realized she was looking at the same linebacker guy she'd bumped into earlier. She nodded, then unwrapped her sandwich. He sat, and his eyes assessed her.

Uncomfortable, she pulled her bag closer and rifled through the contents, acting busy. Notebooks, textbooks, and, at the bottom, a thick paperback novel. *Gone with the Wind.* She'd begun the classic with determination years ago, then life got in the way and she only dipped into it now and again. She pulled it out and flipped through. The pages automatically fell open to a bookmark. No, not a bookmark, but a small snapshot picture of Clay.

She stared at it, almost stunned by the sudden appearance of the very person she kept shoving so hard from her mind. Her eyes couldn't help lingering on his face, so young. Not carefree, but content enough. No scars from Abner yet. No idea prison loomed in his future. He sported a crooked grin and messy brown hair that could use a trim. The picture had been taken before he left for college, she remembered his mom saying.

Margaret had given the picture to her years ago, her favorite one of Clay, she had said. She wanted Charlene to have it as a reminder to pray for him.

Like she'd ever needed a reminder.

She'd prayed herself dry when it came to him.

She automatically took a bite of her sub, then touched the edge of the picture and wondered what it would feel like to throw it out.

"In case you don't remember . . ."

Jolted by the voice, she looked up and recalled where she was and that she wasn't sitting by herself. She slapped the book closed on Clay's photo.

". . . I'm the one who bumped into you earlier," the linebacker clarified.

She nodded, her mouth full.

"Name's Lance, by the way."

Good, she liked no-last-name introductions. Meant she didn't have to give hers. She swallowed. "Charlene."

Lance rested his chin on his big fist. "Don't stop reading 'cause of me."

"I didn't." But she had. She felt a blush.

His lopsided grin showed uneven, though not ugly, teeth. "You got a boyfriend, Charlene?"

She blinked at his bluntness. "Yes," she was quick to say. "Actually, I'm engaged."

Lance whistled. "That serious, hey?" He glanced at her hand. "Engaged, but no ring?"

"Oh, I have a ring. I just—" she thought fast, wanting to avoid the whole messy story—"wasn't able to wear it today. I wanted to," she added hastily.

"You and this guy been together long?"

She nodded and took another bite, not feeling right about sharing personal details with a total stranger, even if he was trying to be nice. Nice, she knew, could come with ulterior motives.

She checked her phone. Her heart skipped when she saw a missed call and message from Ben's mom. Maybe there was an update. And if so, was it good or bad? Her heart hammered.

"I gotta go, but nice meeting you," she told Lance as she hurried to her feet.

He gave a nod. "Likewise. See you 'round, Charlene. Don't forget your bag." He nudged it her way.

Taking it, she wandered out of the cafeteria in a daze. She pressed the phone to her ear and waited for Mrs. Jorgensen's voice. "Charlene, great news. Ben's awake! Come as soon as you can."

Ben's awake!

She stashed her phone in her bag and took off running to the parking lot.

Thank you, Lord! As she drove, she prayed the good news would continue.

When she reached the door of Ben's room, she barely even thought about her terrible previous visit. The Jorgensens looked too relieved at his consciousness to be harboring any grudges against her.

Ben's face lit up the moment she stepped inside, and her throat caught on her words. All she managed was a choked up, "Ben."

"Charlene!"

She hurried to his side and took his hand, very aware that he was still far from perfectly healed. "I'm so glad you're awake."

His hand squeezed hers but his gaze flicked to his family. "Hey, give us a few minutes, will you?" Obligingly, they filed out.

"Ben, I'm so sorry." She brushed hair gently back from his forehead, avoiding the bandage but glad to see that the large one had been replaced by a smaller one. "So you remember what happened?"

"Not much, not the actual fall, but my family filled me in." Charlene hung her head. "It was all my fault."

"If you didn't want to marry me, you could have just said no." He barely grinned before frowning at his tasteless joke. "Charlene, look at me."

She did. It had been too long since she'd looked into his kind, loving gaze. She'd missed it, badly.

"You don't have anything to apologize for. Don't you dare blame yourself. I knew we shouldn't have been that close to the edge, but I was trying to impress you. If anything, it was my fault, not yours."

"No, it was an accident. Nothing more."

They held gazes as she drank in the reality that they were here now, together and safe.

Ben's eyes went to her mouth. "Can I get a kiss?"

"Of course." She quickly leaned in to meet his lips, closing her eyes to savor the moment. Even after days in the hospital, somehow he still smelled like the outdoors.

When their lips parted, she sat back in her chair but kept holding his hand. "How are you feeling now?"

"After that kiss? Phenomenal."

"Come on, Ben. What do the doctors say? When can you go home?" *And when will you walk again? Please tell me you'll walk again.*

Ben's brows furrowed. "I can't feel my legs yet." His voice lowered. "But it's still early . . . too early. There's so much swelling around my spinal cord, but as that goes down—and it can take weeks—there's a good chance I could regain feeling and move-ment. I'm lucky the injury's as low as it is. The higher on the spine, the worse the damage."

She sensed he was reciting something he'd been told. She was sure neither of them really considered the location of his injury "lucky."

"To help my chances, I'll be transferred to a rehab center before I can go home. Lots of therapy for sure." He swallowed. "But I'll be honest, Charlene. There are no guarantees. Everyone's recovery from SCI is different."

His voice cracked and his fingers bunched beneath her palm. "There's a chance I might end up in a wheelchair for good. I—" He broke off his words to look away from her, at the wall. She heard him take a couple deep breaths like he was steeling himself, and her heart palpitated.

"What, Ben? Just say it."

He flung his gaze back to her, a hardened look on his face that she'd never seen before. His lips were rigid as he forced his words through them. "I don't want to lose you, Charlene, but—I can't expect to hold you to a promise of a life with me when I could very well end up being a burden. When you said yes, it wasn't to this." He glanced down at his immobile, sheet-covered legs and grimaced.

"No, Ben." She fought a tremble in her throat. "Don't. I said yes, and I meant it. I want to marry you whether or not you ever walk again. But . . . you will, Ben, I know you will." Tears slid down her cheeks. "Like you said, it's just too soon. We can't give up hope. You're strong, and you'll work so hard."

"I will." His hands squeezed hers. "I promise, I won't let you down."

She swiped at her tears. "I'm so happy you're awake."

"Me too." He looked at her left hand. "I wish I'd caught that ring. It's going to take a little while, but I'll find a way to get another one made, just like it—"

"No, that's not important. I don't need a fancy ring. We'll pick out a simple one, and I'll be just as happy."

His neck muscles flexed. "We'll see. It would only be temporary, till I can get the other one. Once I start earning money again," he added quietly.

"Your job," she lamented, suddenly remembering. He hadn't just lost his ability to walk, but his chance at becoming a fulltime firefighter anytime in the near future. "You worked so hard for that."

"I don't care about that right now. All that matters is I'm still around to have another chance with you." He touched her chin. "Did I ever tell you how lucky I am that you came into my life? You're the best thing that's ever happened to me. And if it weren't for you going to get help, I never would have made it. You're my hero, Charlene."

"That would be heroine," she corrected jokingly, but blushed. It wasn't funny. *Heroine.*

Heroin. It occurred to her to wonder what his family had told him about her arrest. Did he know? If not, she couldn't bear to bring it up right now. And the less she thought about it herself, the better.

At last, after sharing a hospital dinner together, she gave in to the fact that she had pressing homework waiting for her at home, so she said goodbye and promised to visit again soon.

Recharged with hope, her heart and steps felt lighter as she made her way out of the room, confident God's goodness would see them through this trial. She just had to trust.

In the waiting area, she saw Ben's family chatting with a young woman in a dark blue fire department uniform, and as she turned, long ponytail swishing, Charlene recognized Kate. Sheesh, did the girl live at the hospital?

She smiled brightly at Charlene. "So he's still up for visitors?" Kate didn't wait for an answer as she sailed past.

Feeling confused, Charlene heard Ben's mom say, "Kate's been so kind to us. Work brings her here a lot, so she drops in on Ben sometimes."

"They talk firefighter stuff," Lucy said, almost in a challenging tone.

"They talk?" Meaning he talked to her before he even talked to me?

But it wasn't his fault that I didn't get here earlier.

But why is she visiting again?

The thoughts warred inside Charlene, but all she said was, "Okay." She wondered why Ben hadn't mentioned Kate, but it wasn't important. She wasn't important.

Still, Charlene felt unsettled.

She exited the bright hospital into the cool dimness of the parking garage, found her car, and drove home.

Inside, she found Max pacing her living room, talking on his phone. He ended the call, slapped on a baseball cap, and threw her discarded jacket back at her. "Come on, let's go out."

I can't. I've got homework, she almost said, but she sensed his need to go. She shoved her arms in her jacket. "Okay."

He drove them to a bar on Seventh Avenue. As they walked inside, he tugged the bill of his cap lower in an attempt to avoid recognition. "When was the last time you played a good game of pool?"

"Would have been with you. So not a good game."

He cracked a grin. "Your jokes need work, but at least you're trying." He claimed a vacant table and fed in the quarters, then chalked up a cue stick while she racked the balls.

"Go ahead and break." He handed her a stick.

Leaning into a splash of light from the overhanging Budweiser lamp, she positioned the stick and glided the smooth wood over the thumb of her left hand, aiming at the white cue ball. The familiarity of the motion came back to her and she filled her lungs with a satisfied breath. She and Max had grown up playing pool with their dad, who'd loved the game. She cracked the triangle of colorful balls and watched them scatter over the green felt table. A solid red ball, then an orange, clunked into the pockets. A good start.

After Charlene finished her turn, Max lined up his shot while she noticed several women eyeing him from their bar stools.

"Nine ball, corner pocket." Max's cue ball struck the nine, sending it right into the pocket. He followed with two more strategic shots.

Charlene leaned on her stick. "Remember that time we played pool on Grandfather's table, and you tore the felt with that terrible shot?"

Max nodded. "The last terrible shot I ever made."

She rolled her eyes. "You thought Grandfather was going to kill you."

"He would have. But Dad found out first and took the blame."

She smiled at the memory and sunk a blue ball.

While she considered a combo shot, Max circled the table. "I've gotta head back to California tomorrow."

Her aim wavered. She stared at the tiny reflection of her splayed fingers in the cue ball. "Already?" She'd been hoping for at least a few more days. So much for Lake Michigan.

"Yeah." Max switched his hold on his stick. "There's stuff I gotta take care of."

"Oh?"

"A show to get ready for." He tapped a finger. "And a girl I gotta break up with."

"Really?" What else could she say? She hadn't even known he was in a relationship. "I'm sorry."

"It's for the best. You gonna shoot?"

She drilled her ball and it skipped, collided with one of his, and sunk it.

The game continued, but her focus had changed. She realized they hadn't had many real conversations about what was going on in his life lately. She was surprised to learn that his friend Wayne had left their magic act to pursue a comedy routine. But she was more astounded to hear about the sheer number of women Max had dated over the last few years. With the money and fame, it shouldn't have surprised her, but still . . . she shook her head. "Ever thought of going for quality over quantity?"

"That's always been the plan. Problem is, there's an awful lot of gold-diggers out there."

"I believe it."

"I'll probably never get married." He said it like he didn't care. She tilted her head. "But if you found the right girl, you would."

Max shrugged.

"Do you even know what you're looking for?"

He skirted the table and assessed his next shot, then glanced up at her, brows raised. "Seriously?"

"Seriously." She twirled her stick. "List the qualities. Let's see if any real girl has a chance."

"All right." He called his shot and sunk it. "Faith's important, obviously, but she's gotta know how to have fun." He rechalked his stick. The dry squeak put her teeth on edge.

"She can't take herself too seriously. She has to be confident, but not overbearing. Know how to enjoy silence, not have to fill it with lots of meaningless talk." He set the chalk down and hoisted his stick. "While I'm fantasizing here, if she could know me without realizing I'm famous, that'd be awesome." He rested his forearm on the table. "And of course, she's gotta be hot."

"Of course." Charlene snorted. "I'll keep my eyes open for you."

"You do that. If she passes your scrutiny, I'll know she's a winner." There was a little too much sarcasm in his words. He sunk the eight ball, won the game, and gave a fist pump. "Let's get a drink."

She replaced their sticks in the rack and followed him to the bar, glad her favorite drink was water. Her bond papers had been very clear on avoiding alcohol.

Minutes slid by as they relaxed and chatted. She realized, in the drama of the last couple days, she hadn't told Max about her engagement. So she did now.

He set his beer down. "Really?"

"You're supposed to say congratulations."

He eyed her and shook his head. "You're too young."

"Oh, please. Maybe you're too young, little brother, but not me." Her favorite retort, since she had him beat by two minutes of life.

He swiped the back of his hand across his mouth. "Look, nothing against Ben, and I'm sorry he's hurt, but you're moving too fast."

"We've been dating over two years, and I've known him almost four."

"He's your first real boyfriend."

"So? It only takes one. If he's the right one."

Max's eyes drilled hers. "Is he? The right one?"

She stiffened. "Of course."

He turned back to his drink. "I don't like it."

"You don't have to."

"Good, 'cause I don't." He downed his beer.

She bristled. "Not everyone has to live wild and reckless like you. I *want* the stability and safety of marriage."

"Stability? Safety?" he scoffed. "Go live in a convent."

"You're impossible." She blotted a drip of water with a napkin. "If you can't be happy for me, forget I told you."

"Fine." He shoved his empty glass. "I'm not gonna pretend, that's all. You know I know you better than anyone. Talk about your 'twin intuition' crap. Here's what it's telling me: you're still searching for something."

Her mouth opened.

"Or someone."

"That makes no sense."

"Maybe it will if you think about it."

"There's nothing to think about."

Max stood. "You're not ready to get married."

She glared. "You don't know what you're talking about."

"Hey," he backed up and jammed his fingertips to his chest, "I'm not telling you anything I'm not telling myself. Neither one of us is ready for commitment."

"I'm not you, Max." She tossed her hair. "Don't project your insecurities on me."

"Says the queen of insecurities?" He slammed his money on the bar and strode off into the noisy crowd.

"Lover's spat?"

Charlene turned and met the heavily mascara-lashed eyes of a thin blond perched two stools down.

"What?" Then it registered, and Charlene cringed. "Eww, no. He's my brother."

Apparently pleased with that answer, the woman's shiny coral lips quirked. "Wish I had a brother like that." Her brows rose suggestively.

Eww again. Not wanting to encourage conversation, Charlene

pretended to search for something in her purse. She pulled out lip balm and glided it on. Repeatedly. Nice and thick. Obsessive, Max would say.

Perhaps taking the hint, blondie slid from her seat. Her lofty height enhanced by stiletto heels, she clipped past Charlene, creating a breeze of cloyingly cheap fragrance.

Charlene slid a hand past her nose and imagined Max stranding her in this crowded, noisy, stinky environment, knowing how much she would hate it. Would he be that spiteful?

She pivoted on her stool and searched the room. There he was, suavely playing pool with a couple of women who'd been eyeing him earlier. One of them laughed, dropped a hand on his shoulder, and let it linger.

Charlene turned back to stare at her glass. Oh well, at least they'd had one good game. She swirled her water and listened to the clinking ice. The corner of her mouth pulled up. *It wouldn't be like old times if we didn't have a fight or two.*

―――

The brother was gone, and she was alone again. Defenseless. Vulnerable.

Perfect.

It would be time now, any day, when the nosy cow of a neighbor wasn't home, watching and listening.

Nails fingered the shiny new key, rubbed the jagged edge against his skin and contemplated exactly what he would do and say, imagined how she would react. The fear. The trembling. She might even cry.

He'd like to hear that.

Because he didn't want to hear her regular voice again. He shook his head as if he could remove the sound still wedged in his brain. How she spoke. Soft, gentle.

Like her.

He hadn't expected that. His gut tightened.

Hadn't expected her to wake dead memories.

Chapter Seven

*A*s Charlene knelt in church on Sunday morning after Mass, wishing she and Max had parted on better terms, her gaze strayed from the golden tabernacle, up to the crucifix, then to the cherubic angels painted on the ceiling.

Instead of her soul soaring, she felt weighted by something pressing and ominous.

I don't want to go to jail. Please, Lord.

But it was more than that, something she couldn't pinpoint . . .

With a small sigh, she rose to her feet and lifted her purse, but something about the gentle clink of coins made her pause. She counted numerous quarters and decided to light some blessed vigil candles before leaving. The wicks would burn all day, sending her prayerful intentions heavenward on vaporous wisps.

Standing beside the candles, she calculated. At fifty cents each, she could light four. The intentions flowed out easily.

The first candle, she lit with a prayer for Ben. *For a miraculous recovery.*

The next candle, she lit for the Jorgensens. *Comfort them, Lord. Strengthen them. Please.*

One candle for Margaret Morrow's soul. *May she rest in peace.*

When she ignited the last candle, she realized she was lighting it for Clay, wherever he might be . . .

Purse and heart a little lighter, she left church. Her car was one of only a few remaining in the crumbly old parking lot. She was at her door when she noticed something on her windshield.

Tucked beneath her car's wiper lay a single long-stemmed white rose, along with a laminated card of some kind. Curious, she glanced around, saw no one, then slipped the card free to discover it was a gold-edged holy card. Hands clasped in prayer, Jesus' Mother gazed down at her Son's crown of thorns with sorrow, and yet with love, while three wooden crosses protruded from the distant hill behind her.

Flipping the card, Charlene saw a prayer to the Mother of

Sorrow, and her eyes skimmed verses. *". . . stand by me in my last agony. To thy maternal heart I commend the last three hours of my life . . . Ask Jesus to forgive me for having offended Him for I know not what I did . . ."* The card was beautiful, and yet, not knowing who placed it here, or why, it was also mysterious and, truthfully . . . a little creepy. After all, the prayer focused on death. She couldn't help wondering if it was some kind of vague threat.

Nonetheless, a prayer couldn't hurt her. She tucked the card in her purse. Careful of thorns, she laid the white rose on her passenger seat and drove home in deep thought.

When Charlene walked into the library the next day, Geraldine, her boss, stood waiting for her, instead of bustling about as usual. Moving closer, Charlene saw Geraldine's favorite necklace hung about her neck, a little silver book on a chain that, in a nerdy sort of way, Charlene had always admired. Now she studied its polished shine instead of meeting Geraldine's eyes. "You're letting me go, aren't you?"

"I'm sorry, Charlene." The woman smoothed her wrinkle-free suit. "You're a good worker."

But I was arrested. Charlene grimaced. How could she have thought she'd still have a job to come in to today? An arrest didn't mean she was guilty, but she might as well have been for the way she was being treated lately.

She'd been aware of the whispers and pointed fingers whenever she went out. She'd even been getting weird prank calls on her phone.

School hadn't been pleasant, either. She'd overheard some nasty comments.

Geraldine gave a crisp, tactful speech, finishing with, "I wish you well."

Did she? Charlene bit her lip. The drugs had been planted by someone. Maybe someone here at the library. Why hadn't Vivian gotten back to her yet? Hadn't she gone through the surveillance tapes by now? Maybe she'd found nothing and wasn't eager to report the bad news.

Charlene turned to go.

"I'll send you your last paycheck."

Why? So I don't set foot in here again? Am I banned now, too?

But Charlene didn't ask for clarification; she didn't want to know.

She stopped in the restroom to throw cold water on her hot, red face. When a woman entered, Charlene ducked into a stall to compose herself. As she faced the stall door, she came face to face with a picture of herself. Not a flattering one. *Who in the world took this, and when?* Then it hit her.

My mug shot.

Her chest tightened. With increasing anger, she read the few verses typed above the photo:

Come to storytime with Miss Charlene.
Oh, the stories I can tell!
About my recent stay in jail
While I'm out on bail.

Her name, phone number, and address followed.

So that explained the crank calls. And her address . . . she shuddered at the violation of her privacy.

Were there more hurtful flyers like this? She stalked out, and the lady washing her hands gave her a weird double-take before hurriedly leaving, and she knew the answer.

Sure enough, inside the woman's abandoned stall hung another, more vindictive, variation:

Ladies, hide your men
Cuz I'm out on the loose
A spoiled rich girl druggie
A tramp who needs a noose.

Alarm and anger curdled Charlene's stomach. *Juvenile harassment, that's all it is.* She tore up the flyers and flushed them down the toilet.

On her way out of the library lobby, she glared at the replica Liberty Bell. There it hung, silent and cracked, yet taunting her with freedom.

She aimed her car out of town. The town that was turning against her. Most likely, the flyers were plastered all over Woodfield. Someone was out to ruin her life.

Switching on the radio, she shot the volume way up, something she rarely did. Marc Cohn's "Walk Through the World" blared out. Midway through the song, the irony hit her, and she thought of Ben.

61

Walk? *Walk?* Would he ever walk again . . . ? It was too cruel, yet she kept the song on, letting pain eat at her.

On the edge of town, the song over, she was forced to slow considerably. A long row of cars sat parked, cluttering both sides of the street, near Prairie Hill Cemetery. *Must be a big funeral.*

Sun slanted through her windshield, warming her excessively, so she opened a window. Unlike her mood, the May day was nowhere near dreary, but shiny and welcoming.

She recalled the last funeral she'd attended, Margaret's, with the bitter cold, the snow, and the oppressive sadness. But that was across town, at Saint Paul's Cemetery. She hadn't visited Margaret's grave in a very long time, and she felt bad about that. But somehow, visiting always ended up reminding her of Clay, and she didn't want to think about him or how they never did plant those flowers.

Charlene awoke to silence, although she had an unsettled feeling that a noise had broken her sleep. The train? Exhausted, she almost dropped back into oblivion, but scratchy dryness in her mouth and throat begged for relief.

She sat up to sip from a water bottle on her nightstand, only to find it empty. With a groan, she slid on her slippers and, too tired to go downstairs for a new bottle, brought the empty one to the bathroom, where a plastic night light gave a sufficient glow. Tap water would have to do.

The moment she stepped into the bathroom, her body seized. She snapped fully awake, blinking at the sight of the open toilet seat.

To some, the observation would be a minor detail, but for her, who never left a seat that way, the sight sent a chill snaking through her bones. She grasped for a comforting, sane explanation.

Max? But he'd been gone for days now.

Had she cleaned the bathroom tonight? She rubbed gritty eyes. Why couldn't she think clearly? She knew she cleaned almost too frequently, but she didn't think she had tonight.

What could she do? Call the police? What a phone call that would be. *I think there's an intruder in my house. Why? Because a toilet seat is up.*

Even in her mind, it sounded looney.

If something like this had happened in the day, she doubted she'd think twice about it. Nighttime just made everything creepier.

I really hate living alone.

She hurried, too nervous to glance in the mirror or check behind the shower curtain, too afraid she might see something or someone. *I cleaned the toilet and left the lid up. That's all there is to it. So slow down, stupid heartbeat.* The rapid, intense pounding felt borderline painful.

She filled her bottle with a gush of water, then trotted nervously back to her room.

When she climbed into bed, she couldn't plunk her bottle onto the nightstand fast enough. At last, she tugged the bed covers up to her chin and curled up snugly.

Sleepiness soon washed over her.

A whispered rustle of movement barely registered in her foggy mind, but then a faint creak snapped her alert. She strained to hear something more, fearing she would. Fearing someone was in her room.

So turn your head and look.

Just a fraction to the right was all it would take.

No, I'm imagining things. That's all.

Another creak.

Her body lay petrified for a ghastly drawn-out second. Terror lodged in her throat, blocking her breath until air hissed through her teeth, too loud in the potent silence. She balled her fists and swiveled her gaze to the right.

A dark presence lunged, landing on her with a crushing force. Her heart crashed against her ribs. Panicking, she thrashed, but the massive weight suppressed her efforts.

A heavy hand clapped her mouth and nose, stifling her scream. The body drove her deep into the mattress, bedsprings protesting with muffled squeals.

Her struggle to escape turned to a struggle to breathe. One of her arms managed to flail out and topple her water bottle. *Glug, glug, glug,* water flowed out rhythmically.

The intruder's smothering fingers finally slid off her nose, and as she pulled in air, she registered the scent of leather.

An irrational part of her whispered delusions of hope, assuring her that this was all a sick joke. The lights would snap on any moment to reveal—

Who? Who would do this? Only someone with terrible intentions.

Reality returned.

Desperation.

Who are you? What do you want? But she couldn't speak, only wait in blindness for the worst. And her imagination wasn't kind.

Dear God, protect me.

No words came from the shadowed body restraining her, pinning her down. She fought to scratch and claw, but her nails were short and dull, and she couldn't make contact. Apart from a few grunting breaths, her attacker's efforts seemed to take no exertion at all. Was he enjoying this? Did he know that by not speaking, he was leaving her in a terrifying mental darkness?

It occurred to her that he was waiting for her to wear herself out. Forcing herself to go limp, she inhaled rapid breaths.

Warmth tickled her skin as a deep voice whispered close to her ear. "That's right . . . be afraid." A finger ran over her cheek. "It sounds good on you."

A whimper escaped her.

"Shh." While one hand remained over her mouth, cold leather-clad fingers crept over her neck, gently, delicately, then paused to press her throat. "I only want a little information. But if you don't cooperate, I'm going to hurt you."

She racked her tortured mind, trying to catalogue the voice. It was unusually deep and raspy, intended to disguise, she suspected, but had she heard it before?

"I'm going to move my hand off your mouth so you can answer me. Not so you can scream. Got it? If you scream, I'll get angry. You don't want to make me angry, do you?"

She shook her head, but as soon as his hand freed her mouth, she couldn't help herself. Survival instinct took over. She let out a deafening scream.

A sharp blow across her face severed her cry. Two more stinging strikes followed in rapid succession.

"No." He grasped her lips and squeezed hard. "I need you to shut your mouth and listen. Got it?"

Dizzy, she tried to nod, tried to say yes, but only managed a muffled sound.

"Good." He yanked her hair, wrenching her head back.

She stared up into a silhouetted face. Straining her eyes, she made out only the vague shape of his head and broad shoulders, not enough to identify him. The room was too dark. She'd been proud that she'd kicked her bedroom night light habit, but she decided right then and there to return to it.

If she survived this.

The man's breath, close to her face, reeked stale and acrid as he spoke. "Where's your boyfriend?"

A million thoughts tumbled through her mind, a million implications and repercussions. Fear fired from her eyes, shooting pointless pleas into the dark. Her voice refused to work. The man gripped a chunk of her cheek. "Answer me!"

"He's . . . in the hospital," she said, hating herself for possibly putting Ben in harm's way.

"Which one?" His rough fingers ignited a burst of adrenaline. She tried to fight, but couldn't even manage a kick.

"Saint Mary's," she gasped, fairly spitting the lie. "He's at Saint Mary's." *Lord, give me time to warn him.*

The man leaned closer, his facial scruff scratching her cheek as he whispered, "You'd better not be lyin' to me." Hand on her neck, he shoved her deep into the pillow, almost crushing her windpipe, and she thought this was it. She was dead.

Then he shifted his weight and she sucked air greedily, frantically.

He lifted his hand. She saw it coming. Her oxygen disappeared as he pressed a wet cloth over her nose and mouth. She fought to turn her head, but couldn't. Suffocation overwhelmed her. Her lungs screamed for air and she gasped, filling her nostrils with a fruity chemical smell.

He seemed to hold the cloth on her forever. Her skin tingled hot and cold until a thick fog filled her mind and at last she fell from consciousness.

———

She'd put up a decent struggle for someone her size. Nails could still smell her. Her stupid strawberry scented lips. And that hair, reeking of some kind of sickly sweet shampoo. He'd finally gotten to touch the strands, though. Every time he saw her, he wanted to thrust his hands into all those twisted, wild curls. Shining, glinting, taunting.

Like Beth's.

He yanked a whiskey bottle from his bag.

Pretty Beth, the perfect daddy's girl. Perfect. Too perfect for him.

The glass bottle felt chill in his grip. He swigged the drink, felt liquid fire roll down his throat and pool in his gullet. But it didn't warm him. Didn't satisfy. Not even close.

He never should have used the name Lance. He thought it had been long enough.

Clunking the bottle onto a side table, he dropped onto a ratty chair and willed away the tremble in his hands. He remembered Beth perched on an overstuffed sofa, her younger siblings clustered around as she read them fanciful Bible stories. He'd always found reasons to linger near, doing stupid chores like dishes or sweeping. Women's work, but they all had to take turns in that crazy Callaghan house.

All those stories about Jesus. He liked to argue with Beth about Him. The man was supposed to be God, but let Himself be hurt and humiliated and killed. What a wimp. "Weak," he'd scoffed. He could still hear her voice . . .

"Weak? Oh no, Lance," Beth's cheeks pinked with the heat of passionate belief. "There's never been anyone tougher than Jesus." Her wide eyes flashed. "They drove nails through him. Nails. Can you imagine?"

He hadn't wanted to picture it, but the awe in her voice was hard to forget.

"Nails. Can you imagine?"

That night in bed, in the nicest foster room he'd ever had, as he lay awake staring at the ceiling, he did imagine. Nails, hammered right through his palms, through his feet. Would hurt like hell.

"Did you know the word 'excruciation' comes from 'crucifixion'? Because it's the worst torture," Beth had claimed. "Jesus chose that. To suffer for us, to wash away our sins with His blood. One pinprick droplet could have done it, but He chose crucifixion. Can you imagine that kind of love?"

No, he couldn't. Not then, and not now. Choosing suffering wasn't love, or bravery. It wasn't tough. It was stupid.

Stupid.

Seizing the bottle, he downed another swig of whiskey.

Chapter Eight

*T*he sun burned high when Charlene finally awoke. Groaning, and with her head aching, she fumbled to the bathroom to be sick.

Still nauseous, she found her phone beneath her bed. The police responded promptly to her call. They took down her story, and she even told them about the toilet seat being left open. They searched, but found no evidence of forced entry, no footprints outside her window, nothing stolen.

Unfortunately, the fact that the entire incident took place in the dead of night, in her bed, with no witnesses, made them skeptical. She could read it on their faces.

"I didn't dream it," she insisted, "if that's what you're thinking."

She could hardly blame them, though. It did sound like a night-mare, and she was very prone to those.

Additionally, she hadn't reported the incident till late morning, though she assured them the intruder had knocked her out with chloroform or something to make his escape.

While of course she was thankful for the lack of physical evidence on herself, it would have helped back up her claim. She couldn't even find any bruises on her neck, where she was sure she would. For all the police knew, she was merely the victim of a fantastically convincing bad dream.

They were aware of her pending case. She was under a lot of stress lately, after all. Was she taking any medication? Could she think of anyone she'd had trouble with lately? That question made her pause. It was disheartening to realize just how many people probably disliked her. She mentioned the cruel flyers, the random calls, and the strange knife guy from the library, but she couldn't remember his name and she'd thrown his card away.

To her relief, the authorities took her seriously enough to set a guard on Ben at the hospital as a temporary precaution.

Once the police left, she talked with Ben on the phone for over an hour. He had no idea whom the intruder could have been. He sounded steaming mad and frustrated that he couldn't come comfort her. She heard his mom in the background, pleading with him to calm down.

He ignored her. "You can't stay there by yourself anymore, Charlene. I won't let you. It's not safe. He got in once. He could do it again."

True. She ran a hand over her neck, prodding gently at the sore tendons and muscles. She had no desire to stay here alone or even sleep in her bed again, but where could she go? In a hotel, she would still be alone, and she wasn't sure she trusted their security. But she couldn't very well stay at the hospital with Ben.

And Max? She didn't want to keep making him fly back here to babysit her. Because she knew, if she called him, he would.

"You can stay with my family," Ben offered, perceptively sensing that she had nowhere to go.

"Thanks, but shouldn't you talk that over with them first?"

"No need; they'd insist."

Did his mom just say something?

"Still," Charlene attempted, "that's a lot to ask, and we don't know how long I might need to stay."

"Don't worry, the police will catch the guy."

But she couldn't imagine how. They had nothing to go on.

"Don't worry," Ben repeated. "How long till you can get over here and I can actually see you again? It's been too long. I'm having Charlene withdrawals. They can't treat that here, not without you."

She smiled, appreciating his effort to lighten her mood. He always knew just what to say.

An hour later, with one bag of luggage in hand and a still-warm batch of Ben's favorite chocolate chip cookies steaming up a Tupperware, she headed out the door, wondering when she'd be back. But as she turned the key, she had the oddest feeling she'd forgotten something.

With a shake of her head, she stepped back inside. Better to pop through each room than to worry all day. She saw no forgotten items downstairs, so she headed upstairs. She already had her countless hair-taming tools, toothbrush, floss, and toothpaste. From her bedroom, she'd already taken clothes and school books. That should be enough. She didn't want to make herself unwelcome at the Jorgensens' by hauling in a truck load.

In her room, she double-checked drawers and came across her irreplaceable pink pearl necklace, a sentimental treasure that had belonged to her mother. It was one of the very few things Charlene had to remember her by. She slid it into her purse.

Still, a nagging feeling lingered. She caught sight of her Bible. Hefting it under her arm, one other thing gave her reason to pause: Margaret's letter to Clay—that pesky letter that she couldn't get rid of without searing guilt.

She never should have made a deathbed promise without being certain she could keep it. It haunted her mercilessly. No matter how much she told herself Margaret would understand if she didn't deliver the letter, her conscience refused to be convinced.

She snatched the letter and stuffed it in her purse. *Okay, Margaret, but you're going to have to help me find him.*

Soon, Charlene imagined her whispering. *Soon.*

Charlene shook herself and hurried from the room. She'd kept Ben waiting long enough.

———

At the hospital, Charlene left her luggage in the car, shouldered her purse, and wrapped an arm around the cookie Tupperware as she made the familiar trek to Ben's room. She gave the partially open door a cursory tap before peeking in.

Ben rested against the back of his inclined bed, cushioned by pillows. Color had returned to his face, a reassuring sight.

Mr. Jorgensen wasn't in the room. Mrs. Jorgensen excused herself and brushed past Charlene, while Lucy remained in the chair by Ben's bed.

"Hi," Charlene said. "I brought you something." She tried to set the container on the bedside table, but there was no room. The surface was already crowded with flowers, cards, and another Tupperware.

As if noting Charlene's curiosity, Lucy peeled back the lid of the container, pulled out a cookie, and took a big bite.

Charlene smiled. "I guess you can never have too many cookies." She deposited her batch on another table farther away.

"Nope, you know me. Thanks," Ben said. "Chocolate chip?"

She nodded.

"Kate's are *chocolate* chocolate chip." Lucy's tone clearly implied that more chocolate meant better, and Charlene couldn't argue with that.

"Want one?" Lucy extended the container.

"No thanks," Charlene found herself saying, though the large moist cookies looked tempting. The chips still looked melty, too. A muscle near her eye twitched. "So Kate brought those?"

"Yep," Lucy answered, "for Ben."

Charlene turned to him with a stiff smile. She pulled up a chair and sat near his legs, since Lucy still sat munching near his head.

"Only because she's at the hospital a lot anyway. We talk about her emergency and fire calls." Ben cocked his head. "That doesn't bother you, does it?"

Charlene drew her hair out of her face as if to put it in a ponytail, then realized she had no band to secure it. "No, of course not." She let her hair drop.

Ben's smile widened. "I've never seen you jealous before."

She felt herself reddening.

"Looks cute on you. But seriously, you have nothing to worry about. You know you're the only one for me."

Lucy rolled her eyes while making a gagging face.

"And you, kiddo," he addressed his sister, "why don't you go find Mom and give me and Charlene a chance to talk?"

With a longsuffering sigh, Lucy stood, swiped Kate's cookies, and left, banging the door shut.

Ben and Charlene talked for a good hour. He needed reassurance that she was really okay, that the intruder truly hadn't hurt her any more than she'd told him.

"I'd love to get my hands on him," Ben said angrily.

When they finally moved away from that uncomfortable topic, they moved to another unsettling one. He still couldn't feel his legs.

"But I will," he insisted. "It might take weeks, maybe even months, but I will."

She nodded. "You will."

Maybe if they said it enough, believed it enough, they could make it so.

When he told her he'd be transferred to the rehab center soon, she wondered fleetingly if Kate would find a way to visit him there, too. But she refrained from asking, knowing she would definitely sound jealous. She didn't want to be that kind of girl, insecure and clingy.

After a goodbye kiss, Ben told her to go get settled in at his parents', assuring her he'd talked to them and it was all no problem.

At the door, she turned, a sudden pang in her heart, her eyes lingering on him. "I love you, Ben," she said, not knowing why she felt so sad.

Who was she kidding? Unless Kate was blind and brainless, she'd be making moves on him for sure. *Good thing I trust him.* After shutting the door and turning to go, she met Mrs. Jorgensen waiting for her.

"Go on back in with Ben," Mrs. Jorgensen told Lucy. "I just need to talk to Charlene for a quick minute."

As soon as Lucy left, Charlene spoke up. "Thanks so much for letting me stay with your family."

"About that. I'm sorry, but I really don't think that's going to work out after all. We wish we could have you, believe me, but," her voice dropped, "considering what happened, and the fact that that horrible man hasn't been caught, well, it wouldn't be wise. We have to think of Lucy. You have to understand our tough position as parents. We have to do everything we can to protect her." She tucked a thread of brown hair behind her ear and continued.

"Ben's not thinking with his head, only his heart. He has enough to worry about, though, and anymore stress won't help him heal, so please don't mention this to him yet. Can I count on you for that?"

Mutely, Charlene nodded.

"Good. And really, I'm sure you'll find a better fit than our crowded little place. You have your brother. Or your grandfather. He'd have room for you. How could he not?" Mrs. Jorgensen gave a little laugh.

How could he not? Let me count the ways . . .

But Charlene didn't want to.

Every once in a while over the past two years, Ben had encouraged her to reconcile with Grandfather, but persuasive as he was in all other things, he couldn't get her to budge on this. Important and close as his family was to him, he just didn't get how bad it was with her and Grandfather. But then Ben had never met him.

She scrambled to raise her sinking heart. She'd known this was too much of an imposition. She should never have let Ben convince her otherwise.

"Oh, I understand completely." Her tongue tripped over the words. "No big deal."

"Good." Mrs. Jorgensen's dry lips stretched into a smile. "We would take you in, really, if you didn't have any other options, no family at all, but you do, and we have to put Lucy first."

"Of course. That's the right thing to do."

Mrs. Jorgensen patted her shoulder and said, "Thanks for

understanding," before returning to Ben's room.

Charlene retreated to her car, and for a moment, she rested her forehead on the cool steering wheel.

It took her a second to register the note on her windshield. When she did, her gaze slid over the words again and again. *Be careful whose company you keep. You don't know him like I do.*

She glanced around her, searching the shadows of the parking garage. *Be careful.* A threat? About spending time with Ben? It made no sense. She almost hopped out of her car to pull the note from the wiper, then thought better of it. She popped her locks, started her car, and let the wipers swish the note right off the windshield. Then she drove over it.

She had nowhere to go but back home, alone.

At a stoplight, she pulled out her phone and attempted calling Max. Reaching voicemail, she only said, "Hey, Max, I hope you got back safely."

Postponing her return home, she stopped for dinner at McDonald's, something she rarely did. She sat in a corner booth and ate, dragging out the time as she dragged fries through ketchup. She toyed with the idea of seeing a movie next, but she'd only be putting off the inevitable.

Leaving McDonald's, she aimed her car for home. Halfway there, she pulled over for shrieking sirens and flashing lights. A firetruck and police car flew past. Her gaze lifted above the buildings and treetops, and she noticed a dark gray plume of smoke bulging into the night sky. Cracking her window, she could even smell it, a bitter, ashy odor.

Easing back onto the road, she realized the smoke billowed from the direction she was heading. With a rotten, knowing fear festering in her stomach, she sped toward home.

Reaching her street at last, her worst suspicion was confirmed. Her condo was on fire.

Nausea built, but the woman battled it down, closed her eyes and breathed deeply, willing herself to control it. To be in charge. To not be—

"A screw up." She could almost hear her dad saying it.

"Only a screw up would be in this situation."

But she could fix it. She pressed a hand to her forehead. She was smart. The way she saw it, there were two solutions: the clinic, or the man.

The first was the easy option; the second, the challenge.

She pursed her lips and nodded. She was always up for a challenge.

The higher the stakes, the better.

Chapter Nine

*F*lames licked the sky from the roof of Charlene's corner unit, saturating the night with a bright orange radiance. She parked on the street, then sprinted to the edge of the crowd gathered in the cul-de-sac. Riveted by the blazing sight, the blinding light, she already knew her home was gone.

Huge gray hoses snaked from flashing firetrucks and blasted water into the heart of the fire. Maybe there was hope that the firefighters could keep the flames from spreading too much to the connecting units, which still looked okay. She prayed everyone had gotten out in time, and it appeared likely. The damage was concentrated on her unit, now completely engulfed.

The onlookers talked excitedly, many with cell phones up, filming the action. Countless neighbors watched the disaster as if it were entertainment, while almost everything she owned literally went up in smoke.

—————

Nails had followed her home, but the place was crawling with cops. His cue to leave. He swung around and headed for his motel. Now was not the time to make a mistake.

He let himself into his stuffy room, remembering what his last mistake had cost him. Three years in the slammer. All for a gutsy spur-of-the-moment assault and robbery in broad daylight. It shouldn't have happened. But the fool had asked for it. Pushing past him on the street, rude and unapologetic, having the gall to tell him, *"Watch it, son."* Like Mr. Callaghan. Short-circuiting his good sense. He'd socked him an uppercut, then snatched his wallet and bolted.

But he didn't get far.

When the cops clapped the handcuffs on him, he heard Mr. Callaghan's smug voice. *"Consequences, Lance."*

Now he dropped to the motel floor and pumped pushups. Blood coursed through him, muscles bunching and working. Burning with power.

He had lots of years left. Those years inside were nothing. And he wouldn't make the same mistake twice. He grinned. Most cons went into the joint pretending like it didn't scare them—like that Cissy. But Nails always knew who'd be crying into their pillows at night.

He never had to pretend anything. He went in with steel in his veins and iron in his fists, owning the joint, leading a gang in no time.

Cissy had never been gang material. Nails had his eye on him from the moment they hauled him in. He'd been highly amused by all the mistakes the kid made in his first weeks, ignorant of the code of respect, bringing trouble on himself. His case had been high profile enough that he suffered for it.

And high profile enough that Nails knew exactly how to use him. Still, he took his time, studying him, planning his approach, letting him think he hadn't noticed him.

He'd wanted to provoke him that day in the yard, but hadn't expected the powerful reaction. He'd found the kid's greatest weakness. The girl. Of course. It would be the girl.

Something about that rankled Nails in the worst way. Especially the fact that the girl forgave him for what he'd done. What made Cissy so special that he had her to go back to after his pitiful, slap-on-the-wrist sentence?

No, the kid had life too easy.

Something had to be done about him. He had to learn his place.

Nails halted his pushups and rubbed his sweaty face.

He'd never expected the broken jaw. The rumors about it had cramped his reputation. He'd had to quell it fast.

That's where being gang leader came in mighty handy.

The day Cissy was brought back into general population, Nails ordered him a welcome back surprise: a special thirty-second beat-down under the stairs. Thirty seconds, because that was the soonest any CO ever responded to that stairwell.

It was enough. A lot of damage could be done in thirty seconds. Pretty boy wasn't so pretty after that.

It wasn't Nails's best thought out plan, though, for two reasons. First, he didn't get the satisfaction of personally giving the beating. Second, prison staff promptly put the kid in the infirmary, and Nails couldn't get to him.

Then Cissy's time was up, and Nails's bid was extended.

Another three years. Getting caught with that CO screwed it all up. Women had no business being COs, anyway. Chicks, thinking they were tough? Made him gag. Whatever they got, they deserved.

Nails cracked his neck from side to side, then pumped another ten pushups.

No, he wasn't through with Cissy yet.

———

I have to leave town. The thought struck Charlene with great clarity as she watched her condo burn like kindling. So much had already been destroyed: her reputation, her job, now her home. Did she really want to wait to find out what was next?

All she had left was Ben. Maybe the only way to protect him was to leave.

Moisture welled in her eyes, blurring the scene. Still, like the other onlookers, she gazed. She swiped her vision clear and succumbed to the horrible fascination. Because in a terrible way, it was a beautiful, spectacular display. The hungry inferno of ferocious orange-gold flames roared up into the night as if it could set even the moon on fire.

Meanwhile, calmly coordinated firefighters worked together, bravely and efficiently, moving swiftly to battle the blaze. For a brief second, she wondered if Kate was among them. Even from where Charlene stood, the heat was palpable, the scent of smoke thick. She coughed.

The crowd bombarded questions and exclamations, but the police kept everyone back.

"There you are!" Even in the noisy, crackling chaos, that shrill voice refused to go unheard. Charlene turned to see Darla, the head of the condo association, trotting her way as fast as the woman's hefty frame allowed.

"What happened, Charlene? What did you do? How did this start?"

"Uh, I don't know. I only just got here."

"What a disaster!" Darla pulled fingers through her short, feathered hair. "It obviously started in your unit."

"Maybe you left the oven on?" suggested a bystander, one Charlene now recognized as the Harley owner who lived in the end unit.

"I can't believe this!" wailed the single mom from the opposite side of the building. In her arms, her young son watched and pointed at the streams of water shooting into the fire.

But Charlene was still stuck on the oven comment, almost overcome by the possibility. That would be one of the most classic stupid mistakes to make. Surely, she hadn't. But she couldn't deny that she had been in a rush . . . She strained her memory, needing to capture a precise recollection of turning the oven off.

But she couldn't.

"Did you clean out your dryer vent like I reminded you to in the monthly condo memo?" Darla persisted, clearly determined to pinpoint blame. "This is what happens when people don't take the condo rules seriously. I always say—"

"I did clean it," Charlene replied weakly, as she felt more and more eyes turn on her. People nudged each other, not even attempting to whisper.

"That's her."

A finger pointed.

"It started in *her* condo."

"Trouble follows her everywhere."

"I never would have moved into this place if I'd known *she* was living here."

Charlene's nerves seized. She wanted to flee the cruel comments, but where could she go? She had no home. The last of the flames were finally being doused, leaving a dark, pitiful, crumbled shell where her home had stood. Besides, she knew enough about disasters by now to know that the police would want to question her.

She was almost relieved when she spotted them heading her way.

She shook the haze from her mind and answered each question as best she could. What time did she leave her condo? Where did she go? Could anyone corroborate her whereabouts?

It sounded like she was a suspect, but she reminded herself the authorities had to gather facts. This was merely routine. Further investigation would hopefully determine the cause of the fire as electrical or something equally nonblameworthy. She didn't want the fault to be hers, but she also didn't want it to be arson.

With everything bad that had been happening lately, she tried to tell herself that the fire was just a coincidence.

Then she returned to her car and saw the white writing smeared on her back window.

Burn, Witch!

Heart hammering, she looked back at the charred remains of her home. No coincidence. Whether the fire was deliberate or not, someone had hoped she was in there.

Someone wanted her dead.

Her feet pounded the road as she raced back to the police, suddenly not above the humiliation of pleading for protection. With steady composure, the officers listened and jotted notes. They checked out her car and questioned remaining bystanders.

Both the fire marshal and a detective questioned her. When they asked if she'd had trouble with anyone lately, she hardly knew where to start. After telling them all about the intruder, she voiced her suspicions about the knife guy, the note on her car, the flyers which gave her address . . .

It could have been anyone.

A near hysterical laugh threatened ludicrous thoughts. Max had left on bad terms. Grandfather had been insulted when she didn't let him bail her out.

But no, not family. She knew the truth. She heard the voice from less than twenty-four hours ago.

"You'd better not be lyin' to me."

The night intruder.

He did this.

When her swirling mind settled, she heard the fire marshal saying he'd do a thorough investigation come daylight. "I'll be sending some of the burnt wood to the lab for chemical analysis. But I'll tell you now, while arson can be easy to determine, it's usually not easy to nail the perpetrator. Unless they talk. The fire destroys DNA and fingerprints."

She nodded, though it was difficult to even care about the investigation right now. She just wanted to leave.

"We'll take you somewhere safe for the night," Detective Green assured her.

Too bone-weary to concern herself with the snide comments her neighbors made about her being arrested, she trusted Green as he assisted her and her luggage into his car. It felt good to sit, to be safe, and for a moment she let her worries fall away. Her eyes roamed the car's interior, the radio dials, and the hidden strobes.

"Don't forget to call your insurance," Green said. "You could even do that now."

So she did, instead of paying attention to where they were headed.

When the car stopped and they stepped outside, she gripped her luggage and gazed up at an all too familiar gray stone mansion. Green expected her to walk forward, but she hesitated. "I don't know if I want to stay here."

"What do you mean?" He looked at her like she was becoming too high maintenance. "This is your grandfather's."

"But we don't . . . get along," she offered feebly. "He disowned me. He doesn't want me here."

The detective shook his head and led the way up the steps. "Sure he does. We called ahead, and he's expecting you."

"Really?" She recalled how he had visited her in jail. Despite his gruff manner, he had seemed ready to reconcile.

"Really. Not only that, think about how safe you'll be. He's got great security."

The front door yawned open, spilling harsh light. Grandfather stepped into the spotlight of the doorway, smiling a gray-toothed grin and looking genuinely pleased. "Welcome, Charlene."

Green's radio crackled and a voice came through. He put a hand to his belt. "I have to go." With a saluting wave, he departed swiftly down the steps.

Grandfather swept his hand wide, inviting Charlene to enter. Biting her lip, she stepped over the threshold and into the mansion.

As she stood dwarfed in the expanse of the room, the door closed behind her. She glanced back to see the exit blocked by a hefty, square-jawed man. Lines creased his weathered face in too many places. He grinned, and more lines appeared. She wondered how long he'd been working for Grandfather and what type of work he did. *Shady work, I bet.*

"So the prodigal granddaughter returns," Grandfather said triumphantly. "I'll show you to your room. Frank." He summoned the big man to bring her bag.

The mansion décor hadn't changed much, if at all, since she'd been here last. The same cold, unlived-in feeling permeated the place. Ugly pieces of art punctuated the vast space and did nothing to fill it. Grandfather didn't speak, but if he did, she knew his voice would echo. She couldn't shake the feeling of having been sucked into a very beautiful chandelier-lit lair.

She was led to a spacious, luxurious room with its own whirlpool bath. The bed boasted marble pillared headboards. A picture window provided a sweeping view of the partially lit grounds two stories below.

"Make yourself comfortable," Grandfather said.

She eyed him, trying to finger his motives. "So you're really welcoming me back? I still stand by what I told you before. I'm not retracting my support of Clay's defense. Not that it matters anymore. But if you expect me to make some kind of public statement—"

"It's time we move past that." Grandfather waved a hand dismissively.

"Okay."

"We have a new turn of events to negotiate." He steepled his fingertips. "A more pressing, important bit of business. But it can wait till morning. Get a refreshing night's sleep, and we'll discuss it after breakfast."

Ah, so there was a catch. His admittance of the fact soothed her tension slightly. This, at least, was the Grandfather she knew. Whatever the new development, she would deal with it in the morning, when she was recharged. For now, a mile-high luxury bed awaited.

The woman couldn't hold back any longer.

On her knees, she heaved and wretched, spewing her sour, curdled insides, bracing the toilet with one hand while the other hand shoved back her hair, trying to keep it from the line of fire.

Oh, she'd been brought low, so low, but she would rise again. Stronger than ever.

Ignoring the bitter taste of bile, she wiped her mouth and lifted her head, her eyes not seeing the here and now, but the future.

She smiled at herself in the mirror.

It will all be worth it.

Charlene followed the trail of tempting breakfast aromas into the grand dining room, her curiosity piqued.

"Ah, Charlene." Grandfather beamed. "The late sleeper has arrived. You may sit here, my dear."

Frank pulled out the indicated chair for her at the overly long table, then stood at attention. Grandfather sat at the head, of course. She sat beside him and faced an unknown gray-haired guest across the table. The man smiled widely while Grandfather handled introductions. Mr. Flemming was his name, and he turned out to be a visiting investor.

At the end of the meal, she managed a few extra bites while Grandfather spoke in hushed tones with Mr. Flemming near the door. The man then left to attend to a business meeting via Skype in one of Grandfather's offices.

Grandfather approached her with an unusual smile and settled in a chair while she, uncomfortable under his scrutiny, forced down the remains of her last bite.

"I trust you found your room comfortable and the meal more than satisfactory?"

She nodded.

"Good. I'd like you to stay and work for me."

This again? "I already told you—"

"Not just any work," he clarified, leaning forward and speaking low. "I'll train you to take over my business. To run it when I'm gone."

She blinked. "Me? But—"

"It was always supposed to be you." He paused and looked past her, bitterness creeping into his voice. "After your father died, that is. Max could never handle it. Too hot-headed. But you, Charlene," his eyes pinned her, "you can. With the right training."

Her mind skittered over the words, the implications. *Me, a career-driven business woman? Me, in a fast-paced life of corporate power and wealth?* So hard to picture, but when she tried, she went cold. "I'm not right for that. I'm sure you must have any number of qualified candidates—"

"No one else is a Perigard." A hint of color rose at the base of his neck. "No one else is my flesh and blood. Do you even realize what I'm offering? My business is worth more than you can imagine. Someday, all of it will be yours."

"On what condition?"

"All you have to do is live here and work with me."

"But I'm getting married."

Grandfather snorted. "If you actually go through with that, fine. There's room here for both of you." He aimed a finger at her. "But you'll be in charge. And you *will* keep the Perigard name."

Ben would never go for that. She gripped her linen napkin. "What do I know about running any business, let alone a multi-billion-dollar—"

"You're not ignorant, Charlene, though you've certainly made some poor choices. I remember what you're capable of. You have a sharp mind. Like me." Grandfather adjusted the cuff of his suit. "You don't have to decide this second. Try it out. Spend the day in my offices. I'll give you an overview. Show you the possibilities."

He stood and waited for her to join him. She imagined him dangling treasure before her eyes, luring her with glimmering gold and jewels. She knew how wealth could corrupt. She didn't want any part of it. And yet . . .

"My lawyers are even better than Vivian Fenwick." The meaning in his casual words rang clear. An end to her case.

She inched her chair back.

With a nod, Grandfather exited the room, expecting her to follow.

Dropping her napkin, she did.

She was soon immersed in spreadsheets, graphs, and charts, learning about investors, holdings, projections, and profit margins. Despite herself, the work caught her interest. The day slid away.

"You have a head for this, Charlene," Grandfather said approvingly as he locked his office that night. "Start working for me now, then when it's time to take over, you'll be ready. What do you say?"

She swallowed and gave the only answer she could. "This isn't the life I want."

"Are you sure about that? Take some time to think about it."

Her mind spun while she picked at her dinner. Grandfather spoke congenially with Mr. Flemming, but his eyes watched her, waiting for a definitive answer. He wasn't forcing the issue, as if he knew doing so would scare her off. Instead, his nonchalance shook her.

After dinner, she wandered the mansion, almost dazed, hardly realizing that Frank, silent and large, shadowed her.

What am I doing? I need to call Ben and talk to him. But somehow, despite the money, she knew he wouldn't like Grand-father's proposal. *She* didn't like it. It was nowhere near the simple life they'd planned.

She found herself in the theater room. Absently, she flipped through DVDs. She came across a blank case tucked so far back under the shelf that it seemed purposely hidden. Inside the case, she discovered a generic looking DVD labeled with one word, "Justice."

Too curious to contain herself, she slipped the disk into the player and didn't even notice Frank slip from the room. Dire background music played and the opening scene began.

Chapter Ten

*A*s Charlene perched on the edge of her seat, she sensed by the mediocre quality that this was some sort of weird "home movie." The first shot panned down from light snowfall onto skeletal trees, down onto a church cemetery, then onto a lone man standing beside a fresh grave.

Her breath caught. She'd seen this before. Not on-camera, but in real life.

There stood Clay in his black suit, at his mother's grave, after all the mourners had departed. *All but me and Ben,* Charlene realized, as she saw herself step tentatively forward, Ben following slightly behind.

She squinted at the screen. Someone else was caught in the frame, another man, out of focus and distant. Just like on that day long ago, her curiosity returned. Who was he and why was he lingering on the fringe of the cemetery?

The camera zoomed in, losing the man, and her attention returned to herself and Clay. She figured the cameraman filmed from the street at the top of the hill. She puzzled over why Grandfather wanted this footage. Did it provide him some twisted, tangible satisfaction? Did he watch this to rejoice in the misery of his "enemy"?

She and Ben departed from the picture. *The last time I ever saw Clay.* Something like regret twinged beneath her throat.

Clay lingered, then at last made his way out of the cemetery, trekking up the sidewalk, coming closer, shoulders hunched, head tucked low, absorbed in his thoughts, careless of his environment.

Too careless.

She tensed.

A sudden blur of action filled the screen. Two large men, faces hidden by black knit ski masks, rushed him. One man slugged him in the stomach. As he doubled over, the other man clamped his arm around Clay's neck and hauled him from the sidewalk.

The view from the camera flashed to darkness, then to vehicle doors opening. The cameraman was now filming from inside the back of a commercial van. Slow, deep-toned music was suddenly replaced by natural audio, a bumpy, scratchy sound of struggling. The two thugs shoved Clay into the van, then quickly followed, slamming the doors.

One of the men slapped duct tape over Clay's mouth while another twisted his arms back and bound his wrists together.

The scene cut off.

Clutching her seat, Charlene's fingernails dug into the plush fabric.

She'd barely pulled in a breath when a new scene appeared: Clay slamming into a cement-block wall.

The room was large, shadowy, and windowless. Metal shelves, cardboard boxes, support poles, and a dingy stained floor suggested an old warehouse.

Momentarily stunned, Clay blinked, then struggled to his feet. His hands were useless, his wrists still taped together behind his back. Anger overrode the pain on his face as he turned to his assailants.

He braced himself as the two men came at him again.

And again.

Two against one, and Clay bound, were terrible odds. Obviously, he wasn't meant to have a fighting chance.

While the attack wasn't taking place in current time, Charlene still found herself silently mouthing, *Dear God, no, please . . . make it stop.*

As the men came at him, fists striking, boots kicking, Clay's arms strained instinctively to block his head, but it was impossible.

On the floor now, he doubled over and tucked his head to his chest, an attempt to shield himself in the only way possible.

She wished for the somber music again, to cover the sound of the flesh-thudding blows.

Blood trickled onto the floor, and she covered her mouth.

When the pounding stopped, Clay lay still.

And still, the thugs weren't satisfied.

They hauled him up roughly and dropped him on a flimsy folding chair, shoving him up against a crude table. He slumped against it and didn't move.

Charlene's hand lifted. She wanted to reach into the screen and help him, tell him he was going to be okay, but she didn't know if he would be, if he was, if—

A knife flashed and she clutched her throat, but the blade merely slit the duct tape on Clay's wrists. His arms immediately fell to his sides. A man seized them and slammed them onto the table, which she now noticed had tools of some kind laid out, as well as paper, and—

The image froze. Someone behind her cleared his throat.

She whirled to find Grandfather holding a remote, Frank standing beside him at the open theater door.

"Charlene, Charlene, always so curious." Grandfather nudged the door closed. "Do you like what you found?"

She turned back to gape at the screen, still trying to process the cruelty she'd just witnessed, and all she could manage was a strangled sound.

"I always told you he would pay," Grandfather said. "His token prison sentence was nothing. Nothing like what he deserved. For all that boy did to my name and reputation and company; and to you and Max, for that matter—no matter how you both deny it—that beating was a more fitting punishment than anything he could have endured in the luxury prisons of today."

Bile rose in her throat. "That's not justice, that's cold-blooded revenge. You hired thugs to beat him up and *film* it, too?"

Grandfather smiled. "Would you like to keep watching?" He aimed the remote.

She forced her voice through her throat. "*No!*"

"A pity." Grandfather clicked off the DVD, and the room went black. "By the end, he was practically crying like a baby. What do you think of your precious hero now?"

"I think you're a monster." Waves of horror washed over her, crashing, crashing, never receding. "And what do you mean by the *end?* Did you *kill* him?"

Grandfather snorted. "He was merely a little worse for wear." He puffed out his chest. "But he won't dare cross me again. I ensured he would be out of my town and out of my life—and yours—for good."

The words triggered a thought. The letter, the odd, short, abrupt letter Clay had sent. How had he even known her address? The answer fell into place. "You forced him to write me that letter, didn't you?"

"Indeed. I knew how you pined for him, you silly girl."

"I did not—"

"So I ended it. I gave you concrete closure so you could move on."

She shook her head, tears sliding down her cheeks. "You had no right to touch him, to torture him. And right after his mother's funeral—how could you? You think you can do anything, get away with anything, just because you're rich. Well, you can't. And that DVD, that's evidence—" *Shut up, Charlene. Just get the DVD and bring it to the police.*

Lights flicked on, curtesy of Frank, and she saw Grandfather now held the disk in his hands. With a grin, he cracked the evidence in two, then cracked it again. "Easy to dispose of. I suppose I've watched it enough times. It will have to suffice."

You have another copy somewhere. Charlene was as convinced of this as she was of Grandfather's hatred for Clay. Sickened to the core, she couldn't believe she'd considered partnering with him for a second.

"You weren't supposed to find it, Charlene, and I'm sorry it's upset you, but don't let this taint your decision. And don't waste your tears on that boy. He's nothing but a worthless convict."

Her emotions charged into overdrive and she couldn't control them. She shoved her face into her hands, wishing she could destroy the reality of all Clay's suffering as easily as Grandfather had destroyed the evidence of it.

"Now, now, you just need a good night's rest. You'll feel much better in the morning."

She shot up and marched forward, her emotions tattered and raw. "No, I won't. I won't be here—here with you and your cruel, inhuman scheming—" Going slightly insane, her arms itched to fly from her sides and she felt herself on the brink of physically lashing out.

He sensed it, and gave something like a signal to Frank, and the next thing she knew, Frank seized her.

"Get your hands off me—" She felt a sharp prick of pain in her arm, and her words floated away, impossible to retrieve. Her limbs weakened and her eyelids drooped.

She felt someone leading her away, felt herself float down onto something soft, and then . . . she was aware of nothing.

———

Her head buzzed. Her dry tongue sat heavy and tasted bitter. Nausea made her wretch.

Charlene opened her eyes to darkness, a desperation stretching her mind, pulling her here, pulling her there.

She stumbled up from the bed.

Have to. Get away.

She rubbed her aching eyes.

Think. Think.

Her hand grappled for her phone, but couldn't find it. *He took it.* Her body wanted to crash back onto the mattress, her head wanted to burrow into the down pillow. Using every ounce of will, she stumbled to the bathroom and threw cold water on her face. It sloshed all over her body. She moaned, feeling sick, scared, giddy, guilty. *Poor Clay. Poor Margaret. If it weren't for me . . . I'm sorry, so sorry.*

She tried to sling her purse over her shoulder, but dropped it. She frowned at the unexpectedly complicated strap before wrestling it into place. *Stay.*

The droning in her ears didn't let her know how quiet she needed to be, but she tiptoed from the room and didn't see Frank.

She put a hand to her pulsing temple. Could she navigate the maze of the mansion fast enough in her befuddled state? She was aware enough to know someone would be after her soon, but if she could get a head start . . .

She swerved down the hall. Doorways, doorways. *This one?* No. *This one?* Maybe . . .

Ah, into the garage where Grandfather kept his fleet of shining luxury cars. The room smelled of rubber and oil and faintly of gas.

She pulled open the door of a Rolls Royce and glanced inside. No keys, of course, but her brain was too foggy for her to take control of a wheel anyway. She snagged the electric garage and gate openers, and her lips stretched into a smile. No need to attempt climbing a twenty-foot high fence.

She opened the garage door. While it rose silent and smooth, it didn't smother the sound of a yelled curse as she dodged under the rising door and out onto the lawn.

Security lights blazed on. On a dizzy high, she bounced from sparse shadow to shadow.

"Charlene, get back here!" Frank roared.

She chortled. Did he really expect such a request to work? If that was the genius she was up against, she wasn't worried.

Her foot snagged on a low bush and she sprawled onto grass. Gathering herself up, she heard steps pounding close. Hiding in shadows wasn't enough.

She darted under a low tree. Noting the bumpiness underfoot, she reached down and grasped a nice sized stone, about the size of a small baseball. Perfect. She hurled it in the opposite direction from where she was heading, striking and rustling a bush. Her next rock thumped a tree.

She glanced back, hoping the noise had been heard. Yes, she saw Frank hurtle in the direction she'd aimed, not down the hill to her. She'd bought herself a moment, maybe.

Close enough to the gate now, she pressed the remote button and watched the metal bars swing wide, offering escape.

"Hey!" Frank bellowed as she shot toward the opening.

Seconds from freedom, a figure appeared in her path, blocking the exit. The guard from the gatehouse. She tried to dodge, but he caught her arm.

"Let me go!" She strained for freedom.

Huffing, Frank grabbed her, clamping down on her kicking legs and swinging arms, her purse tangling between them. He forced her back up to the mansion, a hand jammed against her mouth.

Grandfather, arms crossed over his bountiful middle, met them at the front door.

Mr. Flemming, in a robe, suddenly appeared at Grandfather's side, squinting at the crazy scene before him. "What on earth is going on here?" He turned to Grandfather, who shot a snarly glare at her before facing the investor and trying to explain away the ugly situation.

"Enough." Mr. Flemming sounded disgusted. He pulled out his phone. "I don't care if she is your granddaughter. Let her go immediately, or I'm calling the authorities."

Frank waited for Grandfather's response. Silent rage trembling his jowls, Grandfather gave the slightest of nods.

And just like that, she was released.

She didn't stick around for Grandfather to change his mind, but ran till the driveway transformed to road. Then she took to the shadows off the sidewalk, avoiding splashes of streetlight.

Her breath came in insufficient rasps and her hair flew wild as her legs pumped, painful and burning. Her purse bounced against her side. She raced over grass, around trees, across streets, till at last she paused, hands on her thighs, to catch her breath. The night air wasn't nearly cool enough on her warm face.

A car drove by, jolting her back into flight mode. Jittery and still not completely in her right senses, she ran, hardly registering a destination, but then there it was.

St. Paul's Cemetery stretched before her, a dark, lumpy expanse punctuated with headstones, towering trees, and glowing memorial lanterns. Stepping slowly at last, she maneuvered carefully around and over stone markers.

Margaret's final resting place was a challenge to find. It wasn't lit with a lantern, and it had been so long since she'd been here—and never in the dark.

She found it eventually, thanks to the inscribed headstone. Only Clay could have had that installed, right? A surge of hope coursed through her.

He's out there somewhere.

She knelt on the brittle grass, a damp coolness seeping through her jeans and onto her knees, and she let the tears flow. "I'm sorry, so sorry," she whispered, unable to articulate the depth of her grief.

"I promise I'll find him. I need to know he's okay, and finally give him your letter. I'm sorry I gave up trying, and that I stopped visiting. It was easier not to think . . . but selfish." Her vision shimmered, and she rubbed her eyes.

Her fingers brushed the gray marble, then touched thin, dry thorny stems attached to a withered, broken rose bouquet. *He was here. Not too long ago.*

More hope bloomed within her. She lowered her head to look closer at the flowers, the papery brown petals, the crinkly veined leaves, and exhaustion coupled with drug remnants caught up with her. Her muscles fell limp.

She lay her cheek against the cool earthy carpet for a moment's rest, and her mind swirled. Sleep pressed in, demanding her eyelids. She fought to keep them open, took in the swath of starry night sky, slender tree limbs swaying in rhythmic harmony, hypnotizing her, and her lids fluttered shut. Then out from the dark canvas of her dreams, he came.

Clay.

He was a mere silhouette, but she knew him, and wasn't frightened.

"I should have tried to find you . . . " she mumbled as a strange tension she'd been holding for so long wafted away as she drifted further into senselessness.

Chapter Eleven

Enveloped in a strange contentment and peace, Charlene surrendered to the dream. Clay spoke, words that couldn't penetrate her thick mental fog, but her soul swelled to hear his voice, his tone gentle and concerned.

She dreamed he touched her forehead tentatively, barely grazing her skin, his fingers warm.

Don't leave me.

She imagined he settled beside her, and they were a strange living pair of souls in a dark desolate cemetery. And she felt nothing but safe and happy.

Her lips moved, then stilled. He whispered comforting words. She sighed, and his hand found hers, so lightly that the touch was more an awareness than true contact.

All was right in her blissful dream world, and as her breathing slowed, she sank deeper, secure in his presence and the thought that he would not desert her again.

I'm alone.

Sure as her head ached, she knew this truth even before she opened her eyes. Musty air entered her throat and lungs, making her cough, triggering pain deep in her temples.

Blinking sleep away, she squinted through the dimness of her surroundings and spied stacks of old books, a plastic draped Christmas tree, and a row of large, chipped statues.

Where am I?

Her getaway came back to her, her tearful visit to Margaret's grave, and then—her hazy recollection brightened and warmed with the memory of Clay emerging from the trees, coming for her.

But it was only a warped dream, threads pulled from regret and woven into a fanciful tapestry of illusion. Cool disappointment filled her as she returned to reality. She rubbed her forehead, then her temples, trying to massage away the headache.

How did I get here?

Surely she hadn't sleepwalked. As she stood clumsily, a check-ered flannel blanket dropped from her shoulders, confounding her further. She left the corner and passed through an open doorway into a simple kitchen connected to a large, familiar room, and she realized she was in the basement of St. Paul's Church.

The lights were off, but faint illumination came from small gutter windows at the top of the walls.

She startled at an array of creaking noises overhead, before realizing these were merely the sounds of people attending Mass above. Kneeling, standing, or sitting—each movement traveled through the old boards.

She pressed her eyelids. She couldn't for the life of her remember how she'd ended up down here, but she supposed she should be thankful. There were a lot worse places she could have woken up. She fingered her neck gingerly; still tender.

She used the tiny, pitifully outdated bathroom, washed her face, finger-combed her hopeless hair, and plucked out a few strands of grass. But something was wrong. Her shoulder was missing some-thing—her purse! She couldn't lose that; it was all she had left after the fire and leaving her luggage at Grandfather's.

Retracing her steps, she was relieved to find her purse sitting in the dusty corner where she'd been sleeping. She brushed it off and shouldered it, ready to be on her way, wherever that might be.

Out of this town, she resolved. She peeked in her purse. Her mother's pink pearl necklace was still there, as was Margaret's letter. So . . . out of this town to find Clay and deliver this letter once and for all.

It was the least she could do.

Her mind began to replay Grandfather's "Justice" movie, but she forced her thoughts to shut down. She couldn't take seeing the images again, not even in memory.

She climbed the creaky, red-carpeted stairs, resisting the inner call to attend the remainder of Mass, and let herself out the side door. Rounding the building, she came in sight of the cemetery once more. Golden morning light barely brushed the hill, reflecting off polished headstones and absorbing into weathered ones.

A lone man stood in the cemetery. Her heart skipped, briefly believing it was Clay. But no, this man was taller, thinner, and much older.

Oddly though, he seemed to be standing near Margaret's grave.

She moved closer, instinctively creeping, shielding herself from sight with trees and bushes, wondering why the man was here, and who he was.

A caretaker, perhaps? But at this hour? And he wasn't taking care of anything. Just standing there. His clasped hands indicated he might be praying. She didn't recall seeing him at Margaret's funeral. Unless . . .

As he began to walk away, up the hill and onto the sidewalk, he reminded her of the man she'd seen lingering in the distance during the funeral. The cursory shot from Grandfather's cruel video had refreshed her memory.

He was almost out of sight now, and she moved forward, making a flash decision to follow him. If he had known Margaret, maybe he knew Clay.

Drawing her purse close so it wouldn't bounce, she hurried across the cemetery. She did a double-take as she passed Margaret's grave. A fresh white rose bouquet lay near the stone, replacing the withered one she had seen earlier.

White roses, like the rose she had found on her car's windshield on that Sunday morning not long ago. She was onto something, and she knew she'd get some answers if she could only keep this man in sight.

He took the sidewalk at a steady clip until he stopped inside a glass bus shelter.

She continued in his direction, yet slowed her steps, instinctively keeping a safe distance. No one else was visible. A tilled field stretched to one side, and a few houses across the street sat silent, with shades drawn. She liked to think that after all she'd been through in the past, she'd learned a thing or two about common sense and taking precautions, even if it made her seem paranoid. She was aware of the fact that she didn't even have a phone on her anymore, thanks to Grandfather.

As she ran out of sidewalk to dawdle on, the bus appeared and heaved to a stop. She jogged to catch up, saw the man climb on board, and followed him.

She'd lied to him, after all.

St. Mary's Hospital? Bull.

She had more guts than Nails had given her credit for. He liked that. Still, he couldn't play games forever.

He crawled the streets in his car and spotted her on the sidewalk.

Just in time, from the looks of the bus she was hustling toward. She appeared to be on some kind of mission, determination straining her face. Interesting.

He turned his car and idled at a crossroads until the bus passed, then he pulled out and tailed it, a smile cracking his face.

The girl was gonna lead him somewhere good today, he could feel it in his bones.

———

Only a smattering of people occupied the bus, so Charlene had a decent pick of seats. The garishly colored upholstery looked as though it belonged in a kindergarten room.

The graveyard man sat near the back. She sank into a seat near the front so as not to miss him getting off.

The bus rumbled away from the curb with a cacophony of gears and took to the highway in minutes. She turned to the chill window pane. If nothing else, she was thankful to be putting distance between herself and Grandfather.

Miles piled up, the bus stopped and started, but the graveyard man never got off. Eventually it was just him and her, many seats apart. She was hyperaware of him and felt him watching her. Prickly tension at the nape of her neck seemed to make her curls coil tight, tugging on her headache. Yet she never actually caught the man's eyes on her the few times she ventured backward glances.

At last, after more than an hour had passed, she saw a "Welcome to Creekside" sign. The bus soon wove through the little downtown, then ground to a halt beside a bus shelter in front of a grocery store.

She heard the man climb to his feet and walk down the aisle, but she didn't look at him as he passed. She pretended to gather her things, which took some acting since she only had a purse. She exited a few moments after him.

Already, he was gone.

She scanned all directions and caught sight of him striding beside trees along the grocery store parking lot. He reached a brown Dodge Ram shielded in shadow to the left of the store.

She realized as he unlocked the truck door that, without a car, her tailing was about to come to an end. If she wanted information, she had to speak now.

"Excuse me!" She jogged forward.

He didn't turn, just climbed inside and slammed the door.

"Please wait!" She waved a hand, but the truck revved. He threw it into gear and the vehicle heaved forward.

Right for her.

Alarmed, she sidestepped just in time. The man's eyes made contact with hers, and she was sure they flashed angrily.

He left her standing there, coughing in exhaust. Just as she thought to catch his license plate, he turned and disappeared down the street.

She released a long breath, not sure what to make of the close call. Had he charged at her intentionally? Surely not, yet the fierce look in his eyes made her think he had.

Her stomach grumbled for breakfast, and she turned to the store, still troubled. Warm yeast and cinnamon scents wafted her way the moment she entered. Though enticed by bakery, she chose a couple bananas and a box of granola bars. The store was practically vacant but for a few elderly shoppers and a smartly-dressed businessman.

There was only one cashier available, and she looked to be about Charlene's age. A few strands of her messy light brown hair were pinned back in an attempt to keep the waves out of her face.

Charlene grabbed a bottle of water and set her purchases on the conveyer belt. The cashier gave a small, mandatory-appearing smile. Her cheery, "Good morning, how are you?" sounded forced and didn't mesh with her dull, tired red eyes underscored with purple shadows.

Despite this, she was still very pretty. Near the corner of her pursed lips was a little brown dot, a natural beauty mark. Her skin was pale, and as Charlene remarked on the delicious bakery smells, the girl seemed to turn a shade lighter. Abruptly, she set down the bananas, turned, and dashed away.

Confused, Charlene watched her go, then glanced down at her items and felt her stomach rumble pathetically.

The cashier reappeared a minute later. She merely said, "Sorry about that," and wouldn't meet her eyes.

"No problem," Charlene assured her, reigning in her curiosity.

Beep, beep, beep. The cashier slid the purchases across the scanner. Charlene noted her crooked nametag read *Brook.*

Charlene was munching on her second banana by the time she hit the sidewalk. The sun shone higher now, and she felt a hint of mounting warmth as she strolled, taking note of the buildings lining the street, particularly the library. *I wonder if they're hiring.* Walking on, she passed an auto repair shop, a bank, a pancake restaurant, Fannie's Fabrics, and a beautiful church at the end of the block.

From the rippled terracotta roof to the textured stucco walls and bell tower, the large building appeared to be constructed in an old Spanish style. The modest steeple held a gray bell. Intrigued, she crossed the grass, moving closer. A cement cornerstone bore the date 1868. Two narrow stained glass windows flanked the front door.

She wandered to a wooden park bench on the front lawn beside a round garden abloom with pink bleeding hearts. In the very center of the garden stood a white statue of the Holy Family.

Glancing heavenward, Charlene's headache dissipated as she rested on the bench. Her fingers stroked the smooth planks, which appeared fairly new despite mild weathering on the varnished surface, and she just knew that this bench, set in such a special spot, had been handcrafted with great care.

A wisp of wind snagged a granola bar wrapper from her lap. As she bent to retrieve it, she glanced up to see a small symbol engraved into the underside of the wooden armrest. Something about it looked almost familiar.

Peering closer, she saw a simple cross with a letter tucked beneath each arm: an "M" and an "A."

MA.

Just like the mark Clay had made in the snow over his mother's fresh grave.

He made this bench.

A thread of anticipation curled around her. She let her finger continue to trace the meaningful mark, and as she lifted her gaze, she spotted another clue that she'd overlooked when she first sat down. An inscription on a small bronze plaque on the center of the seatback read, *Donated in loving memory of M.M.*

Margaret Morrow, of course.

Thoughts racing, she realized it was likely Clay attended Mass at this church and resided in this town. If so, all she had to do was wait till Sunday and look for him here. She didn't want to wait, though, not now that she was so close.

She circled the bench. It had given her answers. If it could give her one more . . .

Dropping to her hands and knees, she scooted beneath the bench and twisted her neck. There on the underside, she discovered the last clue she needed. The words *Sam's Custom Carpentry, LLC* were burned into the wood. Bingo.

———

Her heart's rhythm felt oddly erratic as she followed the gravel shoulder of the road. Weeds rose high among tall grass on either side. Cars passed only on occasion, and the whispery isolation was unsettling.

What if the convenience store attendant had purposely led her astray? The red-haired young man had seemed almost too helpful. He claimed to know the exact place she was looking for and gave her directions easily, almost too easily. He knew she was on foot. She had to hope he hadn't then called a buddy to come snatch her as she walked this rural road.

She sighed. *Once kidnapped, always paranoid.*

She reached into her purse and touched her new phone. At least she'd taken the time to pick this up. Her lawyer needed to know where she was. But first, she would call Ben. Just as soon as she figured out what she was doing.

The road sloped downhill, then back up. A stately tree with new leaves arched far over the road. Just past it, near a driveway, a simple wooden sign hung nailed to a tree trunk. *Sam's Custom Carpentry, LLC* was emblazed on the sign in black lettering.

Her feet carried her quickly to the driveway, her heart picking up pace. Starting down the gravel, she scanned the simple white ranch house. The garage was shut, but a gray Chevy pickup sat parked nearby. Off to the right stood another building. A sign hung above the open double doors, marking the carpentry shop. Her ears picked up the sound of voices—no, music, and she approached nervously, wondering whom she'd find inside.

The doors were propped open with two blocks of wood, allowing a view of wood shavings and sawdust on the concrete floor. The smell of fresh-cut lumber and varnish made a pungent, yet pleasant odor. She spotted tools, workbenches, boards stacked in corners, and a Shop-Vac. Pieces of furniture in various stages of completion lay in unorganized clusters.

She stepped inside, knowing she should call out hello, but her tongue resisted.

A shadow shifted, and as she paused unseen by a wall of hanging tools, she caught sight of a man standing at a cluttered workbench, busy with a piece of wood. His back was to her, but she knew him, knew the color of his hair and the firm, concentrated slope of his shoulders. It was Clay, in a worn flannel shirt, jeans, and a tool belt,

Therese Heckenkamp

working. She found herself watching the rhythm of his muscular arms as he sanded a piece of wood, while a country song played from a dusty boom box in the corner.

Above him hung a simple picture, slightly crooked, of St. Joseph in his carpentry shop of long ago. Jesus, as a boy, worked by St. Joseph's side. Like everything else, the frame could use dusting.

Her fingertips rested on a shelf and she traced the surface, soft with sawdust, and felt a warm gratefulness that after all the time and wondering, she could now see Clay was alive and well.

It was almost enough.

She could turn and creep back out, not disturb this peaceful world he'd found.

How odd that all this time, he'd only been about an hour away. Near enough to make contact, yet he never had. *Grandfather's fault,* she reminded herself.

But still.

Clay stopped sanding and blew dust from the wood, creating a golden mist. He reached up and scratched his head absently. She noticed with some curiosity the Ace bandage material wrapped around the base of his knuckles. She saw this on the other hand, too. Was it a carpentry thing? Protection from blisters or something?

A Blake Shelton song began on the radio, and she felt a mental push to step forward, out of what felt like a cowardly hiding spot. She wasn't afraid. She really wasn't, and yet something in her just wanted to stay still and silent and blend into the wall.

Then Clay turned around.

Chapter Twelve

*H*is gaze was down on the wood in his hand, so he didn't see her. But what Charlene saw caused her to do a startled double-take and blurt, "You grew a beard."

And what a beard. Huge and bushy, it hid most of his face.

His eyes, still a deep, rich brown, jumped to her. His surprise at her silent appearance quickly morphed into a guarded expression.

Realizing her rudeness, she felt a warm blush. "Sorry, I was just surprised. You look so different." Three years older than her, he'd be twenty-five now. He looked every year of it, and maybe a few more.

His brows pushed together. "How'd you find me?" No mistaking the reproach in his voice.

After the mistreatment he'd suffered because of Grandfather, how could she blame him? He probably hated her.

"It wasn't easy," she finally answered. "And I know you didn't want me to. But I had to tell you how sorry I am . . . about what happened after the funeral." She took a small step forward. "I had no idea, until just yesterday, that my grandfather hired those men to—"

"So it was him behind it. Figured. Just didn't know for sure." He spoke as if he didn't much care, then stepped back and indicated a stool. "Go ahead, sit down." The words came out grudgingly.

She sat, but he didn't. When she tried to continue her apology, he stopped her.

"It's over and done with. Not your fault anyhow." He clunked the piece of wood onto the table.

She eyed it. "So you're working as a carpenter? That's great. Do you . . . go by the name Sam now?"

He shook his head. "No, still Clay." He eyed her directly. "I haven't had any trouble in this town. It's small, but people mind their own business. Sam's my employer. I'm lucky he even hired me, with my record." He crossed his arms. "Life's pretty good, all things considered. I can't complain. Not looking for things to change."

She broke her gaze from his mouth—well, where his mouth should have been, if it weren't so obscured by facial hair—and looked up at his eyes as the significance of his last words hit her. He didn't want her, a part of his past, here messing up the life he'd carefully rebuilt. Understandable.

"I go by the last name Smith now, though," he admitted.

"Creative." She tried it out. "Clay Smith." She released a little smirk. The name didn't fit.

"And how're things going for you?" His question felt loaded with, *I don't want to ask, but I guess I'll be polite.*

"Fine," she hedged, not feeling it appropriate to say more. He might think she was angling for help.

Just deliver the letter and leave.

Instead, she touched the smooth piece of wood he'd been sanding. "What are you making?"

She suspected a small smile beneath his concealing facial hair, but couldn't be sure.

"It's a custom order, a cradle. A rush order. They're gonna need it any day." He ran his dusty fingers over the contoured piece, then set it down and tapped it, making it rock gently. When it slowed, he pointed. "See, these grooves here are where the corner posts will fit in . . ."

She nodded as he went into unnecessary detail, more focused on his animated fingers and the rough, dry appearance of his skin, the white cracks around his squared nails. And those strange knuckle bandages. She wanted to ask about them. Instead, she pointed at a nearby black and yellow tool that looked sort of like a big drill. "What's this?"

"A nail gun." He picked it up and showed her how it worked.

Losing interest in that, she asked, "Do you get a lot of custom orders?"

"Yeah, for standard things like tables, chairs, doors, and cabinets. Then there's the creative stuff." He began circling the room, describing pieces. She saw a clever shelf that looked like a canoe sitting up on end, then she spotted a grouping of trains, building blocks, a wooden play kitchen, and a Noah's Ark. Stroking the smooth finish of a rocking horse, she smiled. "You make toys."

He nodded. "They're actually big sellers."

She could see why. They had an old-fashioned charm and wouldn't break like cheap plastic toys.

His knowledge and enthusiasm for his work impressed her. In fact, she'd never heard him willingly talk so much. She was happy he'd found a good place for himself.

She remembered the letter and hoped she wasn't about to throw a wrench in his life.

Maybe it would be a wonderful letter, giving him peace and closure, one last bittersweet moment to share with his mother.

Or maybe it wouldn't.

Either way, it was time.

He'd finished his description of turning spindles on a lathe and was regarding her in a way that told her he didn't know why she was still here.

She averted her gaze and focused on the sharp metal teeth of a table saw. "I do have a reason for coming. I didn't just track you down to get a carpentry lesson—although it's all really interesting." She pulled the bent envelope from her purse, sorry she hadn't managed to keep it in better condition. "I came to give you this."

When he said nothing, she held it out. The distance between them felt huge. "It's from your mom. She wanted me to give it to you if she didn't get the chance herself."

He stared at it, blinked, and then stepped closer. His fingertips avoided grazing hers as he took the envelope.

"I'm sorry I didn't get it to you sooner." She eyed the door. She knew she couldn't stand here and watch him read it, much as she wanted to. She'd done her duty. Now she needed to bow out gracefully.

"Wow." He turned the envelope over. "Thanks for keeping it all this time."

"Of course." She didn't know why her voice came out so quietly. "I'll get going so you can read it."

"Hey."

The word stopped her and she looked back.

He touched his facial hair. "So . . . not a fan of the beard, huh?"

She shrugged and gave an apologetic smile. "It's just—beards are for dads and Amish men. Santa and monks. And mountain men. Not for . . . someone like you." *You have the kind of face that shouldn't be hidden.* She felt the heat of another blush and wished she could control the reflex. "It's so big, it practically covers your face."

"I plan to grow it down to here." He leveled a hand at his stomach.

At the aghast look on her face, he added, "Kidding. I know it needs a trim."

No, a razor. "It's none of my business," she said, embarrassed. "It doesn't matter."

She stepped back, yet had a pointless desire to drag out the painful conversation, simply because she felt like they wouldn't see each other again. But her mind gave her no words. She shifted her feet. "Bye, Clay."

"Wait."

She waited.

He looked uncomfortable, like he didn't know why he'd spoken. He touched the envelope. "Thanks again, and it was good seeing you."

"You too." She turned and stepped gingerly across the sawdust-powdered floor.

―――

Outside, a breath she hadn't realized she was holding trickled from her deflating lungs.

Gravel crunched underfoot as she returned to the road. She wanted to feel happy, relieved that she'd unloaded the burden of the letter and fulfilled her promise. Instead, she felt emptiness. But the emptiness had an oppressive weight.

Long grasses swayed in the wind, rustling. Disguising movement. With no warning, someone yanked her sharply from the edge of the road. Her feet stumbled backward, heels scraping and digging. Just as her scream took form, a hand silenced it.

A strong arm hauled her down into the weeds. She heard a ripping noise right before her captor slapped duct tape over her mouth. More ripping followed as he swiftly crossed and bound her wrists behind her back, then did the same to her ankles, curtailing her struggles. The tape was so tight it restricted blood flow, creating an uncomfortable swelling sensation in her hands and feet.

"Relax. I'm not gonna hurt you. Not 'less you make me." The man faced her and watched, entertained, as recognition dawned.

While she had known at the voice that this was her night intruder, she now knew something else. This was the guy from school, the one she'd bumped into and who'd sat with her at lunch. *What was his name? Lane? No, Lance.*

"So you remember me." He thrust his chin cockily and pocketed the duct tape. "Glad I made an impression."

While her thoughts cascaded, he picked her up, slung her over his shoulder and slunk through the weeds. Where was he taking her? Orienting herself as he skirted trees, she realized he was making his way back to where she'd come from—the woodshop. The noises she attempted through the tape were pitifully ineffective. There was no hope Clay could hear her, not over the music.

Lance moved to the open door, and the next thing she knew, she was shoved inside, onto the cement floor, smashing loudly and painfully into a pile of lumber, which crashed down beside her.

The racket brought Clay to her side in an instant. His focus all on her, he never had a chance.

Look out! she tried to convey with urgent eyes, because she saw what he didn't: Lance approaching, and the look on his face was lethal.

"What the—" Clay's words were silenced by a powerful blow to the back of his head.

Lance worked quickly, taking advantage of Clay's dazed state. The blow hadn't rendered him unconscious, but it had dropped him to the ground, where he lay, stunned.

Lance cinched Clay's wrists with a brown rope, then whipped the other end up over a heavy rafter. He dug the tape roll out of his pocket, then sealed Clay's mouth shut.

"Wakey, wakey, Cissy." Lance slapped Clay's face impatiently. "I've waited too long for this moment to not have you appreciate it fully."

Clay's forehead creased, his eyes opened, and awareness, then recognition, dawned with harsh realization. As if he'd awakened to a nightmare.

Charlene could relate.

At that moment, Lance backed away and yanked the rope taut, heaving Clay's arms abruptly upward. Clay instinctively climbed to his feet to relieve the sudden tension. With his arms tethered up and his boots bracing the floor, he couldn't go anywhere. Lance wrapped the rope once more around the rafter, then tied off the end around the heavy bulk of a drill press.

Panic battered Charlene's stomach. What was Lance planning? And why? She really didn't want to know, yet her mind buzzed with frightening scenarios. She tried to comfort herself with the fact that if his goal was to kill Clay, he would have done that already. Unless

. . . unless he wanted to draw out the pain. She winced.

Lance, taller than Clay by a head, circled him, regarding him with a chuckle. "That's right, it's me, ol' pal. We've got an old score to settle." He rolled up his sleeves slowly, precisely, revealing a scattered array of dark, wicked nail tattoos on his forearms. "But first, I'm gonna have a little fun."

Clay's eyes hardened, then swung to Charlene, flashing a warning, a command: *Get out of here!*

But she reflected only helplessness. Bound as she was, how could she flee? Like a flopping fish? Real effective that would be. Attempting, she scooted along the floor, awakening pain in her knee and shoulder. She searched for something to cut her taped ankles with, but everything at her level was useless wood scraps, shavings, and sawdust.

Lance turned and speared her with a look. Clearly irritated, he shoved her back against the wall.

Clay made an angry noise, muffled by the tape. Lance just shook his head at him and scanned the floor, seeming to search for something. "Ah, here we go." Grinning crookedly, he reached down and swiped an envelope from the sawdust.

He straddled a stool and flipped the envelope over. "Didn't even have the guts to open it yet, hey, Cissy?"

Charlene's heart clenched as Lance ripped into the letter, the letter that she was supposed to guard and deliver at just the right moment. Oh, how she'd failed.

His eyes scanned the sheet. From where she sat, she glimpsed lined paper filled with delicate handwriting—precious words that no one but Clay was ever meant to see. Now Lance read greedily, his cruel smirk growing larger as time passed. Country music played on incongruously in the background.

At last Lance looked up at Clay. "So your old lady finally croaked, hey? This letter she left you is really touching." He let out a low whistle, then stood and stepped closer to Clay. "Apparently, she was keepin' a little secret from you your whole life and wanted to make a deathbed confession to ease her conscience. So get this, your saintly mommy slept around. Your dad wasn't really your dad at all. How you like that? Dear mommy was really nothing but a low-down, worthless, cheatin' tramp—"

Clay's foot smashed into Lance's stomach, sending Lance stumbling back. He crashed into a pile of lumber. The wood toppled around him. He only chuckled. "You don't like that, hey Cissy?

Good."

Lance shot back up with a sledgehammer clamped in his grasp. He approached Clay tauntingly. "You know why I'm here. You know I'm a believer in retaliation. I haven't forgotten our last encounter, and it shouldn't be any surprise that payback's coming." He heaved the hammer to his shoulder and took another swaggering step closer.

Clay's smothered, angry words were futile, indecipherable behind the duct tape. His trussed up arms made him a defenseless, waiting target. He wouldn't be able to avoid or deflect any blows.

Lance hefted the hammer, paused, then swung.

Muscles seizing, he stopped short of Clay's face and snickered at the way Clay had recoiled from the expected blow.

Lance drew back and swung again—and again he stopped short of actually making contact. It was an unnerving game, a cruel, taunting torture. Charlene's fingers curled, her nails pressing into her palms as she watched, helpless. At least the tape over her mouth couldn't stop her prayers.

Readying for another swing, Lance smiled. "Third time's the charm."

Her eyes flinched closed, and she heard a splintering blow.

Terrified, she cracked an eyelid to see him wielding the sledgehammer and destroying furniture and other carpentry pieces, left and right. All those long hours of handcrafted work, gone. Obliterated.

He battered a rocking chair, split a cabinet in two, and smashed Noah's Ark.

She felt the vibrations on the floor, saw the Saint Joseph picture shudder, slide off the wall, and crash into a pile of sawdust.

Next he aimed for the boom box. "If I Die Young" was crushed to silence, and she shuddered. He even pummeled the Shop-Vac.

He moved on to a delicate scrollwork end table. *Smash.* The canoe bookcase. *Smash, smash.*

Clay, his gaze brittle, followed every move of the destruction while the rope rubbed red marks into his wrists.

While here she sat, useless on the floor.

There couldn't be much left to pulverize now. Wood splinters and sawdust rained to the ground. Here and there, even tools toppled and clattered from tables, shelves, and hooks. A hammer, a box of nails, the nail gun.

She swallowed. The nail gun wasn't far from her. She scooted sideways, feeling like a two-limbed crustacean, and swiped the tool behind her back.

Clay caught the move. His brown eyes darkened. Somehow, he knew her plan. His face clearly told her, *No. Stay out of it.* The unspoken words shot at her like both an order and a plea.

But she had to do something.

Lance, finished destroying the shop, headed once more for Clay, the sledgehammer still clamped in hand.

"I enjoyed that. A good warm up." He rolled his shoulders. "I've had a long time to think about this moment. I knew your girl here would lead me to you." He turned to flash her a smug grin and she hastily hid the nail gun close to her back, hoping he wouldn't notice she'd edged forward.

I led this monster to Clay? The knowledge crushed her, but she had to struggle out from under it, had to do something to fix this. Now, more than ever.

"You know your Bible says something like 'an eye for an eye and a tooth for a tooth'? I live by that." Nails touched his jaw. "I wouldn't have thought you had it in you, Cissy, but I'll admit you packed a punch. You shattered my jaw. I even lost a tooth."

Since she was creeping up behind him, she couldn't see Lance's face, but she knew Clay had one eye on her.

"The pain, the swelling, the metal, the wire, living on soup for eight weeks straight—I can't wait for you to experience it. To make it fair, I don't need this." Lance dropped the hammer with a clang, almost making her jump. She was close now. Only a few more feet . . .

Lance socked his palm. "With just my fist, I can pack a stronger punch than you ever could."

Clay gave an almost imperceptible shake of his head. While she knew it was meant for her, Lance noticed and took it for something else.

"Scared? You should be. The pain's wicked. Bones cracked and splintered in your jaw. The blood swelling your face till it feels like it's gonna burst."

So he didn't plan to hit to kill, but to make Clay suffer. How in-control did he think he was? A powerful, vengeful blow to the face could be very damaging. Possibly deadly. Especially from someone built like Lance.

"All I need is one shot. Just one. I'll make it count." He curled his fingers into a knuckle-hard fist.

She was running out of time.

Gripping the nail gun, she edged closer to Lance's legs. With her arms bound behind her, she worked at an awkward angle, and she almost lost her balance and fell sideways. Steadying herself, she lifted and aimed the gun at his right calf muscle while he drew back to deliver his punch.

Right as she pushed the tool to his muscle and squeezed the trigger, his leg moved. With no pressure against the gun's muzzle, the nail failed to shoot. Unbelievable. The safety mechanism cost her her chance.

Her head snapped up. Lance glared down at her, a fistful of her hair in his hand. He snatched the nail gun.

Her heart hammered.

She really hadn't thought this through.

He twisted her hair, forcing her head to look up, up into his hard, merciless face, his blue flinty eyes.

He shoved her against the wall and pressed the nail gun to her chest, over her heart. She watched his finger perch on the trigger, then squeezed her eyes shut. A nail through the heart. What a way to go.

"A nail gun. Creative weapon choice." He almost sounded amused, as if by an inside joke. "You're lucky you missed, or I guarantee I'd be shooting you full of metal right now." He laughed, then clunked the tool down, though not far enough away for her liking.

He still held her hair, and the roots screamed for relief. A silver knife flashed close to her face, sparking a new level of fear. He drew the flat side thoughtfully over her left cheek. "And what a shame that would be, wouldn't it, Cissy?"

Her eyes riveted to the blade grazing her skin.

"Your mommy called this little spitfire a 'rare jewel.'" He looked pointedly at Clay. "Generous, yes, but it would be a shame to ruin such a pretty face." The blade switched to caress her other cheek, while blood roared in her ears.

"Such pretty hair, too. It must have taken years and years to grow it so long." Still holding her with her hair wound around one massive fist, he lifted the knife and slashed.

Slashed right through her hair, she realized as her head fell back, suddenly light.

Her shock prevented her from trying to reach up and assess the damage. Not that her taped wrists would allow her to. But she could see the pile of hair as Lance dropped it to the sawdust, and it was too much. She should have been thankful it was a painless cut, yet her vanity felt sliced in two at the thought of how she now looked. The expression on Clay's face matched her dismay.

Lance picked up the nail gun and a rag and came toward her, twisting the dirty fabric tightly.

Dear God, he's not done.

He shoved her against the composite wood wall and laid the twisted fabric snug over her throat. *Zing, zing,* he shot a nail into each end of the rag, effectively pinning her—collar-like—to the wall. A concentrated varnish odor hit her nostrils.

"There now, that should keep you out of the way *and* give you a good view while I finish up."

Turning, he moved back to face Clay.

She had accomplished nothing but delaying the inevitable.

"Ready, Cissy?"

Clay's face tensed. His eyes glinted defiantly. Then they caught hers, softened, and told her, *Look away.*

"Me, I'm more than ready." Lance drew back, paused for effect, then let his fist fly.

Chapter Thirteen

*C*harlene heard the blow but didn't see it. Didn't want to see it. Her quivering eyes focused on the concrete floor—on the cracks, the dints, the stains. And still, she barely saw them.

Thanks to Lance's previous detailed description, ugly images burst to mind, despite her desire to block them: splintering bone, bursting blood vessels . . .

She mashed her lips together. Clay's pain made her remorse over the loss of her hair utterly trivial.

Her gaze lifted. She couldn't stop herself. She had to know. Why didn't she hear Clay make any noise? Not even a groan.

Then there it was, a deep, guttural sound, harsh and horrible. His eyes swiveled strangely, as if he was fighting consciousness. But he could take this, she told herself, remembering all he had endured in the past.

Unless he'd finally reached his limit.

She shuddered at the sight of him. Defeated. Even with the beard and the tape over his mouth, she could tell his jaw hung limply, awkwardly. He looked like he could collapse, but that wasn't an option. He had to fight the strain of his suspended arms and wrists because dropping his weight would likely dislocate his shoulders.

Lance stepped back and tossed a gloating grin her way. "Don't let anyone ever tell you retaliation isn't satisfying. And while I'm at it—" He yanked out Clay's wallet and pawed through it. "A ten?" He aimed his scorn at Clay's unresponsive form. "That's all you got? Pathetic."

He pocketed the bill, then pulled a paper from Clay's wallet, unfolded it, and scanned it with a frown. "'Clayton Morrow Sentenced to Prison for Accessory to Assault.'" Lance hooted. "What, you thought you'd forget? Needed to keep the article as a souvenir? What an idiot." Still laughing, he chucked the wallet and the article to the ground before moving toward the door.

"Please," Charlene tried to say, her voice restricted by both the rag rope around her throat and the tape on her lips. Lance stepped her way with a purpose that made her stomach flip. He reached out and in one quick motion, ripped the rag from her neck. Then he tore the tape from her mouth.

Ignoring her stinging skin, she hurried to speak. "Please, don't leave him like that." She glanced again at Clay's wrists, saw the rope cutting in. His hands looked like they were starting to swell. "At least untie him."

Lance seemed to consider her words. "Nah." He shook his head, chin hefted high. "I don't think so. You're free to go, though." As if she could go anywhere taped like this. And as if she'd leave Clay.

"Don't forget me, sweetie." He pinched her cheek. "We may meet again someday. I guess I'll forgive you for leading me on that wild goose chase to St. Mary's. This turned out great."

Great? He was a fiend, capable of anything. Fire flashed through her mind. "You burned my condo."

He straightened. "You think I did that?" He laughed and turned away. "And you think I'd admit it if I did?" He sauntered from the workshop, out into the sunlight, and out of sight.

She willed her panicky heart to slow. At least he was gone. Clay wasn't dead. At least not yet.

Wracked with worry, she looked at him. How long before anyone found them? She had no idea when his boss, Sam, would return. They couldn't wait.

Resolved, she strained and tried picking and pulling at the duct tape on her ankles. No good.

She began a tedious search of the shop for something to use. Trying a screwdriver, she only jabbed herself painfully.

Dropping the tool, she shuffled closer to Clay and spoke his name.

He moved and groaned and for that she was thankful. Each time his head began to droop, he jerked it up. But his response seemed to be getting more delayed.

There was another urgency, she realized, from the look of his hands. His arms had given up lifting against the strain, and their weight pulled the rope deep into his wrists.

Spotting a low wooden stool, she managed to shove it over to his scuffed work boots. "Stand on this. Lift your feet." With repeated urges, she got through to him. He stepped up on the stool and the rope slackened, helping relieve the strain from his arms and wrists.

A piercing scream ripped through the air.

Startling, Charlene tried to whirl, but in her bound state it was more of a slow turn.

A young woman raced to Clay's side. "Clay! Are you okay? What happened? Answer me!"

The woman's frantic gaze swung around, hardly registering Charlene, yet processing what needed to be done. She traced the rope to where it was tied, ran to it, undid the knot, then lowered the rope slowly so that Clay's arms went down gradually instead of suddenly. Slight as she was, she tucked herself beside him and helped him step off the stool. He sank to the floor and just lay there, perhaps finally giving in to unconsciousness.

One hand on his shoulder, the woman pulled out a phone and called for help. Then slowly, carefully, she worked the tape off his mouth. It took a long moment before she glanced at Charlene, but when she did, she took in the sight of her taped wrists and ankles. Pocketing her phone, the woman crossed to a workbench. She removed a scissors and came to Charlene's side. "Hold on." She knelt and cut through the layered tape, releasing first her wrists, then her ankles.

"Thank you." Charlene rubbed the stinging red spots and felt the pooled blood drain from her hands and feet.

Watching her, the young woman's slender brows flicked together. A brief narrowing of her eyes revealed recognition.

At the same time, Charlene recognized her. *Brook, the cashier from the grocery store.*

Clay let out a low sound and mumbled something, and Brook moved closer to him. "It's okay. It'll be okay." Her voice caught. "Honey, don't worry, I'm right here." She laid her hand on his chest. "I called for help. They'll be here soon. What happened?"

When his lips didn't move, she glanced at Charlene and repeated, as if realizing she was the only one she'd get an answer from, "What happened?"

Charlene's brain had stalled on the "honey" of a few sentences back, and she studied the beauty-marked girl with her long hair and ruffled blouse. *I wonder how long they've been together.*

Brook stared at her. "Who are you?"

She pulled her gaze away from Brook's hand cradling Clay's head. "My name's Charlene."

Charlene waited. Had Clay ever mentioned her? She watched Brook's face. Not an eyelash stirred.

"And?" Brook prodded.

And what? What could she say? She was a friend? Charlene

doubted she qualified. Her voice came out in an apologetic tone. "I used to know Clay."

Brook waited, wanting more.

Charlene shifted on the cold concrete. "I was in town and stopped by and—and—some horrible man—someone with a grudge against Clay—attacked him." She glanced around at the shambles of the shop. "He destroyed everything."

Brook's expression blended anger with disbelief, then she lowered her mouth to Clay's ear. Charlene felt an unnecessary desire to tell her to be careful. But of course Brook knew to be careful; she spoke softly, comfortingly, and her arm went around him.

Charlene clasped her sore wrists and averted her gaze.

———

Nails's knuckles pulsed with the bruising memory of the punch, and he wallowed in it. A perfect punch. Perfect retaliation.

Forest undergrowth crunched under his boots. Pitiful woodland creatures darted away as he invaded their territory. Squirrels shot up trees. Birds wheeled to the sky. He laughed. *Not hunting you varmints. Not yet.*

The hunt would be on for him, but he wasn't worried.

His time with the Callaghans had taught him well. Make plans. Do what you want. Take what you want. But never get caught.

Never.

I learned from my mistakes, Mr. Callaghan. I learned.

He learned about staying chill under pressure. About not feeling. About controlling others with fear.

About laying low after a job was done, in places no one would ever look, no one would ever think a person could survive.

About not bragging. Not to anyone, ever.

Trust no one.

He rubbed his knuckles and pushed through the woods, deep, deep, to where the old trailer nestled, long forgotten. But not by him. And he'd made sure it was well stocked.

He eyed the rock under the birch tree and smiled, pride swelling.

What made him so good at what he did, was knowing how to plan, execute the plan calmly, then lay low and stay low for as long as it took for the heat to die down. Stay off the roads, out of the motels, and just disappear. Disappear.

And plan the next job.

Charlene hesitated in the entrance of the hospital waiting room. Brook sat hunched in a chair, frowning at her phone. Charlene took a step into the room, assessing. Only a few other people waited, all strategically situated for personal space so that no one sat directly beside anyone else. With the limited chairs available, she would be forced to break the trend. It was unfortunate, as she could really use a comforting bubble of solitude right now.

As she gravitated toward a matronly woman wearing earbuds and swaying slightly, Brook looked up and met her eyes.

"Hey." Brook offered a small smile. "Sit here." With a hand, she indicated the seat beside her.

Complying, Charlene lowered herself into the chair and stared at a wide-leafed artificial plant across the room.

"So how are you?" Brook asked.

"I'm good." Considering all that had just happened, that was almost laughable, but it was her automatic avoid-unpleasantness-at-all-costs response. She tapped a finger on her chair. "Okay, well, I've been better."

But at least she hadn't needed an ambulance to get here, like Clay. The emergency personnel had been swift to arrive. Official questions had been asked, and she gave her statement willingly, but so far Lance hadn't been caught. She'd gotten her purse back from the weeds, but her wallet was gone, and so was her pink pearl necklace. She could only assume he'd swiped them. But she couldn't complain. She wasn't the one in surgery.

"How's Clay?" Charlene asked.

At the same moment, a strong voice broke over hers. "How is he?"

She looked up to see a gray-haired man, his face pulled in worry-lines, explode into the room. His question had been directed at Brook, but the instant he saw her, his face twitched and eyes darkened.

It was the graveyard man, the guy she'd followed to this town. The guy who almost ran her over. She returned his gaze narrowly.

He dropped into the other seat near Brook, beside a rack of messy magazines. His long, jean-clad legs protruded, his dirty clunky work boots a tripping hazard to the general public.

"How is he, Brook?"

"I'm sorry, Sam. They didn't tell me much. They hurried him

away and told me to wait here. They'll let us know."

Something like a low growl stirred in Sam's throat. His eyes met Charlene's accusingly. "Why are you here?"

She blinked. "Excuse me?"

Brook pressed against her seatback, allowing a clear view from Charlene to Sam. He shook his head and looked as if he wanted to spit. "I know who you are. You've never brought anything but trouble into Clay's life. You're a thorn in his side. Now you're here, and he's in the ER. You do the math."

Charlene's stomach rolled. Heat spread through her body. She vaguely sensed Brook's shock, while ears around the room perked up and curious eyes stared.

Part of her wanted to jump up and leave, but after all she'd been through today, she wouldn't let herself be bullied. Cruel insulting man or not, she had to stay to find out how Clay was.

She forced herself to lower her voice in contrast to Sam's. "Are you actually trying to blame me for what happened? Do you know what happened? Were you there?" Her ankles and wrists surged with a stinging sensation, justifying her words, driving her on.

"I don't know what your deal is, but I've been through enough today." She kept her words intensely smooth and even. From too many conflicts in the past, she was learning that the one who kept their cool usually came out the winner in a verbal spar.

Sam's voice was not so controlled. "Why were you at my place? You never should have been on my property."

"Really? Then maybe you shouldn't operate a shop on your property."

Sam's neck flamed red.

"I only went there because I was trying to do Clay a favor. And his *mother* a favor," she threw in for shock value, feeling immediately contrite—not for how it made Sam's face darken, but for using Margaret's memory in a spiteful way.

"Clay's mother is dead."

"I'm well aware. She was a good friend. I was with her through her sickness, her suffering. I was at her funeral." She gripped her left hand so tight she felt her knuckles roll together. "It was her dying wish that I deliver her letter—her last words—to her son. Would you deny her that?"

Sam didn't reply.

"It took me years to track Clay down, and today, when I finally kept my promise—" her voice shook—"that man attacked us. I don't know why. I can't tell you why. But blaming me is—"

"I'm sorry," he ground out the apology grudgingly.

She swallowed more words, her throat a prickly, parched tube. "I'm going to grab a water." She stood up and fled, hyperaware of her racing heart and fiery cheeks.

Her hand dove through her purse, feeling for the small hidden pocket where she kept a few extra bills. *Please...*

She pulled out the folded cash. A small victory.

Moments later, while leaning beside the vending machine and gulping bottled water, Brook appeared beside her.

"Hey, you all right?"

Charlene nodded.

Brook lingered. "Sam's just really upset. It's horrible what happened."

"I know." She capped her water. "So why does he have to make it worse?"

Brook shook her head. "I haven't known him long, but long enough to know he really cares about Clay. I'm sure he feels bad that he wasn't at the shop when it happened."

It. An insignificant, insufficient, sanitized word.

Oblivious to Charlene's jaded thoughts, Brook turned on her heel. "I'm gonna head back. I don't want to miss . . . any news."

The flimsy plastic water bottle crackled in Charlene's grasp as she shadowed Brook back to the artificial comfort of the cheap upholstered chairs. She was almost sure she heard the clock on the wall ticking, until someone turned on the TV across the room and sitcom laughter rattled out.

Sam stared vacantly at the wall, and Brook returned to her smartphone. Gradually, Charlene found herself being pulled to study Sam. She watched him furtively as he stood and paced the room. There was something about him . . .

"Did Clay read the letter?"

Sam's abrupt question startled her into answering. "No, he didn't get a chance."

"Did you read it?"

She sat ramrod straight. "Of course not."

Looking up, Brook remarked, "I wonder what it said."

"It was personal," Charlene answered.

"So you do know something about it," Sam prodded.

Lance's hateful summery of the contents echoed in her mind and she shook herself. She would never divulge the secret. Besides, he could have been making it all up.

"Like I said, it was personal. I didn't need to read it to know that."

"So where's the letter now?"

Good question. Her gut clenched. She rifled through her confused memory. "I think . . . it must still be in the shop somewhere." *If* the detectives hadn't found it and taken it as some kind of evidence. Highly unlikely, though, as she realized she hadn't included the letter in her statement to the police. Fingerprints could be found on any of the other things Lance had touched, anyway. Like the sledgehammer. Or Clay's wallet. Lance obviously hadn't been worried about being identified.

What if the letter was still in the workshop for anyone to read? She eyed Brook and Sam. What if one of them found it and read it? As the caretaker of that letter, a strange protectiveness welled within her.

Just then, a doctor stepped to the doorway of the waiting room and called, "Sam Riley?"

Sam hurried forward. As the doctor took him aside, Brook and Charlene exchanged a glance, then watched and waited for the news.

Chapter Fourteen

"Why'd the doctor call Sam?" Charlene wanted to spring to her feet and insert herself into the conversation so she didn't have to wonder any longer how Clay was doing.

"He's obviously his emergency contact." Brook pocketed her phone. "No living relatives, you know?"

Of course she knew that.

She strained to hear the doctor's words, but couldn't.

Sam nodded, turned, and walked grimly back. "Clay's jaw is broken, all right. They're setting it with metal bolts and his mouth has to be wired shut."

"How will he eat?" Brook cried.

"Through a straw," Sam said in disgust. His own jaw jutted forward. "If I ever get my hands on that guy—" He turned and his growling noises hid what Charlene was pretty sure were curses.

"So can we see him yet?" Brook appeared poised to jump from her chair as soon as the answer was yes. Automatically, Charlene's own foot positioned itself strategically, ready to push off from the floor.

"Not yet." Sam dropped back into a chair. "In a little while. They'll let us know."

A little while in doctor terms could mean hours. For the first time, Charlene noticed her empty stomach. She stood. "I'm going to get something to eat. Want me to bring anything back?"

"No thanks," Brook said.

Sam gave no more than a slight scoffing noise, which Charlene took as a no.

Before grabbing a bite, she stopped off in the restroom and froze in front of the mirror.

Gone were her long, lustrous curls; her hair was shorn, cropped jaggedly uneven above her shoulders. Her fingers touched the locks numbly, then worked them, as if she could caress length from the tattered ends.

Without much weight holding it down, her hair puffed like a

goofy clown's wig. Or an '80s perm.

Ugh.

She struggled to think positive.

It will be easier to care for. Less tangles. It'll dry faster.

What will Ben think of it?

Her hands buried themselves in the mass and tugged desperately. She groaned and swung away from her reflection.

She'd just have to avoid mirrors till her hair grew back.

———

Her stomach appeased with a cafeteria sandwich, Charlene reapplied her lip balm and returned to the waiting room. Not a moment too soon, apparently. Sam and Brook were just leaving.

She caught up to them in the corridor. "Are you going to see Clay?"

"Yes, finally," Brook said without slowing stride.

"About time." Charlene fell in step.

Both Sam and Brook stopped and turned to her.

"What?"

"Actually . . ." Brook began.

"It'd be better if you didn't come," Sam finished.

She shook her head and felt her hair springing every which way. "But I want to see him, too."

"Give us our turn first, is all I'm saying," he clarified. "We don't have to crowd him. Plus, he needs rest."

"I know, but—"

"Brook's his girlfriend. I'm his best friend. Who are you?"

His words stunned her speechless.

"We're the nearest he's got to family, and right now, he needs us."

As they retreated down the hall, she barely heard him mutter, "Not the girl who brings him nothin' but trouble."

She eyed an exit. *Leave this place, hop on a bus, and just go.* But where? Back home? Where was that? Nothing felt like home anymore.

I should go back to Ben. He would never turn her away.

But his mom had . . .

So what. *I'll figure it out.*

But today, she had to finish this. *I won't leave yet. That's what Sam wants.* Maybe Brook, too.

She crossed her arms and leaned against the wall, ready to wait

as long as it took.
My turn is next.

———

The wall wasn't comfortable. Charlene couldn't stand propped against it much longer. Stubbornly, she refused to retreat to the waiting room, with its useless droning TV. At last she slid down to a sitting position right there in the hall, her shoes squeaking on the slick floor.

She received curious second-glances from passing doctors, nurses, patients, visitors, even a custodian. *My stunning haircut.* Or maybe it was her overall disheveled, forlorn appearance.

Her ears picked up distant noises, a medley of life and death, hospital style. Machines beeping, phones ringing, metal carts clattering. Laughter, crying, and everything in between. *Someone's being born right now. Someone's dying right now. Maybe not in this very hospital, but somewhere.*

A rhythm of footsteps drew closer, and she looked up to see Brook and Sam stride past. Charlene sprang up too quickly for her fallen-asleep foot but ignored the pins and needles.

"So?" She directed her question at their backs. "How is he?"

Sam turned, looking inconvenienced and grouchy. "His face is full of metal. He's had better days."

Brook's lips curled down and her eyes shone red and weepy. She sniffed daintily. "He looks terrible."

Charlene's hands grasped each other. "What room number?"

Brook glanced at Sam. His voice was firm. "Leave him be. He needs rest."

Her arms dropped to her sides with a *whap.* "Are you kidding? I've waited all afternoon. I only want to talk to him."

"Talking's hard for him."

"I only want to see that he's okay."

"Take my word for it, he's okay. It's not like this is life-threatening. It isn't comfortable or convenient, but he's gonna be fine."

"What room number? If you don't tell me, I'll just get it from a nurse."

"Go ahead. She won't tell you, either."

"Why not?"

" 'Cause Clay doesn't want to see you. Not now. Not ever. Got it?"

Her lips parted. Breath seeped out. She had to fill her lungs before she could reply. "He said that?"

Sam grunted a humorless laugh. "He can't *say* much of anything. But he made it clear he doesn't want any Charlene Perigard coming around."

She stared at him and he stared back.

It's a bluff. She looked at Brook, but she wouldn't meet her eyes.

Charlene spun and walked away. She found the nurse's station and made her request, only to discover Sam had been telling the truth. Clay had indeed requested that she not be allowed to see him.

"Don't feel bad, hun," the nurse said. "He's been through a lot. Maybe when he feels better—"

"Whatever." She hitched a shoulder. "Doesn't matter."

"First thing he wanted to know was that you were okay," the nurse added.

We're even, then. She gave a nod and turned away.

"I could give him a message."

Charlene didn't want to leave one, but she couldn't be that petty. "Tell him . . . tell him I'm glad he's okay."

She walked away, heading aimlessly down the hall in a mental fog, reading no signs, following no arrows. She wrinkled her face. As if she'd ever wanted to waste her time and effort tracking Clay down in the first place. It was all that letter, that irksome letter.

Sorry, Margaret, but why? Why couldn't you have just sent it by mail?

The letter.

Clay still hadn't read it for himself. He would need to now, to verify or dispel Lance's claims. It likely still lay in the woodshop for anyone to read. Anyone being Sam or Brook.

As Charlene made up her mind, she shook her head in disbelief. What was the unrelenting pull to get the letter to Clay, and only Clay, where it belonged? It wasn't like he was going to appreciate her effort.

———

The taxi pulled over where Charlene directed. "I won't be long," she informed the driver as she exited. "I just have to get something."

Nearing the workshop, she spotted Sam's brown truck parked at the side of the building. Suspicion sprang up like a red flag. Shouldn't he still be at the hospital? She glanced over her shoulder at the taxi, still in sight on the side of the road. Its presence gave her a little reassurance, not that the driver was looking out for her. He was only paid for transportation, after all.

Her steps were soft and muffled as she reached the open workshop door.

Déjà vu hit her, only this time Sam stood where Clay had earlier that day. He wasn't working, though. He was holding Clay's letter.

And reading it.

Incensed, she opened her mouth to speak sharply, when Sam stunned the words dead in her throat by revealing a lighter and flicking a flame to life.

She sensed his intentions a second before he acted, and she dashed forward just as he held the fire to a corner of the irreplaceable letter.

"What do you think you're doing?" she cried as she snatched the paper.

Sam's surprise was quickly replaced by irritation when he recognized her. *"You."*

He tried snatching the letter back, but she scurried away, jumping over wood and dodging tools, trying not to trip on debris or slip on sawdust. Briefly out of sight behind a workbench, she folded the letter and slipped it in her pocket.

Sam loomed over her a mere second later. "Where is it?" he demanded, eyes sweeping her.

"How dare you?" She glared. "That letter's not yours. You have no idea what I've been through to get that to Clay safely, and you—you—"

"And you have no idea—"

"You should be ashamed! Those are a mother's last words to her son. I thought you were Clay's *friend*. I thought—" Seeing his expression of annoyance and anger, the thought came like a revelation, like a punch to her gut. Winding her. Flooring her. "Oh. *Oh!*" She'd seen this look before—on Clay. Her eyelids stretched wide. "You're the one. In the letter. Clay's . . . Clay's real dad."

Sam's eyes closed as weary resignation washed over his face, accentuating the leathery wrinkles and deepening the shadows. "I thought you didn't read it."

Her hand came down on a sawhorse for support. "I didn't." She pulled in a stabilizing breath. "That guy—Lance—he read some of it out loud, to taunt Clay."

"But he never said my name?"

"No."

Sam's face showed a guarded measure of relief. She studied him. How had she not seen it before? In many ways, he was a taller, older version of Clay.

"You have to tell him," she said. "He deserves to know. How could you have known him this long and not told him? He trusts you."

Sam shook his head. "I meant to tell him. I wanted to, but it's never been the right time. I tried after Margaret's funeral." He rubbed work-worn fingers over his face. "I got a letter from her after she died. I never even knew until then . . . about him. She told me someone was going to give him a letter. I didn't want him to find out like that." His voice held agitation mixed with regret.

Charlene let him go on. She sensed he needed to unburden himself, and she, though an unlikely choice, was the only one available to listen.

"She gave me so little time. And it was too late. She was already gone." His gaze wavered. "She was always too hard on herself." His words halted and he regarded her coldly. "After the funeral was the wrong time to tell him." Remembrance flashed hard and hateful in his eyes.

Realization washed over her. "You saw what happened, the men who took him . . ." She lowered her head, not wanting to admit and prove him right, once again, that she, though indirectly, had brought that trouble on Clay. "Did you follow them?"

"I tried, but I lost them. I finally caught sight of them taking off from an old warehouse. When I got there, I went in, and there he was . . . my son." Sam's lip curled angrily. "What they did to him—"

He broke off and looked away. "I took him back here to my place. Took care of him." His mouth tightened. "It's no wonder he doesn't trust easily. I've worked long and hard for that trust, and now . . . I'm in no hurry to destroy it." His words were gruff as his eyes met hers. "Are you going to give him the letter?"

"I have to."

"When?"

"Soon." She bit her lip. She didn't want to destroy Sam and Clay's friendship, but Clay needed to know the truth. She thought of the painful memories he carried of the man he believed was his father. "But it would be better if you could tell him who you are first, yourself."

"I need time."

"How much?" *You've already had so much.*

"Now's no good. Not after what just happened."

She nodded. "There's never going to be a perfect time."

"I know that." Irritation edged his voice. "When I saw you, I knew you were from his old life. I've read the news. Seen the pictures. I figured you might be the one bringing the letter. I'd grown complacent. Then there you were, storming in to upset everything."

"So you tried to run me down?"

"I did no such thing." He grunted, then muttered, "Nothin' wrong with trying to scare you away."

"Why'd you take a bus to Woodfield when you have a truck?"

He regarded her like she was stupid. "I never know when Clay's gonna take off to visit the grave. I don't want to risk him spotting my truck there. He'd have questions." His voice rose. "So can you keep quiet about what you know, or not?"

She could have taken his words as a threat, but she didn't feel it. She felt only sympathy. "I can, for a little while."

"Thank you." Sam glanced around at the workshop wreckage. "He's built a good life here. Come back from so much. He doesn't talk about his time in prison, or before, and I don't want anything—anyone—reminding him of that."

Anyone, meaning me.

She followed his gaze and shivered, recalling Lance's rampage. "He really destroyed this place, didn't he?"

Sam picked up a splintered spindle. He ran his hand over the smooth surface and stopped at the jagged break. "We were already behind on orders. And now Clay's out of commission." He shook his head. "We'll lose business. There may not be any coming back from this. It'll take days just to get the shop cleared and back in shape. Then we'll have to start over. With deadlines to meet, I don't know how—"

"I could help," she broke in, surprising herself.

"What?" Sam looked on the verge of a guffaw.

"I know I don't have any experience, but I learn fast. I'll work hard, and I can do the easier stuff, like clean and organize, sand and stain, handle calls . . . whatever you need to get the business back on track." She crossed her arms. "You know you need help."

Sam set the broken spindle down. "Why would you want to do that?"

She lowered her gaze. "Clay was a friend to me and my brother, when we needed one the most." She almost added, *And it was my fault Lance found Clay,* but she didn't need to give Sam another reason to dislike her. She met his eyes. Brown eyes, like Clay's. Besides, she had to stick around to make sure he kept his promise to tell Clay the truth.

"I can't pay much."

"I'll only need enough for food and rent."

"You can't stay here," he was quick to say.

"I'll find a place in town. So do we have a deal?" She stuck out her hand.

"You're sure you wanna do this?" His mouth lifted crookedly. "It's hard work."

"Then I'll work hard."

They shook, one quick hand pump.

What about Ben back home? her mind whispered disapprovingly. *He has his family, his mom, dad, and sister,* she rationalized. She would visit him plenty, but she needed a break from that town. Nothing permanent. Just a break. This was perfect. Stay busy. Stay productive. Help someone.

Catching sight of a clock made from a slice of tree trunk, she realized how long they'd been talking. "Uh-oh, I forgot I have a cab waiting. I've gotta go. My tab's racking up."

She began picking her way back over the clutter. "Can you recommend any cheap motels nearby?" The thought of staying alone in a motel still didn't agree with her, but with night falling, she didn't have much choice.

Sam nodded. "Sure. Tell the driver Motel 6 on Arlington. And here," he reached her in two broad strides, "for the cab." He thumbed a couple bills from his wallet and pushed them at her.

She hesitated, though she knew her cash was dwindling fast. First thing tomorrow, she'd go to the bank.

"Take it." Sam thrust the bills into her hand. "It's only an advance, and a small one at that. Just remember our deal."

She folded the bills, feeling as if she was taking a bribe.

"You get one day to settle in, so you can start work day after tomorrow," Sam said briskly.

She nodded and stepped around the jagged remnants of a table. Her gaze went to the floor where, earlier, she had cowered in fear. She saw her hair on the ground, a dry puddle of brown strands, the curls flat and forlorn. Grimacing, she left the shop.

Chapter Fifteen

"Charlene?"

Hearing her name, her head whipped around. In streetlight, she saw Brook crossing the parking lot of Motel 6.

"Hey." Brook smiled and shifted a white box in her hands. "I was just picking up some muffins." She indicated the bakery next door. "They have the absolute best banana nut muffins."

Charlene nodded, wondering why in the world Brook was out at a bakery at this time of night instead of at Clay's side. It wasn't like he'd banned Brook as he had her. The muffins obviously weren't for him, either. Unless she planned on blending them into mush.

Brook glanced at the motel's blue doors. "So you're staying? Here in town, I mean?"

Again, Charlene nodded. She didn't feel she had much left in her to speak. She just needed a bed to fall into so this day could finally end.

"How long are you staying?" Brook persisted.

Charlene blew an obnoxious, tickly curl away from her nose. "I'm not exactly sure."

Perhaps it was her imagination, but something in Brook's eyes yearned for more information. Charlene gave in. "A few months."

Brook's eyebrow arched under her thick, sweeping hair. Beautiful long hair. Charlene smothered a flare of envy.

"I know Motel 6 is cheap," Brook said, "but it won't be if you're staying that long."

"The motel's just for a few days. I'll start looking for a place to rent tomorrow."

"Oh, that's good." Brook's forehead puckered slightly as she seemed to debate something.

Charlene glanced again at the motel, envisioning peace, quiet, and sleep.

"Would you like a muffin?" Brook extended the bakery box.

"No thanks." Immediately after saying it, Charlene realized she should have said yes. Her stomach growled angrily. "I really just need to check in, so—"

Brook let out a sigh and flicked a lock of hair from her shoulder. "Look, I probably shouldn't even suggest this, but I need a roommate. It's a small apartment, nothing special, but the rent's cheap."

Charlene cocked her head. "Really?" She had an impression that while Brook wasn't offering whole-heartedly, she genuinely wanted her to accept the offer. But then, what did she know? By now her mind felt about as functional as a ball of fuzz.

Brook nodded. Her green eyes brightened with something like anticipation. "I've been needing a roommate for weeks. My last one bailed suddenly."

"You hardly know me." *And I hardly know you.*

They regarded each other a moment before Brook countered matter-of-factly, "I know you more than I would any potential roommate answering an ad."

"True." Charlene peered down the street. "Is it far from here?" *I could at least take a look.*

Brook's smile held a hint of relief. "No, not at all. Come on, I'm parked over there."

Charlene soon learned that the apartment was conveniently located in the heart of the small town. The building was a long rectangular block, red brick on the bottom half, white siding on the top. Evergreen bushes made a stiff green collar around the place.

Charlene expected a musty, offensive odor when they stepped inside, as many old apartments had, but she detected only a light dusty scent.

Brook unlocked her door and gave a short tour. Though small, the place was decent and cheery with light lemon walls. White gauzy valances topped a picture window. The kitchen was clean and tastefully decorated. A small wine rack held Chardonnay and Merlot beside a bowl of grapes.

Most impressively, the bathroom sink and mirror shone spotless. The spare bedroom was simple and tiny, but empty and vacuumed.

"So what do you think?" Brook asked.

Charlene swept her gaze once more around the room. "I think I'll take it."

A mere half an hour later, Charlene closed the door of her new bedroom and sank wearily onto the freshly-made bed.

Struggling to keep her eyes open, she studied her new phone and brought up the keypad. She stared at the digits, her mind clouding as she tried to pull Ben's number from memory. A three, then a six, then a four—no, a five? Or a . . .

Before she could complete the call, she fell asleep.

First thing the next morning, Charlene tried again. Ben didn't answer, so she left a brief message letting him know she was fine and would call back soon. After a quick shower, she left the apartment.

Her first stop following the bank was a hair salon, and though the hairdresser gave her a wide-eyed once-over, Charlene didn't elaborate on the cause of her current frightful style. She simply asked the woman to do what she could to make her curly mop look as decent as possible without sacrificing any more length.

After approving the results, Charlene headed to a nearby diner for some food. From there, she strolled the sidewalk and spotted a yard sale sign up ahead. A green Trek bike leaning against a tree caught her interest. She ran her hand over the smooth frame and found the price sticker. A bargain. She examined the tires. Firm, and not worn.

"Go ahead," called a woman sticking orange price tags on toys, "hop on and give it a test ride."

So Charlene did, and as she enjoyed a smooth, short ride up and down the sidewalk, she pictured herself sailing through town with the impending summer stretching before her, warm and promising. Her short hair fluttered behind her and she could almost imagine it was long again.

She coasted strategically past rummage items and stopped to pay for the bike. The woman kindly threw in a bike lock for free, and Charlene rode away, jubilant.

She pedaled up and down Main Street in the sunshine and gave herself a little tour of Creekside. Bumping over a plank bridge above a tranquil river, she smiled as she passed people strolling, and they smiled back.

No suspicious narrowing of eyes.

No turning away to avoid her.

No pointing fingers.

She was an anonymous nobody, a girl out for a carefree ride, and it was a wonderful feeling. Joy flooded her lungs like clean air, buoying her mood. For those moments, she didn't think of Lance, Grandfather, or even Clay.

She cruised into a park adjacent to the library, then she set her new bike on the grass and sat on a bench in the shade of a maple tree. Tilting her head, she gazed up at the blue sky and was simply happy to be alive.

Yards away, mothers pushed toddlers on swings. The happy childish cries were a beautiful sound.

Her phone rang, and she slipped it from her pocket and answered.

"Charlene, finally!" Ben's tone held a flood of relief. "Are you really okay? Where are you? I tried calling you all yesterday and just kept getting voicemail."

"I'm fine, don't worry. I'm sorry I didn't call sooner. I just got a new phone; you're the first one I called. So much has happened." She began by telling him about the fire.

"I know," he cut in. "The police questioned me. I've been so worried about you."

A terrible pang struck her. She hadn't realized what she might be putting him through . . . she'd hardly had a moment to think straight. With the subject of the fire exhausted, she moved on to describe her disastrous stay at Grandfather's.

That shocked Ben into silence for a moment. "You told me about him. I just never believed he could really be so, so—"

"Eccentric?"

"That's putting it nicely. What a nut case. You seriously need to report him."

"Right. My word against his, the powerfully influential billionaire." She crinkled her nose. "Look, I'm okay, I got away." Now was not the time to tell him about Lance.

"So where are you?"

She shaded her eyes with her hand and focused on distant daffodils. "In a little town called Creekside, about an hour north. I found a little apartment. My roommate's real nice."

There was a long pause. "You . . . rented a place?" Pure incredulity. "I don't get it, Charlene. Why would you do that? I thought we had everything settled. You were going to stay at my parents'." The agitation in his voice scraped her nerves.

She stood and paced the grass. "I know. I wanted to, really." How to go on without blaming his mom? "But I really think it's best for me to get out of Woodfield completely. There are a lot of people who don't like me there." She switched the phone to her other ear. "It's hard, Ben, and I can't—I don't want to put you and your family in danger. I can't be that selfish. And this is just for a little while. We'll make it work."

"It's just so far away."

She squeezed the phone. "Not really. I can hop on a bus and be back in an hour."

"And how often are you going to do that? How often are we actually going to see each other? I want to be understanding, but it's like . . . I feel like you're trying to put distance between us, when we should be spending more time together, not less. We've got the wedding to plan." He paused. "You still want to get married, don't you?"

"Of course. This has nothing to do with us, or you, Ben." Ouch, that came out wrong. "I mean—"

"When am I gonna see you next? Today? Tomorrow?"

"I . . ." The thought of heading back to Woodfield rolled her stomach. And the drug charges still hung over her head like a guillotine. "Soon, Ben. I promise. I'll always be off Sundays, so I'll come early in the morning and we'll go to churck, then spend the whole day together. Every week."

"Promise?"

"Promise. I want to see you, too, Ben, believe me."

"And what about school? Your classes? You're just going to give all that up?"

"No, of course not. But I'm almost done for the summer. I'll work something out." And she would. Carpentry was not going to be her career. "How are you doing? How are you feeling?"

They talked a little longer, but after she said goodbye, she stared at the blank phone screen, feeling conflicted. She hadn't told him everything, but she'd intended to. They didn't keep secrets.

She wet her lips and made her next call, expecting another earful of a different kind.

"It's about time," her lawyer began. "Why haven't I been able to contact you, Charlene? That is not acceptable."

Back to pacing, she tried to explain, but Vivian broke in. "You'll no longer be needing my services." Her tone switched from severe to triumphant. "Your case was dropped."

Charlene froze in mid-step. "Oh my gosh, are you serious? That's amazing. That's wonderful news!"

"I wish they could all wrap up this nicely."

Vivian went on to explain how the parking lot surveillance tapes had shown a large man jimmying her car open and ducking in the passenger side briefly. "He obviously planted the drugs. Unfortunately, the footage was low quality. We couldn't identify the man. We don't know who was trying to frame you or why, but with that kind of evidence, the prosecutor had no choice but to throw out the case."

After the call, Charlene became aware of a big smile stretching her face. Relief didn't begin to describe her feelings. She promptly called Ben back and shared the news. "This means no more court dates or hearings or bail restrictions."

His relief mirrored hers, but then he asked, "Any chance this changes your mind? About coming back?"

She caught her lip between her teeth. "I still don't know who planted the drugs or why. That person might still be out to get me." The realization tempered her happiness, and after the call, she stared vacantly. She'd left town, but she hadn't gone far. She'd promised Ben she'd visit frequently. Anyone who wanted to find her wouldn't have a hard time.

"A large man," Vivian had said.

Lance? Ridiculously, the thought was nearly something of a comfort. He'd done his damage and disappeared. With any luck, he'd stay gone. Better to think it was him than some unidentified menace.

Charlene realized she'd been watching a little boy and girl swinging vigorously. "Bet you can't swing higher than me!" the boy yelled.

"Can too!" the girl shot back.

Charlene figured they were brother and sister, and they reminded her of herself and Max. The day he'd learned to pump a swing, she'd practiced relentlessly to keep up with him. The blisters on her hands had been worth it. They'd spent a lot of summers swinging side by side.

After the kids jumped off and dashed away to a twisty slide, Charlene wandered to the abandoned swings and settled on a seat. The flexible rubber pressed her thighs and knees together awkwardly, but she pushed off with her toes and glided gently. Holding the chain one-handed, she dialed Max with her other hand.

Reaching his voicemail, she said, "Hey, Max, I just got the best news from Vivian. I'm free! The case was dropped . . ." She rattled off the details till his voicemail cut her off.

Not minding, she pocketed her phone. This was huge news. Max would call her back this time, she was sure of it.

She's trouble. The thought scurried through the woman's mind like a frantic centipede. *Watch her. Don't let her out of your sights.*

But she had.

Irritation clawed.

She couldn't keep an eye on her—or him—constantly, not with work stealing her time.

The woman tugged at her waistband and growled in frustration. She'd lose her slender figure soon and gain countless cumbersome pounds.

No one else will want me.

But that was okay. She didn't want anyone else. Only him. Always him.

Till death do us part.

"Clay was none too happy about my decision to let you work here," Sam commented, speaking the most words he had all day.

Charlene paused in sweeping sawdust from the woodshop floor, but Sam kept right on clamping two pieces of wood in a vise. Satisfied with that, he let the glue set while he hoisted a large pine plank onto his saw table. He slipped on safety goggles, then tugged on ear protection, which looked like plastic ear muffs.

She pulled on her own ear protection just as the saw began buzzing. The wicked teeth of the round blade disappeared into a gray whir and the noise became a shriek. The scent of pine heightened as sawdust rained down.

The first chore she'd done upon arrival that morning was sweep and discard the pile of her shorn hair, glad to have it out of sight, yet, in a ridiculous way, sad to say goodbye. That hair had been with her through so much . . . She shook the ludicrous sentiment away.

She and Sam had cleared a decent path through the wreckage. He'd separated the salvageable wood while she deposited the remaining scattered pieces in a fire pit in the backyard for future burning. She rehung the Saint Joseph picture. Sam, surprisingly patient, taught her the art of sanding and staining.

As she worked, she was acutely aware of Clay's presence in the nearby house. She considered the different activities he might be doing to pass time—sleeping, watching TV, reading, drinking—and she wondered how soon he'd be back at work.

He'd have to face her then. It was only a matter of time.

Chapter Sixteen

"Catch, Charlene." Sam tossed her a broken spindle. It almost jabbed her arm before she caught it.

"Go ahead and take that to the burn pile."

So away she went, glad to snatch a few moments out in the warm sunshine. Tulips bloomed along the edge of the lot and around the base of a gnarly tree. Beneath lowered lashes, she cast a glance at the house. It was basic, somewhat small. A coat of paint would brighten it nicely, and the windows could use washing.

Spindle still in hand, she squinted, focusing on what she thought was a person standing at the window. Clay?

She almost attempted a wave, but he was already gone. Or maybe he'd never been there at all and it was a trick of the dirty windows.

While tossing the wood into the burn pile, her phone vibrated in her pocket. She answered to hear Max.

"Hey Char, got your message. What did I tell you? I knew it'd all turn out. So now that you're free, what do you say you take a trip out here?"

She stared at the woodshop. "That sounds nice, but it's still not good timing. I've got other things going on right now. Maybe when—"

"You haven't ended the engagement yet?"

She bristled, knowing he was trying to rile her. "Of course not."

"Have you at least found me the perfect girl yet?"

"No to that, as well."

"Gosh, slacker. What have you been doing since I left? Nothing but studying and working?"

"I wish." She pulled in a breath and informed Max of all that had happened since his visit, including her condo fire, her stay at Grandfather's, Lance's attack, and her new job.

"And you didn't tell me all this sooner *why?*" No humor in his tone now.

"I tried calling, but you never answered."

"I've been busy. You should've left a better message. How was I supposed to know—"

"You weren't." She paced from the tulips to the burn pile. "Now you know, but you don't need to worry. I'm fine and—"

"Pack your stuff. I'll get you a flight out tonight."

She opened and closed her mouth, trying to form the right words. "No, I can't right now."

"You've gotta be kidding me, Charlene. I can't keep an eye on you from across the country, and I can't keep coming there. You have to come here. I'll buy you your own place if that's what it takes."

He'd called her Charlene, not Char. He was really mad. She spun around and paced faster, careful to regulate her voice. "That's a really generous offer, Max, but you're not spending more money on me. Besides, Ben's already upset I moved an hour away. No way am I moving across the country." She stopped in her tracks. "I'm staying here. Not running. Not hiding."

"You're making a mistake."

"I don't think so."

Max continued arguing, but after a few minutes, he must have known he was getting nowhere. He paused. "You said you're living in the same town as Clay now?"

"Yeah, so?"

"Tell him I said he'd better keep you safe, or he'll answer to me."

She said nothing, knowing she would never relay any such message.

———

"How's Clay feeling today?" Charlene asked Sam a few days later while she brushed stain onto an oak door.

"Fine. He's healing." She mouthed the words silently as Sam said them while putting his muscle into planing a board. It was always the same. He was a man of few words. No wonder he loved putting her on phone duty. She had the delightful task of breaking the news to customers that orders were delayed. Thankfully, most customers were understanding and okay with the wait. She sensed they knew they were getting quality work worth waiting for.

She set her brush down. "I'll be right back," she said as she left the shop for a quick break.

Sam had told her on her first day where to find the restroom.

"Go through the garage door; it's the first door on your right." In those directions, she had heard his implied, *Don't go nosing anywhere else in the house.*

As if she would be so presumptuous.

This time, though, as she left the bathroom and stepped into the hall, she heard a loud, glass-splintering crash from the opposite end of the house. Concern overrode her reservations.

"Clay?" She hurried down the hall into the kitchen. "You okay?"

He had one knee on the brown linoleum, his head bent, as he crouched over shards of glass. In that split second, she knew he was fine and she should have stayed away.

He looked up. His hand hovered over a large piece of glass. His beard was gone, and she saw the large greenish bruises, the swelling, and the odd set of his jaw. "Oh, Clay."

He ducked his head again. "It's not a big deal." His words came out low, slightly muffled.

"Let me help you clean up. Where's the broom? Wait, I'll find it. Don't talk if it hurts." It sure looked like it hurt. Her eyes searched for a broom, her gaze bouncing off walls and cupboards, not registering anything as an uncomfortable feeling filled her throat.

"Relax, I've got it." Clay was suddenly sweeping glass with a broom that seemed to have appeared out of nowhere.

She swallowed, forcing past the tightness. She watched him sweep the fragments into a pan and dump them with a musical *clinkity-clink* into the trash. He hung the broom on a hook, then faced her, arms crossed. "Do you need something?"

She took a step backward. "I wanted to tell you that I'm sorry. I'm sorry Lance found you—"

"Not your fault."

"But he followed me here. If I hadn't—"

"He would have found me. If not then, another time. He's had a grudge for years. Like I said, not your fault."

She ignored the flashes of wire on his teeth, but the metal was like his tone, cold and stiff. He looked thinner already. Not eating enough.

She fingered her knuckles nervously. "Why wouldn't you let me see you in the hospital? And why don't you want me working in the shop? I'm only trying to help—"

"Don't you get it?" he said harshly. "I don't want your help." He shook his head and closed his lips awkwardly, tight over his teeth. He seemed to be debating something. His eyes finally met hers, and flashed. "Bad things happen when you're around, that's all."

Her mind reeled. "I—I don't understand. You just said it wasn't my fault."

"It's not your fault." He ground the words out through his teeth. "You can't help it. It's just who you are." His eyes didn't waver from hers. His stare was rigid.

Cruel.

She wanted to shatter to pieces and be swept from the room.

Doing the next best thing, she turned and left.

———

"Hey, Charlene," Sam barked when she re-entered the shop, "you can't just set a dirty brush down. You've gotta clean the bristles in turpentine or you'll ruin it."

Don't you know that's what I do? Bad things happen when I'm around, that's all.

But she nodded and picked up the brush. While Clay's words blistered her mind, she swished the brush in a bucket of turpentine. The strong smell ate at her nostrils and stung her eyes until they watered.

———

The banana muffins were moldy. Charlene saw the bluish white fuzz speckling the tops through the clear plastic bakery box window. She'd been pulling out a package of bagels when she spotted the box crammed in the back of the cupboard.

Ick. For as much as Brook had raved about the muffins, Charlene would have thought she'd have eaten them days ago. Charlene tossed the box in the garbage on her way out the door, then peddled the five minutes it took to get to work.

Arriving, she coasted to a stop and leaned her bike against a stately oak tree. She paused at the door of the shop, unnerved to hear familiar, but unpleasant, voices raised inside.

"It's too soon," Sam said. "You're not working yet. Get outta here. You need at least a few more days."

"No." Clay's stubborn voice. "We don't have days to spare. I've lost too many already. You can't get all these orders done on your own, and you know it."

"We'll manage. A few late orders aren't a big deal. I'm doing fine. You know I've got help."

A scoffing noise. "*Her?* She doesn't know a thing about

woodworking. How much help can she really be? Besides, you know how I feel about that, about her being here." The anger in his voice came through loud and clear, despite the wires. "You shouldn't be giving her a reason to hang around. We don't need more problems."

Bracing herself, Charlene stepped into the shop and looked right at Sam, ignoring Clay. "What would you like me to start on?" From the corner of her eye, she didn't miss Clay's face flush as he wondered what she'd overheard. The shadowy stubble on his chin hid any lingering bruises. She wondered if he was growing a beard back.

He grabbed a leather tool belt and threw it on. "Sam doesn't need your help anymore. I'm back at work now."

"I'll speak for myself." Sam's tone was sharp, and she thought of the twisted secret they shared. That was probably the only reason he was keeping her here; he likely feared she'd spill the truth if he fired her.

Clay muttered something and pulled out a hammer, then turned away and started pounding.

She spoke so only Sam could hear. "Do you want me gone? I'll go, but I'll have to give him the letter before I leave." Not out of spite, just out of necessity. She was ready to hand it over and be done with Clay forever. She tried to tune out his noisy, powerful swings.

Sam looked from her to Clay and grumbled under his breath. But she knew he realized they were both waiting for his decision.

"She can stay for now," Sam bellowed over the hammering. "We still need all the help we can get." He stepped to Clay's side and stilled the hammer mid-swing. "And if you're gonna be so darn obstinate and work, I need you on the Feldman's dining set over there, not beating up that block of wood."

So it was settled. Clay stomped past her and didn't look her way the rest of the day.

———

After a couple more tension-filled days, Charlene began losing hope that Clay would ever turn civil to her. Maybe prison had changed him, irreparably. A sad thought, but one it seemed time to face.

On her way home from work, she stopped at the library. She'd been feeling the pull for days, not only to find a few good novels to read, but to inquire about any possible openings for summer work. She'd committed to the woodshop, but it wouldn't hurt to know her options, just in case.

She stepped inside and absorbed the quiet calm. How she'd missed this environment. Unfortunately, inquiring for job openings turned out to be fruitless. Disappointed, she browsed books in the ten minutes left before closing. After selecting a few novels, a certain nonfiction book on the "new books" display caught her eye, and despite herself, it gave her an idea.

The next day, she ran the plan past Sam. His brief grunt and nod translated to, *Go ahead, couldn't hurt.*

She wasn't so sure that was true, but she'd give it a try anyway.

After Sam locked the shop, she followed him and Clay up to their house. Clay didn't turn to her, just spoke into the air in front of him. "Your bike's in the other direction."

"I know."

"So where do you think you're going?" he asked as Sam opened the door and entered the house.

"Inside."

"No, you're not." Clay turned and faced her, blocking the doorway.

"I said she could," Sam announced, already down the hall.

Raising her brows, she put on a mock triumphant expression.

Clay narrowed his eyes. His shadowed upper lip twitched in annoyance. He stayed in the doorway, appearing conflicted.

"Lighten up, Clay. I'm not going to hurt you." She could have shoved past him, but she stayed with her feet firmly planted on the stoop, waiting for him to back down.

He gave a slight shake of his head, and she noticed speckles of sawdust caught in his hair like snow. She remembered real flakes of snow in his hair. Felt like a lifetime ago.

"Seriously," she said, "if it's going to be a standoff, never mind. I'll just go."

"No, Charlene," called Sam, out of sight but apparently still tuned in. "Come on in. Clay, get out of the way. All she's doing is using the kitchen for a few minutes." She heard him mutter, "So dang stubborn . . ."

Clay moved aside, confusion, suspicion, and chagrin playing across his features.

"See, there's this book—" she pulled it from her purse and set it on the kitchen counter—"all about making blended food, like smoothies and soups, and I thought you might want to use it. If you're getting tired of juice and canned soup, which you must be."

"You're getting too thin," Sam cut in over the TV he'd turned on.

Clay watched skeptically as she pulled out the ingredients she'd stashed in the fridge earlier.

"You can have a lot more variety this way. Look." She tossed bananas, frozen strawberries, and yogurt into the blender.

"A smoothie." He sounded far from impressed.

"Just wait." She poured in some walnuts, then dropped in a huge blob of peanut butter. She snagged a bag from the fridge. "You can even throw in some spinach." She removed a few tender leaves.

"Hold on. Spinach? That's disgusting."

"No, it's baby spinach. It's mild. It'll blend right in and you won't even taste it. It's good for you." She dropped in a small handful. "You can add celery, too, and carrots."

He made a face.

She added a splash of milk, then set the rubber lid on top.

"Where'd you find this book?"

"At the library."

His mouth moved in an uncomfortable way. "You went to the library looking for it?"

"Oh no, not specifically," she hastened to clarify. "I just happened to see it, that's all. I almost didn't get it," she added, flustered. She didn't want him to think she'd been thinking of him.

His eyes flickered something. The moment felt too long. Too silent. Her fingers fumbled at the blender and flipped the switch on.

With a choppy roar, the machine burst to life and the blades whirred full-speed. The contents rocketed to the top, blowing off the lid. Spinach and strawberries pelted upward and milky-yogurt-banana-mush cascaded and splattered the ceiling—as well as Charlene and Clay.

Alarmed, she hit the switch to off. "Oh my gosh, I'm sorry! I don't know what happened."

"You didn't secure the lid," Clay said dryly.

"And that's why we don't ever let her touch the power saw," Sam remarked from his easy chair.

Ignoring him, she told Clay, "You have spinach in your hair."

"I'm not the only one." He plucked a leaf from his hair and flicked it at her.

Dodging, she watched it flutter to the ground. "You missed."

Looking at him, she felt laughter bubble up and out. Amazingly, his eyes crinkled and his mouth fought a smile—or was it even a laugh?

"Aarghh," he groaned, "my face isn't ready for this." Then it came, a laugh, half-punctuated with pain, but a laugh, nonetheless.

"Clean it up, you two," Sam yelled.

So they tore off paper towels, grabbed a bucket and mop, and went to work tackling the mess.

Her second smoothie attempt blended successfully, after Clay reminded her repeatedly to snap the lid on tight. She poured the thick drink into tall glasses, then he took a straw and tried the concoction. Swallowing, he nodded. "Not bad."

"But not good?"

He took another drink. "Fine, it's good."

"Good."

"It would be even better without the spinach."

"You can't even taste that and you know it." She smiled and tapped the book. "There's so many great recipes in here. Maybe tomorrow—"

"Helloooo," a female voice called into the house. "Hi, you guys!"

Charlene turned to see Brook, a bright smile on her face, sailing down the hall toward them. She held a tray with a couple of milk shakes. "Brought you dinner, honey." She came to Clay's side and put her arm around him before looking at Charlene pointedly. "I thought you'd be home by now."

"I was just showing Clay this book . . ." She dropped the explanation and started retreating as Brook's gaze scanned the cover. "I'll leave it here so you can try more recipes if you want."

"Oh, that would be fun. We'll do that."

"Okay, bye. Bye Sam," Charlene added.

"Hey, Charlene, you have some gunk in your hair," Brook called after her.

Back at the apartment, Charlene took a shower and scrubbed hard enough to rid every last speck of her disastrous idea out of her hair and out of her head.

The woman's skin burned, enflamed by coursing blood as her thoughts smoldered. She remembered how he had looked at her, the other woman, though she was hardly a woman at all. More like a girl. A stupid, stupid girl.

She knew her kind. The girl thought she was really something, with her name that oozed money, her smooth complexion, perfect figure, and hair that curled naturally, bouncing as she walked. Thinking she could have anyone she wanted.

She'd show her.

The woman tossed her own hair, which was growing thicker than ever now. Her long, painted nails were superior, too. Her breast inflated with pride as she admired the impeccable polish. At least in her current job, she could wear any color she liked, wasn't bound by the ridiculous rule of neutrality.

Because neutral she was not.

Not like the tramp. That hussy was just askin' for trouble.

Pressing her nails into her palms, she contemplated just what kind of trouble to give her.

Chapter Seventeen

"So that was really funny, huh?" Brook said when she arrived home late that evening and found Charlene reading in the living room. "Clay told me all about it. Food all over the place and in your hair. Must have been a chore to clean up. But that was really nice of you to think of him like that."

Charlene reread the last sentence of her novel twice while Brook hovered. She seemed to be awaiting a reply, something more than her simple nod. Usually Charlene was already sealed in her room by the late hour Brook arrived home. She hadn't thought much about it, but it suddenly clicked. Brook got home late because she hung out with Clay after work, not because she worked insanely long hours.

"It was nothing," Charlene finally answered. "I happened to see the book and thought he could use it, that's all."

Brook perched on the sofa opposite Charlene's chair and rested her chin on her hand. After studying her a minute she asked, "Do you have Clay's number?"

Charlene looked up from her book. "What?"

"Clay's phone number. Do you have it?"

Charlene closed her book, the spine crinkling. "No, why would I?"

"Well, I just thought since you're friends."

"Are we?" Charlene avoided her eyes. "Did Clay say that?"

Brook studied a tangerine fingernail. "No, but that was the impression I got."

Charlene hated asking, but felt Brook could tell her. "Do you know why he wouldn't see me in the hospital?"

Brook pursed her lips, looking like they contained a secret that was itching to be told, but she'd need a little prompting to spill it. "He just wasn't feeling good. Wasn't thinking straight."

"Evasive answer. Come on, give it to me." She set her book down. "I can take it."

Brook blew a nonexistent wisp of hair from her eyes. "Okay. He didn't say much." She leaned forward and said the next words in a rush. "Just that you were the last person he ever wanted to see."

"Oh."

"It depends how you read into it."

Hmm, nope. Charlene shook her head. No reading required.

"I wouldn't worry about it," Brook added.

Charlene yawned. "I'm going to get ready for bed."

Brook looked a little sheepish, like she regretted revealing Clay's words. "Wait, let me give you his number so you have it in case you need it."

Back to this, were they? "No thanks, I won't need it."

"You can't be sure," Brook insisted. "You're working together. You've gotta have your employer's number."

"Actually, Sam's my employer, and I have his number. That's really all I—"

"Oh what's the big deal?" Brook crossed to Charlene's chair and sat on the armrest. "Just put it in so you've got it if you need it. What if they're both out delivering orders and a customer has a question and—"

"All right. Fine." Charlene pulled out her phone. While Brook watched and recited the number, she obligingly entered and saved it. Charlene noticed she had a missed call and message from Ben. Now that he was settled in the rehab center, he was probably asking when she was coming to visit.

Staring at her phone, she headed to her room. She hadn't realized Brook had already wandered away till a burst of music hit her. Not meaning to, Charlene paused at Brook's open door, caught by the melody of Blake Shelton's "Mine Would Be You," remembering last hearing the song as she tried to work up the nerve to talk to Clay in the woodshop. The day of Lance.

"Need something?" Brook looked up from where she lay sprawled on her yellow and blue paisley bed.

"No." Charlene gave a weak smile. "I just . . . like that song." She did?

"Me too." Brook's expression turned dreamy. "It makes me think of Clay."

"Oh?" Would she elaborate? Did she want her to?

Brook beamed and motioned her into her room, obviously bursting to share.

Charlene sat gingerly on the edge of the bed and noticed a silver-framed photograph of Brook and Clay on the nightstand. He was actually smiling.

"It's kinda like our song." Brook barely lowered the volume. "It was playing when we first met."

"When was that?"

Brook waved a hand. "Back in spring."

Charlene's eyebrows quirked. *How long back? We're still in spring.*

"I was having a really bad day. Like, the worst day ever." Brook's eyelids shielded her gaze. "My boyfriend had recently broken up with me, and I was working, and nothing was going right. Customers were needy and rude, and I was falling way behind. I was stocking this big display of soup cans, and I touched one can wrong, and it all went tumbling down around me. I mean, big disaster, huge mess. So embarrassing.

"Customers were gawking, my manager was barking at me to clean it up fast, and I looked around completely overwhelmed and pathetic and like I was about to lose it and fall apart, you know?"

Charlene nodded sympathetically.

"So I'm scrambling to pick up cans, and suddenly there's this customer, this really nice guy who leaves his cart and starts helping me. He doesn't even say anything, just starts picking up cans. That guy was Clay."

Brook eyed his picture and let out a long sigh. "That was how we met, stacking soup cans. And this song was playing. And everything started to turn around for me after that. Whenever he shopped, he'd say hi to me, and we'd talk. One evening when I got off of work, we just talked in the parking lot forever."

Clay talking forever? Charlene couldn't picture that.

"He bought me dinner. The next night, I made him dinner, and we've just been so happy ever since."

"That's great." Charlene smoothed the comforter and studied the paisley pattern while she sensed Brook studying her.

"So what's your story? How did you meet Clay?"

"My story?" Charlene looked up, almost in alarm, and willed her heartbeat to slow. "Oh, it's nothing near so . . . sweet. Or special." She let out a monosyllable laugh. "In fact, it's really not worth telling at all." She tried to slide off the bed, but Brook hooked her with her arm and tugged her back.

"Hey, no way. That's not fair. It's your turn, so spill it."

Panic pressed in. Charlene's pulse skyrocketed. She'd been so successful lately at keeping everything stuffed and locked away.

Ben knew her past, but he also knew not to bring it up. She could depend on him. He was her safe haven. She'd been away from him too long.

"So?" Brook prodded. "Start at the beginning."

Sweat burst from Charlene's pores. She didn't want to remember it, relive it. But there Brook sat, staring at her, bright eyed and expectant. Charlene cleared her throat and took a deep breath. Brook probably already knew the basics, anyway, she rationalized. She would keep it very dry, simple, and brief.

Get it over with.

"It was more than four years ago." *I remember it like yesterday.* She stared blankly at the wall, which slowly wavered and dissolved, morphing to black as her mind unearthed the petrified, crumbled bits of horror and pieced them back together. She shivered. "It was right after Christmas. My brother had been kidnapped—"

Brook shot up to a full sitting position, eyes wide. "Seriously?"

Charlene nodded.

"Was he—I mean is he—"

"He's fine." She waved away her concern. "It all turned out fine." *Fine? Debatable.* Charlene jumped up. "Know what? It's late. I'm turning in."

"What? No way. You can't leave me hanging like that. That's cruel."

Charlene headed for the door. Brook zipped in front and blocked the way. "I told you my story; you've gotta tell me yours. I won't be able to sleep if you don't."

I won't be able to sleep if I do.

"I'm not letting you go till you tell." Brook spoke playfully, but icy fingers gripped Charlene's heart and squeezed.

"You said it all turned out fine, so come on. What's the big deal?"

Charlene backed up slowly, hit the bed, and plunked down.

"You were telling me about your brother," Brook prompted.

"Right." Charlene licked her lips. "I was looking for him and ended up lost in the woods. It was so cold, and snowing, and I was exhausted."

"And?" Brook urged.

"And Clay was coming through the trees, back from ice fishing on a nearby lake. He let me warm up in his cabin. His family's cabin," she amended, rubbing her arms. "Then his brother showed up."

"Wait—what?" Brook cut in. "Clay has a brother?"

Half-brother. "Had, not has."

"That's *terrible*—"

"It was . . . but it isn't. I mean, he was a terrible man." Terrible? Ha. So inadequate. It didn't begin to describe . . . "It's good that he's gone." She barely registered Brook's shocked expression as she plunged on. "He was the kidnapper, and now he had me, too."

What am I doing? But still she went on, and the words felt like profanity spewing from her mouth.

Brook sat at rapt attention. "How did you survive?"

"Clay tried to help us, but . . ." She swallowed. "Abner tried to kill us all."

"He *what?*" Brook started to sputter another question, but Charlene didn't want to hear it.

Finish this. "We finally escaped. Clay helped us." *I can't ever forget that.* "But there was a trial, and he went to prison."

"What?" Brook gasped. "That's not right! How could—"

"He was convicted on accessory to assault." She gripped the comforter fabric in her hot palms.

"But how could—he couldn't have—"

"He held a video camera and filmed. As Abner . . . did this." Charlene flipped her hand palm-up for Brook to see the pale, melted skin of her scar.

Horror encircled Brook's gaping mouth.

"It wasn't like Clay wanted to film it. He had no choice. It's hard to explain . . . you would have had to have been there—and the jury wasn't. Thus the conviction."

"You didn't testify against him?"

"No, my brother and I both defended him, but the prosecution was relentless. The judge went light on the sentencing. Clay got twelve months and a day, but he'd already served eight of them while waiting for trial." She paused, picturing him as she'd seen him in the courtroom the day of the verdict. "He seemed to take it really well. I think the worst part about it was he was cheated out of being with his mom when she was dying."

Charlene clamped her mouth shut.

Silence wrapped around them, cinching Charlene tightly. So much for keeping the account short, simple, and boring.

"Wow," Brook said at last. "I had no idea . . ."

Queasiness created an acidic pain in Charlene's stomach. "But he must have told you some of this. Bits and pieces, at least . . ."

"No, not a word." Her face was shell-shocked. She would have a lot more questions when the shock wore off, but Charlene knew she'd already said too much.

Way too much.

Charlene's head pounded; her thoughts screamed for escape. Her feet hit the floor. She said goodnight and fled to her own room, where she shut the door, locked it, and pressed her back to the wood. Slumping to the floor, she brought a fist to her lips, feeling like her mouth was the size of the Grand Canyon.

Charlene awoke from the clutches of a nightmare and lay perfectly still, waiting for her heart to slow. Mercifully, her mind blanked out the dream, but the fear remained. Blankets lay piled on her so heavily, she was slick with sweat, yet somehow a chill gnawed deep in her bones.

Her night light threw beams and shadows. Morning light fingered her window shade. Good. Night was over. She shoved the blankets off.

She pulled her phone from her nightstand and opened her contacts. Ben topped the list. Her scrolling finger skipped over Max, then hovered over Clay's name, knowing she should delete him, but she didn't. After a few seconds, she moved to Sam's name and called to ask for the day off. He granted her request with a "Sure thing" and hung up.

An hour later, she was on a bus back to Woodfield to see Ben at last. She called him and was surprised to learn she didn't have to go to the rehab center after all.

"What, they let you go already?"

"No, but it's not a prison," he joked.

She didn't respond.

"My dad's picking me up for the day. I pulled some strings with my charm."

Sure, she pictured his smile that could move mountains.

In town, she scanned the grocery store floral department, wanting to buy him something but feeling at a loss. None of the flowers looked manly enough for Ben, but what had she expected? Settling for a leafy ivy in a plastic pot, she decided to skip inserting the little "get well" card, as Ben had told her he was sick to death of being told to "get well."

"Doesn't anyone get it? Getting well isn't in my control, but I

keep getting told to do it. " Those had been his words a few days ago at the tail end of an unusually cranky phone conversation.

Clasping the small pot, she rounded an aisle and came face-to-face with Detective Green. He didn't look pleased. "The contact number you gave me was no good."

She blinked. "I'm sorry, I had to get a new phone and didn't realize—"

"I need you to come to the station for questioning. Don't worry, it's just a routine follow-up."

Inwardly, she groaned, but nodded. She moved mechanically through the checkout lane. Blocking the fire from her mind hadn't made the mess go away.

At the station, she answered questions and was informed that the fire marshal had concluded that the condo blaze had indeed been the result of arson. No surprise there.

Drained from the questioning, she stepped stiffly out of the station.

———

Nails licked his thumb and counted what he had left of his cash. The rich smell of wealth filled his nostrils. He imagined the stacks upon stacks just sitting in the old man's safe. He couldn't wait.

But he would. He could be patient, very patient.

He wouldn't emerge while he was still big news. Still being hunted. Time would dull the efforts, lessen the resources. The heat would die, as it always did.

He closed his fingers over a cluster of twenties. An unwanted memory, decades old, wormed its way in. Crisp green bills pressed into his sweaty, tired hands.

"That's all yours. You earned it with honest work. How does that feel?"

He threw the cash on the table and stood up, backing away, cursing Mr. Callaghan and his self-righteous words. The hypocrite. Spouting platitudes. Thinking he could make a difference. Could change him.

Memories closing in, his back hit the trailer wall. Nowhere to go. The tight quarters taunted, too much like a cell. He scrubbed a hand over his face, then turned and kicked the wall.

Chapter Eighteen

Charlene arrived at Ben's house empty-handed. She'd forgotten the ivy plant at the police station and wasn't about to go back for it. She heaved a deep breath of the warm grass-scented air and tried to relax, to send her worries away like dandelion fluff on a breeze.

Across the street, a little boy blew iridescent bubbles into the wind. The bubbles came out in a stream, like a string of glass beads and then, *pop, pop, pop,* they were gone.

Turning back to Ben's door, she smoothed her expression. Just in time, too. The red door opened and her face registered surprise when she saw Ben had opened it, from a wheelchair.

It was so good to see him, and yet, to see him like this broke her heart. "Oh, Ben."

He glided back to let her in. She stepped inside.

He ran his hand over a wheel. "Still getting the hang of it, but it beats lying in bed."

"It's an improvement," she managed.

He led her through the house and out to the back deck, into the spring breeze and sunshine. She wove her fingers together. "So how long do you think you'll need the chair?"

Ben's attempt at a smile slipped away. "Long." His gaze drifted from hers and out over the plowed field that backed up to his family's yard.

"But the therapy's helping, right?"

He shrugged. "We'll see."

She followed his gaze, knowing it ran over the highway and up the hills to a thick, newly green forest. He'd told her how he'd grown up hiking those woods, climbing those trees, scouting for animals, even camping. It pierced her to imagine he was thinking of all he might never do again. Culpability washed over her in an all-consuming wave. Her only hope for getting over the guilt would be if he could actually walk again someday. *Please, God. Please.*

"Hey, you cut your hair." He said it as if he'd only just noticed, but she knew it was a purposeful change of subject. "Wow. That's unexpected. What made you do that?"

"I . . . I just couldn't help it. It was time for a change." Self-conscious, she raised a hand to her short curls. "I know, it's really different, but it'll grow back."

"In time for our wedding?"

She blinked.

"Kidding, Charlene. It looks pretty, even kind of wild and spunky. It's a good look for you."

She gave a tiny smile and finally settled onto a plastic chair. They moved on to talk about different, unimportant, safe things, and it felt nice to relax and forget her troubles . . . and then she noticed Ben's inert legs, and the obtuse wheelchair. Like a big, bold sign declaring, *You did this.*

Looking away, she watched a swallow dip and dive, then twirl and swoop, performing a little airshow before it sailed out of sight.

They went over some wedding plans. "Sure makes it difficult now that you're living so far away. I still don't get it. Can't you reconsider moving back?" Ben turned his lake-blue eyes pleadingly on her, and she swallowed; this was the look she'd been able to avoid on the phone. Breaking eye contact, she studied the deck boards at her feet, thinking they needed a new coat of weatherproof sealant.

"Charlene?"

"It's better this way."

"Really? How is it better? How is it possibly better in any way, shape, or form?" He grabbed her hands and brought them to his chest. "I need you so much nearer. I thought you were too far before, when you were minutes away, and now . . . Come on, Charlene. Move back."

"I can't."

"Why not? It's not like you have anything holding you there."

"I have a job. Here, they fired me."

"You'll easily find another job. You're smart and talented."

"I have an apartment."

"So? You can break a lease. You can stay here at my parents', like we talked about. The guest room's all ready. Just say the word."

"The people in this town . . ."

"Who cares? They don't matter."

"It matters when they threaten me," she mumbled.

She wasn't sure if Ben caught her words, but he said, "I'll protect you. Don't you know that? Let me, please." He squeezed her hands. "Move back."

She sighed. "Not yet, Ben. Just, not yet . . ."

He nodded. Slowly, he released her hands. She almost didn't hear him say, "I wish I understood why."

She had to give him more. "I just came from the police station. The fire that destroyed my condo . . ." She met his eyes. "It was arson."

Color drained from his face. "They're sure?"

"They said the fire started in multiple spots, and they found traces of gasoline in the living room."

He seemed to absorb that. For once, he had no comeback.

"I feel safe in Creekside. It's a nice town," she added feebly. "Look, I can show you a few pictures . . . the park, the library, the church . . ." She fished out her phone and began bringing up photos.

Ben shook his head. "No thanks."

Deflated, she set her phone on the picnic table and studied her hands. Her fingers were already turning slightly rough and calloused from working. She made a mental note to use hand lotion.

Birds chirped. The scent of honeysuckle wafted by.

"When we get married," Ben said, clasping the back of his neck, "where do you think we're going to live? Do you hate this town that much that you wouldn't want to settle down here?"

"I—" She stopped to really think her answer through. Something in Ben's expression told her it was important. "I haven't thought much about it, but . . . the way things have been here, the way I feel now . . . I don't like this town much. The only good part about it is you."

Ben nodded. "Family's important. I've said that before. I wouldn't want to leave them behind—not far behind, that is." He met her eyes. "But for you . . . we'll only live where you can be happy."

She gazed at him tenderly. "Thank you. We wouldn't have to move far. I wouldn't ask you to do that."

"Just don't ask me to live in a yellow house, and we're good."

"Um, okay." She felt a little jolt since, for some reason, she'd always loved sunny yellow houses. Apparently, she must not have ever told him that. She wasn't about to now, not if he was serious. She managed a belated laugh. "What do you have against yellow houses?"

"It's just the worst house color ever, that's all. A house should be—I don't know—serious? Manly? Not look like some kind of wimpy lemon dollhouse, you know?"

She raised her eyebrows. "I do now." She touched a finger to her lips. "Okay, well, you probably don't like little white picket fences, either then, hey?" Here was something they could agree on. She never wanted a fence around her home—not for decoration or convenience. She'd come to this conclusion years ago . . . oddly, in a dark moment of confinement, facing death in captivity.

Ben frowned. "Well, no, it doesn't have to be white, but I really like the idea of some kind of fence. Extra security to keep our kids safe, right?"

Her lips quirked but didn't quite make it to a smile. Such a ridiculous conversation, anyway. They'd work it all out just fine another time.

"Do you want some water?" she asked, rising. "I feel like a cold drink."

"Sure, okay. But hey, let me get it." Ben began rolling to the door, but she was already sliding it open.

"No, I'll get it," she assured him.

She said hi to Lucy in the dining room, where she was eating a sandwich. As Charlene filled two glasses, Lucy spoke around a mouthful. "So you moved away, huh? Right after you got engaged. That's kinda weird." She chewed loudly. "How's that gonna work?"

Both glasses full, Charlene turned off the faucet and glided past her. "You'll understand when you're older."

When she stepped onto the deck, Charlene halted, leaving the sliding door wide open.

Ben had an odd, unreadable expression on his face. His hand gripped his phone.

No, *her* phone.

He said, "You might want to close the door."

Concerned, she frowned and slid it shut.

Despite the fact that he grasped her phone tight in his fist, he lifted it for her to see. "You missed a call when you were inside."

"Oh? Who was it?"

"Clay."

She clunked the glasses on the picnic table. A little water sloshed out, puddling darkly on the worn wood.

Before she had a chance to respond, Ben said in a tight voice, "Don't pretend you don't know who that is. You haven't spoken his name in years, but don't think for a second I believe you've

151

forgotten him. I know I haven't." His eyes flashed. "I know it took you forever to move on after he ditched this town and left you all torn up over him. How does he have your number, and why's he calling you?"

She dropped into a chair, feeling as if all her breath had been knocked out by Ben's rough torrent of words. He'd never spoken to her like that before. "It's okay, Ben. Don't get upset. It's nothing." She bit her lip. Confused as she was over why Clay would call, now wasn't the time to wonder. "I'm sure it's just work related."

"Work related?"

Oops.

Ben's jaw slackened. "You mean . . . you're *working* with the guy?"

Her face flushed hot as she started to explain, but he cut her off, his anger-charged voice overpowering her. "And you didn't think that maybe that was something worth telling me? Me, your fiancé?" He plowed a hand through his hair. "Darn it, Charlene, what else aren't you telling me?"

"I—you're taking this all wrong, blowing it way out of proportion."

"Am I?" He looked as if he would have jumped to his feet, if he could. "Then why is it all suddenly making a heck of a lot of sense? Why you moved. Why you hardly call. Why you won't move back." With each point, he jammed his finger to the table, his fingertip turning white and red with the pressure. "What I don't get is why you'd want that guy anywhere in your life. He was nothing but trouble for you—"

"Except for the small fact that he saved my life."

"Okay." Ben clenched his jaw. "I'll give him that. I'm thankful for that. But you don't owe him your life, for the rest of your life."

"Obviously."

"I'm not stupid, Charlene. You like the guy. You always have. I thought I could—"

The patio door zinged open and Ben's mom stood there. "Is everything all right out here? Ben?" But she looked at Charlene, with narrowed eyes that demanded, *Why are you upsetting him? You know it's not good for him.*

"Fine, Mom." Ben's voice was measured. "Go back inside."

Her lips pinched but she retreated. When the door sealed shut once more, Ben met Charlene's eyes at her level, which still didn't seem right. She was used to looking up into his eyes as he stood tall above her.

"I never liked him."

"Ben, please, you're overreacting. You have no reason to be jealous. You have no idea how ridiculous that is." She knew he wanted to believe her words, but he needed more reassurance. "I love you. I'm marrying you. The only reason Clay and I crossed paths at all is because I had a letter from his mom—his dead mother—that I had to give him. I promised her." She pressed her palms flat on the table. "That's all."

"But now you're working for him. Tell me that's not strange."

"No, I'm not working for him. I'm working for his—his employer. His boss. Actually, Clay doesn't even want me working there." She dropped her gaze. "But it's something I have to do. His shop got ransacked. Because of me." She did her best to explain the incident.

Ben looked blown away. "You're only just telling me this now?"

"I didn't want to worry you."

He snorted. "I'm a lot more worried to hear about it like this, so long after the fact."

He was right. Her shoulders slackened. "I'm sorry."

He shook his head. "So you got suckered into working there because you felt guilty? You don't owe them anything. Not a thing. If Clay's got someone after him, it's his own fault, not yours. Another reason you need to stay far away from him. You moved out of Woodfield because you didn't feel safe here. Doesn't sound like you're safe there, either."

His words stirred up fears, but she tamped them back down. "I promise you, Ben, this is temporary. And I told you I'm coming back every Sunday at the very least. We'll go to church and spend the whole day together."

She downed a big swallow of water. It cooled and soothed her stomach, though not nearly enough. She slid a glass closer to Ben. The tense lines of his face were lessening, but still visible. He finally released her phone and took a quick drink.

As soon as he swallowed, he hit her with another question. "Why didn't he answer when I said hello? He hung up on me."

Her lips parted. "You mean, you answered my phone?" She felt strangely miffed.

"Sure, I saw 'Clay' on the display. You blame me?" No hint of apology.

"Considering what I'm sure was your kind greeting, not to

mention the fact that he was expecting me to answer, I can't imagine why he might have hung up." Her tone bordered on sarcastic. "He probably thought he had the wrong number."

"Then why didn't he try again?"

She let out a frustrated noise. "I don't know. Who cares? Can't we drop it?"

"Does he know you're engaged?"

"I—no—I don't know. I mean, why would that even come up? Ben, stop imagining things. Let it go." Her voice softened. "You've got to trust me."

He ran his tongue over his teeth. He raised his brows high, then dropped them. "I know. I know." He shook his head, rolled close, and caught her hand. "I'm not scared of much. I'm not even scared of never walking again. But I am scared of losing you. I love you so much, that that's the one thing I absolutely could not take."

The battle over, she let her neck relax, and her head dipped. "You're not going to lose me," she promised fervently. "I said yes to you, remember?"

"I'll never forget."

Neither would she, nor how she'd sent him plummeting to a horrible fate mere moments after. The two incidents were unavoidably linked. *My fault. All my fault. He's lost so much.* She squeezed his hand in silent reassurance. *He won't lose me too.*

Charlene tried not to wonder about Clay's call, but hours later, after a meal, a movie, and more wedding plans, it tugged at her mind as she tried to leave. Despite discreet glances at her phone, she knew he hadn't tried calling back.

How soon could she return to Creekside? She was aware her car sat abandoned near her burnt condo, but she was loath to return to the spot. Still, she was going to have to get the car sometime. She loved biking, and the bus wasn't bad, but the convenience of her own vehicle topped them both.

"You don't have to go," Ben interrupted her thoughts.

"We've been through this—"

"Just stay tonight, that's all I mean. It's already dark. I'm not going to let you wander the streets at night. It's not safe."

She smirked. "I wasn't exactly planning on 'wandering.' I only need to get to my car—it's still at the condo."

"That's too far to walk."

"Well, I can't stay. I need to be at work in the morning."

His look implied, *Bet you could get out of that if you really wanted to.*

She shifted her feet. "I'll call a taxi."

"No way. I'd drive you myself, if I could," Ben muttered.

Not that he intended it, but guilt stabbed her.

"I'll get my mom to drive you. She won't mind."

This isn't awkward, Charlene thought ten minutes later as she stared at the glowing dashboard clock in Mrs. Jorgensen's Subaru Outback as the woman drove in silence.

She hit the indicator and turned the wheel. "I'd rather you wouldn't visit Ben if you're going to upset him."

Charlene wished they'd stuck to silence. "About that . . . it's nothing to worry about. Everyone has disagreements sometimes."

"Hmm." She turned to eye her directly. "Do you still intend to marry him?" Her look was so intense, her need to know so urgent, Charlene hurried to answer so she'd return her eyes to the road.

"Of course."

Mrs. Jorgensen's gaze snapped back to the sparse traffic. Charlene thought maybe she was going to order her not to go through with the wedding, but she only said, "I don't know why you moved away, then."

Goodness, there was no pleasing the woman. "You didn't want me to move in. I had to live somewhere."

"Yes, but an hour away? Seems rather extreme."

Thankfully, that train of conversation ended as Mrs. Jorgensen pulled into the parking lot next to the rubbly remnants of her condo. With the aid of a streetlight's glow, they both sat and stared at the charred, misshapen form.

"It must have been frightening," Mrs. Jorgensen said, pressing a hand to her stomach.

"There's my car." Charlene clutched her purse and opened the door. "Thanks for the ride."

"Charlene," Mrs. Jorgensen looked her way, "you mean everything to him. Do not lead him on."

As Mrs. Jorgensen pulled away, Charlene was glad the woman wasn't lingering to make sure she got into her car safely. But when she was out of sight, a strange feeling came over her as she realized she hadn't told Mrs. Jorgensen how to get to her condo.

She'd never been here before, despite how long Charlene had known Ben. He must have given her directions, that's all.

Charlene's car was the only one in the lot. She hadn't left it here, though. She remembered it had been parked down the street. Maybe the police had moved it. At least the ugly, hateful words on the back window had been cleaned off.

Closer now, she saw a white envelope tucked under a wiper. Instantly, she tensed into high alert and looked over her shoulder nervously. There would be something awful and threatening inside the envelope, she just knew it.

Oh, how she hated this town.

She felt herself tremble as she ripped the seal. Touching the enclosed paper as little as possible, she flicked the single sheet open and scanned the words.

Relief created a little laugh. The note was only from Darla, condo association president, informing Charlene she'd done her the favor of cleansing the unsightly eyesore from her window and then had her car towed to the lot. Why couldn't she reach her by phone? And enclosed was a bill. This, Charlene could deal with.

She unlocked and opened her door. Interior lights shone, revealing another surprise, this one a large flat manila envelope on the passenger seat.

Feeling watched, she glanced in her backseat, but no one was hiding, lying in wait. She dropped onto her seat and closed the door. Pressing a button, she locked herself in the car.

Studying the envelope, she found no writing or markings of any kind. She shoved her finger under the flap and ripped.

Photographs slipped out in a neat stack into her hand.

She frowned at the first one. It was just a picture of her condo, back when it was still standing. The focal point of the picture was her front door and window. A boring picture. Meaningless.

She spotted herself in the next picture, sitting on her sofa reading a book, oblivious to the picture being taken through the window. Creepy.

The third picture puzzled her a moment, showing simply a beige carpeted staircase, cream walls, and a wooden handrail. Like a punch to her stomach, she recognized it. Someone had taken this picture *inside* her condo.

From outside her home, to inside her home, the pictures were showing an intrusive, frightening progression.

Slowly, she shifted the picture, slid it centimeter by centimeter off the thin stack, hoping she'd reached the end and that she was back to the first picture. She couldn't stand to see another.

But there was one more.

This one showed her lying on her pillow, long hair in disarray, eyes closed as she slept, oblivious to any threat. The picture was a clear close-up of her face. She could even see her lashes resting against her skin.

This picture couldn't have been taken through a window. The photographer had been in her room, watching her while she slept.

Chapter Nineteen

*P*anic shot through her. Charlene slapped the disturbing images, the silent intimidation, face down onto her passenger seat.

After a few unsuccessful attempts, she jabbed her key in the ignition and pealed out of the parking lot with a squeal of tires sure to send vigilant Darla to her window.

As Charlene drove, the anxiety numbing her mind subsided as she reasoned herself into a calmer state. Since the photos showed her in her condo, the pictures were now old and irrelevant. Over a week old, at least.

Whoever had been trying to scare her was too late. She was out of the condo and out of this town.

It was probably Lance. She would never forget the night of his intrusion.

Only . . . she snatched up the last picture as she drove and flicked on a light to rescan the details. The edge of her nightstand had made it into the frame, but no water bottle. She'd had one there the night Lance attacked. She was sure of that, because she remembered knocking it over.

So maybe he'd taken the pictures another night. He obviously had access. She recalled how he'd bumped into her at school. There was a purpose behind that. Only shortly after, he'd invaded her home. But why slip the pictures into her car to scare her now?

She heaved in a big breath and changed thoughts. Maybe it wasn't Lance, maybe it was just Grandfather, spitefully messing with her mind. He certainly had the resources to accomplish practically anything.

Or was it some unknown enemy?

Calm down. She tossed the picture back on the passenger seat, then switched on the radio and zoned out on her long ride back to Creekside. Aware of the wind hissing through her cracked window, she shot the window closed. So that's how the envelope had been slipped in her car. All her fault for leaving it open.

Once parked in the apartment lot, she left her car with a

heightened, hair-prickling sense of awareness and scurried into the building. Her heart rate didn't slow until she was safe in her bedroom. Knowing Brook slept in the room beside her was a comfort, and she was thankful for her presence.

Eight o'clock. Rosary time in the Callaghan household. Nails swore. Why did he still remember that, after all these years?

Why'd he even look at the clock? Time moved slow enough these days. And that infernal ticking. He yanked the thing from the wall, threw it on the floor, and stomped on it. The crunch didn't satisfy him.

"Callaghan." Not even aware he'd said the name aloud, he paced in the narrow confines of the trailer, a terrible energy building inside him.

Why a family stuck with six kids had wanted to bring him into the mix, never made sense. At sixteen, he'd had more attitude and rebellion balled inside him than all those Callaghan kids put together. Yet they acted like they wanted him.

They'd duped him. Briefly. Them and their sickening goodwill. Trying to make him feel welcome. Feeding him home-cooked meals. They didn't hide and ration the grub, like some places. They had a big house, big money. The perfect setup. So he let them drag him to church. He even sat in on their family Rosary, like Mr. Callaghan required. That tyrant always had too many rules.

Nails had never joined in their repetitious prayers, but he sat and listened. He liked when Beth, the oldest daughter, led the Hail Marys. He didn't focus on the words, just the sound of her honey voice. The softness of her face. Her curls sparking copper in the vigil candle light.

He ground his teeth. Beth was only a year younger than him, but she'd had no idea what he was. She was too innocent, too good. He should have hated her. She was always smiling, eagerly caring for her younger siblings, baking, cooking, cleaning, never complaining. Like some nauseating saint. The stark opposite of him. Because of her, his defiance stood out like corrosion.

And still, they kept him. Until . . .

Refusing to finish the thought, he slammed open the door and stalked off into the night. Into the welcoming darkness.

The photo scare knocked all thoughts of Clay's call from Charlene's mind, and she didn't remember it until coasting her bike to work the next morning. Though she had her car back, she enjoyed riding in the open air too much to drive such a short distance.

Her peddling slowed as she reached Sam's drive. Why had Clay called? A thick hesitance lay curdling her stomach as she entered the woodshop.

Both Sam and Clay were already hard at work. Sam gave her a nod, then sent a board shrieking through the table saw. She threw on ear protection.

Clay didn't nod a greeting. He merely looked at her. Something about his tight expression made her stomach flip.

She turned away to work, deciding not to bring up the call. She'd leave it to him. As far as he knew, she knew nothing about it.

"Clay, Charlene," Sam called about an hour later. "Come here." He motioned them with a hammer to his workbench. They stood stiffly, one on either side of him. "Look, you two, after what happened here, I've been staying close, but it's getting old. I can't stay in the shop watching you every day, all day, and I don't want to."

Clay looked monumentally insulted. "You don't need to babysit us."

"I don't plan to." Sam pulled open a workbench drawer. Inside sat a black plastic case, which he opened to reveal a small gun. Several white boxes of Winchester ammunition lay behind the case.

Clay frowned. "I don't need a gun."

"I disagree," Sam countered. "It could have saved you a broken jaw. It could have made sure that ex-con didn't get away."

Clay drilled Sam with a look. "You're forgetting something. I'm an ex-con, too. A felon. And felons aren't allowed to own, use, or even touch a gun."

"Yeah, well that sounds real nice, but while you may respect those rules, the other felon might not. And you're forgetting this isn't just about you. You're not the only one in the shop." Sam glanced at Charlene. "I want you both to have a means to defend yourselves if that lowlife comes back."

He turned again to Clay. "Law or no, you'd use the gun to protect yourself or Charlene, and that would be the right thing to do. Don't tell me you don't want the option. The gun's in my name. You don't have to touch it, but it's here if you need it. I protect my employees." He seemed to stumble slightly over the word "employees." She imagined he had wanted to say "son."

Sam regarded her. "What do you think?"

She glanced at Clay's scowl, then at the gun. "I think it's a good idea."

Sam gave a satisfied nod. "It's a .38 Special revolver. Small, easy to fire, not a lot of recoil, but definitely enough power to kill. If need be. It's not loaded right now. You ever shoot before, Charlene?"

She pictured Abner's gun, a bigger one. Despite how close it had come to her, she'd never even touched it. She blinked to clear the image. "No, but if I had to, I'm sure—"

"Not good enough. Tell you what, I've got to spend the rest of the day making deliveries. We've done a decent job catching up around here. Clay, take her to the outdoor range and teach her to shoot. Make sure she gets plenty of practice." He began walking away and gave a short laugh. "It's safety training day."

"No way, Sam." Clay's hand came down hard on the workbench. "Are you deaf? I just told you, I can't even touch a gun. How am I going to teach—"

"You'll figure it out. Just talk her through it. I gotta go." Sam exited the shop. A moment later, his truck rumbled out the drive.

Clay glanced at her, then shoved the drawer shut with a bang.

She stood rooted to the floor. Her eyes darted to the open door and the bright sunshine bouncing off the driveway. An outdoor range sounded nicer than staying inside. She looked at Clay.

"Seriously? You really want to go shoot?"

She lifted her eyebrows, gave a small smile, and shrugged. "I do. Next time, I'll protect you."

"Oh, that's rich." Clay almost cracked a grin, then sobered and crossed his arms. "I'm not kidding. I'm not touching the gun. So unless you're insanely good at following verbal directions, I can't teach you how to use the thing."

"I want to do this," she surprised herself by insisting, "but if it's too hard for you, I'll find someone at the range to show me." She slid the drawer open and reached for the weapon.

Clay's hand shot out and caught her wrist. "Whoa, hold on." His tone made her flinch. "Never take anyone's word for it that a gun's not loaded. Always treat it like it is."

Slightly unnerved, she swallowed.

Clay released her wrist and pointed. "This here's the hammer. Check that it's down, not cocked. Pick the gun up so the muzzle's pointing away from you and anyone else who's around. Keep your finger away from the trigger until you're ready to shoot. Got it?"

She nodded.

"Go ahead then, pick it up."

All kinds of nervous now, she lifted the silver-barreled gun slowly and carefully by the dark wood grip, sure to keep the muzzle pointed at the wall. The weapon felt heavier than its size suggested.

"To be sure it's not loaded, you'll have to hit the cylinder release button right here." Clay pointed. "Then pop out the cylinder. Try it."

Her right thumb pressed the button, her left nudged out the metal cylinder. Easy enough.

"Good," he said. "Now you can see that each chamber is empty."

True, no bullets rested inside the six vacant slots. She snapped the cylinder back in place. Her new knowledge, slight as it was, gave her confidence. She placed the gun gingerly back in the case and closed it. "So you'll teach me how to shoot?"

Clay's eyes assessed her, darkening. "All right. But I can't drive us. I can't get caught transporting a gun, even if it's not mine."

"Okay." She respected his being a stickler for the law, and she didn't want him ending up back in prison, either. She picked up the case and tucked it under her arm. Then she slid a couple boxes of ammunition in her purse.

"We'll need these." Clay grabbed two pairs of eye and ear protection.

When they walked outside, she realized she'd have to pick her car up at the apartment so she could drive them to the range. It wasn't a terribly long walk, but she considered Clay, still healing, and asked, "You up for the walk to my place? Otherwise I can—"

"It's a broken jaw, not a broken leg. I can walk."

Ignoring a pang, she readjusted her purse strap on her shoulder. "Okay then." She tried to make her words as breezy as the warm, winding air. They set off, side by side, yet a definite distance between them. Tiny embedded granite stones sparkled and glinted in the road. Birds sang. Now and then, a car passed by.

They said nothing for half the walk. Her underarms dampened and she shifted the gun case. She mulled over a few conversation openers, but dismissed them. They'd gone so long without speaking, she couldn't start now.

The thought of an entire afternoon at a shooting range with Clay's tight lips began to loom uncomfortably awkward. When she used peripheral vision to glance discreetly at him, he appeared almost angry. Brooding. Turmoil building like a spring storm.

Then the storm clouds burst and his words rained out, heavy and cold. "I don't get it. I never would've pegged you as a careless, blabbing gossip."

Her stomach plummeted. She knew where this was going. She wanted to dive into the roadside weeds and wildflowers.

"Why'd you tell Brook all those things about me?" His sharp voice cut her. "You're the last person I'd expect that from."

The sense of having betrayed him made her shrink farther from his side, but he slowed his steps and looked right at her, his expression demanding an answer.

She wrapped her arms around herself. "She asked. She wanted to know how I knew you, how we met."

Clay's brows shot up, incredulous. "And you couldn't have kept it simple? Said we met in the woods and left it at that?"

"Sure, because *that* doesn't sound weird at all."

She began moving with powerful strides, wanting this walk over and done with. She knew she should apologize, but his accusatory tone rankled, and an unpleasant pressure built in the back of her throat. The only way to ward it off was to strike back.

"She wanted details, Clay. Girls are different, they talk about things."

"The wrong things."

Her hands clenched. "How was I to know it was some big secret? You never said. We never had an agreement, an understanding that we couldn't discuss it."

"We shouldn't have had to," he practically snarled. "It's common sense. It was bad. All of it. Nothing worth remembering or telling. So why, on earth, would you want to?"

I didn't want to. Her face scrunched tightly and she turned her head aside.

"You had no right," he went on, his words ripping her to shreds. "I came here to start over."

"Oh yeah? Then why do you carry that article in your wallet?"

He flung her a look, eyes smoldering. "What are you talking about?"

"You know." *Me and my big mouth.* "The one about your sentencing. If you wanted to 'start over' I would think—"

"How do you know what's in my wallet?"

"That day in the workshop, Lance stole your money. He found

the article and—"

"It's none of your business. Just like all this is none of your business."

Her eyes followed the random black tar lines in the cracks of the road. *Why* had they walked?

Having realized that silence was preferable, she was aghast when more words burst from her mouth. "You can't build a new life on secrets. Your girlfriend deserves to know. I didn't go into detail. You're being unfair. She could have looked up any part of the story. It's practically all online."

"But she didn't. She wouldn't have. Even if she does need to know, it should have come from me, at the right time, not from you." He raked a hand through his hair. "I wanted her to get to know me first, without all that baggage. We haven't been together long enough for something that huge. I didn't want to freak her out. But you—you just charged in with no regard for—"

"I'm her roommate. We have to talk sometimes."

"Then talk about something else. *Anything* else." He shook his head. "You trying to scare her away, or what?"

Mortified, she almost stumbled. "No, of course not! Never. Why would I do that? No."

"Then what? You want to give her nightmares?" His voice went gruff. " 'Cause she doesn't need that."

She swallowed a tremble in her throat, then whispered, "No one needs that."

Somehow, suddenly, they'd reached her car. She zapped the locks open and fairly wilted onto her seat, turning her head fully away from Clay. What were they even doing? She didn't want to go to a shooting range with him now. He couldn't want to either, so why did she hear him climbing into the passenger seat?

She rested her forehead against the cool window glass, defeated. "I'm sorry. I shouldn't have said anything." She tried to sniff without making a sound.

Why didn't he reply? Surely he had at least a few more harsh words for her. She took a deep breath and focused on willing away the painful throb in her chest.

"Charlene?" His tone was one she hadn't heard in years, a pre-prison tone, something she hadn't expected to hear ever again.

He touched her shoulder. An odd feeling rippled through her.

She blinked rapidly and hoped her eyes weren't red. Keeping her chin steady, she turned slowly to see Clay looking at her with concern.

"What's the deal with these pictures?" His words prickled with restrained alarm.

Her gaze fell to the photos. The creepy stalker photos. She had carelessly left them scattered on the passenger seat, and now he held them in his hands.

"Charlene?"

She scrunched back in her seat while a deep frown creased his forehead, growing deeper by the second.

In a monotone, she explained how she'd found the pictures in her car when she picked it up in Woodfield the night before.

He muttered under his breath, angry again. "So this is from when you lived in your last place?" He held the close-up photo, the one of her sleeping.

"That's right."

"Then I'm glad you moved. Not that that means you're safe." He cursed.

She cringed.

"Sorry." He turned to her. "And I'm sorry I lashed out at you. That wasn't fair. Things have gotten complicated . . . but I shouldn't have taken it out on you. You've got more than enough to deal with yourself."

"It's okay. I understand why you were upset. I shouldn't have said anything."

He slapped the pictures onto the floor. "Let's get you to that range. The sooner you learn to shoot, the better."

A few silent minutes into the drive, he glanced around and remarked, "You *would* have a car this clean."

"Is that a compliment?"

"Just an observation." He rolled his window down, and warm air whooshed in noisily, tugging and tangling her hair and making further conversation pointless.

Chapter Twenty

"Hold the gun steady with both hands, lift it, extend your arms like this, and aim," Clay directed loudly, to be heard above the firing guns and through the ear protection. His ability to speak so strongly with his mouth wired shut impressed Charlene.

She was also exasperated with him. Shooting was harder than it looked, and his weaponless demonstrations weren't helping. So far he hadn't come close to touching the gun, and his obsessive carefulness grated on her.

She adjusted her safety glasses.

His explanations were thorough, but after she repeatedly missed the target, and with her wrists sore from the repetitive recoil, she was ready to give up. *Not a lot of recoil, indeed. Ha, Sam, what a joke.*

Clay shook his head. "You're flinching really bad and that's throwing your aim way off."

Struggling for patience, she adjusted her stance and tried again. She barely hit the edge of the target, and it was only fifteen feet away. Oh well. "Good enough." She set the gun down, ready to lose the unwieldy glasses and clunky earmuffs. Might as well be back working in the shop and actually accomplishing something.

"No." Clay took her off guard by setting her hand back on the weapon. Conscious of his touch, she barely felt the gun.

"You can do this, Charlene. We're not leaving till you get a bull's eye."

"They won't be open that long."

"Look, watch me." Again, he acted out shooting a gun, arms raised and tense, eyes focused. Impressive acting, but it was more distracting than anything. Finger cocked, he pulled an imaginary trigger and absorbed a fake recoil. "Bullseye."

"No!" She clapped a hand to her chest and fanned her face with the other. "And here I was holding my breath thinking you might actually miss. Bravo, Robin Hood, bravo!"

Clay slanted her a look. "Robin Hood shot a bow."

"Then bravo, Annie Oakley."

He faced her head-on. "You just call me a girl?" His eyes flashed, but she was fairly sure she caught a spark of amusement.

She shrugged. "I called you a sharpshooter." A smile escaped her. "You should be honored."

"I'm not." His eyes narrowed. "Daniel Boone, Buffalo Bill, Davey Crockett, Jesse James. Take your pick."

"Jesse James was an outlaw."

"Even more fitting."

No longer amused, she lifted the gun and shot rapid fire, blowing off smoke in a literal sense.

"See, all you need is motivation. Unfortunately, your anger didn't translate to accuracy."

She stomped her foot. "Then help me. Real help, not pretend. Please, Clay. No one's going to know or care."

He studied her a long moment and frowned. "I thought you always played by the rules."

"I try. I do. But I just can't figure this out on my own." She dampened her lips and lifted the gun into position once more.

"Fine." Clay's sudden closeness surprised her. As he positioned his head beside hers, he brought his right hand over hers, guiding her fingers where they needed to go, all without even grazing the gun. "Hold it steady like this." His warm, firm grip tightened.

Despite being disconcerted by a strange current of energy, she stabilized her hand. Somehow, she caught a faint whiff of pine wood and varnish.

"Line up the front sight in the notch of the rear sight. Put the pumpkin on the fencepost."

She choked on a laugh. "Put the what on the what?"

"Put the pumpkin on the fencepost."

"As opposed to putting it under the fencepost? Or baking it in a pie?"

"What?"

Exactly.

Clay's brows knitted. "Look, it's easy. See—"

"Easy as pie?"

He gave her a pointed look that said, *Don't interrupt.* "See the dot on the front sight? That's the pumpkin. The rear sight notch is the fencepost."

She lowered the gun. "Why a pumpkin? Why not an apple or a tomato or a cookie or a pancake? Or a bird. Now that's something that might actually be on a fence. I don't think a pumpkin could balance—"

"That's not the point." He dropped a hand to his hip. "And I think you're stalling."

"I think your pumpkin saying needs work."

"Not mine. Can't take the credit."

"Be grateful for that."

He shook his head. "It's a well-known expression."

"That's debatable."

"Should we debate it all afternoon, or are you gonna shoot?"

Debating was more fun than shooting. "I can't take it seriously."

"You don't need to. Just remember it."

"It's too silly to forget."

"Good." He raised her arms back up, clearly wanting to return to business. His finger touched her trigger finger, annihilating all thoughts of pumpkins and fenceposts.

"And don't close both eyes when you fire. Keep your right one open. And try not to flinch this time. Ready?"

"I think so."

"Be sure."

She fought to cancel Clay's presence and hold the gun still while aiming, nestling the front sight between the notches of the rear sight.

"Okay, I'm sure."

"Then fire."

She squeezed the trigger while remaining braced for the recoil.

Crack.

Bull's eye.

"All right!" Clay shouted.

Her face stretched into a smile.

"A couple dozen more practice shots like that, and you'll be set. In fact . . ." He grinned. "I think you're ready to try the zombie target."

She groaned and rolled her eyes as he lifted the large paper which featured a grotesque, contorted, flesh-dripping face.

Several mutilated paper zombies later, Clay unfastened the latest one from the wooden frame. "Now that, Annie Oakley, is a target to be proud of." He held it out to her.

"Ah, no thanks." She rubbed her aching wrists.

As he rolled the target up, she eyed, for the hundredth time, the cloth strips wrapped around the base of his knuckles. "So what's the deal with those bandages? Did you get those in the hospital, after, you know, Lance?" She knew he'd had them before that, but she was curious as to what his answer would be.

"No." He tucked the target under his left arm. "You ready?"

She nodded and began walking. Once they'd both removed their eye and ear protection, she tried again. "So if your knuckles aren't hurt, why do you wear the bandages?"

He stared straight ahead. "I'd rather not say."

"Why not?"

"It's not important." He picked up his pace.

"Then why can't you tell me?"

"I don't want to."

She blew a strand of hair from her eyes. The more he avoided the subject, the more she wanted to root out the truth. "Can you at least tell me when you're going to take them off?"

"Sure. Never."

"Seriously? That's . . . really strange."

"There's worse things than strange." He gave a humorless smile. "Now can I ask you a question?"

"Sure."

He stopped to face her. "Who answered your phone when I called yesterday?"

"Oh, that was Ben. He's—"

"I remember. Why'd he answer your phone?"

"I was with him. I mean, I wasn't right with him—I'd stepped away—but he would've taken a message. He's my—" she caught herself at the word boyfriend—"my fiancé."

"Really?" His lips pulled into something of a smile. His face looked much better these days now that the swelling had gone down. "That's great. I'm happy for you." He resumed tramping up the hill. "I always knew you'd end up with someone like him."

"Someone like him?" Breathing heavily, she caught up to his side. "What do you mean? And you hardly even knew him. I'm surprised you remember him."

"He seemed like a decent guy. He treats you well?"

"Yes, yes he does." Her heart warmed with a poignant sadness. "He always has." *He always will.*

Clay appeared about to ask another question, then didn't.

So she did. "Why were you calling, anyway?" Her voice dropped. "It was because of what I told Brook, wasn't it?"

He nodded.

"So Brook," she said, to change the subject. "What about her?

169

How'd you meet?" She wanted to hear his guy version of it, wondering if it would be as sensitive and sweet as Brook's story.

He squinted ahead at the shooting range office. "We met in a grocery store."

She waited. "That's it?"

"Yep."

"You're not a good storyteller."

"And my mouth doesn't get me into trouble."

"Really?" She couldn't help herself. "How about that broken jaw?"

"Yeah, how 'bout it." Not taking the bait, he marched ahead to the parking lot.

In her car, he crammed the creepy photos under the passenger seat with a couple scuffs of his boots. He drummed his fingers against the side of the door. "So how's Max these days?"

She turned onto the road and gave a noncommittal shrug.

He shot her a sideways glance. He knew how close she and Max had been. "He still in California, doing magic shows?"

"Yep."

"You been out to visit him?"

"No." Under her breath she added, "Someday."

"You could use the change."

She huffed. He sounded too much like Max.

"There's lots to do there. Great beaches."

"You still trying to get rid of me?" she half joked, yet felt hurt.

Clay faced his window.

She turned on the radio. After a few uncomfortable strains of a country song, she lowered the volume.

"I was hoping to get to the beach this summer," she admitted. She rotated her neck and her tension drained as she imagined relaxing on the sand, soaking up sun, listening to waves.

"Then go." Clay returned to tapping his fingers obnoxiously. "Don't wait on anyone to make it happen."

She tried to entertain the thought. "I just don't know how great it would be to go alone."

"So go with Ben."

"We really need to save for the wedding though, and for a house." She didn't like the thought of being forced to live with Ben's family. Facing the blame in their eyes every day . . . Her grip on the wheel tightened.

Clay's boot nudged the manila envelope on the floor. "You

should take the pictures to the police, you know."

I'd rather ignore them. She kept her eyes on the road.

"You going to?"

"Fine." She'd do it the next time she visited Ben. She knew the drill by now. They'd take her statement, ask questions, maybe check the pictures for prints, and hold them on file. Nothing that would change anything. Every fiber of her tension returned.

"A reminder."

"Huh?" She glanced at Clay, baffled by his abrupt, random statement.

He didn't return the look but kept his gaze out the window. "The article in my wallet. I keep it as a reminder."

Like Lance had said? Seemed rather ridiculous. The sentencing wasn't something Clay would forget. "A reminder?"

"To never be that man again."

"That man . . ." She let her voice trail off, still not understanding.

"A coward."

She stared at the road. "Clay. That was over four years ago—"

"Four years, four decades. Doesn't change the fact that I held that camera. Me, and no one else."

"I forgave you. You more than made up for it."

"You've still got the scar."

She pressed her palm tight to the steering wheel. "I don't care."

"Well I do."

"Throw it away."

"What?"

She tossed her hair. "If you still have the article, throw it away. It's nothing but garbage."

———

A few days later, Clay made his way over to Charlene's work space. His nearness made her fingers still on the sandpaper. She looked up. "What?"

He cocked his head. "Feel like helping me load and deliver an order?"

"Really?" Why wasn't he asking Sam? Not that she minded. She'd welcome any change of pace from her typical workday. She dropped the sandpaper. "Sure."

"Sam's in the middle of drawing up a plan." Clay jutted his chin in his direction. Sure enough, Sam sat hunched over his workbench, scratching paper with pencil. "You never want to mess with him when he's tackling math."

"Good to know."

Clay moved to a group of large blanket-wrapped wood pieces. He gripped one end and she took the other. His muscles flexed. "Ready?"

She nodded and they lifted the bundled wood together. He moved backwards out the door to his open truck bed, where they set the load down and returned for more. None of the pieces were terribly heavy, just awkward and big.

She adjusted her hold carefully and tried not to think about how he might react if she dropped and damaged anything. With the last piece safely strapped in the truck bed, she asked, "So what is this creation, anyway?"

"A bunk bed." He opened her door. "Need a hand?"

"I got it." She hoisted herself up and enjoyed the high view from the front seat. She detected a faint hint of Brook's perfume. As Clay pulled out, her gaze roved the truck's interior. Not bad, but the dash could use dusting. A couple empty water bottles sat in the console. "So what's Sam's story?"

Clay glanced at her. "What do you mean?"

"You know, what do you know about him? Besides the fact that math makes him cranky."

Clay gave a short chuckle and merged into traffic. "I know that he learned carpentry as a kid, from his dad. He did odd jobs for a while, then joined the army in his twenties and traveled after that. Lived out West for a while. Spent time backpacking, hiking, fishing, hunting. Sounds like a great life to me."

"He never got married?"

Clay braked at a red light and draped his wrist over the steering wheel. "Don't think so." The corner of his lip twitched. "Why? You lookin' to set him up?"

Her eyebrows lifted. "No."

Green light. The truck surged forward and she braced a hand against the seat. "So how long has Sam lived here in Creekside?"

"Oh, I don't know. Maybe ten years? Something like that."

"You like working for him?"

"Yeah, I do." He angled her a look. "You?"

She straightened her shoulders. "It's hard work. I don't mind it, but I'm not planning on making a career of it."

His eyes returned to the road. "What did you do back in Woodfield?"

"I worked in a library." A smile touched her lips as she remembered the circle of kids eagerly awaiting storytimes.

A few minutes later, Clay parked in the driveway of a tall blue frame house, and she realized they were going to have to carry the bunk bed up a flight of stairs. The door was flung open by a woman with a plump baby boy perched on her hip and two identical little boys hopping excitedly near her legs. "Where's our bunk bed? Where's our bunk bed?" the twins cried.

"Oh for the energy of a four-year-old," their mom said.

Clay grinned. "We've gotta haul it in piece-by-piece and then set it up." He looked at the boys. "You guys wanna show us where it goes?"

The boy in a blue shirt squinted up at Clay. "Your mouth's funny, mister."

"Kevin!" His mom frowned.

His red-shirted brother added, "It is, Mommy!"

Clay's smile widened and he crouched to the boys' level. "You're right, buddy, it is funny. 'Cause it's full of metal right now. Kinda like a robot, huh?"

"Neat!" Kevin cried.

"I want a robot mouth!" his brother yelled.

Their mom tried to thrust a few strands of hair back into her messy bun and failed. "Show the nice man where your room is, and he'll set up your new bed."

With a whoop, the boys took off, scampering up the stairs to a small toy-laden room. The freshly vacuumed spot on the far wall was obviously the intended location. Charlene and Clay hauled the pieces in several trips, then Clay brought in his toolbox to find the boys armed and ready with their own black and orange plastic tools.

Their mom hovered in the doorway. "Stay back, Kevin and Tommy. Give the carpenters room to work."

"They're fine," Clay assured the woman, and Charlene sensed he was enjoying the boys' eager attention and awe as he bolted the frames together. She was simply amused at being referred to as a carpenter.

Kevin pressed the button of his toy drill and Tommy wielded a plastic hack saw. "Think this saw could cut through a dinosaur bone?"

"Good question." Clay looked thoughtful as she helped him maneuver the top bunk frame onto the lower one. The boys continued to ask a stream of questions that blew her mind, but Clay tried to answer every one. She wondered if she and Max had been this high-strung at four. The woman paced with the baby in the hall, who was fussing and flailing his fists.

"I gotta go potty." Kevin dropped his drill and raced from the room. A door slammed. Not long after, he called, "Mommm, I need more toilet paper!"

Struggling with the energetic baby, the woman eyed Charlene and her empty arms.

"Here, I'll hold him," she offered.

Without a moment's hesitation, the woman deposited the hefty boy into her arms and disappeared into the bathroom. Kevin's voice carried through the door. "It fell in."

His mom said, "No, don't—"

Flush!

There was a loud giggle and then Kevin yelled, "Hey Tommy, come look, it's a waterfall!" Over the gushing noise, Charlene was sure she heard their mom groan.

Tommy hurtled into the bathroom. "I wanna see!"

The baby grabbed for Charlene's curls and squealed in delight.

Clay gathered his tools into his toolbox while she disentangled chubby hands from her hair. "You're just too cute," she muttered into the child's impish face. But she realized when she was a mom someday, she'd have to tie her hair back. Extremely well. *And what are my chances of having twins?*

The boys came flying out of the bathroom, hollering excitedly when they saw the finished bunk bed. They scaled the ladder like a pair of monkeys. Their mom emerged and admired the completed bed. "Thanks so much." Then her desperate eyes glanced back into the bathroom. "You wouldn't happen to know anything about plumbing, would you?"

"Let me take a look." Clay rolled up his sleeves and moved through the hall to the bathroom.

As the boys started to follow him into the cramped and wet room, Charlene spied a pile of books in the corner of the bedroom. "Hey you guys, want to hear a story?" She settled on the floor and started reading about dinosaurs, successfully luring the boys to her side. The baby even focused on the colorful pictures and forgot her hair.

Two stories later, Clay emerged with a plastic action figure in hand. "Found this hero taking a swim."

"Yay!" Kevin jumped up, grabbed the toy, and started swooping him through the air.

"Thanks so much. Both of you," said the boys' mom. She showed Charlene and Clay to the door with a laugh. "Come back any time."

"Bye!" the boys chorused. One of them added, just before the door closed, "You're a real neat robot, mister!"

"Whew." In the truck, Charlene sagged into her seat, buckled, and pushed the hair back from her face, enjoying the peaceful hum of the motor. "That was . . . quite a call."

"You never know what you're gonna get." Clay eased onto the road and smiled. "Thanks for your help. You did a great job."

"Huh." She shifted in her seat. "You weren't bad either, mister robot."

On Sunday, the woman eased away from the curb and followed the girl out of town, observing from a distance and soaking up what she needed to know.

So the girl came back to Woodfield every week to go to church and pretend she was perfect, while the floozy had two men dangling on the side.

Her man wasn't enough? She really was a piece of work. The audacity. The self-entitlement.

The woman's fingers grappled the steering wheel. Her nails dug at the faux leather, picking, picking. How would the girl like it if someone interfered with one of her men, hmm?

She just might have to find out.

Chapter Twenty-One

Spring days slid into summer, and intense sunshine crinkled the grass into prickly, tawny blades.

Inside the woodshop on the first of July, Charlene felt like she was working in a sweatshop. Lack of circulation caused pent up air to hang heavy and smothering, but it didn't seem to bother Sam or Clay at all. While their foreheads and biceps shone with sweat, they worked on, focused, driven, and never complaining.

Unlike her.

"I can't take this wretched heat," she moaned to the cabinet she was sanding. Damp curls tickled her forehead and neck. She could barely breathe the stifling air. Missing her old job, she dreamed of the cool library. "I can't take another day of this."

"If you can't take the heat, Charlene, take the day off!" Sam barked.

His hard manner didn't faze her anymore, but she could take a hint. She dropped her sandpaper, gave a quick wave, and was out the door. Better to chill in her air-conditioned apartment and read a book than to roast in that shop.

She was surprised to find Brook lying droopily on the sofa, one hand hanging over the edge. "Hey, Charlene," she said listlessly.

"You're off today?" A thought crossed Charlene's mind. "Any plans?"

"Staying cool and lazy. That's about it."

"What do you say we go find a beach and cool off? It would be fun. We could pack a lunch. Interested?"

Brook perked up. "Know what? That's actually a good idea. Know what would make it even better?" She pulled out her phone.

Charlene soon overheard her inviting someone, so she slapped together a few extra sandwiches.

Through the window several minutes later, she saw Clay pull up to the apartment in his gray truck.

"Can you believe I actually convinced him to come? He's usually all, 'I have to work,'" Brook confided. "This is going to be awesome."

"Awesome," Charlene parroted. *I get to be a third wheel.*

Clay helped Brook up into the front seat while Charlene clunked and clambered with her bags into the narrow back seat.

Brook cranked up the radio and began singing along. Charlene admired her ability to be so unselfconscious. For a fraction of a second, she wondered what it would be like to simply open her mouth and join in. Instead, she opened a novel and hoped the book was thick enough for what was shaping up to feel like a long day.

Over an hour later, Brook groaned, "Why's it taking so long to get there? This better be some special beach you're taking us to, Clay." She nudged him playfully. "Or are you lost? Please tell me you're not lost."

"I'm not lost. Look." He pointed to the right.

Charlene glanced up from her page to the window, just in time to glimpse a huge sapphire ribbon shimmer over the grassy horizon.

Brook gasped. "It's . . . like an ocean!"

Clay chuckled. "Lake Michigan."

Charlene watched out the window, transfixed. Rolling country-side stretched wide around them, but past it, the deep blue expanse dipped and disappeared, peeked tauntingly between two hills, then vanished. She moved closer to the glass, watching for a reappearance.

"What do you think, Charlene?" Clay caught her gaze in the rearview mirror.

Such an easy question, yet her tongue felt tied. "It's beautiful," she managed.

Clay stepped on the gas. The lake—it really did stretch as magnificent as an ocean—surged back into view.

A short time later, they exited the highway. They drove a few more miles, turned off on a country road that swooped through bobbing trees, and eventually parked in a little rectangular lot tucked into a stretch of woods.

Charlene and Brook tumbled out excitedly. A restroom and a picnic table sat on the edge of the lot. A wooden sign pointed to a cordwalk through the trees, another pointed to sand dunes, and yet another pointed straight ahead to the beach.

"There's even sand dunes? Wow," Brook gushed. "What's a cordwalk, though? Don't they mean boardwalk?"

"Nope," Clay said, loading his arms with a bag, then a cooler, "though that's basically what it is. The boards are connected by thick ropes—cords—and so you get cordwalk."

Brook spun around with her arms outstretched, her sundress twirling prettily. "This is great! Charlene, I'm so glad you talked me into this. And Clay, you picked the best spot." She dove at him with a kiss and he set down the supplies to take her in his arms. Charlene quickly fixated on searching in her bag for her sunglasses.

When she dared look up, Brook was trotting up the beach path, her hair swooshing in the warm breeze. Clay turned to smile at Charlene gratefully. "I haven't seen her this happy in a while. Thanks."

"You bet." But he was already out of earshot, catching up to Brook, putting an arm around her shoulder. Charlene glanced down at her feet as she walked, till the parking lot gave way to matted grass, which gave way to a sandy path bordered by tall waving prairie grasses. Sand grit slid into her flip-flops and under her bare feet.

When she crested the hill and saw the huge, seemingly endless glimmering water speckled with white sailboats, awe washed over her. After standing still a moment and absorbing the sight, she picked her way down the uneven wooden steps, hazardous with blown sand. On the wide shore, Clay set down the cooler. She saw a couple colorful shade umbrellas and only a few other people up and down the vast beach.

Her ears welcomed the constant rush of waves. She breathed in an enormous lungful of fresh air and savored the peacefulness, marveling at how God had spared no beauty in creating this.

She lifted her face to the sun, her skin absorbing the warmth. So she was a third wheel. So what. She would enjoy this day anyway, and be grateful for it.

With each step she took, sand squeaked underfoot. Brook's happy chatter floated her way. Brook dropped her towel, tugged on Clay's arm, and raced into the waves.

"It's freezing!" she shrieked, before splashing him and insti-gating a wild water battle. Charlene watched for a minute, then shook out her towel and laid it down smoothly. Reclining, she looked up at the delicate clouds powdering the blue sky with fanciful shapes. Castles. Angels. Dragons.

"That water is ice," Brook declared when she returned, dripping, to her towel. "Liquid ice. My skin was turning blue."

"I'm hungry," Clay said, apparently not bothered by the water. "Let's eat." He plunked down and sand stuck to him. Again, didn't seem to bother him. Charlene's skin crawled just imagining the clinging grit.

She noticed him tug his knuckle bandages tight and secure before unpacking the cooler. "All right," he said. "Real food and not a blender in sight. This is living." He'd healed fast, and just had the wires removed a couple days ago. It had been a wonderful sight when he first smiled to show his wire-free teeth.

As if the seagulls had sensors, they began swooping and landing nearby, boldly ambling closer, trying to snag a morsel. "Scram," Clay told the birds. "I've got a lot of eating to make up for."

Charlene mainly listened while Brook and Clay chatted through the meal, but as the food dwindled, she noticed they'd become very quiet. Then she realized Brook had fallen asleep.

Charlene tucked the remains of their picnic away, speaking to Clay without looking at him. "Your explanation about how the lake never freezes completely over in winter must have bored her to sleep." Glancing at Brook, she added, "She looks so peaceful." Indeed, she had a visage of sweet innocence, of a pure soul who'd never been wounded or damaged or traumatized by life, who only dreamed of rainbows and moonbeams, never haunted by nightmares.

"You're frowning," Clay said, and Charlene flinched, taken unaware by his sudden nearness. "What's wrong?"

She smiled. "Nothing." She slipped off her flip-flops and stood on the sand. "Ouch!" Without soles to protect her, the sand scorched her feet. She scurried to the water. Breathless at the cold temperature contrast, she stepped out of the lake onto the saturated, wave-washed sand. Glancing up and down the seemingly endless stretch of shore, she began strolling, ready to be alone with her thoughts.

"Hey," Clay caught up to her, "I've been wanting to ask you something." He squinted against the sun's glare, the skin around his eyes crinkling. "You haven't found my ma's letter anywhere, by chance, have you? I thought Nails left it in the shop, but I haven't been able to find it."

Panic billowed inside her while she put on a thoughtful face and continued walking the sun-kissed sand. For whatever reason, Nails must be what he called Lance. That wasn't important right now. Her mind churned furiously. She couldn't lie to Clay, but she'd promised Sam she'd give him time to break the news tactfully. She reproved herself for thinking so little of the letter lately. If she didn't keep the pressure on Sam, he may never tell Clay the truth.

"Charlene?" Clay waved a hand near her face.

Snapping out of her thoughts, she chose her words carefully. "I'm sorry, I haven't seen the letter in the shop since that day. Do you think Lance—Nails—or whoever he is—maybe took it?"

Clay grunted. "Maybe." He began to work his jaw slowly, as if testing it.

She dug her toes into the wet sand as they walked, gouging little troughs. She debated voicing a question she'd been wondering for a while. When she spoke, she couched it in several questions. "What's the deal with that Nails guy, anyway? Why did he come after you like that? And why did he think—how did he know—that I'd lead him to you? Why did he say . . ." she let the last words fall out in a rush, "I was your girl?"

"Because he's an idiot. He's deluded. I don't know." Clay shoved his hands into his pockets. He glanced over the water, then back at her. "He thought he was a big shot in prison. Rumor had it he liked to try and get friendly with the female COs, and most of the inmates looked up to him or feared him. They called him Nails. He picked fights all the time. When he went after me, I busted his jaw. Not long after that, my time was up, but he ended up having to serve extra time. He held a grudge, and he didn't get his chance to really pay me back till he got out."

She kicked a piece of driftwood. "You don't think he'll come back, do you?"

"Nah." Clay rolled a shoulder. "He got his revenge. And if he's smart, he'll stay away, now that you're a sharpshooter."

"Oh, please."

Rushing waves filled the ensuing silence. Hardly realizing it, they'd walked a fair distance and were now approaching a young family. A little boy of about six was digging a hole in the sand with his little sister. Another sister, probably almost two, was busily spooning sand into a bucket. Colorful floppy sunhats topped the girls' wispy golden hair. Their mom wore a straw hat with a brim so wide, Charlene expected the wind to pick it up at any moment and send it sailing like a flying saucer. Their dad sported a monstrous beard, reminding her of the one Clay used to have.

When she smiled and said a polite hello to the family, the little boy perked up. "I'm digging for pirate treasure."

"My name's Gina," announced his sister. "I'm five. Look what I can do!" She flung herself over in a wild blend of a summersaultcartwheel.

"Wow, good job," Charlene said.

The littlest girl stared at them and said, "Hi! Hi! Hi!" over and over.

"Can we bury you in our hole?" the boy asked excitedly. "I can dig it really big." Sand began flying in every direction.

"How about after you find your treasure, you bury her?" Clay pointed at Charlene.

"Hey," she admonished, elbowing him and lowering her voice. "The poor kid's not going to know you're joking."

"Who said I'm joking?"

"Then they should burry you." She walked on with a friendly wave. "You're still covered in sand." Her skin itched and prickled at the sight. "Gosh, how can you stand that?"

He shrugged. "Doesn't bother me."

She couldn't help glancing back at the happy family scene. Once upon a time, that had been her and Max.

Someday, in a different way, she wanted that again.

She came to a cluster of rocks and driftwood, and the thought of sitting and resting, her feet dangling in the water, lured her closer. "We should probably head back before we walk too far." She almost hated to say it, and belying her words, settled on a rock and stared out over the sparkling water, taking it all in.

Clay shaded his eyes and gazed too, saying after a moment, "There's sure something about wide open spaces . . ."

Indeed. *Especially after serving time in a cell,* Charlene found herself thinking, but she merely nodded.

Her skin tingled with heat. She dipped her hand in the water and patted her brow with the cool liquid. In mere seconds, it evaporated, leaving her skin more parched than before.

Stepping away, Clay plucked a small piece of driftwood from the dry sand and turned it speculatively in his hands before returning and propping himself against the rock beside her. He pulled a tiny pocketknife from his shorts and flicked open the blade. He began swiping it along the wood, shaving off curls.

The flash of sharp silver summoned an unpleasant memory. She swallowed and looked away to the hazy horizon. "Did anyone ever approach you about Abner's knife? You know, the black snake-handled one?"

In her peripheral vision, she saw Clay pause with his blade in the wood, his calm countenance transformed with tension. She couldn't help glancing at the scar on his ring finger. The perfect match to hers.

"No, they didn't." His gaze skewered her. "Why would they?"

Regretting that she'd brought it up, she hastily explained her strange encounter as Clay's eyes narrowed.

"It was weird and creepy," she finished, "but I only saw the guy that once. He probably gave up searching by now."

"I don't like it. You ever see him again, call me. I'll take care of him." Clay's eyes wouldn't leave hers, like he was waiting for her to say something.

"Okay," she agreed.

Slowly, his hands eased back into carving, but his face didn't relax.

She sighed and lifted her hair off the back of her damp neck, holding the short strands up so the breeze gave a little relief as she prepared to drop her other weighty question. "So I was wondering . . . do you still think bad things happen when I'm around?"

The corner of Clay's mouth dipped. "I shouldn't have said that."

"Then why did you?"

He bent his head over his carving and she stared at his wind-blown hair.

"To make you leave."

"Okay. I got that. But why? If it's because of my grandfather—"

"No, it's not. It's just—we shouldn't see each other. It's better that way." He looked directly at her, but she couldn't decipher his expression.

She stayed silent a moment. "Do you still wish I'd go?"

He broke eye contact. "I should. Look what happened with Nails. I don't want to put you in danger."

Despite the heat, a chill touched her. "So you do think he's coming back."

"It's a possibility."

"I'm not going to live in a bubble. I've done that . . ." She glanced around at the beautiful beach. "I feel safe." *Right here. Right now.*

"Feelings mean nothing," he said shortly. "I've got no right being anywhere near you." His brow furrowed. "After everything, how do you even look at me without hating me? I don't get that. I can't make it up to you. I know that. The least I can do is stay away. You don't need to be reminded—"

"I don't care," she said, almost fiercely. "Stop thinking of me as some kind of victim. I'm not. It's over. I'm not going to let it rule my life. It's been long enough. I can look at you and not think of all that." Her tone softened. "If you can do the same . . . maybe we could be friends. Finally." Her voice held a hint of hope.

She waited.

Waves surged and receded. Misty lake droplets sprayed her legs. Clay's head angled so that she couldn't see his face at all. Just when she was ready to stand up and walk away, he spoke. Grudgingly. "I'll try."

Not exactly the answer she'd hoped for, but it was something. Progress. She swirled the water with her toes.

At last, she slid off the rock. "We'd better head back."

Clay nodded, then he lifted his carving and blew it clean. "What do you think?"

"Oh," she breathed. She accepted the wood gently and turned it in all directions. "It's perfect. It's . . . a little park bench. What made you decide to carve that?"

He snapped his knife shut, pocketed it, and shrugged. "The driftwood was the right shape."

"You could specialize in this. 'Clay's Custom Dollhouse Furniture'," she quipped as they began their trek back.

"Very funny. I'll pass."

"Well then, if you have a daughter someday, you'll make her very happy."

She tried handing the carving back, but he crammed his fists into his pockets. "No, keep it. Or throw it away. I don't care. It was just something to do."

On their way back across the beach, they sighted the young family, but they were in no danger of the shovel-wielding little boy even noticing them. He was too busy racing around, kicking up clouds of sand as he played tag with his mom, who held onto her floppy hat onehanded as she ran. The dad was giving the little girls a ride on a float a couple of yards from shore. Happy squeals carried on the wind.

Clay watched the little boy as his mom caught him in a big hug. A muscle on the side of Clay's jaw twitched.

When the laughter faded behind them, he spoke up. "I should have read the letter when I had the chance. Nails could have made it all up, you know? To mess with me." He rubbed his hair roughly.

She strolled with heavy steps, grinding her heels in the sand. Keeping this secret was killing her.

"I shouldn't doubt her," he went on, "but . . . what if I always have to wonder? That's just a heck of a way to wreck my ma's memory. What if I never find out the truth?"

"You will."

He looked up at the sky. "I don't know, Charlene. I just don't know."

She had the answer he needed, but with it would come a hundred more questions, and she didn't have those answers.

Fingering the miniature wooden bench, still in disbelief at the skill of Clay's hands, she felt unworthy of the gift . . . if she could really call it that.

Slowing, she turned and walked backwards a few steps, just to see their footprints side by side for the briefest moment before they were washed away by the waves. As if they'd never been.

Chapter Twenty-Two

"It's about time," Brook huffed as soon as they came within earshot, and Charlene felt an incredible jolt of guilt as she realized she'd forgotten all about her. She palmed Clay's carving, feeling an odd need to keep it from sight.

"Where were you?" Brook demanded.

"Just walking the shore," Clay said. "We didn't want to wake you."

"Well you should have. I slept way too long without turning over. Look at me, I'm baked." The front half of her fair skin had indeed turned a painful pink shade.

Clay's face flashed concern and regret. "Let's get you out of the sun. Want to head back home?"

Brook glanced at Charlene and nodded. Clay draped a gentle arm around Brook, careful of the sunburn, and she turned with him to walk back to the towels and cooler.

They packed up, then trudged up the hill. Charlene lagged behind. At the crest of the sandy hill, at the last possible point, she turned for one last view of the beach, emblazing a mental picture to remember the day by.

The trailer was a sweatbox this time of year. Worse than the hole. Even with thick foliage keeping the sun off, the interior still baked. He spent as much time out of it as possible. Wearing camouflage, gun ready, Nails roamed the woods.

His thoughts roamed, too. Too freely. This was the time of year for lame picnics and potlucks, like the ones the Callaghans had hauled him to. As if he could ever make friends with any of those churchgoing pansies.

He'd gotten out of one of the picnics by pretending to be sick. So easy. He remembered how it felt to be sixteen and finally have that great big house to himself.

It was all he'd wanted from the start . . .

Finally free to search, he found it, like he knew he would: a fat stack of money stashed in the back of a drawer, such a predictable location. Gleefully, he began counting the bills.

"What are you doing?" The voice froze his grasping fingers.

He looked up to see Mr. Callaghan's disapproving face in the doorway.

"What's it look like?" Lance sneered, masking an unexpected spike of shame and fear. He braced himself. He was big, but Mr. Callaghan was bigger—and stalking toward him with tensed muscles, clenched fists.

Gripping the cash, Lance stretched taller and stood his ground, half expecting a blow. His gaze flicked to Mr. Callaghan's leather belt. The heavy buckle. Maybe he'd slide the belt off and go at him like the last foster dad who'd caught him stealing. "Think you're so tough? Not so tough now." *He sliced the memory away.*

Mr. Callaghan crossed his arms and eyed the cash. "Put it back."

"Make me." He bared his teeth.

Mr. Callaghan studied him a long time, making him sweat. "It's not your money, Lance." He held out his hand.

"I need it." I took it. That makes it mine. *He should have pocketed it right then and bolted.*

"Haven't we treated you well and given you everything you need?" Mr. Callaghan's lips pressed tight with disappointment.

He scowled and looked away. "Go ahead, call the cops."

"That's not what you want, Lance."

The stupid man had no clue what he wanted. He swallowed as Mr. Callaghan pried the money from his grasp.

"We can work this out." Mr. Callaghan put a hand on his shoulder, making him stiffen.

"Don't touch me." He shook the hand off and stepped back, breathing heavily.

Mr. Callaghan nodded. "We're going to take a ride."

"No." He backed away.

Mr. Callaghan reached for him again.

Anger flashed, and Lance swung his fists.

Before he could make contact, Mr. Callaghan seized his wrists and turned his arms behind him, twisting him so he faced the corner.

It didn't hurt until he started to struggle. He hated being captured. Like an animal. "Get off me!"

Still clamping his wrists with one hand, Mr. Callaghan brought his other arm around him, pinning his arms, pressing his chest. "Hey, hey. Settle down. I'm not going to hurt you."

Lance swore and kicked backwards.

"You have to learn you can't just swing out when you're scared."

"I'm not scared." Lance seethed. He willed his muscles to burst him free.

The hold tightened. "If you don't learn to control your anger, it'll end up controlling you."

Lance writhed and twisted, turning wild with panic. "Get your hands off me. I'll kill you!" He wanted to. With everything in him, he wanted to see the man dead. If he only had a gun . . .

"When you're done with the temper tantrum," Mr. Callaghan said calmly, "we can go downstairs."

Cursing the man, Lance fought desperately, but he only wore himself out. Heart hammering, he finally slackened.

"Good." Mr. Callaghan angled him to the door. "Let's walk."

Jaw set, Lance trudged from the room with Mr. Callaghan still pinning his wrists. Grudgingly, he stalked down the stairs, his face hot. He was glad the Callaghan kids weren't home to see him like this. Especially Beth.

In the garage, Mr. Callaghan released him at the passenger side of his truck. "Get in."

Glaring, Lance slumped onto the seat.

Mr. Callaghan climbed in and turned on the engine. "Seatbelt."

Lance's nostrils flared. The guy thought he was a baby.

Mr. Callaghan's brows rose. "Do it, or I'll put it on for you."

Hell. Lance yanked it on.

———

"You sound happy," Ben said that night after Charlene recounted her day over the phone.

"I am. It was so nice to have a day off, and the beach was beautiful."

"So you said you went with your roommate?"

"Right, Brook. She had a good time, except she got sunburned."

"Anyone else?"

"Anyone else get sunburned?"

"No, was there anyone else at the beach with you besides Brook?"

"Well, sure . . . We saw a few other people there."

"You're dodging the question, Charlene." Ben muttered something she couldn't make out. Then he said, loud and clear, "He was there, wasn't he?"

She perched on the corner of her bed and released her breath. "If you mean Clay, then yes, but—"

"Why were you hiding it? You said there's nothing going on between you."

"Because there's not. I just knew if I told you, you'd act exactly this way. Quit it, Ben. Quit being jealous of nothing." Remembering Brook was in the next room, she lowered her voice. "I told you he's dating Brook. She invited him along, that's all."

Her gaze brushed over his little wood carving, which she'd set on her dresser.

"You'd tell me if he made a move on you, right?" Ben persisted, "Because wheelchair or not, I'd be there in a second to kick his—"

"Ben," she cut in sharply, "enough. This is getting really old. Me and Clay, we're just friends. Probably not even that."

"You believe that? Do you have any idea how beautiful and amazing you are? I'm not the only one who sees it."

"Beautiful and amazing? What about trustworthy? That would mean a lot more. Trust me, so you can stop worrying about nothing."

"Nothing? What if I told you I was hanging out with some girl and just calling her a friend? Would you be okay with that?"

"Are you?" She thought of Kate.

"No. That's not the point. I could if I wanted, but I don't. And that's the difference. You should honor that."

She paused to consider his reasoning. Should she promise to avoid Clay at all costs? To ease Ben's mind? Was that the right thing to do? Somehow, that seemed like such an awful lot to ask. She moved her foot back and forth, skimming the carpet with her toes. "I hardly have any friends here."

"You don't need any friends there. Come back here with me. I'll be the best friend you ever had, and more." Waiting a few heartbeats, he added, "You got this sudden day off of work . . . why didn't you come here? We could have spent it together." He cleared his throat. "That kind of hurts, Charlene. Did I even cross your mind?"

Her mouth fell open. She'd enjoyed a light, happy mood at the start of the call, and now she felt like slime. What kind of fiancée was she? "I'm sorry, Ben."

"Is it because I'm no fun? Because I can't do as much anymore? Is that it? Because—"

"No, of course not! And that's not true. You can do plenty—"

"I can't swim."

"You can still go to the beach. You can still enjoy the water." She put a hand to her forehead, feeling a little frantic. "Look, Ben. The Fourth of July is almost here. I'm driving back and we're going to spend the whole day together, I promise. We'll have a picnic, watch the parade, see the fireworks—we'll have the best day ever. How does that sound? Is it a date?"

He took his time, but at last he agreed, "Okay, it's a date."

After they hung up, she let out a long breath. Their relationship hadn't been this tricky back when she saw him almost every day. This weekly thing just wasn't cutting it.

Her phone chimed, and she almost didn't pick up. Then she saw it was Max, so she answered.

"Hey, Char. Found the perfect girl for me yet?"

She rolled her eyes. "Working on it. What have you been up to?"

He shared his schedule of rehearsals and shows, so hectic it made her shudder, then mentioned a new trick he planned to debut in February.

The sucker punch came out of nowhere. "You called off your engagement yet?"

Not what she needed to hear tonight. Her defenses rose, sharp and rigid, and her words came out vicious. "I'll tell you when that'll happen. When I find your nonexistent dream girl." She hung up. The phone trembled in her hand a moment before she dropped it.

Almost immediately, it beeped, signaling a text.

Knowing she'd regret it, she glanced at the message from Max: *Geez, someone's sensitive.*

Her teeth perched on edge and she clunked the phone onto her nightstand. *And someone needs to mind their own business,* she thought as she went to get ready for bed.

On her way back from the bathroom, Brook called her into her room. She began lamenting her sunburn, then asked, "Did you get burned at all? Your face looked kind of red when you came back from your walk."

Charlene touched her cheeks. "I should have used sunscreen." She ran a finger over the bridge of her nose. "I'm sure I'll have a new batch of freckles by tomorrow," she added ruefully.

"So did you and Clay talk much on your walk?"

"Oh, you know Clay. He's not much of a talker."

The way Brook stared, waiting, made her uncomfortable. She had to give her something. "He talked a little about wood carving."

Brook turned slightly, then gently slid something across her dresser. A small wooden angel came into view. Her fingers traced the wings, which appeared feather-soft, even though they couldn't be. "He's very talented. Look what he carved for me."

Charlene peered closer. The detail was amazing. This had to have taken much longer to make than the tiny bench. In fact, it made her token carving look like scrapwood in comparison.

"That's really something," Charlene said. The drape of the angel's robe looked soft and natural. The angel's expression was simple, yet serene. Peering closer, she noticed a heart carved into the palms of the angel's hands.

Brook lifted the figure and held it close to her stomach, in a sheltering position. "Do you like him, Charlene?"

Her brows pushed together. "What do you mean? Do I like who?"

"Clay."

The answer should be easy, but she sensed it was a loaded question. "Yes, I like him," she said slowly. "He's a nice enough guy."

Brook gave her a dissatisfied, steely look. "You know what I mean. Do you have feelings for him?"

Alarmed, she took a step back. "No, definitely not. He's your boyfriend, Brook. Why would you ask me that?"

"Precisely because he *is* my boyfriend. I need to make sure you don't forget that."

"We're barely friends." She shook her head. "Believe me, most of the time, I think he hardly tolerates me."

Brook appeared doubtful. "I don't know. Sometimes he looks at you . . . and you look at him a certain way . . ."

He did? She did? No, it was all in Brook's head. Like Ben, she was simply prone to jealousy.

A weariness descended over Charlene. What was it with people tonight? Was the unbearable summer heat getting to everyone and melting their minds? "Don't you know I already have a boyfriend in Woodfield? Actually, he's my fiancé. I'm *engaged*."

"Really? And how would I know that? You never said anything. Why didn't you tell me?" Brook narrowed her eyes at her left hand. "And why aren't you wearing a ring?"

"It got lost. Long story. But it's being replaced. Trust me, I'm engaged." She clasped her left hand to cover her ring finger scar before Brook peered closer and asked about that. Charlene rubbed the thin raised ridge, as if she could smooth it away.

"Does Clay know you're engaged?"

"Yes. Brook, please, don't worry. Clay and me—that's just ridiculous. Wouldn't happen in a million years." She forced a laugh for Brook's benefit, though she felt deflated, run over by interrogations. Twice in one night was too much to deal with.

After a little more reassurance, she managed to extricate herself from Brook's room and turn in to bed. While she may have appeased Brook, Charlene was sure Brook wouldn't ever include her in anymore outings with Clay.

Ben would certainly be happy about that.

———

Secrets. Deception. Lies. He owed her more than that. So much more. Nothing was going right lately. She felt him slipping so far away from her.

Torturing herself, she recalled the way he had looked at the girl. Hungry. Wanting. The way he should look at her.

He had once.

He would again.

I can't lose him. He belongs to me. She touched her belly. *To us.*

Smiling fake smiles at customers, she brainstormed as she worked. All the while, her blood curdled. The situation was more serious than she'd thought. So much was at stake.

Only one thing to do.

Time to step up my game.

Time to play hardball.

Chapter Twenty-Three

The grass was long. He'd ventured to the edge of the woods and stared out at the field, the vast openness of it, and knew he had to turn back, back into the covering of trees and leaves. But he stared at the rippling blades, something seizing inside. Staring, staring, like that day long ago . . .

He stared out the truck window and didn't really care where Mr. Callaghan was taking him. Dumping him back in the system, no doubt, to be someone else's problem. About time.

During the drive, Mr. Callaghan shook his head and preached about honesty, trust, and morality, all because of the money he'd tried to swipe. "If you don't start making better choices, Lance, you're going to regret it."

Lance rolled his eyes and didn't acknowledge him. The only thing he regretted was getting in the truck with this sermonizer.

At last, Mr. Callaghan killed the motor at the Catholic Church, which sat on at least two acres of land.

Lance snorted. Was this the lame plan? Drag him to confession? Like that'd solve anything. The naïve fool. Lance jumped out and spat on the shaggy grass. "I'm not talking to no priest."

"So don't. I'm not asking you to." Mr. Callaghan crossed the lawn. He unlocked a shed and wheeled out a push mower. Stepping away from it, he glanced at his watch, then at Lance, expectation written all over his face. "Better get started."

Lance's jaw slackened as he surveyed the huge lot. What? Cut all this by hand, in this heat? The guy was cracked.

Mr. Callaghan angled him a steady, stern gaze. "Actions have consequences, Lance." The man's hands landed on his hips. "You're not setting foot back in my house unless you can own your mistakes. Accept the consequences and learn from them. Can you do that, Lance? Can you be a man?"

Again, Lance wanted to let his fists fly. Why not make the fool get rid of him now? If not, it would only be a matter of time. He swore.

Mr. Callaghan started the lawnmower, and the roar drowned out the curses. The man stepped to the side and waited, brows raised.

Lance crossed his arms and glared, channeling hatred to his eyes.

Mr. Callaghan shook his head and climbed back in his truck. The abandoned mower conked out. The truck engine burst on. Tires rolled.

Lance's chest jolted. The man really would leave him in this scorching heat, near the stupid church. Walking back to the house would be as grueling and humiliating as cutting the grass.

With another curse, he grabbed the mower, yanked the cord, and shoved it forward.

From his comfortable air-conditioned seat, Mr. Callaghan watched him like a slave driver. Lance plodded over the land in a slow grueling pattern of endless repetition.

Those hours in the burning sun were the longest and hardest he ever worked in his life. Sweat poured from him, soaking his shirt front and back, making the soppy fabric cling to him.

At the end of it all, after he thrust the mower back into the shed and wiped the sweat from his eyes, Mr. Callaghan approached him and nodded. "Good job, son."

Son. His heart almost skipped a beat. All the profanity he'd been about to let loose died in his throat.

He stared mutely as Mr. Callaghan counted out a few bills, then pressed them into his damp hand. "That's all yours," the man said, as if it was a lot. It was nothing. Not near as much as he'd tried to take. Mr. Callaghan smiled. "You earned it with honest work. How does that feel?"

Lance's fingers closed over the money and squeezed. For the first time, he could almost imagine what having a father might feel like. His tongue touched the corner of his lip, tasted the salt of sweat. For the first time, he thought maybe he could give up stealing. Maybe . . .

Maybe the sun had fried his brains.

"Lance?"

He shoved the cash in his pocket and scowled.

Mr. Callaghan opened the truck door. "Come on, let's go home."

Sam left on another delivery, and it was just Clay and Charlene and country music in the woodshop, till the phone rang. She picked it up. "Sam's Custom Carpentry, how may I help you?"

"I kind of have a carpentry emergency on my hands." The woman laughed. "One of my kids broke the stairs banister, and I need it fixed right away. Can you send someone?" Her words radiated hope. Charlene jotted her address, then told her to hold on a moment while she checked with Clay.

"Oh, Clay. Perfect. He does real nice work. My husband bought me one of his wonderful bookcases—the kind that lock. The kids haven't managed to get into it yet."

When Charlene ran the request by him, she expected Clay to nod and load up his tools, but he stayed at his workbench. "See if she can wait till Sam gets back."

"Why? She doesn't care who comes. In fact, she said she likes your work."

Clay scratched the back of his neck, but she saw him eye the drawer. The one with the gun. "Sam will be back soon. I'll go then."

Realization dawned. "You don't want to leave me here alone."

He shrugged, not denying it.

She pursed her lips. "I don't need a babysitter." She returned to the desk. "I'll tell her you'll be there in fifteen minutes."

He pivoted on his heel and regarded her with amusement. "When'd you turn so bossy?"

"Sam's not around." She spread her hands. "Someone's gotta do it."

With a shake of his head, he gathered tools while she assured the woman he was on his way.

The feeling of having the woodshop to herself was peaceful, not frightening as it could have been if she'd entertained worried thoughts. Instead, she hummed along to the country music. As often as it played, she was accustomed to it and even growing begrudgeingly fond of quite a few songs. They weren't all depressing, as she used to think.

Her wrist moved rhythmically, varnishing an end table in time to the music. Before long, her lips began moving and she sang familiar, upbeat lyrics. For fun, she exaggerated the southern twang, the song sounding so funny that she smiled, remembering Brook's easy, carefree harmonizing in Clay's truck.

With exaggerated fervor, she belted out lyrics involving tail-gates, backroads, and beer. She even swung her hips and sashayed her feet. The mock dance move caused a person to slide into her vision, a lanky cowboy leaning against the doorframe with a lazy smile. Clay.

Embarrassment surged through her. He'd repaired the banister and returned already? The fun she'd been having must have made time fly. How long had he been watching? More importantly, *listening?*

Her mouth dropped, the last lyric dying of humiliation in her throat, till Clay stunned her by picking up the line and striding back to work with the tune now coming off-key from his lips.

Like it was no big deal. Nothing to be ashamed of. So she was having fun. Why not?

It's okay. Relax. Forcing her voice back to life, she sang past her self-consciousness and returned to work.

"My gosh, what's that darn awful screeching?" Sam's voice broke through their talentless duet a few moments later, his expression disgusted. "You two should have your lips stapled shut. Thank the Lord for ear protection."

As Sam threw on the plastic earmuffs, Clay and Charlene glanced at each other, their singing canceled by laughter. Then they caterwauled the next song. Simply, she thought, to irritate Sam.

It was a good day.

And that evening, as she peddled home from work, she realized her cheek muscles were sore from too much smiling. Her face stretched into a grin.

No such thing as too much smiling.

―――

Armed with a package of fireworks, Charlene made sure to arrive bright and early at Ben's house on the Fourth of July. The sun still hung low enough near the eastern horizon that it hadn't baked the air yet.

Ben's mom opened the door and eyed the fireworks disapprovingly. "How funny, I would have thought you'd have had your fill of all things fire-related for a while."

Charlene forced a halfhearted laugh. But she was glad she'd brought the fireworks because when Ben saw the box of roman candles, cherry bombs, and bottle rockets, his eyes lit up like a little boy's. Their date was off to a good start. They left the package in the backyard, to use after they returned from the town's fireworks display that night.

As they made their way down the sidewalk into town, Ben told her how glad he was to be living at home again, now that it had been modified for his needs, though he still went to the center for daily rehab. "And I have some good news." He slowed his chair. "The therapy's working. I can feel my feet. I even moved a toe yesterday."

She halted, astounded. "Really? That's amazing!"

"It is. Any feeling below the injury is a huge deal. If this keeps up, who knows? I might even walk again. We'll keep hoping."

She nodded rapidly. "We will." In a daze of grateful wonder, she resumed strolling alongside him, envisioning the day he would walk again. Then a question edged its way in. "Why didn't you call me and tell me right away?"

"I almost did, believe me, but I wanted to tell you in person. See your reaction." He smiled. "It was worth it."

After a picnic in the park, they lined up along Main Street to await the afternoon parade. The performance was well underway when the firetruck made an appearance, creeping along with red and white lights flashing and earsplitting sirens warbling. Charlene gripped Ben's arm and felt the display was slightly bad taste for anyone who associated the sight and sound with the memory of an accident, but she knew she was probably being overly sensitive.

In contrast, Ben appeared highly riveted by the shiny red truck. Again, like a little boy. The endearing thought evaporated on the tail of regret when she recalled the job he'd lost. And then she recognized a certain female firefighter with her abundant chestnut hair smoothed back in a bouncy ponytail.

Kate.

She smiled Charlene's way, but she wasn't looking at her. Kate's eyes were on Ben. Somehow, the fire department's regulation polo shirt and pants appeared entirely feminine and flattering on her.

"Hey look, it's Kate," Ben informed her unnecessarily as he waved.

Walking along behind the firetruck, Kate tossed candy to kids from an overturned fire helmet. A large chocolate candy bar landed in Ben's lap. "All right," he said, and this time Charlene was not amused by his enthusiasm.

"That's not typical parade candy," she pointed out.

"Yeah, we lucked out. Want some?"

"No thanks." She waited. He should know that if she turned down chocolate, something was wrong.

He bit down on the candy. "That was actually a pretty good throw, hey?" he managed around a mouthful. "But she plays softball, so I guess—"

"Wait, what? How do you know that? And why is she singling you out to get the best chocolate?"

He raised his eyebrows as his lips spread into a gloating smile. "Not jealous, are you?"

She folded her arms and turned to face him squarely, her back to the parade. "She was flirting with you. I saw her batting her lashes."

He chuckled and chomped off another hunk of chocolate. "So how does it feel to be on the other side?"

"You've got to be kidding me." Heat crawled up her neck. "What are you even talking about?"

"You and Clay. Me and Kate. Sure, it's nothing, but see how it feels?"

She shoved a hank of hair behind her ear. She didn't mean to raise her voice, but found it necessary to be heard above the garish parade. "Are you trying to 'get back at me'?" She used finger quotes, something she never did. "Because that's really childish, Ben. You and Kate," she scoffed, "are nothing like me and Clay. We have a history—"

"Somehow, that's not really helping your case," Ben said, visibly irritated now.

"He saved my life—"

"*Helped* save it," Ben clarified. He chucked the remaining chocolate to the ground. "Give Max the credit he's due, too. And did you forget who it was who helped rescue me from that cliff back in April? Does that count as 'saving,' Charlene? Because I think it does."

"Clay and I went through so much more than—" She bit off her words, but it was too late.

Ben's knuckles whitened as he clenched the sides of his chair. His voice growled low, but she heard the words. "You're actually *comparing* our pain and suffering? I didn't know it was a contest." Something horrible rippled over his face. "Okay, if it is, you win, Charlene." His gaze speared her. "How's that feel? You get the most emotionally damaged award. Congratulations."

She recoiled. He had never struck out at her like this before. Devastation filled her, yet she knew she deserved it. Her lips parted, but she couldn't find words to fix the piercing pain.

"Thanks, Clay," Ben muttered.

Her heart throbbed. "Maybe we have some issues to work through," she attempted, her voice hoarse, "but he's not the problem."

"I say he is." Every muscle in Ben's neck and arms pulled taut. "What if I said you had to make the choice: him or me?"

Her ears roared, the sound like beating waves. "You're giving me an ultimatum?"

"I've given you so much, Charlene." He shook his head. "And it still doesn't seem to be enough." His anger faded to sadness. "Will I ever be enough? Or are we done?"

Her insides crumpled in on themselves, and her heart collapsed to dust. *Are we done?* Her feet moved backwards, and she felt herself turn.

She couldn't face this, but if she fled now, she knew she might never be able to get Ben back.

And still, she couldn't stay.

She took off, weaving through the surging crowd of ridiculously happy people. As she ran, she was glad Ben couldn't, and she despised herself for the wicked thought. Her lungs burned, but it didn't mask the sorrow searing her soul.

Ben, her steady rock. Her guiding light. He'd loved her unconditionally. What had she done? They'd been together so long. He'd listened to her rehash her torments, the nightmares. He'd soothed her emotional scars. Maybe she had been wrong to burden him with all that. But he had helped her through, he really had. As he guided her to hope and happiness, she had healed. Or so she thought. And now that he was wounded and hurting—because of her—she couldn't even stay by his side.

Her steps eventually slowed, and she walked dazedly, perspiring in the heat, wandering through town, just thinking, thinking, and praying. For guidance. For answers.

Ben needed an answer. He needed—he deserved—a fiancée who would choose him above everyone and everything. If she couldn't do that, how could she ever be his wife?

Her hands clenched. She could do it. She would. Why throw away their happy future? For the sake of a fragmented friendship that Clay hardly wanted? There was no reason to cling to that.

Resolved, she began to feel that a sense of peace might be within reach. She had to find Ben and tell him her decision. Tell him she was sorry.

If it wasn't too late.

She popped into the air conditioning of an ice cream shop and then into the restroom, where she splashed her face and blotted it dry with a crispy brown paper towel. She finger-combed her scraggly curls, then she slicked on ChapStick. With a deep breath, she composed herself.

At the ice cream counter, she bought two bowls of chocolate ice cream with caramel sauce, Ben's favorite, and resolved to find him before the peace offering melted.

Shouldering her way out the door and into the July furnace, the race was on. *Look for a wheelchair.* The ice cream wouldn't last long. How could she have been so heartless, leaving him alone in this heat with no one to—

There he was.

But he wasn't alone.

Under the dappled shade of a birch tree, Kate reclined on the grass and gazed up at Ben, whose back was to Charlene. Steeling herself, Charlene set her shoulder blades and strode forward. She didn't get far. The tail end of Ben's words to Kate stopped her cold.

"Stockholm Syndrome."

The hated, horrible phrase socked her in the gut. The definition echoed from her past. In a courtroom, a doctor on the stand defined it, attempting to describe her as a victim who had developed "a positive emotional attachment" to her kidnapper.

Kate murmured something back, and Ben replied, "It's not healthy. She needs professional help."

Some gentle words rippled from Kate, meant to comfort him.

He shook his head. "She's messed up."

No. He didn't just say that. Not Ben.

Betrayal stabbed her. Her limbs trembled. The two Styrofoam bowls dropped from her hands, splattering the grass and her toes a chocolate brown, right before she turned and ran.

Chapter Twenty-Four

The Fourth of July traffic made Charlene's drive back to Creekside take longer than usual. She could have used the time productively, to mull and process everything, but she wasn't up to it. Her response was to flee, even her thoughts.

She cranked up the radio and let the songs erase Ben's scathing words from her brain. But they burned on, blistering her heart.

And how dare he talk to Kate about their private problems. Or, more accurately, apparently, *her* problems. She kept picturing him, over and over, as if he were a doctor detachedly pronouncing a diagnosis. Her diagnosis.

"She's messed up."

She slammed the steering wheel with one hand and accidentally hit the horn, jolting her back to her environment in the congested traffic and earning a vile gesture from a nearby driver.

Once in Creekside, she fared no better. All the people in celebratory moods thwarted her need to curl up in a ball and disintegrate. The police had road-blocked Main Street for the festivities, and cars jostled for parking spots.

She gave up and took a spot when she found one. If she went home, she might encounter Brook, and she couldn't face any questions right now.

Dusk settled, and while the air outside cooled, her car remained stuffy and hot. She blew her nose, then sagged out the door. She blended into the crowd hiking up the huge park hill. At the distant top, families reclined on blankets or sat in chairs. Kids threw balls and waved glow sticks wildly. Others whipped burning sparklers amid happy shrieks and plumes of smoke.

Stepping over a popcorn spill, she moved away to a weeping willow on the fringe of the firework anticipation and sank into the generous shadow. She swatted mosquitoes, then pulled out her phone and found three missed calls from Ben. She dropped the phone back in her purse as if it had burned her.

She hoped to remain unnoticed in her non-optimal fireworks-gazing spot, but as she fingered a little white clover flower, she caught sight of someone wandering in her direction. When she recognized him, the flower snapped off in her hand.

She turned her face away and used what hair she could to shield herself.

Go away. Go away.

Cowboy boots stopped in front of her.

"Charlene?"

She peeked up at Clay, but couldn't even muster a feeble hello.

"I thought that was you. What are you doing all the way over here by yourself? Brook said you were spending the day with Ben."

"Yeah, well that didn't exactly work out." She glanced around warily. "Where's Brook?"

"Talking to a friend. She wanted me to go ahead and find a spot." He held a folded blanket clamped under his arm.

"Better hurry. The best spots are almost gone." Shadows thickened, and she was grateful for the face-masking cover. Now she only had to guard her tone.

Clay sat down on the grass a safe distance away, yet still too close. "Are you okay?"

She tried to force the words *I'm fine* from her throat, but she couldn't lie to him. "I don't want to talk about it." Barely breathing, she drew her knees to her chest and waited for him to leave.

He didn't.

They sat side by side in the gloom, and it reminded her of a time years ago, locked in a dark, earthen room. Silently, she cursed the memory.

"Clay, do you think we're messed up?" A tear leaked out. "You know, from everything that happened with Abner?" She pulled in a breath and tried not to let herself shudder.

"Maybe." She saw his silhouetted profile glance up at the sky. "Probably. But I hardly think we'd be normal if we weren't a little messed up from that."

It wasn't what she wanted to hear. More treacherous tears escaped. "I don't want to be like this," she whispered.

He moved closer. "Hey, so we're a little messed up. Who isn't? That's what we are just by being human, right? Original sin's got us all messed up. That's why we need God. Didn't you tell me something like that once?"

She rested her wet cheek on her knees. "I don't know. I don't know what to believe anymore. Life just keeps getting harder. God isn't supposed to give us more than we can handle. But He does."

Clay was quiet a moment. "Maybe He knows you're stronger than you realize."

"I'm not."

He shifted on the grass. "I think you are." He cleared his throat. "Strong enough to face the truth, the darkness, to know it for what it is. And to know . . . the light is stronger."

She sniffed, unimpressed. "Empty, abstract words. That's all you've got?"

"All right." He rubbed the back of his neck. "Then I'll be blunt."

She waited.

"If you want to be happy, you've gotta be willing to fight for it. Feeling sorry for yourself, giving in to despair—that crap won't get you anywhere but down."

Her head came up and bumped the tree. She wanted to be offended by his words, but instead, she stayed silent. Because there was something in his voice . . . something driven, and real—

"Sure, life can be hell. Sure, there's hardships. But that's no excuse to be blind to the good things, the blessings—they're all around us, and we forget to see them."

The good things. She pulled in a jagged breath and noticed the fireflies blinking gold lights.

"It's hard to hear the truth. Some days, we want to give up. I get that. I do." The fingers of his right hand barely grazed the bandage on his left.

Sorrow panged within her.

"I know you've been through a lot, Charlene. Just remember, you're not alone. And who you are doesn't change by what someone thinks or says. Not what your grandfather says, or Max, or me. Or even Ben."

Ben.

She pressed her back hard into the tree bark. Ben wouldn't be happy if he saw her sitting here with Clay. "I thought Ben understood, but now . . ."

"Don't be too hard on him. He loves you."

"How would you know? You only saw him that one time."

"I could see it. Even back then."

She puzzled over that for a moment. Looking up at the dim sky, she clasped her fingers together and worked her knuckles. "Do you ever wonder . . . do you think about . . . what if you hadn't left Woodfield? What if you hadn't gone away?"

He scuffed a boot heel in the grass. "I try not to wonder about things I can't change."

And me, I wonder too much.

It was as though he picked up on the turmoil still radiating from her. "You had a hard day today. But tomorrow you'll get up and you'll start over."

She pulled her tangled hair back from her sloppy face and sniffed. "But I'll still be me." *And I'll still be messed up. If my future husband thinks I am, what hope is there for me?*

"Hey, look at me." Barely touching her chin, Clay rotated her face to his. "You survived Abner. You can survive anything this world throws at you."

"I don't want to just survive anymore." She didn't care if he saw her tears, if he thought she was weak. "It's not enough anymore. It's just. Not enough."

"I know."

For a second, she thought he was going to wipe her tears away, but his hand lowered and his voice dropped. "I know. And that's why you need God. Don't shut Him out. 'For though I should walk in the midst of the shadow of death, I will fear no evils, for thou art with me.'"

Irritation prickled. Bitterly, she thought of Ben, who couldn't walk. Might never. "Since when did you become such a theologian?"

"Since serving time." He could have shot the words out angrily, but he didn't.

She bit her tongue.

He pulled in a breath. "I had time to reflect, in there. To read the Bible. To talk to a priest. Really talk. Father Grady would charitably say we debated." His voice took on a hint of amusement. "But truthfully, it was me arguing with him every chance I got. And that's what it took. That, and all the prayers I know my ma said for me."

And she had. So many. The prayers Charlene herself had said crossed her mind as well. And now here he was, trying to bolster her faith.

"I never would have made time for facing the truth if I hadn't been in there." He drew up a knee and rested his forearm on it. "And I realized . . . I had no control of the outside. Where I was. There was no point in fighting that battle. But on the inside—" he stabbed his chest with a thumb—"my soul—*that* I could do something about. I could keep it dark, shackled with anger, with hatred, with sin." He paused. "Or, I could choose to fight my way out of those chains, by turning to God. That's where the real freedom is. The only freedom."

He forked a hand through his hair. "Dang, it's not always easy, Charlene." He faced her full on, his eyes brilliant. "But I'll tell you this: it's worth it. I know that now, and now that I do . . . I can't *un*know it."

She swallowed.

His eyes still intense, he went on. "You know it, too. I saw you and Max, the faith you had when you were facing death. A faith that strong doesn't disappear. It might be tested, it might be attacked, but God knows it doesn't disappear." The raspy fervor in his voice traveled through her like electrical charges. "You may have to fight to find it again, but it's there, Charlene. Don't ever doubt it. It's there."

A stillness settled over them like a blanket, till a startling *zing* sliced through the night, followed by an explosive *bang*. The reverberations practically shook her. She looked up to see fireworks burst, sparkles raining down, sizzling and crackling, etching the sky.

She and Clay watched a few more colorful explosions, which illuminated lingering smoke patterns, until she touched his arm. "Shouldn't you be getting back to Brook?"

"I should. I was just about to." With one arm, he pushed up from the ground. "Hey, look at that one." Colorful falling stars twirled and dove to earth with a high-pitched shriek.

He looked down, his plaintive expression tugging at her. "Come on, come sit with us."

She didn't move. "Does it bother Brook, that you were in prison?"

He didn't react to the apparent randomness of the question, only shook his head slowly as blue and gold fireworks burst behind him. "No, it doesn't." He sounded amazed.

Good. She's not stupid. "Go on. Go find her. She's waiting for you."

A shower of jewel-toned fragments reflected luminous in his eyes as he stood, still hesitant. "Come on, don't sit here all by yourself."

"Really, I'm fine now." She smiled up at him so he would think it was true. "Go."

He walked away, glancing back a couple times until he

disappeared into the crowd on the hilltop.

Mosquitos bit her. She swatted them away, then hugged herself close. Overhead wavered radiant, shivering streamers of red, white, and blue fireworks.

Let freedom ring.

With a sigh, she turned her face up to the vibrant bursting lights and tried to find warmth in them. Wanting to. Needing to.

Failing.

Like brilliant stardust, the beauty cascaded down, then burned itself out in an instant, leaving a vacant dark nothingness.

After a while, she heaved herself up. Her legs prickled at the sudden rush of blood. If she left before the show finished, she could get a head start on the inevitable after-fireworks traffic jam.

She crossed the hill to the restroom, where a couple people stood in the shadows of the building.

"Come on, Brook," a man's voice pleaded. "I promise we can make it work this time."

Despite the fireworks, her ears tuned in to the familiar name. As she paused near the corner of the restroom, she heard Brook's voice, low but adamant. "I told you, I'm not getting back together with you. I'm happy with Clay."

"But I miss you. Come on, we'll start over. It'll be different this time, I promise." The man reached for her arm.

Brook stepped back. "No."

"One more chance, that's all I'm asking—"

"You're out of your mind if you think I'd break up with Clay," Brook said firmly. "He treats me better than you ever did. And besides . . ."

Shamefully, Charlene stepped closer, her ears straining.

Brook rested a protective hand on her abdomen. "I'm pregnant with his baby."

The fireworks finale created a ground-vibrating boom, but Charlene barely registered it over the shockwaves going off in her head.

—————

"You have to tell him." Charlene confronted Sam the next day while Clay worked in the driveway, loading Sam's truck with a completed order. "I'm done keeping the secret. I can't do it anymore. Tell him or I'm giving him the letter tomorrow." *And then I'm gone for good.*

With a grunt, Sam plunked down a stack of boards. He gave her a sweeping, critical glance. "You look bad. Like you didn't sleep at all."

She prickled at the obvious truth, but her eyelids drooped. There was no mistaking the redness in her eyes and the lavender crescents beneath them. Just thinking about it, she stifled a yawn, unsuccessfully.

Astonishment at overhearing Brook had kept her mind awake, churning, unable to reconcile the Clay she thought she knew to the announcement Brook had made.

Not my business.

But she couldn't pry the questions and disbelief from her head. Clay and Brook having a child together? The thought hacked a cavity in her chest.

With unhappy fascination, she remembered the first time she met Brook, her sallow appearance and sudden dash from the cash register—to the bathroom to get sick, probably. She remembered Brook's weariness, as well as the muffins she claimed to practically crave, then didn't eat. It made sense now.

Sam still stared at her.

"You had plenty of time," Charlene said curtly. "But you obviously forgot all about the letter."

"Wrong. It's all I've had on my mind." His face turned thunderous and his voice grated like a wood file. "For over three years, it's all I've had on my mind." He glanced to the door and lowered his voice. "I've got this. I asked Clay to go fishing with me this Saturday. I'll tell him then, if you can wait that long. Can you?"

"I guess," she conceded.

"Hey, Charlene," Clay hollered from the driveway.

As she neared the door to see what was up, he headed toward her with a stunning arrangement of yellow roses, the full blooms billowing from a large glass vase.

Reacting to the confusion on her face, he explained, "They were just delivered. Must be from Ben."

Of course . . . Ben.

She accepted the flowers with a small nod, not even able to meet Clay's eyes for fear of what he'd read there. Too many frightening emotions whirled and warred within her. She hadn't a clue which one might surface, obvious and unsuitable, in her eyes.

She dipped her nose to the soft petals and tried to enjoy the sweet scent. She plucked the little card from its plastic prongs and read:

Charlene, I'm sorry. I love you. Please call me. Ben.

All she could see was how it read with a simple removal of a period: *I'm sorry I love you.* As if to say, *I don't want to love you, but somehow, I'm stuck loving you. You and all your messed up baggage.*

So maybe she was reading into it, but she couldn't help wondering if there hung a thinly veiled, subconscious truth there.

She barely heard Sam's disgruntled remark about allergies and bees as she set the vase in the corner of a workbench.

Her work that morning was halfhearted as she tried to avoid thoughts of Clay. Sharing a workspace, this proved to be highly difficult. She had to consciously fight to keep her eyes averted from him.

Her day was only half over when Brook burst into the shop, an odd, resolute look on her face. Sam stopped his power drill. Clay switched off his handsaw, and Charlene set down her varnish brush. As if sensing Brook had something important to say, they all removed their ear protection.

Brook flicked a pointed glance Charlene's way before fixing her gaze on Clay and announcing in a high-pitched voice, "I found the letter you've been looking for." Her hand lifted to prove it. Sure enough, she held the slightly bent "My Dear Son" envelope secure in her grasp.

Charlene flinched, and as her thoughts reeled, she heard Clay's bewilderment. "My ma's letter?" Amazed, he stepped forward to take it. "Where'd you find it?"

Brook cast Charlene a look of triumphant spite, and her stomach dropped.

"Charlene had it. Hidden away in one of her drawers. I accidentally came across it when I went looking for a shirt of mine that ended up in her laundry."

A likely story.

Clay faced her in disbelief. "Is that true, Charlene? Did you really have the letter all this time?" As his hand slid the envelope into his pocket, his expression practically begged her to deny it.

Unable to stand his gaze, she bent her head. "I'm sorry, Clay. I wasn't trying to—I mean, I only meant to—"

Her confusing jabber was made more perplexing when Sam spoke over her. "Now hold on. Don't go blaming—"

But Brook overrode them both as she sent a cutting look Sam's way and plowed ahead on her strange, destructive mission.

"Charlene wasn't the only one hiding something from you. There's an important detail you need to know. About Sam."

She wouldn't. Not like this. Charlene felt like her chest was being squeezed in a vise.

"What about him?" Clay's voice sliced the air.

Suddenly, Brook looked like she didn't want to finish what she'd started.

"Brook," Clay barked.

"Sam . . . he's your dad."

Clay's face blanched. His gaze shot to Sam. He stared at him for what felt like forever, the muscles near his eyes tightening. The pulse in his neck pounded. "Is that true? Are you . . . ?"

Sam's chin jutted forward. He gave one curt nod. "It's true."

Clay's jaw went slack. His gaze ping-ponged from Sam, to Charlene, to Brook, reflecting incredulity and then the devastating pain of betrayal. "How did you know . . . ?" He addressed Brook as realization dawned.

"It's in the letter, isn't it?" Outraged disapproval flashed across his face. "You read the letter?"

How presumptuous and invasive. Quick as it came, Charlene exterminated the self-righteous thought.

Clay's gaze speared her next. "I asked you. Directly. You told me you didn't know where the letter was. You lied."

Her lips parted for a feeble response, but he had already dismissed her from his sight.

He moved on to Sam.

"How long have you known?" A red flush crept up Clay's neck, then took over the white of his face as anger consumed his shock. "My whole life?" His hands curled into fists. "You worthless—" He cursed. "How could you do that to her? To me?"

"It wasn't like that," Sam said.

"Then how was it? 'Cause I can't see any excuse that makes it right. Tell me. No, on second thought, I don't want to know. You obviously weren't planning on telling me." His eyes flamed, a frightening, scorching brown.

Sam remained quiet as Clay continued blasting him with his words. "You thought you could just jump back into my life when it suited you, and lie some more. I thought you were a good person. I thought I could trust you."

Clay smashed his fist on a workbench. "I thought I could trust you all."

Clamping his mouth shut, he stormed out of the shop.

"Clay, wait!" Brook, a glimmer of *What have I done?* in her eyes, turned to dash after him.

Charlene knew better.

A door slammed. Clay's truck roared to life, then tore out of the drive, tires spitting gravel. Very soon, the angry engine faded away, leaving them all to face a deep, unsettling silence.

—

His ears perked, instantly alert. Time in prison had taught him to sleep light, to always be on guard. He searched the shadows of his trailer and listened for the sound.

There it was. Something scratching on wood, like little pinprick claws. Just a critter of some kind, that's all. Settling back down, Nails closed his eyes, and the memory ambushed him . . .

"Don't you dare!"

Not heeding Beth's cry, the kitten shot out the door left open by one of the younger Callaghan kids. The fur ball bolted across the grass, a wild gray streak heading for who-knew-where.

Good riddance, *Lance thought as he chomped an apple.*

"No, Gossamer, come back!" Beth flew from the house, skirt flapping as she sprinted after the critter.

He slumped against the doorframe and watched, amused by the ridiculous chase. What kind of name was Gossamer, anyway? It was ten times too big for the scrappy creature. As Beth charged through a neighboring field, he tramped outside lazily. A couple acres later, he caught up to her. She still didn't have the kitten.

"The more you chase, the more she'll run." He chucked his apple core at a tree.

Beth turned to him, visibly flustered. "She doesn't know what she's doing. She's so tiny and defenseless. I have to catch her."

Yards away, the kitten whipped her tail as she crept into a ditch. She lingered a moment, batting blades of grass, then slunk up to the highway.

"No, Gossamer, no!"

A paw touched the pavement.

Beth pressed her hands to her cheeks. The kitten pranced to the middle of the road and paused, suddenly in no hurry.

"Come back, Gossamer!" Beth yelled. "A truck's coming!"

Lance shook his head, unconcerned. "She'll move in time."

"What if she doesn't?" Beth rushed to the ditch and began clambering up to the road.

He sprang forward and cut her off. "I'll get her." He took off, running across traffic for a lame ball of fur. He was a fool. The truck bore down, horn blasting. And sure enough, the kitten shot to the other side of the road.

Lance followed, trying to keep the dumb animal in sight, though he was tempted to turn and give the finger to the honking truck as it whizzed past him.

There went the streak of fuzz, right up into a tree. Real creative. And people thought cats were smart.

He huffed an exasperated breath and climbed after the thing, hardly knowing why. "C'mere stupid cat." He reached out and was rewarded with a lightning-fast swipe of a razor-sharp paw. Blood welled in three long, thin tracks on his forearm. He grabbed the creature by the scruff as it yowled and struck out again, catching his other arm. More stinging, more beading blood. Man, for such a tiny creature, this thing could do damage. Defenseless? Bull. He should wring its neck.

Instead, he maneuvered the kitten and pinned its paws so it was immobile. With a pitiful mew, it trembled in the crook of his arm. He dropped to the ground, crossed the road, and handed the ball of trouble back to Beth. "Careful," he warned, but the thing didn't even try to strike her.

She beamed and cradled the kitten like a baby. Then she noticed his arms and her big brown eyes saddened. "Oh Lance, I'm sorry."

He scoffed. "No big deal."

She trailed her slender fingers along his arm, unnerving him. The cuts didn't bother him. Her soft touch did.

"Thank you for saving her."

He hadn't, but if that's what she wanted to think, let her.

Suddenly, she hugged him, the fur ball sandwiched between them, and he didn't know what to do. He stood rigid, but she lingered, her silky head right under his nose, smelling sweetly of vanilla and cinnamon. Her hand lay warm on his shoulder, then slid again to his arm.

When she spoke, warmth even radiated from her words. "I'm so glad you're here, Lance. So glad." She tipped her innocent face up at him. "You're special, and someday you're going to do great things." She sighed dreamily. "I just know it."

Chapter Twenty-Five

*C*harlene entered the apartment to find Brook had already shut herself in her bedroom for the evening. When she heard low weeping, she tapped on Brook's door. Brook didn't answer, merely muffled her cries, perhaps with a pillow.

Clay will get over it, Charlene wanted to tell her. *He'll cool down and eventually forgive us all.* In her room, Charlene ran her fingers over the little bench wood carving. *I know him . . . he will.*

The next morning, and the morning after that, he still hadn't come back. From the little that Charlene glimpsed of her, Brook looked drained, frail, and despondent. Sam threw himself into his work with a deep furrow in his brow. Even more silent than usual, he pushed himself to do too much, nowhere near stopping when Charlene left at the end of the workday.

On Friday, she climbed in her car and headed up north, into the land of thick pine woods and countless lakes.

Turning off the highway, she drove backroads of increasingly rustic appearance, till at last a windy path through an overhanging, shadowy forest led her to a weed-choked gravel drive. She rumbled up it slowly, her car bumping and rocking till she cut the engine.

For a long moment, she simply sat, unmoving. Then she lifted her chin and faced the nightmare-infested cabin of horrors from her dark past. *I must be crazy.* Even in the warm sunshine, it was a somber, dingy sight.

But sure enough, her hunch had been right. There, off to the left, Clay's mud spattered truck sat in the shade.

Daisy heads bobbed randomly between long grasses. She stepped out into the itchy overgrowth. Trees and leaves swooshed and sang an ominous, breathy ballad. Weeds grew up through the gaps of the wooden porch steps, tickling her ankles as she climbed.

The sagging porch creaked and her nerves sizzled. Shadows sashayed and fell on her with no apology, giving the sense of an almost physical, unwelcome touch. With a shake of her shoulders, she approached the cabin window.

Boards nailed over the inside barred even a glimpse of the interior. She rapped on the door, but no one answered. "Clay? Are you in there?" Her hand reached for the doorknob, shivered, and fell back to her side.

I can't do it.

She put her mouth near the door. "Clay?"

When he didn't answer, she turned and trudged down the steps. If he wasn't in the cabin, there was another, perhaps more likely, place to look. She hiked down the overgrown driveway onto the desolate dirt road and followed rutted curves to the lake.

Wet grass gave way to pebbles and mud, then a slimy little shore. No welcoming sand here. Fat flies buzzed. An old canoe lay tipped over on the nearby slope. She walked out onto a rickety pier, which swayed questionably.

At the end of it, she shaded her eyes and peered over the glimmering water. She couldn't find a single boat on the lake. Then off to the left, in a southern inlet, she spotted an aluminum boat. She squinted and saw a fisherman. Even from this distance, she was sure it was Clay.

She sat down cross-legged on the pier, resigned to waiting out his return. Water lapped a lulling rhythm beneath her. The sun beat down and the weedy lake began to tempt her with cool relief. She dipped her fingers in the water, but this lake . . . it was probably full of huge monster fish, ready and waiting to nibble her. She pulled her fingers out.

She'd been in this lake once in her life, and that one frigid time was more than enough. The water masqueraded as a completely different lake in summer. She scanned the dark expanse, an unpleasant murky green.

Tired of waiting, she cupped her hands around her mouth and hollered, "Clay!" Her voice echoed, and while his head turned, he made no move to acknowledge her or move his boat closer.

He's ignoring me.

With a huff, she walked over to the beached canoe and assessed it, hands on her hips. As long as it wasn't too heavy . . .

She tipped it right-side up and found a paddle beneath it, then dragged the canoe over stones and muck to the water. Her flip-flops sank in gunk as she stepped into the shallows. Squishy, sucking mud curled her toes.

When the canoe no longer touched bottom, she climbed inside and started paddling.

Moving away from the shore was tricky. She'd never navigated a canoe before, and steering was all trial and error as she attempted to aim for Clay's boat. She paddled on one side, then quickly switched to the other. In this way she zigzagged tediously over the water. But at least her palms were used to hard work and didn't blister.

She finally came close enough to see Clay's face, shaded under the bill of a camouflage ball cap. He didn't turn to look at her, even as she splish-splashed clumsily beside him.

"So much for fishing." He reeled in his line with a whirring sound. Her eyes followed the movement of his tan, muscular arms.

He tore a piece of lake weed from his hook. "You just about scared away all the fish in a two hundred yard radius."

"Maybe we could talk, then," she attempted.

"Nope." He set his pole down, pushed his cap lower over his eyes, sat back with folded arms, and proceeded to disregard her.

She stared at his stubborn, stubbly chin. "Come on, Clay, don't be like that. Give me a chance." A distant loon warble was the only response.

Her canoe drifted quietly for a few minutes, the current gradually gliding her away. She seized her paddle. Slicing the water, she brought her canoe as close as possible to the side of Clay's vessel. The boats connected, and the *bump* made him thumb back his cap and glance up. The hat perched oddly, like it was about to fall off.

She set her paddle down and gripped the side of his boat. "I'm not going anywhere."

"Suit yourself." His lips jammed together in a disapproving line and he looked away.

Her tense shoulders fell, remorse filling her. "I'm sorry about the letter. I didn't want to mislead you, or lie to you. I was only keeping it safe until the time was right. I thought it would be better if you heard it from Sam, so he could explain his side."

"I'm not interested in hearing his side of anything. He's had years to tell me, and he never said a word."

The canoe rocked ever so slightly. The breeze blew light and warm, but she almost shivered. "He planned to tell you, he really did."

"So what."

She waited, studying his surly face. "I can see him in you. Especially when you look like that."

His scowl deepened.

"Yep, there it is."

He grunted.

"Oh, that too. Definitely."

The slightest glint escaped his sullen eyes. "Keep it up, and you're gonna swim back."

"Oh, and the threats. Just like Sam." She closed her mouth. Maybe she'd gone too far.

He stayed silent, gazing in the general direction of the cabin, though they couldn't see it through the clustered pines. She sensed his thoughts were long ago and far away.

She wracked her brains for the right words to cut through the standstill and bring his mind back. He really needed a friend right now, a friend who knew just what to say. As he had, for her.

And then she had it. "A wise man once told me, 'Feeling sorry for yourself won't get you anywhere but down.'"

He snorted. "How wise could he be if he didn't have the sense to know his words would be thrown back in his face?"

"No, not thrown, Clay." She softened her voice. "Never."

He rubbed his forehead and eyed the bottom of his boat. "Thing is," he said quietly, "I know Sam too well now. And he is a good guy. The kind I always wanted my dad to be." He flicked open his tackle box, stared at the array of hooks and lures, then clunked it closed. "Why'd all those years have to be wasted? And how could my ma—" He grimaced.

"Did you finally read the letter? Did it . . . help at all?"

His neck muscles moved. "It wasn't enough," he said dismissively. "Now the ma I thought I knew, she's not the same person to me anymore."

Hearing the hardness in his voice, Charlene couldn't help rising to defend the woman she'd grown to love. "You mean, she wasn't perfect."

His brows plowed together. "You can't understand."

"I do." Her gaze glimpsed a hawk sailing high above, cutting clean arcs through the air. "Your ideal image of her is shattered." She leaned forward, her grasp on the side of his boat tightening. "It doesn't change her love for you. Or," she hesitated, "her love of God. If He could forgive her . . . how can you not?"

Clay angled away from her.

"And Sam," she went on, surprising herself. "It was only because he cares so much, that he didn't tell you sooner. He just didn't know how."

Clay shoved his fishing rod to the bottom of the boat. "I can't change how I think of him. He's Sam, not my dad."

"Oh Clay, he's not going to care what you call him. Either way, he's the only parent you have left. And that's something. More than you thought you had. It's like having time back that you thought you never could." She met his eyes with a plea. "Don't throw that away."

"He's too late. Twenty-five years too late. I don't need him anymore."

Her gaze trailed off, and she found herself noticing Clay's hands. The bandages had shifted, and she focused on a dark inkiness that was partially revealed. If she wasn't mistaken, it looked like the edges of a tattoo.

Catching her gaze, he drew his hands up. He readjusted and tightened the bandages roughly so that, once again, she saw nothing.

His last words ran through her mind, sorrow twinging her soul. "It's not weakness to need someone," she said softly. Overhead, she noticed clouds gathering in dark bunches to the west. "And maybe . . . maybe he needs you."

"How'd you know where to find me?"

"It wasn't hard to figure out." Her hands growing tired, she repositioned her hold on his boat. "I remembered you came here before . . . to get away, to fish . . . And the cabin's all yours now." She suddenly registered the shadows under his bloodshot eyes. "You've been sleeping there, haven't you? Clay, that's horrible." When she thought of all the twisted memories . . . "How could you?"

His shoulder hitched. "It's just a place. A place to crash." He worked his jaw. "I'm gonna sell it, though."

"Honestly?" Her heart palpitated. "Do you really think anyone would buy it?"

"Sure, it's got this lake access. I may have to take less because of the creep factor now, but I'll get something. Then I'll use the money to buy some land and build my own place."

"Where?" Concern washed over her.

"I was thinking the outskirts of Creekside." A muscle near his eye twitched. "That was my plan, anyway, before I found out about Sam. I don't know if I can keep working for him."

"You can." Sunlight faded. "Of course you can. He loves you, you know. Like a dad. He's thought of you like a son for years. I can tell. You can tell, too, I bet . . . if you'd just stop and think about it."

His face hardened.

"You need to come back and talk to him. And Brook." She focused on a tattered leaf floating in the grimy water at the bottom of his boat. "You shouldn't have left like that." *Especially with Brook in her condition.* But did he know? She gave herself a little shake. *Not my place. Not my business.* Head bowed, she watched him through her lashes.

"I know," he admitted, rubbing the back of his head. "That wasn't right."

"They're both worried about you. You need to come back."

He gave a nod.

At that moment she became aware that clouds had overtaken the sky and were darkening heavily. "We'd better head back before it rains." She released her hold on his boat, creating an immediate gap between them.

He assessed the sky. "You won't make it in time."

"Thanks for the vote of confidence." She picked up her paddle.

He shook his head. "Climb in. I'll give you a ride back." He reached out and gripped the edge of her canoe, bringing it flush against his boat. "Be careful. Go slow."

"Okay." She eased up off her seat, then clambered over the edge gracelessly and plunked, relieved, onto a metal bench. "But the canoe. We can't just leave it floating out here."

"I've got it." Using a rope, he tied the canoe to the rear of his boat. Then he cranked the motor and aimed for the dock. They chugged noisily over the lake, skimming and bouncing, reaching the pier just as the rain crashed down, instantly drenching them.

Clay secured the boat with a swift knot and then helped her out. Next, he hefted the canoe and tipped it over on the shore. Together they dashed for the little road.

The scent of rain on hot dirt filled her nose. Silver beams of rain sliced down, pulverizing the ground and stirring up mud. They ran all the way to the cabin porch and stood under the narrow overhang, watching rain pour, battering the tall grass and crushing the bright daisies. Thunder cracked, shaking the air.

Clay opened the cabin door. "Come on, let's get out of this." He stepped in without a second thought, while she stepped back with an overpowering aversion, as if she saw evil leaking from the interior in plumes of black smoke.

In her mind's eye, she did.

Understanding dawned on Clay's face. Still holding the door open, he stepped back out beside her.

She clutched her fingers and tried to work up courage. The last time she'd entered this cabin, she'd almost lost her life. *So long ago. Forget it.* She sipped short breaths and willed her muscles to relax.

"Hey, it's all right. It'll be okay." His hand lightly stilled her worrying fingers. "If you'd rather stay on the porch, we will."

She nodded, grateful, but his touch infused a calmness that even the next crash of thunder didn't shake. In a way she couldn't understand, her fears shrank, then subsided.

With the wind slinging rain at them, she turned, stepped through the opening, and entered the cabin. Right behind her, Clay closed the door on the wild weather, but the noise remained, like shrieking demons circling the cabin, rattling the windows, clawing for entrance.

She edged close to Clay's side. He still hadn't released her hand, and she was glad for the warmth of it. Her lifeline to composure.

But then he slid his hand away, muttering, "Let's get you some towels." In the kitchen, he loaded her up with three dingy dish rags from the musty cupboard, and she smothered a smile at his well-intentioned effort.

He pulled off his drenched cap and made a sorry attempt to wring it out, then laid it on the counter. His bedraggled hair dripped rivulets down his face. She blotted her face, hair, and arms grudgingly and tried not to cringe when she noticed mice-gnawed holes in a corner of a towel.

All the while, Clay stood puddling rain on the scuffed floor, watching her. Impulsively, she reached out and swiped at his flat, drenched hair, rumpling it and preventing the water from dripping into his eyes.

As he ducked out of reach, she smiled at how pitifully soppy his black t-shirt and jeans were. "Aren't there any bigger towels somewhere?"

His eyebrows flicked together. He put up a silencing hand and cocked his head. "Did you hear that?" he whispered.

"What?" Instantly fearful, she clutched the wet, pungent towels to her chest.

Frowning, he crept forward and peeked in the bedroom, then bathroom.

"It's just the rain. Or the wind." Her tone pleaded for him to agree.

He shook his head. "It came from the cellar." He circled back to the trap door in the kitchen floor.

"You're not going down there?" She tugged at his arm, seized by muddled nightmare visions of what might await, including mobs of rats, demonic specters, and Abner's ghost.

Clay took her by the shoulders and moved her back gently, whispering, "Go to your car. Lock yourself in."

She gave an emphatic shake of her head and he didn't look pleased. Dropping the towels, she reached for her phone, ready to call for help if there was, indeed, a reason. Not finding the phone on her, she realized it was still in her purse in the car.

"Go," Clay ordered, then he eased open the squeaky cellar door. As he peered into the dimness, she heard the distinct, steady *creak, creak, creak* of footsteps.

Someone was walking up the steps toward them.

The woman lay in bed, torturing herself.

She didn't know what was worse: not knowing where he was, or suspecting he was with the other woman.

It was too long since he'd held her. Way too long. All because of the tramp.

I have to find him.

His presence gave her comfort. His touch gave her strength. Both things she needed.

Desperately.

Getting out of bed was so difficult these days. She was tired almost all the time now. Her hand fluttered to her temple, then her belly. For such a tiny thing, the baby was powerful, leaching all her energy.

Her only hope was that the child would be worth the trouble, would be enough to make him forget the other woman and stay with her forever.

With him by her side, she would finally have everything. Her heart panged.

I'll finally be happy.

Chapter Twenty-Six

Startled, Clay and Charlene stumbled back as a man emerged from the cellar shadows.

"Howdy." The stout, bespectacled man doffed his derby hat, greeting them as if they'd met casually on a stroll. He stood shorter than Clay and appeared to be middle-aged. Crow's feet cut deep at the corners of his eyes. Then he sidled a little closer, and Charlene caught a whiff of a telltale smell.

"Who the heck are you?" Clay demanded. "And what are you doing on my property?"

Her eyes riveted to the undeterred man, and she tapped Clay's arm. "I know him. He's the knife guy."

The man gave a short, one-syllable chuckle. "Hmm, an interesting nickname." She noticed dirt in the creases of his hands and under his nails as he fingered his string-thin mustache. "But I do recall I introduced myself to you as Horace Cain. Why, I even gave you my card." He *tsk, tsk*ed. "You mislaid it, didn't you? I was highly disappointed you didn't follow up on what we discussed."

"You followed me here, didn't you?"

He laid a business card on the kitchen counter. "I've simply been doing a little, shall we say, sleuthing, on my own."

"Enough," Clay said gruffly. "I don't know who you think you are, but you can't just go breaking into places and—"

Horace gasped. "I would never. The door wasn't locked." He glanced about the dingy, unkempt place with a disdain that was laughable on a man who smelled as he did. "You really can't blame me for assuming the place was abandoned."

"Oh, but I do." Clay's arms tensed, veins rising. "Whatever you did or didn't think, you're still trespassing." Finger pointed, he stepped close to Horace, and all Charlene could think was, *How can Clay stand the smell?*

Horace stepped back and smoothed a hand down his front. "Now, now, don't get ruffled. I'll be on my way."

"You bet you will."

She caught Horace honing in on Clay's scarred finger, the pale old cut just barely visible past his knuckle bandage. Was it her imagination, or did the sight please the man?

"I just want to make sure you're aware that I'm willing to pay generously for that special little article I'm seeking."

"The ugly old knife?" Clay moved till he stood toe-to-toe with Horace. "How do you even know about it?"

"You're brother and I, we moved in similar circles."

Highly unsettling.

"Still . . ." Horace tapped his fingertips together greedily, his beady eyes harboring deep, distant thoughts. ". . . it took me time to realize its value." His slender tongue slid over his gapped teeth as he grinned. "You don't have the slightest idea where it might be?" His gaze darted about the room.

"No," Clay said firmly, "and you're not welcome to search. My brother took it with him to the bottom of the lake, for all I know or care."

"Gracious, such thoughtless unconcern is disturbing. I would think you'd be more cautious, considering the little lady."

As Clay sputtered, "What do you mean?", Horace slipped into the bedroom. "Hey, where do you think you're going?" Clay stalked after him.

Following Clay, Charlene scanned the room. It was dominated by a drab, saggy bed. Abner must have replaced it after the fire damage (courtesy of Max)—and done a little redecorating. An ugly taxidermy goat head now hung oddly low above the bed, quite a thing to have looking down on you as you fell asleep.

Maybe that was why she'd seen Clay's sleeping bag in the main cabin room. She'd have to remember to suggest he remove all remnants of Abner's macabre existence before attempting to sell this charming place.

Horace prowled the room like a rat, his eyes wandering the walls and floor. Clay's expression was disturbed and slightly stunned, as if he didn't understand how the man had gotten this far. Clay's fists clenched. "Get out of here."

As if he hadn't heard Clay's raised voice, Horace said, "You are aware of the curse, aren't you?"

Clay's arm moved, but Charlene caught it. "Wait." His bicep felt rock-hard under her hand, but her thoughts were all on Horace. "What do you mean, 'curse'?"

Horace's eyes almost twinkled. "The knife is very old, with a long, rich, and tragic history."

"Give her the short version," Clay cut in, "and make it shorter."

"Very well." Horace grinned. "It's the dagger of Satan himself. Possessed. And whoever is cut by it, is forever marked to suffer the evils of hell—in this life, and in the next."

She swallowed and released Clay's arm. He made a scornful sound.

"You weren't cut by it, were you, dear?" Horace's fingers walked the log walls like thick fleshy spider legs. He tapped and even put an ear to the wood. "He would have kept it in a secret, safe place." He spoke in hushed tones now, as if to himself, or . . . *someone.*

"So is there a way to break the so-called curse?" Not that she believed his claim for a moment. She was humoring him. Or, more accurately, she was strangely, unwisely, fascinated—as if by a dreadful ghost story or horror movie.

She tried to rub the goosebumps from her arms.

"Break the curse?" Horace faced her. "Perhaps . . . but first you have to find the knife."

Clay's hands came down strong on the man's shoulders. "Get out. Now."

Horace sent Clay a sizzling look that belied his odd, mild-mannered attitude. "Careful, Mr. Morrow. You wouldn't want to face another assault charge, now would you? They won't go so easy on you a second time."

"My property. I'm well within my rights." Clay's tone was clipped. He propelled Horace out of the bedroom and to the front door.

"Perhaps . . ." the word came out of Horace's mouth like a hiss.

Clay opened the door.

"I'm a very determined man," Horace said. "You *will* let me know if you find it. I'll make it well worth your while. And don't forget about the curse." He met Charlene's eyes and said solemnly, "Bad things will happen."

"Is that a threat?" But Clay didn't let Horace answer. He gave him a hard shove down the steps, then slammed and locked the door.

Clay pried a board from the window and he and Charlene watched silently as Horace strolled down the weedy drive. The man's shiny wet form reminded her of a slimy snake in the grass.

"He's a new nightmare to add to my collection." She released a short laugh. "This cabin of delights is going to be a real catch for someone."

"Why I didn't kick him out the second I saw him, is beyond me," Clay berated himself.

"It was like he had us under a spell."

Clay glowered out the window, making sure Horace reached the road and kept walking. "If I ever find that knife, I'll destroy it."

She was silent a moment. "What did you think of the curse?"

Contempt covered his face. "He made it up to scare you, that's what." He finally moved away from the window. "Look, I'd better check in the cellar and . . . the other room down there, make sure he wasn't up to anything else. He's probably just a harmless kook, but you never know."

You never know, indeed. You might find a dead body down there.

Clay regarded her indecisively. "You'll be all right up here? It's just for a few minutes."

She nodded. She wouldn't tell him her veins iced at the very idea of him leaving her side, not when he was going *down there.* Alone.

When he left, she stood ramrod straight in the middle of the room and stared into the grimy filmed window of the cold wood-burning stove. Her eyes fixated. Her heart forgot how to beat properly. She thought she saw a flicker of flame curl to life. It rose up, licked the glass, and prodded, seeking a crack to escape from, to slither out and—

"Charlene." Clay clasped her arms and she gasped. He peered into her face, concerned. "You okay? You looked—"

"I'm fine." She blinked and shook herself. "Did you find anything down there?"

"Just some holes in the dirt. He must have been digging for the knife."

She traced the scar on her ring finger. "All that curse stuff . . . it's nonsense, I know. But when you think about all our rotten luck . . ."

"No such thing as luck. Rotten or otherwise. Life's what we make of it, with God's grace. Trials and crosses got nothing to do with a curse."

"I know, but still." She shuddered. Her mouth pulled down at the corners, out of her control.

Before she knew what was happening, he wrapped her in a hug. A strong, protective hug. "Hey, don't worry about it. Forget him. Forget the knife. The curse. Forget everything."

Finding herself in Clay's arms was so pleasantly bewildering, that forgetting everything else was suddenly very easy to do. Her cheek pressed against his firm shoulder. He smelled of lake water, rain, and trees. Even though they were both still wet, she felt warm. She shivered, but it wasn't related to cold or fear.

"Come on," he said in a low voice. "Let's ditch this place. You shouldn't be here."

She felt him letting go, and reluctantly, she slid back to reality.

His gaze skimmed her face. "When did you last eat?"

It took her forever to recall. "This morning."

He plucked his wrinkly wet cap from the counter, almost tugging it on before thinking better of it and stuffing it in his back pocket. "Let's go get some food."

He locked the cabin behind them and walked her through the drizzle to her car, where he gave her trunk and backseat a thorough onceover to calm her nerves and assure her she was safe to drive alone. She wished she could ride with him.

Her wipers swiped water beads from her windshield, and she tailed his truck out of the winding woods and back to the main road. She felt a sense of rightness that she had found him and helped convince him to return home. She thought of Sam and Brook. Then, not strong enough to stop herself, she replayed his hug in her mind, such a brief, strange moment. Pleasant confusion stirred within her, warming her again.

As the rain tapered off and stopped, she turned her wheel and followed Clay's truck into a gas station. Good timing. Her car needed a fuel-up, too.

"Be out in a few," Clay called as he headed into the building after filling his tank. He soon emerged with a plastic bag, which he slung into his truck before they took off again.

Her stomach growled. *And just when are we going to get that food you promised?* She'd assumed he would have pulled into a fast food place by now. They'd certainly passed enough of them.

Finally, he took an exit off the highway, but he soon turned off the country road onto a hidden dirt road with not a single building in sight, only fields and forests. Despite her gnawing hunger, she was curious. *What are you up to?*

Her car jostled along with occasional sharp bumps till they emerged in a clearing bordered by aspen and pine. Clay's brake lights glowed red, then he shut off his engine and stepped down to the ground. She parked beside him and got out to see him gathering branches and clearing a patch of dirt. The rain storm hadn't come this far south, apparently, because nothing here was wet. Before long he had a little fire burning briskly in the dusky clearing.

Crouched on one knee before the flames, he cocked an eyebrow. "Ever tailgate before?"

She shook her head. "Don't people do that in parking lots, before games?"

He crossed to his truck and dropped the tailgate with a *clunk*. "Sure, but I'd choose this spot over crowded pavement any day." He ducked back in his vehicle for the plastic bag and flipped on a country music station.

He brought the bag to where she leaned against the truck. Fishing inside, he drew out a pack of hot dogs, then hauled out a cluster of cans. "Got us a six pack, too."

"Oh." She felt flustered. "I don't really drink."

"Sure you don't." He winked. "It's root beer." He popped a tab and handed her one.

They stood around the fire, the heat finally drying them as they roasted hot dogs on sticks till the meat blistered. Then they hoisted themselves onto the tailgate to eat and washed the food down with root beer. Before she knew it, stars appeared, bright little pin-pricks in the velvet sky. The warm humid air gradually cooled with the darkness to a pleasant temperature.

"This is nice." She swung her dangling legs. "Much better than fast food."

He raised his soda. "To tailgating."

Her hand lifted her own drink. "To tailgating with you." She blushed. "I mean, since this was your idea and everything. And it's really nice." *Clunk,* she put her can down. She might as well be drunk, the discombobulated way she was feeling. It was just so perfect and peaceful, though, with the cozy little fire—nothing at all like the specter flames in the cabin stove—and the twinkling stars and the curtain of trees all around. Like there was no one else in the world but them.

"It is nice," Clay echoed, contentment in his voice.

"Just to clarify," she touched the condensation on her soda can and spoke softly, "you do forgive me, then? For keeping the letter from you?"

"Yeah, sure I do. It's all right. I know you meant well."

She tipped her face to the sky. *"The good things, the blessings—they're all around us, and we forget to see them."* His words from the Fourth of July rippled through her like a refreshing breeze. She filled her lungs with sweet night air. *This. This right now. This is a blessing.*

She turned to eye his profile. "You're a good guy, Clay."

He gave something like a snort. "I wouldn't go that far." He turned and dug out a plastic bag. "Ready to roast some marshmallows?"

"Definitely."

After torching too many marshmallows into charcoaled lumps, she managed to toast a perfectly light brown one. She savored the burst of warm gooey vanilla before settling back on the tailgate, full and satisfied. She gazed up at the stars, and a random question popped into her head. "After you build your house, what color are you going to paint it?"

"Hmm. Haven't thought too much about that." He shifted beside her. "What color do you think it should be?"

She couldn't help herself. "Yellow?" She waited for his reaction.

"Yellow," he repeated, thoughtful.

"I don't mean a glaring yellow," she felt the need to clarify. "Something sunny, but still subtle."

"That's doable."

"With white shutters?"

"Why not?"

Away in the distance came the forlorn whistle and rumble of a train, blending with the truck's soft radio music. The moon glowed, a huge gray pearl above. Crickets chirped. Night was beautiful, and it had been forever since she'd thought that. Normally, the sinking sun signaled a descent into darkness and fear, memories and nightmares. But not tonight. She sighed. If every night could be like this . . .

"Do you ever have nightmares anymore, Clay?"

He was quiet a moment as the train whistle died. "Well, sure. Sometimes."

Grateful for his honesty, she nibbled at her lip and tasted marshmallow residue. "I sleep with a night light." She studied her knees and didn't tell him that the main thing she was looking forward to about marriage was always having a strong man nearby at night to protect her. The silly thought stirred up a flood of mixed emotions that sparked like the fire.

She eyed her bare ring finger. She didn't even know where she and Ben stood anymore.

Her eyes jumped to Clay's fingers, to his one hand resting on the edge of the tailgate, rather close to her hand. She could reach over and touch that infuriating bandage. She could . . .

She did.

Clay's head turned.

She didn't meet his gaze, but brushed the bandage with her fingertips. "Can't you tell me about it? Please?"

Surprisingly, he didn't pull his hand away. She listened to him breathing, debating.

"It's really no big deal," he said at last. "Nothing you don't already know anyway, I guess."

The flickering yellow glow of the fire, mixed with the moonlight, gave just enough visibility. He loosened first one bandage, then the next, and removed them, revealing a row of harsh tattooed letters. They formed a word on each hand, right below the knuckles. He fisted his hands together and faced them to her, something vulnerable on his face as he waited for her to read the ink.

Worthless Convict.

She almost said the words aloud, but stopped herself in time. There was a familiar ring to the ugly expression. She'd heard it enough times to know who was responsible.

"Oh, Clay." She recalled the cruel DVD and how she hadn't finished watching it. This tattoo must have been what had happened next in that warehouse. She put a hand to her mouth. "Grandfather." *He had you branded. Like an animal.*

Clay brought his arms back to his sides. "He didn't think justice was served. He thought I got off too easy. Maybe he was right."

"Clay, don't say that. Not ever." Was that how he thought of himself, as a worthless convict? A doleful melody flowed from the distant radio, and she tried to tune it out. She moved her hand to his and touched the "W," felt the slightly raised letter of the ink-injected skin. "The words aren't true. You know that, right?"

His pause was too long. "Sure."

She knew he was only appeasing her.

The sadness that came over her was so intense, she couldn't bear it. "You can't think that, not for a second. God made you. In His image and likeness." Her grip tightened on his hand. "He made you worth so much. So much that He died for you."

The corner of Clay's mouth tugged. "Now who's being the theologian?"

She flushed and loosened her grip, yet didn't take her hand away. She touched the tattoo again. Her mind played out the scene as she imagined what had happened in the warehouse after the film was turned off. Thugs holding Clay's arms down. The buzzing, sharp needle. How long had it taken? "Was it really painful?"

He didn't make her feel bad for asking the stupid question, just gave a short laugh. "It wasn't pleasant. Wasn't meant to be. But it could have been worse."

She refused to think how. And now Clay had to bear this stigma for life. Unless . . . "Can't you get it removed?"

His voice was doubtful. "It's inked pretty deep. It would take a lot of costly sessions, and I'd still have scars from that. Don't know that it would be worth it." He shrugged. "Maybe someday."

He eased his hands away. "So now you know."

Now I know. She dropped her hands to her lap.

"Promise me something, Charlene. Don't ever get a tattoo."

How could he take this so lightly? She watched as he began rewrapping the bandages. Anger at Grandfather boiled inside her. "He went way too far. This isn't okay—"

"It is." Clay finished securing the last bandage and leaned back on his arms. "It's over. I'm not locked up. Not in prison. If this is the worst I've got, I'm doing all right."

Prison. That dirty word again. She hated to think of him there, but she'd never asked, and tonight she felt like she could. Her one night stay in jail had been bad enough. But Clay—he'd spent twelve months and a day locked up. She couldn't imagine. "How bad was it?"

He was silent a moment. "Tolerable." A shadow flickered across his face. "Don't get me wrong, I wouldn't ever want to go back." He looked up at the stars. "But like I told you before, some good came out of it."

He crushed a soda can under his hand. "It took me losing everything to understand. When you lose it all, when you hit rock bottom, it's black and empty. Lonely. That's when I found out . . . I wasn't alone." He shot her a guarded look. "Does that make any sense?"

"It does."

His hands went into his pockets. There was a pause between songs on the radio, and her ears filled with a lively medley of chirping insects.

"You still pray the Rosary, Charlene?"

A change of subject? "Sometimes. Not every day anymore . . ."

"Remember those marks you scratched on the wall, down in the hole? To keep track of your prayers?"

She waited for her heart to seize at the memory, but it didn't. She found herself nodding calmly. "You called religion just another form of captivity. Didn't want anything to do with it."

"I didn't. For the longest time." He lowered his chin. "Then I found out what real captivity was."

She stayed very still.

"When Father Grady offered me this . . ." He drew his hand from his pocket to reveal a cheap plastic rosary, the black beads and crucifix held together with white cord. "I almost refused it. I wanted to throw it back in his face. But you don't get much to call your own in prison."

He ran the beads through his fingers. "Never even knew there was such a thing as a prison regulation rosary, but apparently there're people out there who take the time to make and donate these, some kind of prison ministry. Who would take the time to do that? For worthless convicts?"

She heard the smile in his voice, but still hated his using the expression. She studied the string of dark beads and thought it wouldn't be that difficult to put together. But she wasn't impressed by the somber color choice. "They couldn't have made it a little cheerier looking?"

"What would you suggest? Pink?" He chuckled. "Gotta be black to avoid gang colors."

The crucifix dangled and twirled in the breeze. He watched it for a moment. "Obviously, I could have prayed without this. Wasn't anything stopping me. But there wasn't much motivating me, either. Having something tangible, something to remind me . . . something to hold on to. It made the difference. Especially in that bereft world."

His fist closed over the beads. "I hope I won't ever take prayer for granted again. Or life, for that matter." He tucked the rosary back in his pocket.

"You always carry it with you?" She thought of her own rosary, the blue beads that had been with her through so much, now hidden away in her nightstand drawer.

"I do." He fingered one of their forgotten marshmallow sticks.

"And if you lose it?" Her gaze slid away from him.

"Father Grady could always hook me up with another one."

As if it could be so easily replaced. "You still talk to him? Still see him?"

"Sure. There's no one better to debate religion with. He set me up with all the best books, too."

"The Bible?"

"Of course."

"*Lives of the Saints?*"

"You bet. I even read about Saint Tarcisius. I'll still never like the name, but you were right, he was courageous." Clay cleared his throat. "And there's worse to be named after."

Something about his tone put her on alert. He broke the stick, then chucked half at the fire. It hit with a whack, and sparks flew. The flames popped, hissed, and settled. "Now I know why my dad—or whoever he was—picked my name. And why he always seemed hardest on me. He must have known the truth, or at least suspected, that I wasn't really his son." He tossed the rest of the stick at the fire, missing this time.

She edged a hair closer. Not really wanting to, she asked, "What do you mean?"

"He told me once . . . I can't recall what I did to tick him off, but he'd had a few drinks, so it wouldn't have taken much. He yanked me upside down and started jabbing at my face. Being the smart kid I was, I grabbed his finger and bit it.

"He dropped me to the ground and started mashing my head in the dirt. Man, I thought he was gonna scrub my face right off." He swiped a hand over his cheek. "I can still hear his exact words. 'You're dirt, boy, nothing but dirt. That's what clay is. That's all you've ever been and all you'll ever be, and don't you forget it.'"

She was stunned into silence. A single tear trembled on her lashes, afraid to fall.

Turning to her suddenly, Clay looked ashamed. "I shouldn't have told you that. I don't know why I did." He pressed the heels of his hands to his forehead. "Sorry. I'm sorry—"

"No, Clay, I'm sorry." Her words came out full of the swelling ache in her throat. She didn't know what she was doing. It was simply an instinct.

His sad face, all too often wounded and hurt, was right there, draped in conflicting shadows and firelight, mere inches from her.

How could she resist?

Reaching up, she cupped his chin in her hands, drew him to her, and kissed him.

Chapter Twenty-Seven

Clay broke away, knocking into soda cans, clattering them to the ground. "What are you doing?" Alarm flashed in his eyes.

Charlene couldn't believe what she'd just done, yet she shared none of his panic. Her lips still tingling, she absorbed the blissful moment. They'd melded together, and all had been right. But if he hadn't felt what she had . . .

Her eyes opened fully. Her hands fell to her sides.

She should tell him she was sorry, but she wasn't. Not yet.

She should be embarrassed, but she didn't feel that, either. She was still clinging to the memory of the kiss. And it overpowered everything else.

She started to speak, then stopped. She wasn't going to make excuses or apologize for something that had felt so right, still felt right.

It was what it was.

And apparently, Clay thought it was terrible.

He sat speechless, appalled by her bold behavior. A deep sadness returned, creeping over her heart.

"What's the matter with you?" he demanded, although she didn't think he really wanted an answer.

So she gave him one. "You kissed me back."

The distress in his eyes was swept away by outrage. "Don't ever do that again."

"Don't worry, I won't." She dropped to the ground. "If you don't."

"What? What's that supposed to mean?" He jumped off the tailgate. "Don't even try to blame that on me. That was all you—"

She spun around to face him with a glare, while hating herself for glaring at him. "It was *not* all me. You took me to this remote location, with the music, the fire, the moon and the stars. Like the perfect . . . something. And then feeding me your—your heart-breaking story. How can you not—" She turned to hide her brimming eyes. "Never mind."

How could he be so blind? What had felt so beautiful, now rankled, sour and ugly. She swiped away her tears. She just needed to be anywhere but here. Anywhere but with him.

He stalked to his truck and cut the music.

He had a point, though. What *had* she been thinking? She was engaged, and Clay was with Brook, having a baby with her, for crying out loud. Kissing him wasn't right. Not at all. It was as wrong as could be. Deep in her mind and soul, she knew that. The truth wrung her heart.

I really am messed up.

Whatever these feelings were that she had for him, they were dangerous. They'd crashed over her suddenly, but she suspected they'd been building stealthily for a very long time. Others could see what she couldn't—or didn't want to—face.

The memory of Brook's voice floated out of nowhere. *"Do you have feelings for him?"* She pictured the angel Clay had carved for her. The heart cupped in loving hands. He'd given his heart to Brook, and Charlene had given hers to Ben.

Glowering, Clay attacked the little fire, smothering it brutally, extinguishing all flame. Just like that, she'd have to stomp out any stray feelings she had for him. She'd had a hard enough time convincing him to be a friend; how could she think he would ever see her as more?

She would be satisfied with friends. She would.

And yet, he had returned the kiss. For the briefest, most thrilling moment, he had. She was sure of it.

But what did it matter now?

And why wouldn't he speak? He only cast her a cryptic, offended glance before they climbed into their respective vehicles. Their headlights burst on, and they drove, leaving the no-longer-enchanting spot behind, swallowed by the night. As if it had never existed. And it shouldn't have.

Soon they left the country road for the mind-numbing stretch of double lane highway that would take them back to Creekside.

She kept her radio off. No music could possibly pair with her heavyhearted thoughts. A knot of pain sat in her middle, hard and palpable.

Mile upon mile she drove, till there was nothing to do but squeeze out a prayer past her stiff, cold soul. A prayer that Clay would find peace and happiness, even . . . even though it couldn't be with her.

They parted ways when he turned onto the street that led to Sam's, and she continued on to her apartment.

She slid into her spot beside Brook's car. She couldn't bear the thought of rehashing the day with her, though technically she brought good news of Clay's return. She hoped Brook was sleeping. As she opened her door, she heard her phone chime, muffled in her purse.

Could it be Clay? Did she want it to be? Part of her leapt with hope. She dug it out and thumbed the answer button without checking the screen.

In her peripheral vision, she barely noted the bounce of headlights as a vehicle turned into the lot.

"Charlene, something terrible happened."

She floundered to identify the woman's strained voice on her phone, realizing it was Ben's mom just as the woman choked on her words. "Someone broke in. When Ben was here alone."

Alarmed, Charlene tried to pry more details out of her. Infuriatingly, Mrs. Jorgensen only said, "You need to come right away. I have to go." She hung up.

Charlene gaped at the "Call Ended" screen and tried to process Mrs. Jorgensen's words. She hadn't even said if Ben was okay. But surely he was. She would have said if he wasn't. No, she would have said if he *was*, and she hadn't—

The sound of approaching footsteps made her look up.

"Hey," Clay said from several feet away. He cleared his throat, but his voice still came out rough, ragged like his expression. "I didn't want to leave things like—" His words cut off and his focus shifted. He crossed to her side in two strides, a hand going to her arm. "What's wrong?"

Lips compressed, she gave a little shake of her head. *Not now.* He'd come back, but she couldn't do this now. "It's Ben." She slipped back into her car. "Something happened. Something bad. I have to go to him."

Clay released her arm. His disconcerted expression said, *What was I thinking?* "Yeah, of course. Go. I hope he's all right."

She put her hand on the door and he backed up.

"I just wanted to make sure you got home okay. That's all. Drive safe." With an abrupt up-then-down of his hand—a lame attempt at a wave—he headed back to his truck.

After pulling out onto the road, she glanced in her rearview mirror and saw his silhouette just standing there, watching her as she left.

Ripping her gaze away, she aimed for the highway, blinking rapidly. She had another long, lonely drive ahead of her.

No, I'm not really alone.

She made a shaky sign of the cross and began to pray.

A police car hunkered in Ben's driveway, setting Charlene's heart to a discordant beat. It was one in the morning, and all the house lights blazed.

She sprinted to the door. Ben's mom let her in, no judgment in her eyes, only relief at seeing her.

"He's okay, right?" Charlene asked, before her jaw dropped at the sight of a brutally banged up wheelchair. Ben's wheelchair. It looked as though it had tumbled down a flight of stairs. And he wasn't in it.

Something like a squeak escaped her throat.

"It's all right." Mrs. Jorgensen patted her arm. "It's not what it looks like. He's okay, but he's been asking for you so urgently. He'll tell you everything. Thanks for coming as fast as you did." She took her arm and hurried her past the disturbing wheelchair, down the hall, and to Ben's room.

A silver-haired officer was just closing his notebook. With a nod at her, he left the room with Ben's mom and dad.

Once the door closed, she faced Ben, who sat propped up in his bed. He didn't look hurt. No cuts or bruises, but there was something in his eyes that shook her. "What happened?"

The moment she stepped close enough, Ben's arms seized her with a desperate strength, tan arms that looked more muscular than ever. His lips landed on hers, and she couldn't breathe.

Nothing like kissing Clay. The thought slammed into her. She hurled it away, powered by shame and the fear that Ben would somehow know she'd betrayed him.

He released her at last and she gasped a quick breath.

His eyes drank her in. "Good to know I can still make you blush." His hand remained on her arm as she dropped into a bedside chair. "You've got to forgive me, Charlene. For the Fourth of July. I know I was way out of line and—"

"No, Ben, you were—" *Say it. Say he was right.* It was the perfect time to confess, but cowardice shushed her. She let him take over. The earnestness in his face was too powerful.

"I thought I was going to die, and all I could think was, I didn't want things left like that between us. Let's make things right." He squeezed her hands. "I can't lose you. Not for anything. I couldn't stand it. I'll do what it takes, whatever it takes to keep you. Please tell me you forgive me."

She rushed to assure him. "I do. It's already forgotten. I'm just so glad you're all right. When I saw your wheelchair . . ." She shuddered. "What happened?"

He began the story in animated detail, complete with hand gestures. He'd been alone in the house. His mom and dad were out on their monthly "date night," and Lucy was at a sleepover. He had just fallen asleep when the sound of breaking glass woke him.

"I called out, thinking it was my mom and dad. I switched on my light. There was no answer, but I heard noises, doors opening and closing, footsteps coming down the hall. Just as I reached my phone, someone burst in here and grabbed it. He was wearing all black. Black mask, black gloves. The last thing I saw before he crashed my lamp over and the lights went out, was the sledgehammer in his hands. I expected it to come crashing down on me at any second."

His voice lowered. "I thought I was dead."

Her hand went to her throat. A sledgehammer. Nails? Was he back? But why here, attacking Ben? Wasn't Clay the one—

"I kept asking what he wanted," Ben continued, "but he never said anything."

"How big was he? Really big?"

He gave her a quizzical look. "No, just average, but strong enough to slam that hammer and pulverize my chair."

Just average? Then it couldn't be Nails. She felt a small measure of relief.

"My ears are still ringing from the noise." He put a hand to his head. "It felt like forever, but it was actually over pretty quick. When he left, I kept expecting him to come back, to do something worse. All I could do was wait in the dark till my parents got home. I mean, I could have dropped out of bed and crawled with my arms. I thought about it, but what good would that have done? It was crazy." He shook his head. "Just major crazy.

"I mean, what was the point, you know? Break in, shake me up, destroy my chair? If someone was mad enough to do all that, why didn't they hurt me?"

She caught her bottom lip between her teeth. "I don't think it's you they're mad at." She had to say it. "I think it's me. I think they were trying to hurt me, through you." She looked down at her finger, at her "cursed" knife scar, and her hair fell in her face.

Ben reached out and tucked a curl behind her ear. "I don't know. Maybe. But even if that's true . . . that's not going to keep me from you. I don't want you to worry about it. The police will catch him."

Then at the very least, they'd need to talk to her. Again. "This is why I should stay away . . ." She sighed. "But even that's not working." She bet once Ben's family realized the attack was her fault, they'd turn cool to her. And she wouldn't blame them at all.

She wasn't worthy of Ben and his adulation anyway. She never had been. But now, after kissing Clay, guilt was a screwdriver twisting deeper in her gut with each endearment from Ben's lips.

Confess, she exhorted herself. But Ben had already been through too much. Yes, he was remarkably strong and resilient, but she knew her betrayal would crush him. He'd rather endure another intruder, she was sure, than know her lips hadn't been true to his. She couldn't bear to tell him.

It would never happen again, she reasoned, and it wasn't so terrible—it wasn't like they were married yet, thankfully.

But she had to give him something. It was the least she could do.

"I decided to quit working at the woodshop." Intertwining her fingers with his, she went on before she could change her mind. "And I promise I'll never see Clay again."

Charlene's pledge didn't make Ben as happy as if she'd decided to move back to Woodfield, but it came close. She also agreed to stay with him a few days if his mom allowed it.

Surprisingly, she did. So Charlene slept in the guest room and she and Ben filled their days with wedding plans, board games, TV, and—thanks to the new wheelchair his dad procured the very next day—they went for "walks" together. They also went to church, where she went to confession with a heavy heart and left with her soul cleansed and renewed, ready to face life with a fresh start.

When she called Sam to give him her resignation, he said he was sorry to see her go. She couldn't read his voice, but she hoped he and Clay had had a good long talk and were well on their way to working things out, but she didn't ask; and, of course, Sam didn't volunteer the information. He thanked her sincerely for the months she'd been there. "It made a difference, and we're back on our feet now."

His last words made her wince as she thought of Ben. He wasn't making any more progress, and he seriously doubted he'd ever be back on his feet.

She wept tears over that, late at night, but she didn't give up praying for a miracle.

———

Back in Creekside, Charlene went job-hunting and ended up with a position at Fannie's Fabrics. She found she missed the smell of sawdust and varnish, but the agreeable scent of crisp new cotton compensated somewhat. And Fannie was a delightful, grandmotherly woman, always trying to interest her in knitting, crocheting, quilting, and crafting.

Charlene signed up for online classes to continue working toward her library science degree. Then, because she couldn't get the idea out of her head, she researched online and ended up ordering a rosary making kit, one with black plastic beads and crucifixes.

The days passed, the heat waves of August gave way to the glowing colors of autumn, and Brook's pregnancy began to show, her belly swelling like a little October pumpkin.

While they'd settled into a routine, it was slightly strange being roommates. For the most part, they avoided each other. Brook's cheeks became rosier and she looked content and healthy. Occasionally, Charlene glimpsed Clay picking her up in his truck outside the apartment, but he never came inside. She wondered if he ever brought her tailgating under the stars.

At last, she tucked the little wooden bench carving away in the back of a drawer, behind the towel she'd brought to the beach that warm day so long ago.

The best thing about the passage of time was that her hair was growing. Little by little, but it was something.

———

Hangers clicked together as the woman's fingers glided over the soft clothes, rifling through, imagining, coveting. So many things, so many beautiful things for her little one, if she only had the money. Stores like this taunted, with their jacked-up prices and ludicrous lists of "essentials" that made having a baby rank up there with impossible privileges of the rich and famous.

Of course, most first-time moms were at least granted the luxury of a baby shower.

But not her.

She sniffed.

She had no family to throw her one. No true friends, either. No one cared enough. Not even her man.

Pain stabbed. The baby punched.

Her man thought he could just deny the truth. But she didn't blame him. He was bewitched by the conniving girl.

No matter. He'd have to face the truth soon enough. They both would.

Paternity tests don't lie.

Chapter Twenty-Eight

"Exculpate? That's not a word," Ben scoffed when Charlene finished playing her Scrabble tiles.

"So bring on the dictionary."

Ben pulled out his phone and searched online. "'Exculpate. To clear from a charge of guilt or fault; vindicate.'" He exhaled and spread his hands. "How do you know this stuff?"

She shrugged. "I read a lot."

"You retain a lot."

"Should have known better than to challenge me," she teased. "My turn again." She studied her letter rack.

"Exculpate," Ben muttered, shaking his head.

After she won the game, she began dropping tiles back in the pouch. "I've been thinking."

When she paused, he urged, "About . . . ?"

"About . . . maybe moving back."

His eyes lit up. "Yeah?" His eagerness was evident, and so was his hesitance as his hand stilled, no longer collecting tiles. She could tell he didn't want to push her too hard.

Her heart softened. "I was thinking maybe you could help me look for a place, if you want."

"Of course I want." He moved closer and kissed her.

She tried to relax, but her lips refused. She didn't enjoy Ben's kisses any more. She wanted to, but every time his lips touched hers, guilt and unworthiness battered her heart. *Tell him, tell him,* had become a constant, internal chant.

She drew back and pulled in a deep breath. "I have to tell you something."

He rested his forehead on hers, his skin warm. Eyes clear and undisturbed.

She eased away and wiped her damp palms along the fabric of her skirt. "It's about that night, back in July . . . when you were attacked."

His smile faded and his eyes clouded. "Yeah? What about it?"

"I was with Clay that night. And I kissed him."

Ben's face reacted with the barest twitch of a muscle. He waited in silence, as if expecting her to detract the words. As if she were pulling a tasteless prank.

"I'm sorry," she went on. "I shouldn't have done it. I don't know what I was thinking. But nothing else happened, I promise, and—"

"Get out."

She startled as Ben pushed fiercely from the table and wheeled to the front door. She hurried after him. "Ben, please. I'm so sorry. It was so wrong of me. I know that."

His neck muscles pulled and his nostrils flared. He opened the door. "Get. Out."

Her lip trembling, she turned and did as he said.

———

A lonely week later, her phone vibrated on her nightstand. She snatched it up, but saw it wasn't Ben responding to her numerous messages. It was his mom.

Doubting her wisdom, she accepted the call. "Hello?"

"Charlene?" Mrs. Jorgensen's voice was low, as if she didn't want to be overheard. "What happened between you two? Ben isn't speaking and he's barely come out of his room. I'm going crazy with worry. Is the wedding off?"

"I don't know." Charlene pinched a corner of her shirt and worked it, twisting and pulling. "It's up to Ben."

"You need to fix this."

"He doesn't want to talk to me."

"Did you cheat on him?"

Charlene dropped onto her bed. Her eyes scanned the ceiling as she fumbled for words. "I can't talk about this with you. This is between me and Ben."

A loud, disgusted sniff hit her ears. "You don't deserve him. You never have." Mrs. Jorgensen hung up.

———

On a late October morning two weeks later, Charlene crossed paths with Brook as she snagged breakfast in the kitchen.

With one hand, Brook held a bagel to her mouth, but it paused as her other hand went to rest on the curve of her shirt stretched tight over her belly. "The baby's moving."

"Really? Wow, did that just start?" Charlene asked to be polite.

Brook had never actually announced the pregnancy, making the situation awkward. If she hadn't overheard her informing her ex-boyfriend on the Fourth of July, Charlene would have naïvely thought Brook was merely growing plump, till the pregnancy became obvious. Not that she owed her any explanation. But it felt odd, like an elephant in the room that they silently agreed not to speak of.

And now, out of nowhere, Brook was.

"Oh no, the baby's been moving for months, but the kicks are much stronger now. Here, feel right here."

Not knowing how to avoid it, Charlene set down her yogurt, hesitantly laid her hand flat on the side of Brook's belly, and waited.

She felt nothing. Then suddenly—*bump!*—a little hand or foot socked her. It was an uncanny feeling, and she almost flinched. "Wow." She meant it this time. "That's amazing."

Her hand lingered for a few more punches or kicks. She couldn't help wondering if the baby was a little girl or boy. A little Brook or—

"You haven't asked if Clay's the father," Brook said quietly. "I would have thought that would have been your first question when you realized I was pregnant. But you never asked."

Charlene's hand retreated. "I figured you'd tell me . . . if you wanted to." A dreadful anticipation clutched her as she awaited Brook's response, but she merely patted her belly and offered a tiny, ambiguous smile before assuring her, "Clay's going to be a wonderful father."

With a slight nod, Charlene dropped her spoon in the sink, tossed her yogurt, grabbed her purse, and left. She had the day off, but no plans. Missing Ben, she sat in her car and wondered where to go.

Her phone chimed. Since she'd given up on Ben calling, she took her time picking it up. When she saw it was him, she whipped the phone to her ear, heart hammering. "Ben."

"I forgive you."

She dropped her head and stared at her lap. "Thank you," she whispered. "I'm so sorry."

"I don't know why, but I can't stay mad at you."

She held her breath.

"I miss you," he added.

"I miss you, too."

"We're gonna make this work."

Tension slid from her neck and shoulders. "We will. I'm so sorry and—"

"No, I don't want any more apologies or explanations. Let's forget it ever happened."

She put a fingernail to her lips and almost nibbled. "So . . . I'm exculpated?"

Silence for two beats, then a short laugh. "Yeah, you're exculpated. And happy birthday, by the way."

Her lips quirked. "Thanks."

"Got plans?"

She stared out at the emaciated trees lining the parking lot, at rusty leaves falling to the pavement. "No."

"You do now."

———

She'd been given a second chance she felt she didn't deserve, and the day was almost perfect. Ben crammed it with things he thought she'd enjoy—a museum tour, a trip to an apple orchard, a fancy restaurant dinner—but between them all, Charlene checked her phone repeatedly and almost keyed Max's number. They hadn't talked since she'd hung up on him back in July.

As a twin, she couldn't feel right on her birthday without Max being part of it. For as long as she could remember, it had always been a joint event. Surely, today he would call.

It wasn't like Max to hold a grudge, but even if she did owe him an apology, she figured he also owed her one for harassing her about her engagement. She stared at her phone but refused to make the call. She pictured him doing the same. Like they were locked in some ridiculous silent standoff that just might last till they were old and gray.

At the restaurant, she slipped her phone back in her purse as a waitress set down a slice of cake bearing a flickering candle. To Charlene's relief, the woman moved away without any "happy birthday" singing spectacle. This restaurant was too classy to do something like that. Thank goodness for Ben's choice. She smiled at him. He knew her so well.

After the cake, he passed her a square package. She unwrapped the gift, knowing it was too large to be a ring box, which was what she had half suspected he might give her.

Inside sat a heart-shaped silver box with her initials engraved on the top. A jewelry box. She lifted it and opened it very, very slowly.

No ring nestled on the black velvet lining.

In fact, nothing at all lay inside. Mild surprise, but no disappointment, touched her.

"There's a little winder thing on the bottom," Ben pointed out. "It plays a song."

Tilting the box, she cranked the petite golden knob. As the melody began tinkling out sweetly, she felt her eyes shine as she thanked him. This would be the perfect place to keep her mother's pink pearl necklace—if she ever got it back.

Her ears prickled and a bad feeling swept over her. "What song is this?" Her fingers pressed tight to the cold metal. "Is it . . ."

Ben nodded, looking very pleased with himself. "That's right. 'Glory of Love.' You remember that first time I finally convinced you to come over to my house and we ended up watching *The Karate Kid* together?"

She remembered. She'd enjoyed the movie, but not the theme song. It wasn't his fault; he had no way of knowing. Really, it was a beautiful song. Wonderful. She simply had a tendency to lug senseless emotional baggage.

"This song makes me think of you," he said.

Her heart constricted. Oh, how he would hate it if he knew this song made her think of Abner. And Clay. How it had been playing in the background during captivity . . .

She choked on her words. "That's so thoughtful." *It is. I'm just messed up.* She lowered her eyes, pretending to study the jewelry box's lovely etched details.

She wouldn't ever play the music again, that's all. It was that simple.

She would be okay.

Later that evening, Ben and Charlene streamed a movie to the widescreen in the Jorgensens' living room, but it wasn't very entertaining. Halfway through, Ben dozed off and Charlene's eyes strayed to the family computer in the corner of the room. She eased herself from the sofa and sat down at the keyboard, knowing Ben wouldn't mind.

If nothing else, she'd get an update on Max's life by checking his website. In a few clicks, she was there. A flashy headshot of Max appeared prominently at the top of the homepage. Below this was a wide-shot of him performing on stage. She clicked on "latest news," then "show times." He was slated to perform an all-new trick that promised to be his most daring and death-defying yet, to be unveiled in a February show.

She hovered the pointer over the option to "buy tickets now." His shows often sold out fast. She checked the date and availability, working her tongue over her teeth. Then she pulled out her credit card and bought a ticket.

Happy Birthday to me.

Now she would have to go see him.

She was just about to close the window, when, on a sudden whim, she typed in an image search for "snake handled knife curse." Countless irrelevant pictures popped up. One of them, though, looked like Abner's knife. She clicked on it and was transported to a black page with a blood red heading that read, "Satanic Museum."

She should have closed the page right there, at the ominous, sick feeling traveling from her fingers to her toes and whirling in the pit of her stomach. But she didn't.

On the top of the screen, black candles burned beside an ugly horned goat head. Her eyes, however, were captured by the picture of the knife. The site referred to it as an "athame," otherwise known as a ceremonial dagger.

She read the article (if it could it be called an article and not utter rubbish), the claim of the curse, and it was all as Horace had described.

Then she came across something he hadn't expounded on:

> *Those who have been sliced by the black snake-handled athame, are marked by Satan as his own. The only escape from the damning curse is a sacrifice—some may say murder. Very specific conditions must be met:*
>
> *One must obtain and use the very same athame with which they were cut with.*
>
> *If one who bears the scar of Satan's athame is able to locate another soul, likewise scarred, he or she must use the knife and stab them in the heart while calling on Satan's mercy with the words, "Deliver me, O Mighty Lord Satan from this, your almighty curse."*
>
> *Only then can one hope to appease the wrath of Satan.*

Her hand froze on the keyboard, repulsed. Save yourself from hell by murdering someone? Twisted logic from the Father of Lies. Her eyes returned to the picture of the knife. At the bottom of the web page, the site noted that the Satanic Museum was working on obtaining the authentic snake-handled athame. Perhaps, then, Horace worked for—or even owned—this museum. She could certainly picture him in such an appalling line of work.

Locating the "about" tab, she clicked it. Skimming the screen, she learned that the museum was located in a neighboring state—and that the museum had been growing its collection for thirty years under dedicated curator Horace Cain.

As her mouth grimaced, a ghastly thought emerged like a snake from a hole. What if Horace wanted the knife for more than just museum display? What if . . . what if he believed he was one of the cursed, and he was looking to break the curse? She strained her memory to see if she could recall noticing any scar-like mark on Horace, but she couldn't.

Still, if he seriously believed this nonsense and wanted to free himself from the curse, he might think of her, or Clay, as a victim to sacrifice.

She swallowed, then swallowed again, telling herself her theory was farfetched.

But that didn't make her thoughts any less disturbing.

Chapter Twenty-Nine

"*What* are you looking at?"

Charlene jumped guiltily, bumping her knees against the desk and quickly clicking the satanic window closed. Engrossed as she'd been, she hadn't heard anyone approach. Now she turned to see Lucy and her accusatory eyes over her shoulder.

The girl crossed her arms. "If I tell my mom you were looking at evil stuff on our computer, she'll freak. Like, big time. Especially if she knows you let me see it." She leaned in closer, craning her neck as if she could still glimpse something evil on the standard home screen. "What was that, like devils and spells and stuff?"

"Lucy, please." Charlene propelled herself away from the computer by means of the rolling chair. "I was just doing some research. On the history of something, that's all. Purely a fact-finding mission, nothing to worry your mom about. Trust me, okay?"

Lucy tilted her head. "You're really not as nice as you pretend to be." With a flip of her hair, she turned and left the room.

The corners of Charlene's mouth turned down. She missed the cute, innocent little girl that Lucy used to be only a few brief years ago. Wilting into herself a bit, Charlene turned off the monitor, brushed a kiss to Ben's cheek, tucked a blanket around him, and left for Creekside.

For someone prone to nightmares, the website had been a terrible thing to visit, but she couldn't help feeling grateful for what she'd learned. If she ever caught sight of Horace again, now she'd know to run.

As an antidote to the taint of malevolence now in her mind, she prayed St. Michael's prayer, invoking the warrior angel's protection.

Call Clay. Warn him.

The thought appeared from nowhere, but couldn't be brushed away. Despite her promise to Ben, it was only right to let Clay know what she'd discovered about Horace and the knife. She dug out her phone.

Calling him isn't seeing him.

But he didn't answer. She drove ten more minutes and tried again. He still didn't pick up. She continued this pattern all the way home.

She let herself into her apartment with a heavy weariness, not near as alert as she should have been. As she clunked her keys on the kitchen counter, she caught a reflection of movement in the microwave door. "Hey, Brook," she mumbled, about to call Clay one last time.

"Hey."

At the unmistakable, hard masculine voice, her head whipped up, her wide eyes landing on none other than Nails.

He smirked. "Long time no see."

She made a petrified dash for the door, but he cut her off all too easily. He grabbed her close, squeezing her arms, bruising them as he spoke into her ear. "I've got a real special job lined up, sweetie. One last perfect heist before I leave the country for good, and I need your help."

―――

Her apartment intercom buzzed.

Nails shot Charlene a look. "Expecting someone?"

She gulped. "No."

"Then we ignore it."

Several minutes later, as she ran ChapStick nervously over her lips and Nails quietly detailed what was expected of her to help pull off his grand scheme, a sharp knock interrupted.

His gun jammed into her side and he whispered, "Not a word." He hustled her to the door and checked the peephole. Cursed quietly. "Get rid of him. Make him suspicious and he's dead."

Nails cracked the door, keeping a firm grasp on her left arm as he stayed hidden and ready behind the door.

Hyperconscious of the gun, she swallowed and willed her voice steady, willed color back into her face. She couldn't fail. She couldn't.

"Clay."

"Hey." He already looked too concerned. "I couldn't get ahold of Brook all evening. Then I saw you tried calling me a bunch of times, and you didn't answer when I called back."

Because Nails took my phone.

"So I thought I'd swing by and check if everything's okay." His eyes locked on hers. "Is it?"

Nails's fingers dug deep in her arm. She broke eye contact and clenched her teeth. "We're fine."

Clay's brow dipped, unconvinced. "Why didn't you answer the intercom?"

"Did you buzz?" She yawned. "I was sleeping. How'd you get in the building?"

"Came in behind someone." He glanced down the hall. "So you slept through the buzzer but you heard my knock?"

She forced out a breath through her teeth. *Don't do this, Clay. Go away. For your own sake, go away.*

"Why'd you call?" he persisted.

Why indeed? Her petrified mind wouldn't dredge up the reason. No time to think. *Tell him something. Anything.* "I had a nightmare."

Head tilting slightly, he seemed to consider that. "Why not call Ben?"

She blinked. Scrounged for an answer. "I tried him first. He didn't answer." Her gaze wavered from Clay's scrutiny. "I needed someone to talk to. Anyone."

"Where's Brook?"

A very good question. But for her sake and the baby's, she lied again. "She's sleeping. I won't wake her. You know how much she needs her rest."

"Right." Clay paused. He tried to peer past her into the apartment. "Come on, Charlene. Talk to me." His voice turned gruff. "What's really going on?"

Fix this, ordered Nails's jabbing gun.

"I told you, it was just a nightmare."

"Then let's talk about it. Can I come in?" He took a step forward.

"No!" She pressed the door and felt her face blanch. "I don't want to talk about it. I'm over it."

His face tensed. "I don't like how you look."

"That's the nicest line I've ever heard."

"Cut it out. Tell me what's wrong."

You're right, Sam. He's dang stubborn.

She drew herself up and narrowed her eyes. Forced them to sizzle. "The only thing wrong here is you. Thinking you can come here in the middle of the night and give me the third degree." She stunned herself at how cold her words sounded. "Go away."

As she closed the door, his hand shoved it open. She stumbled back, horrified as he pushed his way in.

Nails threw the door shut and brandished his gun. "Not a smart move, Cissy."

Clay jolted, then froze.

"You must have a death wish." Nails locked the bolt. "How's the jaw?"

The thunderous expression on Clay's face drew weak words from Charlene. "I'm sorry. You should have left—"

"Shut up and sit." Nails indicated a chair with a thrust of his chin. Obeying, she crossed to the living room and sank down.

To Clay, Nails said, "Hands on the wall." The gun drilled his back. "Do it."

He frisked Clay, found the black rosary, and flung it to the floor. "Still a little church boy, I see." Then he found Clay's pocketknife. As he took it, Clay went for his gun. Nails immediately cracked him on the back, and he went down.

Nails yanked him up, shoved him to the wall with a beefy forearm, and pressed the gun barrel to his neck. "Stupid, stupid kid. I was generous last time. And the time before that. I let you live."

Clay's throat moved.

"I gave you a chance to be a part of this, the job we talked about way back in the joint, but you didn't want in." Nails's saliva sprayed Clay's grimacing face. "You lost your chance, and now . . . now you're nothin' but in the way."

Charlene heard a click as Nails cocked the gun. Her heart stopped. "No, please. Don't!"

"Your fault, girl." Nails's gaze never left Clay. "You didn't keep him away. I warned you."

Clay's eyes fixated on the gun. Sweat beaded his brow.

She fought for breath. "If you kill him, you'll never get into the mansion. I won't help you. I won't!"

"Oh, but you will. I don't need Cissy for leverage. We already went over this. I've got one of my buddies with Brook. One word from me, and he'll blow her pretty brains out. Cissy here knows the kind of guys who work for me, don't you?" The gun pushed his throat, and Clay sucked air. "There'll be no hesitation, no matter how lovely or pregnant your friend is."

Clay's fists balled. A vein pounded in his temple.

"I won't help you if you kill him," she repeated in desperation. "But if you let him live, I'll do exactly what you say. Please." Her voice faltered. "Please, Lance."

He shot her a look that made her press herself as far back into the chair as possible. She didn't know why she'd called him that. Maybe because it sounded more human. And that's what she needed him to be. So he could find a speck of compassion. But his look told her she should have kept her mouth shut.

Clay picked that moment to gamble. He threw himself to the side, then dove for Nails's gun arm. With a curse, Nails wrestled him to the ground and kicked him a couple times. "Give it up, kid." Nails loomed over him, brandishing the gun like he wanted nothing more than to shoot him, and she lost all hope.

But her tongue moved, and she pleaded again. "Please, Lance."

To her amazement, he thrust the gun in his pants and pulled something from his pocket. "More trouble than you're worth," he muttered, crouching down and wrenching Clay's arms behind his back and zip tying his wrists. Such thin, laughably dinky looking pieces of plastic, but so effective. Then he bound Clay's ankles before forcing his feet to meet his hands. With one more zip tie, he cinched Clay's ankles to his wrists.

Nails swiped a dish towel from the kitchen as Clay groaned, opened his eyes, and cursed. "If you hurt her—"

"I'll do whatever I want." Nails crammed the towel in Clay's mouth, wound a strip of duct tape around his face to keep the gag in, then hauled him to the closet, where he shoved him in among the boots and broom and vacuum cleaner and slid the door closed.

Crossing his arms, Nails strode to her side, kicking Clay's rosary out of sight. "There now, happy?" He looked like he expected an answer.

"Not happy," she managed around a lump in her throat. "But grateful."

"You should be. Now it's time for you to make good on your end of the deal." He whipped out his gun and leveled it at her. "Let's go visit Gramps."

Charlene drove her car. Nails sat in the passenger seat, his gun aimed at her the entire ride.

He said, "You might not want to hit any potholes if you can help it."

Each minute of the drive felt like an hour.

Glancing at him, she caught a very strange expression on his face. A pensive blend of savage hunger and pleasure. Suppressing a shudder, she knew she didn't want to know what he was thinking.

———

He'd come close. So close.

He'd imagined himself squeezing the trigger, the blast, the blood. The kid's expression, the scream.

She'd saved him. With that voice. Those words. So like Beth. How often had she suckered him in with those same words?

"Please, Lance. Could you open this jar for me? Oh, and could you reach that box on the top shelf?"

"Please, Lance. Will you help me mop the floor?"

"The little kids want you to play hide and seek with them. Please, Lance."

It had been forever since anyone had called him Lance.

He shifted in his seat and steadied the gun, kept it trained on the girl. He didn't intend to shoot her. But guns talked. They put the fear of God into people like no priest ever could, no matter how much fire and brimstone they spouted. Guns got things done.

He'd never killed before, but he'd always been willing to, if it came to it. And he'd always been curious, but that was never quite enough. Too risky. Although he'd come close with that one CO. With his bare hands. If the other COs hadn't shown up when they did . . .

But when he'd held the gun on Cissy, drilled to his neck, hard metal to pliable skin, it was a feeling like no other. More than the usual intoxication of power, tonight he'd had a craving to destroy. He hated the kid with a passion, and wasn't sure why. Normally, he didn't feel anything. He'd trained himself not to. Anger was okay, but this was more than anger. More primal. Something about the kid and his attitude, his piousness, needed obliterating.

He could only hold out so long, he realized.

If Cissy ever crossed him again, he wasn't going to be able to resist.

———

Charlene didn't know where her audacity came from, but she heard herself speaking. "I want my necklace back. The pink pearls. You have no idea how much they mean to me. Please, it was my mother's necklace. It's all I have left of her."

"Ain't that sweet." Nails didn't look at her. "Shut up and drive."

At last, there it was: Grandfather's grand estate, regal, gated, and guarded. One misstep or misplaced word, and Brook and her baby would die. Charlene didn't need a reminder. She planned to follow Nails's plan to the letter.

At the gate, she buzzed the guard.

"Who is it?" he asked through the intercom.

"Charlene Perigard and a friend, to see my grandfather on a very urgent matter."

Knowing how she'd last fled here, it was suspicious that she was now asking for entry. What would she do if Grandfather refused? She swallowed. Nails would be far from happy, and someone would pay.

To her relief, the gates swung open, enabling her to proceed up the driveway.

Nails grinned. "One last thing I should mention. We're on a time constraint. If for any reason my buddy doesn't hear from me with the all clear by four a.m., it's buh-bye Brookie. And then I'll send him over to work on Cissy."

Her teeth clenched together. *Lord, help us.*

Her heart went out to Brook, wherever she was, with an agonizing sympathy. As one who'd been kidnapped, Charlene wouldn't wish the cruel experience on anyone. To save Brook and her unborn baby, this robbery had to be a success. Money was expendable; lives were not.

She hoped Grandfather would see it that way.

Heaving a bracing breath, she parked at the top of the drive. Nails followed her out of the car, his gun hidden, but still ready. He planted himself behind her at the towering front door.

Her old nemesis, bulky bodyguard Frank, opened the door with an assessing gaze, but he stepped aside. "Follow me."

Nostrils flared, Nails strode in with a powerful, in-charge air. When Frank stopped outside the sealed doors of Grandfather's office, about to knock, Nails drew out a Taser and zapped him. He went down in a stiff, stunned heap on the marble tile. In a second, Nails drew his gun. He threw zip ties to Charlene. "Cinch him up, ankles and wrists. Good and tight." He watched her do the job, and she felt like a criminal-in-training.

Nails smiled. "Show time."

She swung the office doors wide and led the way into Grandfather's spacious, book-lined lair. Grandfather sat not at his desk, but in a brown leather chair, a thick robe over his pajamas, his hands blue-veined talons on the arm rests. "What have you gotten me out of bed for at this ungodly hour, Charlene, and who—"

His eyes went wide as Nails drew both guns.

"Open your safe, Gramps." Nails flashed a toothy grin.

Grandfather sputtered and turned five shades of tomato red. "Frank!"

"Pointless," Nails remarked.

Grandfather leapt to his slippered feet. Snarling, he turned to Charlene. "What's the meaning of all this? Why'd you bring this scum here? What's the matter with you, always taking up with lowlife convicts . . ." as he chastised her, he stealthily backed up to his desk.

"Stop right there, old man," Nails ordered, wagging his firearm. "Any alarm you plan to trip, or gun you plan to grab, I recommend against it. 'Less you like the idea of being riddled full of lead."

Nails thrust his chin at her. "Tie Gramps up. Wrists and ankles." He tucked one gun away and tossed her two zip ties. Apparently, he had a limitless supply.

Thinking of Brook and her baby, she followed orders and plucked up the thin plastic strips. While Grandfather blustered, she secured him to his rolling desk chair.

Nails began to spin him around tauntingly so that his wispy gray hair zinged out by centrifugal force.

"Stop it," she said, disgusted. "That's not necessary. Just get what you came for and leave."

"Old man's gotta tell me where the safe is, first. Then the combination. Just tell me what I need, Gramps, and I'll stop the ride."

"Never!" Grandfather's skin took on an increasingly sick gray hue.

Nails remained amused for less than a minute. "My patience is wearing thin, old man. Ready to talk yet?"

"When hell freezes over. With you in it."

"Stubborn old geezer." Nails threw back his shoulders and sent the chair, with Grandfather in it, careening across the floor. It smashed into the wall, and Grandfather let out an *Oof.*

"Bet that felt good on your old bones, didn't it? I've got lots more where that came from." A flicker of thought shadowed Nails's brow. "Or . . ."

He turned to Charlene. "I could use the method that's always the most effective. Damsel in distress."

She tried to scurry from his grasp, but he caught her in two swift steps. An arm bear-hugged her upper body, pinning her arms to her sides. He smelled of decay and sweat.

"Talk, Gramps." Nails pressed the cold gun barrel to her temple.

Her heart crashed against her ribs. Her brain screamed with panic as adrenalin ricocheted through her. If she'd learned anything from her kidnapping experience years ago, it was that Grandfather would not come through for her when it mattered the most.

I'm as good as dead.

She closed her eyes, forcing a stream of tears down her cheeks. Twenty-three years of life. Exactly. That was all she was going to get. A prayer on her lips, she prepared to be blown apart.

She heard a growling noise that turned into Grandfather's angry voice. "The fourth bookshelf on the east wall, behind the row of encyclopedias. That's where it is. The combination is . . ."

Her mind muted his words with a drone of sheer relief as Nails released her. He prodded her forward, the gun now on her back, a slightly less frightening spot. Weak kneed, she moved to follow the directions.

Her hands moved mechanically, tipping books from the shelf, punching in the combination, opening the safe, revealing a bountiful, astonishing stash of thick wads of cash.

"Get it all." Nails pulled a folded canvas bag from within his coat and threw it at her. It flopped open to a huge size. Greed dripping from his gaze, he watched her fill the bag, hurrying her with threats. The satisfaction on his face was sickening, yet she clung to the hope that this entire episode was almost over.

She leaned into the safe. "That's all of it." A glimpse of something shiny pulled her eyes upward, where she spotted a flash drive taped to the roof of the safe. Squinting, she made out the word "Justice" written on a tiny label.

The police just might be interested in this, she realized. If she ever got the chance to give it to them. She swiped the drive and palmed it as she backed out of the safe.

Nails didn't give her a second glance, merely grabbed the bloated bag and surveyed the safe to confirm it was empty. As he did so, she slipped the flash drive in her pocket.

After swiftly zip tying her to the foot of a leather sofa, he shook the money bag in Grandfather's face. "Thanks, Gramps." He looked at her. "And thanks for your cooperation. Couldn't have done it without you."

"You'll let Brook go now?" she called after him.

He grinned and snagged her car keys. "Thanks for the ride." The study door slammed shut.

She turned to Grandfather, pale and slumped in his chair, and said, "Thank you."

"Bah!" His head snapped up. "Now look what you've cost me. You're always costing me. I'll go broke yet because of you. If you'd stayed with me and worked for me, things never would have come to this. You have no idea the effort I put into making sure you were ready and disposed, everything I did to get you here, and you still couldn't see the golden opportunity."

Exhausted as she was, the tirade of words jolted her. *Making sure I was ready and disposed? Everything he did . . .* An incredible realization surfaced, like sharp icebergs jutting up from a frigid sea, the bulk of danger shrouded beneath the depths. The deception.

He *had* been ready for her. So ready.

She met his eyes and saw a spark, like the memory of a flame. That's when she knew. He'd smoked her out, driven her to him.

"You," she gasped. "You burnt my condo."

Grandfather snorted. "As if I would stoop to such a menial task."

"No, but you were behind it. You . . . you sent someone."

He didn't deny it. She thought of Frank. The big, bulky hench-man carrying out Grandfather's dirty work. In fact . . . she recalled Vivian's description of the person in the library parking lot surveillance video. That could have been Frank.

"You had drugs planted in my car. So you could play rescuer and win me back. But that attempt didn't work. So you burnt my condo. You wanted me in trouble so I'd come crawling back to you for help. Of all the low, conniving—"

"If your mind moves that slow, it's just as well you aren't working for me after all. Need sharper minds than that."

"Devious criminal minds, you mean."

"I merely did what I had to do to get results. I tried contacting you by civil means, but you ignored me every time. Don't blame me. You forced my hand."

"Were you behind all those other horrible things, too?" Trembling, she rattled off the threats: the note on her windshield, the cruel writing on her car, the sneaky photos, even the attack on Ben. She would put nothing past Grandfather now. Nothing. But he denied everything.

Her teeth clashed. "You expect me to believe you, when you committed arson?"

"Stop overreacting. No one got hurt and you got the insurance money, didn't you?"

I don't know, they're dragging their feet. The least of her worries. "Don't try to change the subject. And don't think for a minute I'm not going to tell the police about this."

"By all means, tell them any fanciful story you like. My lawyers will emphasize that being disowned and disinherited might make one inclined to be bitter enough to make such wild accusations. The little matter of proof will be a stumbling block, as well."

Indeed. For the arson and the drug operation, she had nothing. But when it came to justice . . . all she needed was the flash drive.

Her mind spun into a headache as she fell silent and waited, wondering how long it would be before help arrived.

Chapter Thirty

*H*elp came hours later in the form of the morning maid. Her scream ricocheted outside the study doors, and a disgruntled Frank and a slew of police officers soon flooded the study.

Nails, of course, was long gone.

"Why can't they ever catch him?" Charlene lamented to Brook days later, when it looked as though, once again, Nails had vanished from the face of the earth.

Or at least the country. Which, honestly, would have pleased her greatly if she could believe it was true.

It was the not knowing that tortured her.

"I mean, seriously, they've got his fingerprints, his name, his picture . . . why can't the police just catch him and lock him away forever?"

All they'd found so far was Charlene's car, abandoned on a highway. They returned it to her, no worse for being stolen, but she detested the thought of living her life in fear of when Nails might next appear. For the millionth time, for one of a million reasons, she wished Clay had never served time.

Grandfather was, of course, newly fired up to see Clay sent back to prison, once he learned the connection; but the police didn't go for it after releasing Clay and grilling them on the entire incident. No one was charged. Charlene gave the police Grandfather's flash drive, though, so that was something.

"Just breathe, Charlene," Brook said now. Charlene was impressed with her resilience. She'd been snatched from their parking lot, blindfolded, and held in captivity in the trunk of a car. Never even saw her abductor. Many hours later, she was dropped off in a ditch along the side of the road. When she heard the car drive off, she worked her ropes and blindfold off and began walking. The police eventually picked her up.

Despite her traumatic scare, both she and her baby were, thankfully, found to be in perfect health.

Charlene regarded Brook with a fondness that crept up on her.

"You're the one who's going to need to 'just breathe' soon enough. Labor's getting close." If she were her, she'd be worried about that.

Brook smiled and rubbed her rounded belly. Although she and Charlene had grown closer since the robbery, there were some things they didn't speak of, topics they still avoided—Clay being the main one.

―――

Fools believed anything. He had no partner helping him, as he'd told them. The only partner he'd ever considered was the kid, back before he'd blown his chance. Nails had easily kidnapped the pregnant girl himself, then turned her loose after the job was done.

Now with the money stashed, it was time to lay low again.

Time to pass time.

He opened a drawer and drew out the necklace. The strand slipped and slithered, the pearls rolling under his fingers like fat rosary beads. They were valuable, but he twisted them. Couldn't help himself. They were important to her? All the more reason to destroy them.

He heard her begging for them. That voice . . .

He flung the necklace away, focused on something else. Anything else.

Cans and boxes of bland food sat in his cupboards and on the grimy counter. If he had to eat one more meal of ramen noodles, he'd puke.

The hiding and waiting was the hardest part of what he did. It didn't usually get to him. Not like this. Not like tonight. The rain and the cold and the emptiness converged, pressing in on him.

He swept the cheap food from the counter, banged open a cupboard and yanked out a bottle.

It was that Charlene's fault. Always reminding him of Beth.

Beth.

Normally, it was only once in a while that she crossed his mind. Lately, it was all the time. He ran fingers over his close-cropped head, rubbed his prickly scalp. He didn't want her in his brain, in his thoughts. He didn't want her anywhere.

He didn't want to look her up or track her down. He probably wouldn't recognize her even if he saw her. She was probably fat and ugly now. He swilled the whiskey, then slammed the bottle on the table.

Twenty-two years ago. He cursed. She would have married some upstanding church boy long ago. Raised a bunch of brats. Forgot he existed.

Good.

'Cause he knew what she'd think of him now. She'd look down her pert little nose and shrink away. Repulsed.

He grabbed the bottle and threw more whiskey down his gullet. *Drown the memories. Drown them all.*

———

The woman stared at the rosy liquid in her glass, remembering, considering. The cravings were bad tonight. She'd been through too much lately. She deserved the taste of a real drink. Just a taste. One glass.

She'd abstained so long, and she still had so many weeks to wait. Her fingers reached out and encircled the glass.

The baby kicked.

Releasing the drink, she put a hand on her squirming belly, searching for the lively contact of a little foot or hand. The child was growing strong. Pride—and something else too elusive to name—shimmered within her.

She closed her eyes. Once her man saw the amazing thing they'd created together, he'd never look back. When he was all hers and only hers, and they were a real family, they would toast and drink champagne together while their baby slumbered nearby.

A celebration.

The girl would be forgotten, left out in the cold to wallow in rejection.

Thrilled at the thought, the woman bundled herself for the weather and stepped out to visit him.

———

Charlene's life settled into a steady, though slightly numbing, pattern. Thanksgiving and early December came and went without any drama or danger more pressing than her spending days with Ben's family and navigating ice-slicked roads and vision-impairing snow.

When a Christmas card from Max showed up in her mail, it was the highlight of her week. His hastily scrawled message settled her worries as she read between the lines. He wasn't holding a grudge, just booked solid with shows. He was sorry he couldn't get away to visit over Christmas, but promised to see her in the new year.

She sent a card back, and they exchanged a few brief texts, but Charlene couldn't bring herself to call him. She knew if she did, she'd spill everything, the robbery, her near-death . . . and Max would insist she move to California; and this time, he would talk her into it. She wouldn't be strong enough to resist. She'd do it. She'd run . . . losing everything she'd worked for. She'd become dependent and cowardly, always wondering if she'd only stayed and been strong, what her life could have been.

So she didn't call, and she stayed in Creekside, making frequent visits to Woodfield and Ben. They perused wedding reception locales and finally chose a hall near a lake. Waterside trellises strung with little white lights would twinkle like stars, and it would be beautiful. Perfect.

The day after Christmas, she tried hard to picture the summer scene as she sat at the kitchen table. Instead, all she saw was the rosary making supplies spread out before her. Then the lock clicked, the door opened, and Brook stepped into the room.

Charlene's hands froze on a half-completed rosary. "I didn't know you'd be home this early." She felt guilty, like she'd been caught gorging on a gallon of ice cream.

Brook shrugged out of her coat, which didn't button all the way shut now that she was close to her due date. "Work was slow. My manager let me go early." She studied Charlene and the table, the bag of black beads and crucifixes, the roll of cord. "What are you doing?"

Charlene tugged a knot tight. "Making rosaries."

"Black ones." Brook's expression registered the truth. "For prisoners. Clay told you about . . . that."

She nodded.

Brook pulled out a chair and settled across from her. "Can you show me how?"

Charlene looked up, surprised. "You had a long day. Wouldn't you rather rest? The knots are kinda tricky and they're really tiring on your hands."

"I don't care. Sitting is resting. Might as well be productive."

Indeed, Charlene understood the desire. Along with the hope of easing someone's suffering by sharing the love of prayer. She measured out a new length of cord, then leaned forward and explained the process.

Brook caught on quickly, and she chatted as they worked. "So what did Ben give you for Christmas?"

"A winter coat." Charlene caught a bead from rolling off the table. "And a pair of opal earrings."

"But . . ." Brook leaned forward and scrutinized her ears. "Your ears aren't pierced."

"That can easily be fixed." Charlene touched a lobe and her lips hinted at a smile. "His way of encouraging me. How was your Christmas?" Since Charlene had been in Woodfield the entire day and night, she had no idea what Brook had done.

Brook beamed. "It was great. I spent it with Clay and Sam."

Of course. Charlene lost count of the beads she was stringing as she pictured the scene, the warmth and laughter, the fireplace crackling. A real cozy, down-home country Christmas. For some reason, she imagined Sam cooking, in an apron, and the picture was priceless.

She and Brook worked on in a peaceful rhythm, and she thought with a trace of wonder, *This is what it would be like to have a sister.*

Brook's chair squeaked as she shifted her weight. "So you bring all these rosaries somewhere yourself, or send them, or what?"

"I send them. Usually in batches of fifty. I found a prison ministry address online."

Brook picked up a bead and rolled it between her fingertips. "It was nice of you to think to do this, Charlene. Real nice. Most anyone else would hear Clay's story and not—"

Charlene glanced up to see Brook's lips pinched and throat working.

"—not get this out of it."

Charlene shook her head, feeling Brook was blowing things out of proportion.

Brook sniffed. "It's easy to forget about people in prison. To think they're less than us. But . . . 'as long as you did it to one of these my least brethren, you did it to me.'"

Charlene dropped a bead, and it *ping, ping, ping*ed across the table.

Brook handed it back, her eyes shimmering. "You care, Charlene. You have a big heart. You . . . I . . ." Her voice wavered.

Charlene put her hand on Brook's, sensing she wanted to say something more. "What is it, Brook?"

"It's nothing." She bent her head. "I just . . ." She looked back up and heaved a breath. "I'll go with you tomorrow, if you want. To get your ears pierced, I mean."

"Oh. Okay, thank you." Charlene squeezed her hand. "I'd really like that."

———

He burned with fever. He dropped onto the flimsy mattress and couldn't get up again.

Out of nowhere, Mrs. Callaghan's round face bobbed above him. "You poor boy."

He wanted to spit at her. Cuss her out for calling him that, but he didn't have strength to do anything but groan.

Then she was gone, and it was Beth, sweet Beth, caring for him, laying a cool washcloth on his fiery forehead. He relaxed then, and slept, though he wanted to stay awake and look at her, talk to her.

Maybe she would tell him one of her lame stories. He wouldn't mind. Had nothing better to do. What was that one? The one about . . .

"The Good Thief," whispered Beth.

Right, even the title was lame. The good thief. As if there could be any such thing. He was either good, or a thief. Couldn't be both.

Beth's voice began the story in her harmonizing way . . .

"The soldiers crucified two robbers right next to Jesus on Calvary. One on His right, and one on His left. They didn't use nails for the robbers, only ropes. Jesus got the nails." Beth always paused at that part, like it was supposed to mean something profound.

Then she went on, quoting her Bible as she did so well. "One of the robbers mocked Jesus, saying, 'If thou be Christ, save thyself and us.'

"But the other man, the good thief, rebuked the first. 'Do you not fear God, seeing thou art under the same condemnation? And we indeed justly; for we receive the due reward of our deeds. But this man hath done no evil.'

"Then the good thief spoke to Jesus. 'Lord, remember me when thou shalt come into thy kingdom.'

"Jesus replied, 'Amen I say to thee: This day thou shalt be with me in paradise.'"

A thief in paradise? The story was as stupid as they came.

Still, it stuck with him.

"Remember me . . ." And he drifted into sleep, where the fever couldn't burn.

On a Tuesday evening in early January, Charlene ventured out to a specialty baby store, part of a row of old-time storefronts built of yellowed brick and featuring fabric overhangs and large window displays. All the after-Christmas sales and slashed prices called to her. Even when she'd had plenty of money, she'd always enjoyed the thrill of a good bargain.

With Brook's baby overdue, it was high time she bought a gift, but when she stepped into the store, she knew why she'd put the chore off for so long.

The modest sized place was literally crammed floor to ceiling with the cutest array of pastel items she'd ever seen. From car seats and cribs, to tiny outfits and shoes, to books and toys, it was more than overwhelming. At the same time, the downright adorableness of it all pricked her heart and awoke a yearning for a baby of her own.

She wound her way past a young couple wielding a registry scanner, a grandmotherly lady piling her cart with toys, and an obviously-pregnant blond woman frowning at a price tag. Reaching the clothing racks, Charlene fingered an ultra-soft outfit that looked like a miniature bear costume, complete with paw feet, and marveled that any human could be born this small.

After taking much too long to decide, she chose three outfits, a stuffed duck with a soft tuft of fuzz on its head, and a classic board book that had always been a library favorite.

Before leaving the shop, she rebundled herself in her coat and pulled on a wool hat that hid her new earrings and most of her hair. With the plastic bag looped over her arm, she stepped out into the cold night to see snowflakes drifting lazily from the sky, fluttering like tiny white fairy wings. She lifted her face to them and barely felt them brush her cheeks before they melted.

She told herself she dreaded winter, the cold, the weak sun, the lack of color, the snow—but when winter came, there were occasional magical moments like this when it charmed her.

"Excuse me," said a man trying to enter the store, which she was mindlessly blocking.

"Oh, sorry," But as she answered, she realized she knew his voice. Well.

Clay.

Their eyes met.

They both paused, the snow falling between them. A curtain. A gauzy wall so thin, yet so thick.

They'd done an admirable job of avoiding each other in this small town, but every once in a while . . . She sighed, suddenly realizing at the squeeze of her heart, it really was time for her to move back to Woodfield.

As they sidestepped at the same moment, she attempted a small nervous laugh. "Doing some last minute shopping for the baby, too, huh?"

Clay scratched his knit cap. "Yeah, gonna try." She watched his eyes go to the store window and catch a glimpse of the impossible selection. His face fell.

She was about to offer to help him pick something out, when her brain stopped her. This was something he should do on his own.

"Well, good luck. I'll see you around." *Or not.* She started to walk away, down the vacant, snowy sidewalk, when he came up beside her with brisk, tramping steps.

"I'll walk you to your car. Since it's dark and snowing."

Really? She'd survived much worse. Her brain told her she shouldn't accept his company, but it didn't win this time. "Okay, thank you." The snow continued sprinkling down as they walked side by side.

He cleared his throat. "So how have you been? Did you have a good Christmas?"

"I did. You?"

"Yep."

That was a good spot to give up on, or so it seemed they both decided. The snow squeaked underfoot, reminding her of the sand at the beach all those long months ago.

She turned her face to the glass storefronts, to window shop as they walked, and a sparkling jewelry display caused her to slow. "Look at that," she breathed, pointing to little baby footprints on a dainty silver pendant. Entranced, words slid from her mouth before she could weigh whether she really wanted to say them. "You should get that for Brook."

Clay almost pressed his face to the window. His breath fogged the glass. He pushed open the shop door, and she found herself following, wanting to see the necklace up close.

Almost instantly, she knew she'd made a mistake.

As he spoke with the woman behind the counter, a long, obtuse case of glittering, taunting engagement rings assailed her. Countless facets captured and redirected the light in a thousand blinding rays.

She shot a desperate look his way. How long did it take to buy one necklace?

Struggle as she did to ignore them, the rings pulled her. Amongst the sparkle of sharp angled diamonds, a smooth, soft, calm pink sheen almost glowed, drawing her closer.

Her fingertips pressed the glass as she stared, fixated on a pink pearl ring. A cluster of three little diamonds hugged the pearl on each side of a tapered gold band. Her heart tugged at the bittersweet thought of her mother's necklace, heartlessly stolen by Nails. She doubted she'd ever see it again. But this ring would go so well with it . . .

"Would you like to try it on?" the sales woman asked brightly.

Embarrassed to be caught gaping, Charlene shook her head.

Clay appeared at her side, a little jewelry bag crinkling in his hand.

"Let me know if you want me to take any rings out so you can see them in the true light." The woman beamed at both of them. "Have you set the date yet?"

Charlene blinked three times before catching her meaning, then felt herself engulfed in an instant, furnace-hot blush.

"Oh, no," she choked out.

"We're not—" Clay attempted.

The woman tilted her head, waiting expectantly.

"We should get going," Clay said. "Thanks for your help."

He and Charlene turned away from the sales woman in unison, practically tripping over each other in their haste to hustle out the door.

Charlene found it a wonder the snowflakes didn't sizzle on her burning cheeks. Tugging on her gloves, she walked vigorously, trying to expunge the last few minutes from her mind. The incident had been so utterly humiliating, the only thing to do was ignore it.

Unfortunately, Clay didn't.

"You were looking at that pink one, right?"

She clapped her hands to her arms. "I noticed it, yes. Because it reminded me of my mom." She cleared her throat, trying to mask the catch in her voice. "Of a necklace she had, that's all."

Clay remained quiet for a few steps. "You told me a while back that you were engaged to Ben." She heard him cram the jewelry bag in his pocket. "Why don't you wear a ring?"

It stunned her that he had even noticed a detail like that. "I had one, but I lost it."

"Yeah? How long ago?"

"A while."

He shot her a sideways glance. "And he hasn't replaced it yet?"

Her defenses rose. "Engagement rings aren't cheap. And I was stupid and careless for losing it in in the first place." She kicked the snow.

"All I know is, you've gotta have a ring if you're engaged. It warns other guys to back off. If I were Ben, I'd be getting you a ring right away. Just sayin'." He coughed. "Tell him you want the pink one."

Her lip quirked. "It's not a classic diamond engagement ring. I don't think he'd really go for that."

A short, harsh noise escaped Clay's throat, sounding slightly like a laugh. "He's not going to be the one wearing it."

She narrowed her eyes at the snow drifts glinting severely under the street lamps, like piles of pulverized glass, and decided the subject needed changing. "So you bought the necklace. Brook's going to love it."

"Hope so."

"So do you think you'll be shopping for a ring for her anytime soon?"

A car drove by, spraying dirty snow. Five steps later, he still hadn't answered. She began to wonder if he'd even heard her. Then he said, "No." The single word hung heavy in the air.

"No?"

"No."

She slowed her steps, wondering if she dared venture further into the subject. Something warned her there'd be no turning back if she did. Still, she persisted.

"So are you thinking like maybe in another year or so . . . ?"

His jaw flexed. "No. I'm not going to be buying her a ring. Ever. I'm not in love with Brook."

He stepped in front of her and stopped walking, which forced her to halt. He tugged the hat from his head and scrunched it in his fist. He looked her directly in the eye. "I'm in love with you, Charlene."

Her lips parted. Misty breath escaped, but no words. She simply watched the snowflakes powder his rumpled hair and gather on his shoulders.

His stance was firm, his face pained, but resolute. "There, I said it. It's about time." His eyes flicked away for just a moment. "I don't expect you to say it back, and I'm not asking you to." His Adam's apple bobbed. "I've got no right telling you this when you're engaged. But I'd rather tell you than regret not doing it."

Her gloved hand traveled up to her mouth and she pressed her lips, trying to squelch the whirr of emotions warring within her. "We've been through so much together, Clay . . . that's all. I don't really think what you feel could be—"

"I know what I feel." His voice lowered and held a touch of hope. "Does this really come as such a shock to you?"

"I—I don't know." Her hand crept down to her throat. "I don't understand." Her gaze scuttered over the snowbanks. "Then why . . . when I kissed you that night . . . did you get so angry?"

He smacked his hat against his leg. "Because it was nothing but a pity kiss." Disgust lay thick on his voice. "That's worse than no kiss at all. The last thing I want is your pity."

She sensed his eyes searching her now, afraid to find more of that pity. His wary vulnerability just about crushed her. "Oh Clay, I care about you so much, but . . ." She took a step forward, and he took a step back, frowning.

She moistened her cold lips. "I wish I knew what to say, but . . . I don't. There's Ben. We set the date. For June. And Brook, and Brook's having a baby . . ."

"The baby's not mine, just so you know." He scrubbed a hand across the stubble on his face and she heard the scratch. "She knows I'm always here for her as a friend, but we've been over since July."

July? That long ago? She thought back . . . July was when they'd kissed. July was also when Brook had stormed into the workshop with the letter. Had a broken heart driven her to it? "But you still see her. You spent Christmas together."

"She would have spent it alone. I couldn't let her do that."

Of course not. He wasn't that kind of person.

"When I first met Brook," he said in a worn voice, "I was trying to build a new life, and I thought she and I had a chance. I never meant to hurt her. I wanted it to work, but then you showed up. And then one day I realized what had first attracted me to her." He looked away, then back at her with haunted eyes. "She reminded me of you."

"Clay—"

"But she isn't you." His hands jammed deep in his pockets, his shoulders hunching. "I know I'm no good for you. You deserve a heck of a lot more than an ex-convict." His voice turned husky. "I've been fighting this too long. It was time you knew, that's all." He waited a heartbeat, then tucked in his chin and turned away.

Her hand left her side, then fell back. Her mind and heart fired erratic, discordant signals. She didn't know what to do.

Hurt Clay, or hurt Ben.

She didn't want to hurt anyone. She'd already promised herself to sweet, reliable, devoted Ben.

But Clay . . .

No, she couldn't. It wasn't right.

How could she do that to Ben? She'd already taken so much from him.

Gripping a storefront ledge mounded with snow, she observed Clay's back, the stiffness of it, and floundered for words. It had taken so much for him to tell her this, and she didn't feel worthy. She wasn't. If he truly knew her . . .

"Clay, you don't even really know me . . ."

He threw her a glance over his shoulder, clearly insulted, and tugged his hat back on.

"Clay, wait." Her hands moved mindlessly, pressing snow together in agitation as she stuffed her feelings away into a remote, frozen place. "I'm sorry I can't say what you want to hear. I wish I could." *I wish I could.*

He hitched a shoulder, the motion saying, *No big deal. Forget it.*

"I wish things were different." Her voice wavered. "Don't sell yourself short. You have so much to offer. So much. When you find the right girl . . ."

He shook his head.

"I don't know how to say what I need to say," she pleaded.

"Then don't." He turned just long enough for her to see his eyes glint moist in the streetlight. "Just don't. I'm fine. I'll be fine."

She felt a tear roll down her cheek, saw it drop onto the misshapen snowball in her hand. She felt so inept. So sad. How could she help him see? "All these feelings and thoughts from right now . . . like this snowball, they'll melt away . . . in time. And you'll forget all about—"

He stalked over and gave her a look that shut her up. "I don't want to forget." He clamped her hands, and as he leaned in, she sensed he was about to kiss her.

She whipped her head back while releasing the snowball and pulling her hands free. "I'm sorry."

He'd never know how sorry.

She took off, leaving him standing alone on the sidewalk, leaving him with nothing. Nothing but the worthless snowball.

Chapter Thirty-One

*B*one weary and feeling that her heart had just been bled dry, Charlene chucked her shopping bag onto her passenger seat. Grabbing her snow brush, she attacked the fluffy accumulation on her car, clearing each window with a vicious sweep.

Back inside, she almost turned on the engine, needing the heater, but didn't make it that far. Sealed in her vehicle with no one around in the vast night emptiness, she crumpled into a pathetic ball and sobbed aloud, hot tears pouring out.

Her heart ached with excruciating pain, and she couldn't even sort out why. It was a terrible blend of a great sense of loss over a might have been that could never be, and anger at the cruel way life taunted and tricked. Love wasn't simple or predictable, safe and reliable; love sliced and slashed, twisted and gouged. Like a knife. A cursed knife.

But she didn't have enough tissues in her purse to keep crying like this. She had to stop and pull herself together. Sniffing deeply, she blotted her eyes, then nose, with her last sodden tissue before shoving her emotions away. Then she picked up her keys, cranked the ignition, and thrust her car into gear.

Her phone chimed cheerily as she pulled into the sloppy street, but she didn't even check it, fearing it was Clay.

She'd been so careful, rarely letting herself venture into thinking of him as more than a friend, but now she realized how much she'd wanted to. Maybe, if they'd had a different history, and different timing, maybe . . . But there was no point entertaining thoughts of something that could never be.

She couldn't break up with Ben. She couldn't.

And no matter what Clay had said, Brook was her friend, and she wouldn't hurt her that way. Even if they were over, she knew Brook still loved him. There was a line friends simply didn't cross.

Her phone rang again. And again.

She went to silence the incessant noise, but saw it wasn't Clay calling, after all. It was Brook.

So she answered.

"Charlene, finally! Oh my gosh—" she broke off with a primal cry, making Charlene cringe.

"Are you okay? What's going on? Are you—"

"I'm in labor." She paused to pant and breathe. "At the hospital. Can you come? Please, Charlene, I don't have anyone to be with me, besides the nurses, and I really—" She cut her words off for another agonizing cry.

"I'll be there as soon as I can." Charlene dropped her phone and stepped on the gas.

She'd bought the baby gifts just in time.

———

Tossing and turning, Nails sweltered as feverish thoughts coursed through his mind . . .

His mother only ever came to him in nightmares. Always holding the syringe, driving the needle at him. "It will make you happy, Lance. So happy." She pulled dry, cracked lips into a smile, a terrifying smile in her pale, hollow face.

A child again, he ran.

She chased him.

He tripped and fell, and she loomed over him. Her wasted arm stabbed, the needle's sharp silver tip piercing him through the heart with a fierce, radiating pain.

His eyes flew open to darkness. Wild breathing. His own. He gritted his teeth and flipped his sweat-soaked pillow, kicked the hot sheets off. Lay there, still sweating. The Callaghans had given him his own room. After all the rooms he'd shared with other foster kids, it was a luxury. But nights like this, the quiet was too much. He punched his pillow and cursed.

Sleep refused to come. He tipped himself out of bed and rubbed his head, paced the floor. At last he opened the door and slipped into the hall. A strip of dim light glowed from Beth's room. Peaceful light. It drew him nearer. He stood at the cracked door and saw her face, her smooth brow, her eyelids closed in oblivious tranquility.

Something in him ached. He swallowed and nudged her door wider, stepped closer, his bare feet muffled on the carpet. Her hair cascaded, soft ripples fanned all around, draping her pillow, her forehead, her cheek, her shoulders.

Across the room, he glimpsed her little sister Gracie curled in her toddler bed under the window. Sound asleep. Her night light bathed the room in a gentle glow.

Looking again at Beth, he realized there was room in her bed. He sucked in a shallow breath. What would it feel like to lie beside her?

He took a step closer. Then another. His heart skipped a beat.

Slowly, he eased himself onto the rosebud mattress sheet. The slight creak made him freeze, but she didn't stir. He relaxed.

She wouldn't know. No one would know. He would just lie there for a second, soaking up her serenity. Till he forgot the nightmare.

He fit perfectly, almost touching her, but not quite. He was close enough to feel warmth radiating from her, to smell her scent, vanilla and cinnamon. He fingered one of her curls, like smooth ribbon. Tension drained from him, and his breathing evened out, grew shallow, and his lids drooped . . .

Wrong, so wrong. It wasn't supposed to be like this. The pain surpassed every suffering she'd ever experienced. She screamed and pleaded and swore, to no avail.

The doctor didn't care. The nurses didn't care. No one cared. No one. She was a patient. A room number. Nothing more.

She flailed from side to side, her eyes searching wildly, as if her frenzy could make him materialize. He should be here with her, helping her through this, but he wasn't. Worse yet, she knew where he was, and who he was thinking of. She had heard the way he said the other woman's name, and it gutted her.

She would never forgive him.

Charlene entered Brook's hospital room and wished she could turn right back around. Brook writhed on the narrow, inclined bed. Her eyes squeezed shut and her face contorted. Making horrible sounds, she didn't even notice her. Charlene edged closer and saw her forehead and upper lip beaded in sweat.

When Brook finally caught sight of her, she choppily explained that her contractions had come on sudden and strong at work, and a coworker had called an ambulance.

"*Aargh!* The pain's gonna kill me!" Her white-knuckled hands gripped the bed rail and her lavender fingernails looked as if they'd break from the pressure.

Charlene glanced around the small, clinical room. Confined here with Brook in this frightening state, she felt a stomach-curdling anxiety. "Why don't you get the epidural?"

"Too late," explained a sympathetic-faced young nurse in maroon scrubs. "This baby's coming fast."

Charlene hurried to situate herself near Brook's head and felt helpless. "What do I do?"

"Just be here for her," the nurse said. "Encourage her."

Charlene pulled a chair close. "You can do this, Brook," she said, trying not to reveal her doubts and distress as Brook moaned like a tortured animal.

Charlene's eyes darted to the door with each in-and-out of the nurses. She wished someone could reassure her that *she* could do this—be a support person for a woman in labor without fainting. *Pull yourself together,* she reprimanded herself. *I've got the easy job.*

Time slid into nonexistence, a stand-still, as the contractions reached an insane peak. In horror, she watched them rise to incredible heights on the graph paper sliding from a machine.

Brook twisted, haggard and gasping, "I—can't—do—this!"

Charlene believed her. Why didn't the nurses believe her? And hadn't a nurse said hours ago that the baby was coming fast? This wasn't fast, not at all.

What was going to happen if Brook really couldn't do this? Charlene glanced, worried, at a nurse, and was astounded at her smooth composure as she once again assured Brook that she could, indeed, do this.

With her next breath, Brook cursed someone named Connor. She didn't dare ask, but Charlene guessed he was probably the father. She wondered briefly what Brook's plan was for supporting herself and the baby; but everything, even that, waited on the birth.

The doctor arrived with a calm, businesslike air, and in a whirl of efficient synchronization, the nurses produced tools and even removed the end of the bed and raised it to the doctor's lofty height.

Suddenly Brook stopped wailing, flooring Charlene as her entire face mashed into pure determination. She pushed, her eyes bulging. Stringy strands of hair plastered her face.

Charlene held a cool cloth to her head between pushes. This cycle seemed to go on forever, until Brook's tense features finally wilted into relief and wonder. Charlene dared let out her breath and turned her gaze to see a tiny, damp baby in the doctor's grasp.

"It's a girl," he announced.

In a matter of seconds, a nurse suctioned the baby's airway clear, and the newborn let loose a robust cry. Then the baby was toweled and laid on Brook's chest, where Brook encircled her gently within her arms. The baby quieted as Brook gazed in awe at the scrunchy little face, and the baby peered at Brook with curious squinty eyes.

And Charlene knew, for the both of them, in that instant, it was as if no one else existed. Vanished was Brook's wild, desperate, defeated insanity. Though worn ragged, she somehow appeared the picture of serenity.

"Hello, little Gabriella," Brook whispered. "I love you."

Almost an hour later, Charlene held Gabriella for the first time, as Brook looked on with pride.

"She's perfect," Charlene murmured, studying her closed, wrinkled eyelids. The baby fit light and snug in her arms, and she felt as though she could hold her and gaze at her forever.

Brook's tired face lit with an inner glow. While Charlene could tell it was a challenge for Brook to tear her eyes from her new daughter, Brook looked at her with an expression of admiration and gratitude.

"Thank you so much for coming, Charlene. You didn't have to do that, and I know it wasn't fun for you, but it meant the world to me."

"I wish I could have done more, like give you an epidural. But I'm so glad it all turned out well."

"It did," Brook said in amazement, eyes back on her baby. "And it was worth it."

Recognizing the yearning in Brook's gaze, Charlene relinquished Gabriella back to her. "Is there anything else I can do for you before I head home?"

Caressing her baby, Brook barely appeared to hear her, but she answered, "Thank you, no. You already did so much more than I can ever repay. The nurses will help, so we'll be well taken care of." She glanced at a text on her phone. "And Clay's on his way."

Charlene nodded. Then it was time for her to leave her gift and say goodbye.

Despite all her personal turmoil, after just witnessing the miracle of new life entering the world, Charlene found her thoughts sliding into perspective. Life wasn't all about her. God blessed the world with miracles every day.

She went home to bed feeling a sense of acceptance. *God's will, not mine, be done.* And she slept peacefully.

———

My daughter . . .

She gazed down at the tiny angelic face. So real. So perfect. How could a baby have such long, thick lashes? Such flawless skin? She stroked the fuzzy head, the plump hands, the curled fingers, the soft little dots of fingernails. Rolls of skin at every joint. Exquisite.

But such beauty couldn't last. Beauty never lasted. The thought pierced her, and a tear rolled down her cheek.

———

When Charlene picked Brook up from the hospital and brought her and Gabriella home to the apartment two days later, Brook gave her a set of earplugs as she apologized in advance for any cries in the night she might happen to hear.

Charlene assured her not to worry. "I used to live next to a train."

Two days later, Brook's aunt surprised her with a visit. The tiny woman arrived with a huge casserole, then dedicated herself to caring for Brook while oohing and ahhing over the baby. Brook's eyes glowed. Charlene was glad to see she had some family after all.

"I called her after Gabriella was born," Brook explained after her aunt left. "I was afraid to, but she didn't judge me. Not like my parents. Still, I didn't expect her to come all the way from Bloomington." Brook smiled all the rest of that day.

When Charlene wasn't working at Fannie's Fabrics or studying, she busied herself tending to Brook and making sure she had groceries, encouraging her to nap when Gabriella did, and keeping the apartment tidy. Holding beautiful, downy-headed Gabriella was more than enough compensation.

Sundays, though, were still reserved for Ben. She rose early and made the drive to Woodfield to sit beside him in the back of Saint Paul's Church during Mass. Numerous families with children filled the pews in front of them. Thinking of Gabriella, her eyes sought out the babies with new wonder.

The toddlers, however, were impossible to ignore. One mother wrestled an energetic pigtailed girl onto her lap and tried to show her a picture book. When the girl shoved it away, her mom tried to interest her in a bag of Cheerios. The girl took the cereal eagerly, then tipped the bag with a loud, "Oops!" Cheerios rained down on the floor, bouncing and rolling, some landing at Ben's feet.

Despite herself, Charlene's lips twitched with a smile and she glanced at Ben. He frowned.

"Chee-os!" the little girl shrieked so loud that Charlene thought the stained glass windows just might shatter. The mom clapped a hand over the child's mouth and whispered something in her ear as she shot a frantic glance at the dad, who sat with eyes closed. Either deep in prayer, dozing, or blissfully oblivious.

"Want Chee-os!"

The mom hustled the girl awkwardly out of the pew, crunching Cheerios to dust as she went.

Bang!

With a flinch, Charlene's gaze turned to another child, a blond little boy slamming wooden puzzle pieces on the pew. He looked up with the cutest grin before hurling a piece. Right at Ben.

Charlene picked up the wooden car shape as Ben muttered, "Don't give it back."

But she did.

On the sidewalk after church, Ben made a disgusted noise. "What kind of dumb parent brings a puzzle to church?"

"That's not nice, Ben."

"Come on, Charlene. I wouldn't do that. Would you?"

"I—"

"No. You'd have more sense." His wheelchair crunched over rock salt on the sidewalk. "And those Cheerios. My gosh. You can't tell me the kid's gonna starve if she doesn't eat for one hour." He shook his head. "Some people need to learn to control their kids. Man, I sure wouldn't stand for that."

She flicked him a glance. "So you expect perfect behavior? They're kids, Ben. We don't know what it's like to be parents. It can't be easy. I'm sure they're all just trying to do the best they can. At least they're taking their kids to church."

"And teaching them it's nothing but playtime and snack time."

Compressing her lips, she let the subject drop.

Chapter Thirty-Two

*O*ne afternoon when Gabriella was about three weeks old, Brook and Charlene lazed about in a patch of sun on the floor, admiring the baby as she lay like a cute bug on her back on the middle of a blanket, her plump arms and legs waving randomly. Brook danced a jingly monkey toy past her face.

As Brook moved, a flash of silver nestled at her throat caught Charlene's eye.

"I like your necklace." This was the first time Charlene had noticed her wearing it. Since this was actually the first time Brook had changed out of pajamas for the day, this was no great surprise.

Brook fingered the silver baby footprint pendant with a wistful smile. "Thanks. Clay gave it to me." Her smile lessened and her fingers slowly released the pendant. "Charlene, I think you know this by now anyway, but I have to apologize for leading you on and letting you think Gabriella was Clay's baby. That was so wrong of me." She reddened and lowered her head.

"I wanted her to be, wanted us to be a real family so bad, but . . ." She shook her head. "Maybe you already know, but he and I are just friends now. That's all we've been for a while."

The forbidden subject, now broached, was so touchy, Charlene wasn't sure what to say. Brook went on, eliminating her need. "I wanted to be bitter and mad at him, but I just couldn't."

She leaned down to caress Gabriella and give her a kiss. "If it weren't for him, I wouldn't have my little angel."

Charlene tilted her head as if she'd heard wrong.

Keeping a loving hand near Gabriella's body, Brook explained. "When I first met Clay, I was going through a real rough time. I'd left home to be with my boyfriend, but then he broke up with me. Everyone had warned me Connor was bad news—but after he left and I found out I was pregnant, I didn't want to go crawling back home in defeat, proving everyone right, that Connor used me and left me."

Brook lowered her voice with a nervous glance at Gabriella, as if afraid she might understand her next words. "I wasn't going to go through with the pregnancy. The night when Clay took me out after work, I spilled the truth to him. He was a good listener, but he told me not to do it. He gave me lots of reasons, but nothing convinced me. I told myself I'd be doing her a favor by not bringing her into this terrible world. And it was so early in the pregnancy, I thought it couldn't matter." Her eyes became glassy and distant.

"Then the day I was about to go to the clinic, he gave me the angel carving. He said it wasn't much, just a simple piece of wood that couldn't compare to the reality."

Her eyes misted over and her voice trembled. "He said my baby already had a beating heart. He said God already loved her so much, that He'd given her a guardian angel of her very own, the very second He created her, to be with her and watch over her and guide her always, to protect her heart and soul—just as He'd given me one, too."

Charlene remembered the angel carving, with the heart in the palm of the angel's hands, and it took on a new meaning.

Brook sniffed. "That really hit me. I'd never thought about that before. If God gave us our very own angels to be with us and help us through life, He must love us so much. How could I walk in that place and . . . stop that little heart from beating?" She paused. "I couldn't. I took that carved angel as a reminder of God's love and care. And I didn't feel alone anymore."

"Oh, Brook." Charlene slid to her side and hugged her.

Brook swiped a tear away. "So you see, I can't be mad at Clay for not falling for me the way I did for him. After we stopped dating, he still came by to take me to some evening classes at church, to help me learn about the Catholic faith. I had so many questions." She paused at Gabriella's cute cooing noises and took a deep breath.

"And while I'm bearing my soul, I might as well confess that when I first asked you to be my roommate, it was for selfish reasons. I was jealous of you from the start. You know the saying, 'Keep your friends close and your enemies closer?' Well, I thought what better way to keep an eye on you than to live under the same roof?" She scuffed a toe. "I also thought maybe I could get some inside information on Clay from you, since he never likes to talk about himself."

"I understand, Brook, and I don't blame you for any of it."

"You're a really good friend."

Charlene traced her finger over a little lamb on the baby blanket.

She wondered guiltily if Brook would feel that way if she knew she'd kissed Clay. She had to say something, but the words that came out were a stalling tactic. "How did you find me at the motel at just the right time? That wasn't really coincidence, was it?"

"No. Sam actually called and told me. He seemed to want to keep an eye on you too, for his own reasons. You know Sam, always more worried about Clay than he wants to admit."

"He knew I had the letter. He was afraid I'd break the news too soon."

"Like I did." Brook dipped her head. "That was a low blow to you all." She placed a finger in Gabriella's hand and let her squeeze it in her chubby little fist. Brook glanced at Charlene, then down again at her daughter. "Obviously, I'm not good at keeping secrets, and maybe I shouldn't tell you this, but . . . the reason I went so wacko and did that, was because I was jealous. The evening before—"

"Wait." Charlene couldn't listen to another word without revealing her own secret. It had been weighing on her for too long. "You were right to be jealous of me," she admitted in a small voice. "Back in July, when I went to find Clay, I . . . I kissed him."

Silence stretched. Charlene looked up to see Brook's averted gaze.

"I can't say that doesn't hurt."

"I'm sorry."

Brook shook her head and turned to meet her eyes. "You were always the one he wanted."

"I shouldn't have kissed him. It was wrong of me."

"So you're not perfect." The edge of her lip crooked. "If I were in your place, I wouldn't have been able to resist, either."

"Still, I—"

"It's okay, Charlene. You'll understand if you let me finish what I was trying to tell you. The night Clay and I were hanging out after the fireworks, Sam called him to the shop to help with something, and I came across some papers. I realized Clay had them because he cared . . . really cared, and that's what hurt so bad." She swallowed, then steadied her gaze.

"They were letters, Charlene. Letters to you. He started so many, some very impersonal, others telling you he wanted to see you. Obviously, he never sent them, but he must have wanted to. They were dated, and they stopped when he started seeing me, but still . . . he still had them.

"After that discovery, I was devastated. I knew he was going to break up with me, and it was only a matter of time. Maybe if he didn't feel so sorry for me, he would have done it sooner." Brook closed her eyes. "Without meaning it, that's the cruelest thing of all. Realizing someone is with you only because they feel bad for you." Her eyes opened.

"As much as it hurts to know we won't ever get married like I dreamed . . . I think if we did . . . and he didn't really love me, I would know it. In time, I would come to resent him, and him me. We wouldn't be happy."

Even as Brook's words appeared to lighten and free her own conscience, they hung heavy as bricks on Charlene's. Little did Brook know that she was describing her and her lingering attachment to Ben.

Charlene saw herself in a new light, and it was ugly.

"I'm free now," Brook went on, "and I have my little angel girl. Clay's faith gave me faith, and I know now I don't need to hold onto him to have that faith. It's bigger than him."

Brook swept up her baby, twirled, and hugged her. "I'm going to be baptized, and so is Gabriella. I want her to have the gift of faith. So she can know God . . . and her angel."

"I thought there was something worthwhile in you. I was wrong."

Nails shoved his fists to his ears, but it didn't silence the condemning voice from his past. He awoke alone in the trailer, on the cold, narrow, lumpy mattress. Alone. Always alone.

He swore, because he remembered the night when he wasn't alone . . .

"Lance!" the voice hissed warm in his ear. Hands pushed and shoved. "Wake up!"

He mumbled and turned over. So comfortable.

"Lance, you have to wake up. Now!" Her voice rose, panicky. Fists battered at his back, so light it was laughable.

"What were you thinking?" she demanded. "You can't be in here! If my dad finds you—"

"Huh?" He flipped over and cracked an eye. Brain foggy, he rubbed his head. Where was he? What was going on?

A door slammed open.

A squeal. "Daddy, no!"

Heavy hands clamped his arms and tore him from the bed. Someone dragged him, disoriented and stumbling, into the hall. A brute force shoved him against the wall, jerking his head. He blinked and saw Mr. Callaghan's face. Too close to his own. His gut clenched. There was something in the man's eyes that he'd never seen before. Something dangerous.

He swallowed and tried to find his voice, sensing he'd made some huge mistake, but he could clear it up, if only—

"You sneaky little bastard." Mr. Callaghan's breath hit his face.

Lance's heart pounded as the man shook him, rattling his thoughts. What had he done to make him so angry?

Then it hit him, as sure as he knew the man was about to.

Beth. He'd laid down . . . fallen asleep beside her . . . How had he thought that was a good idea? His face flushed hot.

"Daddy, no!"

There she was, tugging at her father's shoulder, eyes saucer-wide, face pink, voice desperate. "You don't understand. Nothing happened. He didn't mean—"

"Get back in your room, young lady," Mr. Callaghan thundered. At that moment, Mrs. Callaghan appeared and corralled Beth, still pleading, into her bedroom and closed the door.

Leaving him to Mr. Callaghan.

Lance knew he should say something, but his tongue was knotted. Before he could manage a word, Mr. Callaghan seized the back of his neck, the savage grip practically tearing his skin as he forced him down the stairs and into the garage, into his truck. He almost slammed the door on his foot.

Breathing hard, Mr. Callaghan cranked the engine and pulled out. "How dare you, boy." His hand hit the steering wheel. "I opened my home to you. Gave you countless chances because I thought there was something worthwhile in you." The vehicle careened around a corner, throwing Lance against the door. "I was wrong. You only ever wanted to take advantage. I can forgive most anything, but not that."

"I didn't—"

"Don't even try to defend yourself. I know what I saw. You're out of here."

Words died in his throat. His shoulders sagged. It was useless. The back of his neck stung where Mr. Callaghan had gripped him.

At last, he was being kicked out. Why had he let himself think that maybe this time, it might not come to this? It always did.

Early morning sun flashed through the window, bright daggers of light. He thought of the big house full of laughter that had begun to feel like a home. Maybe, if he finally said the words that seemed to come so easily for others . . . he licked his lips. Licked them again. "I'm sorry."

"Bull."

Lance shut his eyes and thought of Beth. His fingers gripped the seat. He wouldn't ever see her again. Giving it one last shot, he heard his voice come out pitiful, weak. "Please."

There was no answer. He jolted forward as the truck ground to a halt. He opened his eyes and saw the familiar gray building. Social services. Bands of steel squeezed his chest.

He almost begged for mercy, but clamped down on his tongue as Mr. Callaghan pulled him out roughly, making up for all those times he'd treated him so well.

Inside, the man pushed him onto a hard seat and ordered him to stay, like a dog.

And he did, slumping low, in a kind of shock which crept over him, covering him in a hard shell, glazing him with numbness. He didn't hear much of what Mr. Callaghan said to the woman at the desk, but what he did hear was enough: "I don't want him anymore."

Without a backward glance, Mr. Callaghan left him there. For the system. With the troublemakers, the losers, the worthless rejects of the world.

Where he belonged.

He thought he heard his mother laugh.

Still in his pajamas, he hung his head and stared at his bare feet, feeling nothing.

Charlene sat in her idling car in Ben's driveway, eyeing his house and dreading what she had to do. Stalling, she rolled on lip balm. She'd hardly managed any sleep the night before, and she had a headache. She was drained and tired, and it was only ten o'clock in the morning.

On Valentine's Day.

Not the day she would voluntarily choose to do something like this. For breaking an engagement, it rated right up there with a birthday, Christmas, or New Year's. The opposite of romantic, for sure. But she hadn't been able to get off work till today, and Ben was expecting her.

As much as she didn't want to face this, she couldn't bear to drag this out, stringing him along for even one more day.

Ironic or not, she hoped Saint Valentine didn't mind her turning to him with her desperate plea. *Ask the Lord to help Ben understand. Help me to say the right words.*

If she were more of a coward, she would do this over the phone. Giving herself a little shake, she gripped her purse and picked her way over ice patches to the front stoop.

Without her even knocking, the door swung wide, revealing a virtual garden on wheels. Ben sat in his chair with a huge bouquet of red roses on his lap. "Happy Valentine's Day!"

Thoughtful. Sweet. She was going to miss that about him. She entered, stomped the snow from her boots, and then pulled them off.

"Don't just stand there on the wet rug. C'mere." One of his hands secured the vase of flowers while the other opened wide for a hug. She lowered herself compliantly and rested her head on his shoulder. He nudged her face with his, maneuvering so that their lips touched, and they kissed.

Her heart wept that he didn't realize it was their last one, a goodbye kiss.

She eased herself away, removed her coat, and ran hands over her sweater, smoothing and tugging it down. "Hey, so I really want to talk to you about something." She glanced at Lucy reading a book in the living room and lowered her voice. "Can we go talk in private?"

A hint of concern crossed Ben's brow, but he nodded. "Yeah, sure. No problem." His voice lowered. "Just don't tell me you want to change our invitation selection, or my mom will freak."

In that case, this might kill her.

Then again, she might be delighted.

Charlene's clammy hands twisted together as she gave a belated, insufficient little laugh. She heard Mrs. Jorgensen moving around in the kitchen.

"So what's up?" Ben asked after he'd closed the door to his dad's study behind them.

She nibbled at her bottom lip and scanned the floor-to-ceiling bookcase before forcing her eyes back to Ben's expectant ones. She heaved in a breath. *Just say it.*

"I'm sorry, Ben, but I can't marry you."

Chapter Thirty-Three

*B*en's face appeared paralyzed. It barely even moved when he forced out, "You don't mean that." His hands clutched the arms of his wheelchair, tendons protruding starkly.

Sinking into a chair so she wouldn't be looking down on him, Charlene expelled a breath. "I do, Ben. I can't go through with it. It's not fair to you."

"No, you're just nervous, that's all, now that we're counting down and the invitations are almost ready and—"

She stopped his words by laying a hand on his forearm. He just looked at it.

"Then why?" His voice strained. "We're so good together, can't you see that? Don't doubt us, please. You've never been able to see how perfect we are together. You've always made me work so hard to convince you—"

"Exactly. Ben, don't you see?" She held his gaze. "You should never have had to 'convince' me. I never wanted this—you—enough," she admitted softly. It was always more the idea of finding that safe happily-ever-after that she'd yearned for.

Ben shook his head and took her hand. "If it's because you're mad about still not having a ring, I haven't forgotten. It's in the works. It will be worth the wait, I promise. Just give me a few more weeks. That's all—"

"Oh Ben, it's nothing to do with the ring. I never should have said yes in the first place. It's my fault. You just . . . you did everything right . . . I couldn't see . . ."

"Excuses." He dropped her hand. "You've just never forgiven me for the Fourth of July, have you? How many times do I have to say I'm—"

"This has nothing to do with the Fourth of July."

"Doesn't it?" Anger crept into his tone. "Maybe it has everything to do with it. You're breaking your promise to marry me, let me ask you this. Did you break your other promise, too?"

"I don't know what you mean."

"Don't you?" he said tersely. "Have you seen Clay since you promised me you wouldn't?"

She swallowed. "Not intentionally. Our paths crossed a couple times, but—"

Ben smacked the arm of his chair. "Perfect. I saw this coming. I warned you not to move away, not to move near him, but you did anyway." He turned hard eyes on her. "Like you wanted this to happen. And that kiss. You don't just have commitment issues, you have all sorts of issues. You have ever since I've known you. I've treated you like spun glass. No one else is going to do that for you, Charlene. Not another guy, certainly not your precious ex-convict."

"Ben—"

"Let me finish. You told me I could trust you. You led me on all this time, wasted years of my life. I'm supposed to be okay with that?"

"I'm so sorry." Her thumb rubbed her palm, heating her scar with friction. "I didn't realize that's what I was doing. That was never my intention."

"Then what was your intention? Because I tell you, mine was always honorable." A single tear leaked from his eye. He dashed it away. "Always."

Her throat tightened to a dangerous point, and she didn't know how much more she could take. "We're not right for each other, that's all. You can't tell me you haven't sensed that. How we've changed, drifted apart—"

"Drifted? More like ripped. Ripped apart by you and that loser."

"Don't. He's not."

"So you'll stand up for him. You'll be loyal to him. But me, nah. Forget about me. Forget about us." Ben spread his hands. "Nothing worth holding onto here. Just three years' worth of nothing. If it's that easy for you to walk away, then go ahead. Do it."

Knowing words would fail her, she pleaded with her eyes for him to understand, but was met with a stony stare.

"Do it," he repeated.

Despite the bitter words, she knew he didn't want her to accept the challenge. Her feet stayed braced against the floor. "Can't you see I'm trying to make this right?"

"But you can't. There's no making this right." His tone mocked. "Not like this. You're only trying to ease your conscience, that's all. What do you want me to say? 'I don't mind, go ahead and dump me and marry the guy you've been seeing behind my back.' Is that it?

Is that what you want to hear? 'Cause you'll be waiting a long time if it is."

She pulled in a jagged breath.

"And why don't you even cry? At least pretend this is hard for you?" His tone dripped disgust. "I swear, Charlene, sometimes I think your heart is ice."

Her voice came out in a tiny whisper. "If you think that, then you don't know me at all." The burning at the back of her eyes intensified, unbearable, but she fought it with everything she had. No way would she let tears fall now.

His words echoed in her head. *". . . your heart is ice."*

But even a heart of ice could break. Her chest wrenched with a pain like her heart shattering, for everything they had shared that she thought had meant so much. Worthless now.

"I should go." She could say she was sorry a thousand more times, but it wouldn't ease their suffering. She rose on weak knees and headed for the study door.

"Wait, don't leave." Desperation filled Ben's voice. "Would it make any difference if—"

Something told her she had to turn and look.

She did. And what she saw made her mouth drop open. At the same time, she stumbled back against the door with a hard *bump*.

Ben no longer sat in his wheelchair, but stood unaided in front of it. He let the image sink in, then took two unfaltering, strong steps to her side.

"How long?" she gasped up at him. She never thought she would see him stand over her again. "How long have you been able to walk?" Her feeling of what should have been happiness for him was blotted by incredulity and something else, something far from joy.

"Only a few months. It happened so gradually, with all the therapy. I didn't believe it could, at first. The chances were so low, but—"

"Why didn't you tell me? You told me there was no hope. All this time you had me believing—"

"I wanted to surprise you." He ducked his head.

"No." She studied the shameful expression he was trying to mask. "There's more to it than that. You don't hide something like that. Not from your fiancée."

His head whipped back up. "If you'd been a better fiancée, I wouldn't have felt like I had to." His words cut deep, and he looked regretful the moment they escaped. He put his hand lightly on her shoulder, and she winced.

"You don't realize how well I know you, how well I can read you. My being unable to walk, and the guilt you felt . . . that was the only thing keeping you with me. Don't deny it. If you had known, you would have already been gone. I needed the extra time to win you back."

Her disbelief at the monumental scale of his deception gagged her. She couldn't wrap her mind around it. "And your family's known all this time . . . you've all gone along with this façade when I've visited. And at church . . ." She pictured him in the wheelchair. He'd gone to such elaborate lengths to keep the secret. "All along, I've been the brunt of this huge, cruel joke." She shook his hands off her.

Pain flashed over his face. "Why can't you just be happy for me? For us?"

Because there is no us.

Then like a punch to her gut, she was struck by a horrifying thought. She put a hand over her mouth. "The break-in. The damage to your wheelchair. Tell me that was real. You didn't make all that up too, did you? In some twisted scheme for pity or—"

"No!" His eyes snapped. "I would never stage that. It was real, I swear."

She believed him, but wasn't comforted.

"Please try to understand," he said earnestly. "I was going to tell you."

"How do I know that?" She put a hand on the cold doorknob. "If I hadn't broken up with you—would you have just gone on with the sham till you—you'd caught me and married me?" Her voice faltered. "We always promised to be honest with each other, Ben."

"Yeah, well, then we both failed. But that doesn't mean we have to throw everything away."

A thought crackled through her, shocking like static. "Kate." She turned back. "Did she know?"

"Know what?"

She could see the dread forming on his face.

She had her answer.

But she would make him say it. "Did she know that you recovered, that you can walk?"

At least he was man enough to meet her eyes. "Yes."

She gave a short nod and whispered, "She's been there for you."

"Charlene, please. We can work through this."

"No. There's nothing left to work through." She turned the knob and stepped into the hall. "I'm done. I'm saying goodbye, Ben. But I'm glad you can walk again. I really am."

"Of course you are." He spat the words. "It's all very convenient for you. Now you can run back to your kidnapper, guilt free."

Teeth clenched, she strode down the hall as Ben hurried after her. As they passed the living room, Lucy looked up, saw him walking, and chimed in mockingly, "Well alleluia, it's a miracle!"

Indeed, and I prayed for that miracle.

Sometimes it was funny how God answered prayers.

―――

The woman was so tired, but the baby was crying again. So loud, so heartbreaking, wails of sorrow that couldn't be quenched, pulling at her, tugging her from the insulating cavern of sleep where she didn't have to feel. Didn't have to remember . . .

She pulled her eyes open to darkness. Ears straining, she heard only silence and realized she didn't have to get up after all.

But she was awake now. Her hand slid beside her over the cold mattress and her heart panged. Awake and alone in her bed. Always alone. Would he ever take his rightful place beside her?

She released a quivery sigh and rested her hand on her stomach, her saggy, slack-skinned belly like an empty, floppy bag. Empty like her heart.

She squeezed a fistful of skin. The plan hadn't worked. Yet she was like a moth drawn to his treacherous flame. Returning again and again, despite her singed wings.

Tears leaked, wetting her pillow. She remembered when he was all hers. Only hers. He would be again. She couldn't give up. All she needed was a new bargaining chip to ensure his return.

There had to be something . . . some way . . .

She sat up suddenly, knowing what she had to do.

―――

Was he dying? He'd heard life flashes before you when you're dying. Didn't seem worth it, but his brain flashed anyway. The lonely house. The rancid smells. Hunger gnawing. The witch of a woman, the needle scars in her arms. Her screams. *"I'm your mother! Respect me!"*

He never did.

He was glad when she was gone.

Foster homes. So many. So many things for the taking.

The Callaghans. They had the most. If he could have taken all their money . . .

None of the others had as much as them, but there was always something to take. And nothing to stop him. The fools knew it was him, but they couldn't prove it.

He took to the streets, learning real life skills. Fighting. Building brain and brawn. People started to fear him.

Fear gave him power.

At eighteen, he was free of the foster system and celebrated with a needle to the arm. But not like the witch. Never like the witch.

The tattoos pleased him. The nails looked right. Hard. Sharp. Tough. He'd chosen the old Roman kind—rugged and barbaric.

He robbed his first convenience store that week. The rush was better than any drug. An invigorating high. And he was just getting started . . .

Now he sat up on the edge of the mattress, his head murky. His arms rubbery. Belly so starved it felt like it was eating itself. Pitiful. Weak. But he wasn't dying after all. Just as well. He had big plans before he'd be ready for hell.

He pushed aside the musty quilt, then rubbed his jaw and found a stubbly beard. How long had he been out? He stumbled to the window and saw sludgy snow, dripping branches.

His tongue felt like it was growing fungus. He scraped it against his fuzzy teeth, then moved to the cupboard and rummaged for food. He chomped down on a stick of jerky and ripped it in two. A few days to get his strength back, to make arrangements, then time to uncover his money, time to leave the country.

Time to start living at last.

—~~—

"Miss, you'll need to turn your phone off now," the flight attendant said pleasantly as she paused near Charlene's seat. "We'll be taking off momentarily."

Complying, Charlene powered her phone down. She'd seen no messages of importance, anyway, just more missed calls from Ben.

Sighing, she settled back in her seat, thankful she was getting away. Not running away. There was a difference. Taking a break. Gaining perspective. This California trip couldn't have come at a better time. Saying goodbye to the cold, snowy Midwest and hello to the sunny West Coast was just the therapy she needed.

The one and only thing she had to worry about in California was reconnecting with Max.

He still didn't know she was coming, or that she would be sitting in the audience tomorrow night when he debuted his new trick, but she planned to surprise him by visiting him backstage after the show.

In the shuttle from San Francisco International, she popped on her large movie-star shades and took in the sights. Tall, top-heavy palm trees and countless historic buildings flashed by, and she was glad she wasn't the one navigating the steep roads, where drivers zipped and wove brazenly through congested traffic.

If Max had known she was coming, he might have sprung for a classy beach hotel, but she was content with what she could afford, a small one-room place with a view of a brick wall. She'd mainly be using it for sleeping, anyway.

That night she found that the street her motel was on didn't settle down at dark. A steady din of honking horns, revving motors, and loud voices thrummed through the night. The dingy drapes didn't prevent lights from flashing into her room and across her bed, either. Though she preferred a night light, this glare was too much. It made her realize what a sleepy little town Creekside was.

And when she thought of Creekside, she thought of Clay. And those feelings were nothing but conflicted. Despite Ben's certainty, she had no intention of pathetically turning to Clay.

She hadn't seen him in over a month—the night he'd told her he loved her. And she still didn't know what to do with that.

Having just ended a long, serious relationship, it was too soon to think about starting another. Clay deserved more than a desperate rebound. She couldn't do that to him. He already thought he loved her. If she couldn't follow through and commit, it wouldn't be fair and she'd end up hurting him even more.

The pain she'd seen a month ago was already too much.

She needed time.

She tramped down her internal mess and closed her eyes. Someday, if Clay was still waiting for her, then maybe . . .

But she wouldn't blame him if he wasn't.

Lying in bed, she rubbed the blue beads of her rosary between her fingers as she murmured prayers.

When she closed her eyes, she saw herself, years and years from now . . . never married. Spending her days as a librarian, the storytime kids her children for an hour. She'd fill her nights peacefully, reading, sewing, praying. Stability. Safety. More blessings than many had in life. It would be enough. She would thank the Lord and be content.

―――

Nails bit his cheek. Something wasn't right. The dirt under the rock looked suspicious, almost freshly disturbed. He flung off the earth, ripped off the bucket lid, looked inside the ten gallon space, and cursed.

The money was gone.

Enraged, he plunged his hand into the emptiness, scrabbling his fingers through the mocking traces of dirt, refusing to believe the cash was missing.

But it was.

All of it.

Nothing here but a hole and dirt.

Pawing feverishly through the surrounding soil, his eyes caught a bright fleck of blue. He plucked it up and studied it. A ragged crescent of some kind of tough fibrous material. Like a . . . fingernail. A broken, painted fingernail. *What the . . . ?*

Then he saw something else . . . something that made him forget all about the nail, something plastic—a red tube of familiar lip balm.

Strawberry.

―――

The surging river of anticipation swept her with the crowd into the huge building, above which Max's name blazed in lights. It still seemed like a huge joke that he had somehow pulled this off, duping everyone into paying money to see him, her ridiculous brother, perform illusions on a stage. That was the greatest trick of all.

Judging from tonight's turnout, he was doing well. His initial success, it couldn't be denied, was primarily due to the fact that he was a survivor of the shocking Perigard kidnapping. But five years later, she figured something more drew them, or he wouldn't have lasted this long. He'd always had enough charisma and personality for the two of them, and as his twin, she'd often suspected he'd somehow snatched her share right from birth.

Inside the grand auditorium, an usher led her to her seat in the center of a distant middle row. Settling in, she scanned the room. Old ornate lighting cast a honeyed glow. Balconies swooped from the walls. A dusky stage curtain hung in thick folds.

The air of expectancy in the large space was palpable as she waited to be amazed and mystified as promised. Lights dimmed, the steady hum of audience voices hushed, and the curtain spread open with a soft wing-like flutter, much like her heart fluttered in nervous anticipation. Even knowing Max had performed countless times, she still felt stage fright for him.

An eerie dry-ice mist hung low on the empty stage. Deep, mysterious tones of music swelled. A wide spotlight settled mid-stage.

"And now," a loud voice boomed, "the amazing Max Perigard!"

Poof, a plume of smoke appeared. As it dissipated, there stood Max, finely dressed and exuding a presence that owned the stage. He flung out a silk handkerchief that grew into a huge rippling satin sheet. The second he released it, he disappeared in a burst of smoke. The fabric floated down over the empty stage, but as it did, a large form of something appeared beneath it.

With a startling *vroom*, a Lamborghini burst from the fabric. The driver's door opened, and out stepped Max, to wild applause. He flung out his arm, directing attention to the passenger door. It opened, and out stepped his sparkling assistant.

An array of impressive illusions followed, including a levitation trick, a box pierced with daggers, and Max passing through a mirror, till at last the time came for the highlight of the show: Max's first-ever performance of what he called the Glass Casket.

After presenting the long, clear casket from all angles for the audience's scrutiny, Max climbed inside and lay down, deathlike. His wrists and ankles were handcuffed by his beaming assistant, who then closed the lid of the casket and locked it.

Charlene didn't like it.

Next, four muscular hooded "pallbearers" marched solemnly onstage and upended the casket so that Max was upside down, and the audience now saw him standing on his handcuffed hands.

While the pallbearers moved off to the side of the stage, his assistant attached a tube to the top of the casket, and everyone watched as blood red liquid pumped in.

Charlene squirmed. Max took one last breath right before the liquid covered his face. At that point, she held her breath, her timer for how long he could go without air while he worked his escape. Of course, she realized he'd trained to increase his breath-holding endurance, but the thought didn't comfort her.

Tense, somber funeral-like music played. Time ticked, her lungs burst for air, and the red liquid now reached halfway. Max moved and turned, splashing as he did so. She gave in and gasped for breath.

When liquid reached the top of the casket, the tube was removed. Everyone waited.

For dramatic effect, his assistant picked up a sledgehammer and handed it to one of the pallbearers, who stepped forward and poised as if ready to smash the glass and set Max free.

Charlene wished he'd use it.

Her knuckles came to her lips, where she pressed them against her teeth.

The beat of the music intensified to an agitating extreme while the entire audience stayed hushed.

Too long. It's taking too long.

Like an alarm going off in her lungs, she felt her chest burn.

Something's wrong.

Just as she was about to shoot to her feet, the pallbearer smashed the glass. Shattering sounds rang out amidst audience gasps. The red liquid spewed onstage, revealing—no one.

Two pairs of empty handcuffs lay amidst the shards of glass. Max was gone.

The pallbearer whipped off his hood, and there he stood. Calm, jubilant. Successful. Max.

Relieved, Charlene released a wavering breath. Sweat chilled her body while the audience went crazy.

Now she knew why she didn't watch his performances. Way too nerve-wracking.

When she finally found her way to him after the show, she attacked him with a hug.

———

So she was on vacation, was she? The boy Nails had paid to inquire at Fannie's Fabrics gave him that much at least, which explained why he hadn't been able to spot her no matter how long he staked out her apartment. Of course, with that kind of money, why not go on vacation?

He squeezed the lip balm. Had she left it on purpose to taunt him, or dropped it by accident? Either way, a stupid move.

A deadly move.

He scratched his newly shaven face. Her Corolla still sat in the lot. But when she came back, when it moved, he'd know, and he'd follow, and then she'd never come home again.

Fresh rage filled him, as it did every time he thought about her sneaking onto his territory. Her betrayal.

They'd had an understanding. He'd spared Cissy for her, and she dared steal from him? And the trailer was no good to him now. He couldn't go back. She might have talked. She'd taken everything from him. Everything.

He wouldn't be merciful again.

Never make the same mistake twice.

—————

"You were right. Ben wasn't the one," Charlene admitted. "I broke up with him."

Max could have taunted, "told you so," but he didn't. He hugged her, said, "Man, I'm sorry, Char," and left it at that.

She stayed with him for a month. They made up easily for lost time, and when he wasn't performing, they spent time wearing ball caps and concealing sunglasses while enjoying the San Francisco sights.

As they walked the Golden Gate Bridge one damp, misty morning, Max admitted he hadn't dated anyone in over half a year. A record for him.

On Fisherman's Warf, they ate soup out of bread bowls as they had as kids. Then they toured the acclaimed wax museum on Jefferson Street, though she could have done without the chamber of horrors.

When Max couldn't convince her to visit Alcatraz, he settled for the Ghirardelli Chocolate Factory, then took her out of San Francisco, cruising coastal roads in his McLaren convertible. The wind tangled her hair into hopeless snarls, but it was worth it when they ended up at a beach.

Sitting on the sun-warmed white sand, she filled Max in on the craziness in her life, and he shared his unfiltered opinions on it all. Especially when it came to Clay.

"He told you he loved you?" Max's tone sounded angry, but for once, she read him wrong. "What took him so long?"

She scooped up some sand and let it trickle out, a dry waterfall through her fingers. "Come on, Max, seriously. I don't know what to do."

"What's the big problem? Go see him. Talk to him. You want to, don't you?"

"I don't know." She brushed her hands clean. "I mean, I wasn't sure about Ben, and look how that turned out. How can I be sure with Clay?"

"You kidding me, Char?" Max turned an exasperated expression on her. "You don't have to be sure. Not right now. You haven't even dated the guy. If he ever proposes, that's when you need to be sure."

She watched the frothy waves and considered his words until he interrupted. "I guess what it comes down to is, you've gotta ask yourself if it's worth the risk."

The risk? Her stomach whirled. She gazed out at daring surfers riding the waves. She'd never been one to take risks.

Max rotated a Frisbee in his hands. "So much for convincing you to move out here. Guess there's no chance now. Not with Clay waiting for you back there."

She opened her mouth, but she couldn't honestly protest.

And Max knew it. He nudged her and grinned. "So I'll just have to find a way to make time to visit you. Which reminds me. You found the perfect girl for me yet?"

She rolled her eyes. "That's a tall order. Give me a couple more years. At least."

"I'll give you twenty. I'm in no hurry." He jumped up. "Come on, let's go toss the Frisbee."

Chapter Thirty-Four

*C*harlene returned to Creekside with a decent tan and the hope that Max might visit soon. The last of the ice and snow had melted in her absence, and recent rain greened the grass. The air was laden with the scent of spring and new beginnings.

While Charlene recounted her trip and snuggled Gabriella, Brook sat cross-legged on the carpet, folding burp cloths, blankets, sleepers, Onesies, and an impossible array of miniscule socks.

"If Max ends up coming to visit on a regular basis, maybe he'd like to rent this place with you," Brook suggested.

Puzzled, Charlene stroked a finger over Gabriella's petal-soft cheek. "But you and Gabriella—"

"We can't stay here much longer." Brook smoothed a flannel burp cloth and proceeded to fold it excessively into a compact square. "I want Gabriella to have her own room eventually, and a yard, and my aunt in Bloomington invited us to come stay with her. My uncle died last year, and she's lonely. She never had any children of her own. She even said she would take care of Gabriella so I can go back to school."

"But—"

"I think it's best." Brook looked up with a steady smile. "Gabriella's real dad lives here, but he's no good for us." She swallowed, her smile slipping slightly. "Also . . . it's only a matter of time before you and Clay—"

Charlene tried to shake her head but couldn't quite manage it.

"It's okay, Charlene. And anyway, I think . . . I think you loved him first."

Charlene's lips parted, but no words came.

"It's okay," Brook repeated. "I'm okay with it. I . . . I just don't want to be here to see it."

An ache in her heart, Charlene cradled Gabriella tighter and buried her face in her sweet baby-shampoo scent, relishing it.

Memorizing it.

———

Leaving nothing to chance, the woman stuck a GPS tracker on the bottom of the girl's car. Like a fat boxy beetle, it held tight. Right next to the other one.

Inside her apartment, she settled near her window, a pillow plump and heavy in her lap, sewing it shut with precise, tiny, strong stitches, and imagined the future. So close now. So close.

Countless stitches later, she stabbed the needle through the fabric one last time and pulled the thread taut before biting it off with a satisfying *snap.*

The girl was finally going to get what was coming to her.

———

On a shiny April day, after finishing an early work shift, Charlene walked out to her bike to find Ben in the parking lot leaning against the hood of his car.

"You up for a hike?" he asked nonchalantly, as if they hadn't parted on bad terms over two months ago.

Amazed at his persistence but dreading a confrontation, she merely reached to unchain her bike. The weather had been so mild ever since her return, she hadn't even used her car yet. Ben stilled her hand. "Come on, Charlene. Just talk to me. I hate how we left things."

She wiggled her hand out from under his. "I have nothing left to say. That's why I didn't answer your calls."

"But I need to apologize. I'm sorry I let my temper get the best of me. I want to make it up to you. For all we've been to each other, can't you give me that? A little bit of your time? You don't have anything else planned right now, do you?"

She should have made something up, but instead she admitted she had no plans besides cleaning her apartment.

"Knowing you, it doesn't need it."

She almost laughed. He had her there.

"So let's go on a hike. For old time's sake. Just this one last time, please. No strings attached."

She squinted into the sun, pretending to debate. His request was so solemnly heartfelt, she didn't have it in her to refuse. Besides, if humoring him for a final farewell was what it would take for him to accept they were over, she was willing to give him that.

Reading the answer in her eyes, Ben opened his car door, and she slipped in as she had so many times in the past. He tossed her bike in the trunk, and they were off.

She wasn't expecting him to take her all the way to Sunset Lookout, though. She didn't know what he was thinking—if he still thought he could rekindle their dead romance, or if he was just oblivious to the last time they'd hiked this path to the rocky outcropping. Either way, it wasn't a place she wanted to revisit. Yet he led her to the same ledge he'd proposed on.

"You're not going to push me off for some kind of crazy revenge, are you?" she quipped, and he looked stricken.

"Don't joke like that, Charlene. I brought you here to show you something." As he spoke, he produced a harness and rope from the bushes. He preceded to strap the harness on, then attach the rope securely around the base of a tree.

"Just wait." He flashed his best smile, then approached the ledge. He turned around, grasped the colorful rope, and began to rappel over the edge.

Fear fluttered within her. From wheelchair to rock climbing in a matter of months. *That's Ben.* She wasn't sure whether to be impressed or concerned.

She crept as close to the edge as she dared, and waited, hands at her stomach.

"Stand clear, I'm coming back up," he announced, to her relief.

She backed up to a giant coppery rock. When his flushed face appeared, she wondered if this whole episode was a return-to-conquer-your-fears kind of thing. As if he had to show the cliff who was boss.

Musing, she didn't register the transformation on his face as he approached. Stopping in front of her, still in rope and harness, he dropped to one knee on the pine-needled rock. As he held out a ring, she regarded him incredulously. "What are you doing?"

"Exactly what it looks like." He cleared his throat. "It was one year ago today, exactly, that I first proposed to you. I want us to have a fresh start. This is our second chance. We can get it right this time." A trickle of sweat dripped down his forehead.

"Charlene Elizabeth Perigard, will you marry me?" He held up the ring, pinched between his thumb and forefinger, and waited.

"Is this . . . the original ring?"

"The one and the same. I didn't want to settle for a replacement. You deserve the original."

"And—is that what you were doing? You just found it now?

How could you have known—"

He shifted uncomfortably on his knee. "Okay. I found it weeks ago, with hours of searching and the help of a metal detector. That's not important." He swiped a hand across his forehead, leaving a dirt streak, and sighed. "Try not to overanalyze it. I did this today for the effect."

As in, to impress her. As in, look-what-lengths-I-went-to-for-you. As in, I-love-you-this-much. Undeniably romantic.

And sadly desperate.

Her voice came out soft. "Thank you, Ben, but I still can't marry you."

"Why not?"

"I don't love you."

His crestfallen look was replaced by determination. He squinted intently. "Marry me anyway. Please."

A small sound moved her throat. Her heart broke to hear him beg so pitifully. "You can't mean that. You're asking me to chain you to a loveless marriage. I would never do that to you. You deserve—"

"But I want you. I have so much to offer you. I'm even starting fulltime with the fire department next month. We can forget this year ever happened. We're right for each other. Maybe you can't see that now, but I'm sure you'd come to love me over time." His hand without the ring squeezed into a fist. "That's enough for me."

"And if I didn't, you'd come to hate me. And resent me. You would."

"*Never.* You're all I need. You're—" His voice cracked. "Look—look inside the ring. The inscription you never got to read. Look at it now, and . . . reconsider."

The wet shine in his eyes and his distressing plea were tragic. If she'd known she was in for this emotional turmoil, she never would have agreed to the hike.

Acquiescing, she took the ring from him and carefully looked inside the band, tilting it to read the words engraved in gold.

The sun caught the inscription: *The answer to a prayer.*

He thought she was the answer to his prayer.

Her heart squeezed.

"Oh, Ben." She lowered the ring and took his hand gently. "Sometimes, the answer to a prayer . . . is no."

She laid the ring in his palm and curled his fingers around it before letting go.

The day after Ben's proposal, Charlene detected an odd odor, like a bad perfume, in the apartment hall when she came home from work. Entering her place, she almost slipped on a sheet of white paper lying on the floor just inside her door. The white rectangle stood out starkly on the gray linoleum. Jadedly, she wondered if Ben had pushed a letter under her door. She sincerely hoped not. Amazingly, he hadn't tried calling once since the disastrous hike, and she was fairly sure she'd finally gotten through to him.

When she flipped the paper over, she saw no penned or typed words of any kind, only a simple printed picture. It wasn't even a photograph, but a clip art image of an old-fashioned hourglass with sand running through.

Time running out? Fear skittered over her skin.

It wasn't an obvious threat, yet she sensed it was sinister. Maybe she was reading into it. She had thought—dared hoped—the cruelties of last year were done, that they wouldn't follow her to Creekside, but now it seemed they'd caught up to her at last.

Not wanting to study the picture any longer, she flipped it over and laid it on her counter.

That night as she sat missing Brook and Gabriella, the ticking wall clock brought to mind the hourglass, and she wondered how many more tense nights she'd have to endure alone.

Overflowing with nervous energy, she jumped up and began cleaning, sweeping floors that didn't need it, vacuuming carpet that was already spotless, even moving the sofa in search of dust bunnies.

And there on the floor among the puffs of gray, lay a black rosary. She dropped to her knees and scooped it up, knowing instantly that it was Clay's, remembering the night he had told her about it.

That strange, wonderful, awful night.

She brushed the dust off, watched the particles float down, then stared at the beads dangling from her fingers and realized the rosary must have ended up under the sofa the night Nails had kicked it, the night of the robbery.

She remained on her knees, head bowed. All this time, Clay had been without it. But knowing what it meant to him, her grasp tightened, knowing something else.

Whether she wanted to or not, she would have to give it back.

Cutting fabric yardage for customers the next day, Charlene's heart alternately sank and bobbed with dread and elation. Today, after work, she would return the rosary. Today she would see Clay.

"Excuse me? Miss?"

Her scissors stilled and she looked up at a customer.

"I said I needed three yards of flannel, not two."

"Oh, sorry." She swiped the piece off the cutting table, unraveled the flannel bolt, and began again. *Concentrate this time. Don't think about Clay.*

So instead, the unpleasant hourglass popped to mind. She could pinpoint two people who might want to frighten or threaten her: Nails or Horace. Ben flitted through her mind, but she immediately dismissed him. She knew him too well. Though he may be feeling hurt, he would never stoop so low.

Nails was still unaccounted for, but by his own admission of intent, he was likely gone from the country, enjoying Grandfather's money. The more time passed, the more secure she felt accepting that.

Her scissors paused. Maybe Grandfather had left the picture. Although, if he was going to threaten her, she would expect something much more elaborate.

Which left her with Horace, who—creepy as he was—had faded to the back of her mind. Since she hadn't seen him in so long, she doubted he was a concern. Unless he wanted her to grow complacent, unsuspecting. Maybe he had found the knife.

She folded the fabric, pinned on the price, then handed it to the waiting customer. As the woman walked away, Charlene realized something. She'd never told Clay about her online discovery and her suspicion that Horace might be deluded enough to believe he could break a curse by using her—or Clay—as sacrificial victims.

Now two reasons she had to see him today. Maybe the Horace theory was crazy, but she'd rather warn Clay than regret it.

Or maybe, she thought as she peddled home, she was looking for excuses to see him that wouldn't appear desperate and needy.

After showering and taking extra time with her clothes and hair, she slipped in a pair of new hoop earrings, tucked Clay's rosary in her purse, and headed out to the parking lot.

She climbed into her car for the first time in two months. The interior smelled stale, and she opened her windows. As she drove, excess energy made her hands skittish on the wheel.

All over Sam's front yard, the first dandelions of spring flaunted bright yellow heads. She parked and exited to the buzz of a distant saw. Passing Sam's truck in the drive, she did a double-take at a magnetic door sign advertising *Sam and Son's Custom Carpentry.*

Well . . . now that was something. A sense of contentment descended on her. Clay and Sam must have reached a very agreeable reconciliation indeed. She was glad, but then disappointed when she didn't see Clay's truck anywhere.

The buzzing saw ceased and she knocked on the door frame to announce herself as she stepped into the shop, which was once again much messier than she'd ever allowed.

Sam looked up and caught her disapproving glance. "Come back for your old job? I'll hire you anytime."

She smiled but stayed hovering near the entrance, scanning the shop. "I'm here to talk to Clay. Is he around?"

Sam tucked a short pencil behind his ear. "Nope."

She waited for him to expand on the statement, but he didn't.

Like prying a pearl from an oyster. "Is he out on a delivery? Will he be back soon?"

"You could call him." Sam hefted a board. "All I know's, a guy stopped by to talk to him, and soon after that, Clay took off. Didn't explain nothing to me."

Sensing Sam's gritty irritation, she stepped back. "The guy, was he a customer?"

"Never seen him before, and he didn't place an order."

"What did he look like?"

Sam's wrinkled brow said, *You think I got time to notice things like that?* Yet, humoring her, he replied, "Young."

So not Horace.

"Was he real big?"

"Tall, but not huge."

Not Nails. "His hair?"

"Real dark. Black, I'd say."

She immediately thought of Ben, his hair so dark brown, practically everyone mistook it for black. Her chest seized. Whatever Ben might have wanted, she knew it wouldn't have been good. Of course, the visitor might have been no one she knew, and meant nothing, but she couldn't ignore her concern.

"Thanks, Sam."

Hands occupied, he jutted his chin in acknowledgment. "Don't be a stranger 'round here."

Back in her car, she slipped out her phone and did what she'd been telling herself for months that she would not do. She called Clay.

"Hey," he answered.

She assumed his phone had shown who was calling, but she clarified anyway. "Hi, Clay, it's Charlene."

When he remained silent, she pressed on and tried to keep her nerves from disrupting her vocal cords. "Where are you? Can I come talk to you?"

While she waited uncomfortably for his answer, she heard a distracting background noise, similar to phone static, but more natural, more like wind.

"Sure." He didn't sound eager. "I'll be home tonight."

"Oh." She didn't want to wait that long. "So you're busy right now?"

"Not busy. Just far."

"Oh." She slid her thumb along the steering wheel. "How far?"

"Lake Michigan. I was out this way to drop off an order and figured I'd stop."

She pictured him walking the beach alone. "Would you care if I joined you?"

"Why would I care?"

Choosing to ignore the stiffness of his tone, she let out a breath. "All right, I'm heading that way. Will you meet me in the lot?"

"Don't drive all the way out here. I'll drive back."

"No, it's fine." She could use the time to think. "I want to, really. I'll call when I get there."

Hanging up, she felt a strange anticipation. Hopeful thoughts rolled through her mind, and the drive didn't feel nearly as long as it was.

When she arrived, she didn't need to call, because Clay was already waiting, leaning against a tree trunk on the border of the lot. Theirs were the only vehicles.

"You made good time." He kept his arms folded across his chest as she walked over. "Weren't speeding, were you?"

She shook her head, so glad to see him that she wanted to just stand a moment and study his face. Feeling foolish, she looked down at her shoes and remembered why she was here. She dug the rosary from her pocket and held it out to him. "I found this."

He took it, not commenting.

"I thought you'd be missing it."

He shrugged and shoved it in his pocket. "I've got other rosaries. One's as good as another."

Despite the splash of sun on her shoulders, the breeze chilled her. Or perhaps it was his words.

He tilted his head. "You got your ears pierced."

She touched the silver hoops and nodded. "In December." So long ago. It shouldn't matter if he liked them or not. But she didn't want to stand there as if waiting for his statement to lead to a compliment. "Can we walk?"

They fell into step and trod the weathered, uneven boards of the cordwalk, which reminded her of a small-scale railroad track winding off into the trees, then out into open grass and weeds. The path was just wide enough for them to walk alongside each other, but narrow enough to make the side-by-side feel almost too close.

Neither one of them, though, made the move to go ahead or fall back. Clay kept his hands in his pockets. As they meandered, she heard waves surging and caught occasional glimpses of vibrant blue water. As she explained what she'd come across about the snake knife on the Satanic Museum website and laid out her theory, the entire thing sounded ludicrous to her ears.

He listened with few comments, and when she was done, he said in a worn voice, "That's what you wanted to tell me?" His fists jammed deeper in his pockets. "You couldn't have told me that over the phone?"

"I—I—" He was right. Why had she come all this way? Her brain scrambling, she cringed at the thought of admitting anything further. Her gaze fell on bitty bursts of purple flowers. "I wanted to give you the rosary. And see you." Her heart picked up speed. "I haven't seen you in months."

"I was in town all that time. You could have stopped by. Any time."

"I know." But she hadn't. She looked off to the fuzzy horizon. "I wanted to," she confessed. She slanted him a hesitant glance as her face heated. "I just wasn't sure if you'd really want to see me. After everything . . ." *After I rejected you.*

Maybe now it would be his turn to reject her. Could she risk that? Was it worth it? Her stomach knotted. "Did Ben come talk to you today?"

Not even asking how she knew, he answered, "He did."

Trepidation filled her. "I don't know what he said to you, but I can imagine."

"I don't think you can."

Did he have to make this so difficult? "I'm sorry."

He squinted up at the sky, then down at the grass. "For what?"

She wasn't even sure anymore. Yet there was so much sorrow inside her, it was all she could think to say. "For Ben. For you. For everything. But whatever he said, just realize he didn't mean it. He was probably angry, and venting. I . . . I broke off the engagement."

"I know. He told me."

She bit her lip and braced herself. "What exactly did he say?"

"Exactly? Besides the breakup, he told me three things: First, that I won. Second, that he always knew you had your heart set on me. And last of all, that if I ever hurt you, I'd have to answer to him."

Her face flamed. Before she could sputter out something to deflect the situation, Clay halted and looked her straight in the eye. "Is it true?"

She knew he wasn't referring to the part about answering to Ben. She almost wished he was. Unable to avoid his gaze, she stood statue-still. All she could manage was a nod.

As if that wasn't sufficient, he prodded, "So you do care about me?"

Again, she nodded.

He rubbed a hand against the side of his stubbly chin. "As a friend? Or more than that?"

She was done with nodding. *Lord help me, here comes the honest truth.* Summoning every thread of courage, she laid her hands on his shoulders, whispering, "More."

Right before she kissed him.

Chapter Thirty-Five

*C*lay returned the kiss. His hands wove into her hair, caressing gently yet strongly, pulling her closer. Needing her, like she needed him.

"Easy there, cowboy," a man's voice smashed the moment. "Don't start something you ain't ever gonna be able to finish."

In agony, Charlene recognized the voice. *No, not Nails. Not now.* She flinched at the sharp jab of something in her spine, between her shoulder blades. A gun.

Her eyelids didn't want to open to the nightmare, and her heart pounded against Clay as she tightened her grip. His arms wrapped her protectively, and she pressed her head against his shoulder. If she could just stay like this . . .

"Get the gun off her," Clay growled.

"Back away from her," Nails countered, "or I blast you both with one shot."

Clay whispered in her ear, "It'll be okay," before slowly releasing her. His hands spread wide as he stepped away, anger sparking from his eyes. "What could you possibly want now?"

"As if you don't know." Nails's arm cinched Charlene to his chest. His other hand jammed the gun to her temple. She tried not to tremble.

"Toss your phone on the ground in front of you," he directed Clay. "You too, sweetie." They did as he said, and he crushed their phones beneath his massive boots.

"Into the woods, Cissy," Nails ordered. "Move it."

Clay stalked off the path and into the trees, throwing back glares at Nails that said he'd like nothing more than to annihilate him. She knew he was scrambling for a solution. But a gun to her head didn't leave much leverage.

The frantic pulsation of her vein against the cold barrel only accentuated her fear as she walked deep into the woods. When there was nothing but thick wilderness around them in all directions, Nails ordered Clay to face a tree and put his hands behind his back.

Nails spoke in her ear, his breath hot. "I'm gonna release you now, but my gun's ready. Run, and your boyfriend gets the bullet." He let go of her and tossed a roll of duct tape at her feet. "Wrap his wrists, good and tight."

She plucked up the roll, praying that Nails would follow his previous pattern and as long as they cooperated, do no more harm than he had in the past. She hated the work her hands did, hated the ripping sound of the tape pulling from the roll. She watched herself go through the motions as if it were someone else wrapping around and around Clay's wrists until Nails told her to stop.

"Turn around, Cissy. Press your back up against the tree."

Clay whipped around like he couldn't wait for a confrontation. "Feel like using me as a punching bag again, that it? Feel like you don't stand a chance unless I can't swing back?"

Nails's mouth quirked. "Gettin' worried, are you? Maybe it's time you started prayin'." A look passed between the two men that Charlene couldn't decipher, but it chilled her.

Nails eyed her. "Wrap him to the tree."

Clay braced his back against the trunk.

"I'm sorry," she whispered to Clay as she began, remembering the times Abner had forced him to follow orders, and she'd had no comprehension how it felt to be on this end, powerless and hating herself. "I'm so sorry."

"Not your fault," Clay told her steadily. "None of it. Whatever happens, remember that."

Whatever happens? Her hands faltered, sticking to the tape. *He thinks he's going to die.*

Terror leaching into every part of her, she worked in a daze. Nails watched and nodded when she finished. "Good." He grasped her again and pulled her back several yards, pushing away her hair to speak in her ear. "Take a real good look, and know you did this to him."

She swallowed hard. "You made me."

Nails shook his head. "I would have left you both alone, if you'd left me alone."

She strained against his grasp. "What are you talking about?"

"Where is it?" His fingers traced her hair, the motion unnerving.

"Where's what?"

"My money."

"Your money?" Her mind blanked. "How should I know what you did with your money?" *Not that it is yours, you thief.*

He shoved something in her face. Strawberry ChapStick. "This is how. Found it where my money should've been."

She sputtered. "So? Is that supposed to mean something?"

"It does mean something." He shook her. White flecks ricocheted through her vision. "Your ChapStick was there, and the money's gone. So's your precious pearl necklace. The evidence says guilty."

"But I didn't—" It made no sense. "Why would I—"

"I don't want excuses. I want the truth." He clutched her jaw, puckering her lips. "This time, there's no second chance if you lie. Tell me where the money is, or pretty boy dies."

"I don't—"

He aimed the gun.

"No!" She shot Clay a desperate look.

"She knows nothing," he hollered. "I took it."

What? What was he doing? Instantly, she knew. Trying to protect her. "No, that's not true!" She glared at him. *Don't give him more reason to hurt you.*

He looked steadily at Nails, ignoring her. "It's in my cabin, up north. Let her go, and I'll show you where."

She stared, slack jawed. He was taking the lie and running with it, digging himself into a deadly hole. He had to know if Nails took him there and found no money, he would kill him. He was trying to save her.

Two could play that game.

"No, I took it. I'll take you to it. Just let Clay go."

Clay burned her with a look.

Nails chuckled. "You're both pitifully amusing, but I don't have all day. No one needs to be a hero. I want my money. That's it. Very simple. And I don't need the both of you to show me. I only need one. And I choose . . . you." He tapped her head. "Meaning I don't need you."

He leveled the gun at Clay, who glowered and said, "Go to hell."

"Sure, just not today. Today, it's your turn."

No. Her heart dropped to her feet. She'd hung onto the hope that Nails was a ruthless robber, but not a murderer. *Please, God, no.*

Nails's iron grip intensified, snatching her breath and incapacitating her arms. She felt like a useless rag doll as he peered down his gun at Clay. "Go on, beg for your life. Let your girl remember you like that, the true, cowering sissy you are."

Clay clenched his jaw and remained silent.

Charlene, however, lost it, struggling as tears coursed down her face. It couldn't end this way. Not after everything. "Stop," she implored. "Please, don't shoot." Struck by inspiration, she drew in a breath. "Please, Lance." It had worked before; maybe it would again.

She felt the jolt through his muscles. "You're out of luck, girl. I'm not Lance. Never will be again," he added softly.

"Coward," Clay spat. "Trying to settle a score with a gun." He strained against the tape. "Fight me like a man."

"Tough words." Nails sounded amused. "But you know who'd win that fight." He adjusted his aim. "You gonna grovel or not? It's that or meet your maker."

Clay scowled. "Why they thought it was okay to let you out of prison, I'll never know."

"No, you never will." With a swift, metallic thrust of the gun slide, Nails chambered a round. "Any last words?"

Clay's gaze was steady as steel, landing not on Nails, but her. "I love you, Charlene."

"Pathetic. And pointless." Nails squeezed the trigger.

The gun's sudden blast deafened her.

"No!" she screamed. *I didn't even have a chance to—*

She gasped in horror as the bullet made impact, all thoughts obliterated by the painful lurch of Clay's body. Then, worse, by his scream of agony.

And the blood.

Blood on his shoulder, on his chest, blooming like a macabre flower over his heart as he writhed and yelled.

But at least he wasn't dead.

Not yet.

Losing all sense of her own restriction, she tried to run to him, but couldn't.

Nails cussed and aimed again, obviously intending to finish the job. Frantic, she tried to slam him with her body, to jostle his aim, but she could barely move. Cinched against him as she was, her effort was pitiful.

The gun clicked, but didn't fire. Nails squeezed the trigger repeatedly and nothing happened. Not even a click. As he spewed profanity and gave the slide several rapid thrusts, Charlene realized the weapon must have jammed.

Clay's gasping cries continued, wringing her soul, shredding her heart.

Nails marched forward, dragging her with him, and stopped right in front of him.

"Shut up and die." Nails drew back the gun and pistol-whipped him with a resounding *crack* to his skull.

Instantly silent, Clay slumped against the tape.

Drowning in horror, Charlene shrieked and struggled.

Nails smacked a strip of duct tape over her mouth, muffling her cries, and hauled her away.

She fought to turn around, her mind a blaze of raging panic. Was Clay still alive? Was there any hope at all? Straining insanely, she felt like she was tearing her muscles. But she needed to see him. Needed a sliver of hope.

Nails's fingers dug into her arms. "You gonna walk nice, or should I knock you out and carry you?"

She stopped struggling. Dejected, sick with shock, dead inside, she plodded forward.

"Thought so."

They crunched noisily through the forest until she glimpsed the parking lot through the trees ahead. Before emerging, Nails surveyed the lot. Despite her desperate prayer, no one was waiting to save her.

Or to save Clay.

If that was still even possible.

Dear Lord, send angels all around him. Guard him. Protect him.

Nails shoved her to the ground, crushing a knee to her back while binding her wrists and ankles together with tape. After pawing through her purse and snatching her keys, he picked her up and strode to her car. He deposited her on the floor of the backseat before climbing in the front and locking the doors.

Her ears prickled when she heard the metallic sounds of the gun. He was unjamming it, readying it to use again. Dread pooled in her belly, jelling, then solidifying in a hard lump.

The car rumbled to life, and she felt every bump and jolt acutely. At her low eye view, she scanned for something she could use to free herself, but her car was too clean. All but the carpet. Her forehead grazed it and her nose registered that it needed odor control.

Shifting, she spotted, wedged under the front passenger seat, a black book. Her Bible, left and forgotten long ago during her impulsive move from Woodfield. The fact that she hadn't even realized it was missing till now, saddened her.

Despair clamored for admittance into her soul. She needed to fight it, but couldn't do it alone.

"For though I should walk in the midst of the shadow of death, I will fear no evils, for thou art with me . . ."

She gained strength from the memory of the verse Clay had quoted, knowing as she stared at the Bible, it was in there somewhere, along with all manner of suffering, miracles, hope, and salvation.

Trust in Him. All things are possible with the Lord.

She worked her way to an awkward sitting position. Nails reached back and ripped the tape from her mouth in one swift, stinging motion. The gun jabbed her head. "Give me the directions."

She rattled off the route to the cabin easily, since she'd driven it recently. Satisfied, he removed the gun. At least the drive would be long, giving her time, because when they got there and there was no money . . . she'd be all out of time.

She stared at her knees, wanting to ask if there was a chance Clay could still be alive, but not wanting to hear Nails's inevitable cruel reply. Her heart twisted. There was no one to notice she was gone or to report her missing. Not today. Same with Clay. Sam wouldn't think anything odd until it was far too late.

She tried to compact herself behind the driver's seat, to avoid any more incidents of a gun to her head, and to give herself a little support. From her odd angle, she watched bright shafts of sky slide past the opposite window. Snapshots of life. Here one second, gone the next.

After a long while, she whispered, "How did you get in my condo that night?"

Nails chuckled. "A simple key. I swiped yours and made a copy that day I bumped into you at school, then returned yours at lunch. Admit it, you liked my attention. It made you feel special."

The ludicrous claim wasn't even worth addressing. "You took pictures of me, too." She tried to ignore a fierce, inaccessible itch on her shoulder blade. "And you slipped that hourglass picture under my door. Why?"

He snorted. "Whatever you're talking about, that wasn't me."

She didn't know whether to believe him or not, but didn't argue. She focused on the itch and tried to rub it away against the seat.

"If my money's not at this cabin, you're gonna wish you were the one I shot."

She wet her lips.

His seat shifted. "Didn't spend any of it, did you?"

"No." *Couldn't spend what I didn't have.*

Her misery increased with each mile. What was she doing? She was backed into a deadly corner. He didn't want to believe the truth. If she convinced him of the truth now, he'd kill her. If she didn't, he'd kill her later. All she was doing was borrowing time.

So make use of it. Pray. Like your life depends on it.

The passion in her prayers drove her lips to move, to mumble, and Nails must have realized what she was doing, because he laughed. A horrible sound.

Be with me, Lord. She thought she was fortifying herself, steeling her soul with armor, but when she recognized the distinct, slow rocky crunch of the tires over gravel, her cramped muscles seized and she felt no bravery, only panic.

Nails left her locked in the car as he exited to case the cabin out. Much too soon, he returned to haul her from the vehicle and up the steps. Inside, he deposited her jarringly on the floor and slung her car keys on the kitchen counter. "Where's my money?"

"Cut me free and I'll show you."

"That's not how it works." Anger narrowed his eyes.

"Yes, it is." She squared her shoulders. To have a sliver of a chance at escape, she couldn't be bound. Willing her eyes to radiate confidence, she held his gaze unflinchingly. His gun was tucked out of sight, but she knew it was on him. She'd have to move very carefully. He'd proven that he wouldn't hesitate to shoot.

Producing a pocketknife, he wielded it near her neck. "Looks like you've got an old scar here on your throat." The blade touched. Pricked. "I could open that back up."

She pulled air through her teeth. "Kill me and you'll never find the money."

He slid the knife slowly down her body, making her tremble and sweat, then slashed through the tape at her wrists.

"Careful." She cringed at his rough haste.

"A little nick's not gonna kill you. Find my money or you'll get more than a nick." He patted her cheek and she recoiled.

She glanced around the cabin, desperate for inspiration as he cut her ankles free. How long could she exploit this bluff? Standing slowly, her long restricted muscles stretched in tingly protest. She pursed her lips, wandered to the trap door, and pointed. "Down there."

"Ladies first."

"I need light."

He produced a small flashlight. "Go ahead, lead me to it."

She caught the edge of her lip in her teeth and tried to ignore a high-voltage shiver. She eased the creaky trapdoor open, then paused.

"Go on," he prodded.

Down she stepped. One step, two. Into cold, clammy, musty air, with Nails at her back. The flashlight beam speared past her, thin and weak, stirring up shadows, dust, and memories.

Old horrors mixed with new.

Fear inflated her lungs. What would happen when she couldn't produce the money? *I won't be leaving this cellar alive.*

"Move it." He gave her a nudge that made her lose her footing. She stumbled onto the packed dirt floor and scanned the crooked wooden shelves. They were bare, but for dirt. On the floor and in the dirt wall were random holes—from Horace's previous searching, no doubt.

The largest hole in the wall, though, was not Horace's doing. She remembered only too well the gaping portal which led to the connecting earthen room where she and Max had spent so much of their captivity.

"It's in there," she whispered, not approaching the spot, merely motioning. His interest was caught by the odd sight, and he shone his light into the cavern.

With a curse, he whipped out his gun and aimed into the depths, demanding, "Who're you?"

"Don't shoot," came a voice from within. "I'm coming out."

Stunned, she watched as Horace climbed out, streaked with dirt, his eyes magnified behind his glasses as he took in the sight of Nails, so huge compared to him.

She shook her head. So he'd come back, broken in, and continued searching, despite Clay's warning. A very bad decision, and she sensed he knew it. He looked like a confused, disheveled old man. Why had she ever been frightened of him? His eyes reflected fear when he looked at Nails. She could relate, and almost sympathize.

"Who are you?" Nails repeated. "And what are you doing here?"

"I'm not doing any harm." Horace's voice wheedled. "Just looking for something."

"You old fool," Nails muttered, not lowering his gun. "You're in my way."

Horace spread his hands. "Please, son—"

His words were severed by a blast from Nails's gun.

The power of the close-range bullet flung Horace back against the wall and threw his hat off his head. Collapsing on the floor, his lifeless hands whapped the dirt.

Charlene shrieked, turned, and bolted up the stairs.

Nails stormed after her in an instant, footsteps thundering. She made it to the kitchen before he reached her. Seizing her hair, he yanked her back, forcing her to look up at him, into eyes of blue flint. "Is my money down there, or not?"

"No!" She'd dragged this out as long as she could, but what was the point? Help wasn't coming.

"No?" He growled. "Then where is it?"

I don't know. I don't know!

She strained with her limited head movement and looked desperately at the door, but it might as well have been a mile away. Defeated, she said the words that would likely get her killed. "I don't know where your money is. I never did!" Anger zapped through her. "Don't you think I'd tell you if I could?"

His nostrils flared, but the logic must have struck him, because he swore and kicked a chair, toppling it. He raged through the room, pulling her painfully with him as he trashed their surroundings. A grown man having a temper tantrum. Things definitely hadn't turned out as he'd planned, and she sensed he'd soon take his wrath out on more than just the furniture.

His teeth clashed together as he faced her. "Then you're useless to me. Useless."

She waited for the gun to plow into her head.

"I could kill you so easily. Maybe they'd even think your convict boyfriend killed you. After all," he paused to kick the wood burning stove, "this is the scene of his crime, isn't it?"

She swallowed and resisted a response.

"I could kill you," he repeated. The muscles of his face twitched and contorted as he stared at her. "But first . . ."

With a frightening glimmer in his eyes, his hands dove back into her hair and he dragged her into the bedroom. "You're gonna have to give me something to make my time here worthwhile." He shoved her backwards onto the saggy bed. The springs squeaked with a bouncy, taunting rhythm. His gaze never left her as he grappled his way onto the mattress after her. Like a savage beast.

Instinctively, she scrambled back, clunking her head on the wall.

He grinned.

Horrified, she tried to hurl herself from the bed, but his beefy arm rammed her back against the thin pillows as he laughed. "Look at your face. I'm really gonna enjoy this." His hands pinned her down.

Dear Lord, no. Blood roared in her ears. Vision flickering, her head tipped back as her body prepared to pass out. The course-haired goat mount hovered on the wall above her, its ugly little beard hanging like a devil goatee, its dead black mouth open in an evil, gloating chuckle, its tongue . . .

She gasped. Her vision cleared. At this angle, she could see that its tongue was not really a tongue at all, but the black, snake-like handle of—

Nails shifted his weight. His hands released her arms and crept down her body.

Lightning quick, she reached up and seized the knife.

Chapter Thirty-Six

*B*lade in hand, Charlene swung left and right in a fevered frenzy. Almost with a mind of its own, the knife ripped through the air, slicing and stabbing at Nails's leering face, his groping hands, his monstrous, tattooed arms.

He backed off her with an enraged howl of pain. She didn't even register his expression through her blind, quivering attack. Crimson blood flashed.

She sprang from the bed and fled the room, still clutching the knife, the hideous, precious, wonderful knife that had saved her from the unthinkable.

Still running, she swiped her keys as she raced through the kitchen. She flew from the cabin and scrambled into her car with hyperventilating sobs.

The knife still trembling in her bloody hand, she hit the lock neurotically. She dropped the weapon on the console and swiped her sticky hands on her jeans before cranking the engine and tearing down the driveway. Her foot slammed the gas. Power thrummed beneath the pedal. Swerving onto the road, she narrowly avoided crashing into a tree.

She was in no state to drive.

But she had to.

Have to get away. Have to get back to Clay.

Other than those few thoughts, her mind was numb with repulsion, refusing to replay the horror of what had just taken place. Tears cascaded from her eyes, and she blinked furiously to see the road that would take her where she had to go.

———

The woman wrenched herself from the edge of the cabin, into the trees, just in time to see the girl burst out the door. Her Corolla hurtled out so wildly, she'd never notice her own vehicle tucked into the brush off the shoulder of the road.

Dissatisfied, the woman pursed her lips and crept forward. What had the girl been doing here? And where was she going now? The GPS tracker had allowed the woman to stay far out of sight to avoid being spotted, but that also meant she was many steps behind. Too many. She'd missed something important.

She skirted the cabin and peeked in a strip of grimy window. Nothing moved inside. The door stood open, so she stepped through.

"Honey?" she called hesitantly, not sure if he was there. Her adrenaline rush dwindled with an unsettling dread. "Honey?"

A moan answered. The bawdy sound mingled with profanity and then, venturing deeper into the cabin, she saw him.

Her hands clapped her mouth and she screamed.

Charlene had no sense of how long she drove before some semblance of rationale crept in and her tears and frantic heart rate began to slow.

He isn't in my car. He isn't following me. He's probably dead. I hope he is.

She noticed her dashboard display for the first time and saw the orange fuel warning light, the needle on empty. Hardly able to process such a simple obstacle, she let a remnant sob escape.

She took the next exit and pulled into a gas station, hating the delay. Although she wanted to personally reach Clay as fast as she could, a 911 call would be the smart thing to do. She would have thought of it sooner if her traumatized mind had been working normally.

Not that she knew exactly where to direct emergency personnel to find Clay in the depths of the vast Lake Michigan woods, but they could start a search. She should let them know where to pick up wretched Nails, as well, she thought with a grimace. And Horace. Poor, foolish Horace.

She tumbled out of her car and tore into the gas station, where she placed her emergency call amidst gawks and whispers on the state of her dishevelment and blood stains. She tuned out everyone but the dispatcher on the line.

In choppy, ragged sentences, Charlene explained the emergency, frustrated that she couldn't make the dispatcher understand instantly. The exchange took too long. She felt an intense need to get to the site herself, to help guide the rescuers to Clay's side. And she had a much longer drive than the local police and rescue team.

Only when she clunked the phone down and started for the door, did she realize she couldn't go far. No purse meant no money. Yet staying here was unthinkable, and everyone's eyes were still glued to her. What were they waiting for? More bad news? She thrust her hands through her hair as she paced, fuming. "I need gas, but I can't pay for it."

"I've got it. Go ahead," said a man as he took out his wallet and headed to the counter.

Dumfounded, she thanked him, then hurried back outside. The transfer of gas felt like eternity. She watched the price rise, the cents zinging by, the dollars plodding, till she finally reached half a tank. Good enough.

As she drove, a string of prayers left her lips—the only thing keeping her from going insane.

Her heart hammered her chest as beautiful scenery flew by. Sunset sky flashed in her rearview mirror. Intense, yet serene. Like a fringe of heaven.

She gripped and re-gripped her wheel.

Let him live. That's all. Just let him live.

The grayness of evening leached the colors from the sky, trying to drain her hope. *Like blood draining away.* Dusk settled in, blurring the edges of scrubby bushes and gaunt trees. By the time she was only a couple miles from the parking lot, the shadows had thickened.

Lights glared in her rearview mirror, suddenly very close. A car on her bumper. The silhouette of someone leaning out the passenger window. *What . . . ?*

With a bang that made her jump, her car lurched to the right, her wheel pulled. Her tire . . . it hadn't popped, it had been shot.

Her fingers shook and tightened on the wheel, fighting for control. Because she had no doubt who was in that car.

It can't be.

But she knew it was. She careened off the shoulder of the road, squealing to a lurching halt. An overhang of light green buds, full of new life, brushed her windshield—tender green fingertips waving goodbye.

She hadn't stabbed him well enough.

He's here. Coming for me.

Somehow, through the petrified realization, her mind worked. If she could escape into the forest shadows and work her way to where Clay was, there would surely be police on the scene by now. Her hand grabbed the knife, and she threw open her door, diving into a sprint. She crashed down a slope of snarly weeds, running for tree cover, but she didn't make it.

He grabbed her.

No, not he.

She.

The woman wrenched her around and Charlene caught sight of waxy coral lips as the woman twisted her wrist and knocked the knife from her hand. So easily, as if she'd expected the weapon. It fell to the grass. Still in sight, but unreachable.

Charlene's head pounded in time with her heart. Panic overriding confusion, she fought, but despite the woman's willowy body, she was strong. She seemed to know just how to hold her to cut off her struggle. An odor hit her, the distantly familiar scent of a cloyingly cheap perfume . . .

Her ears perked. Had she caught the crunch of approaching footsteps? Scanning the shadows, the form of a person flicked past her. *Someone's coming!* For one second, her heart leapt. Then the silhouette turned visible, and her hopes plummeted. Not help. Not rescue.

Nails.

He lumbered down the hill toward them. The woman straightened, jerking her forward, presenting her to him. Like a cat proud of a mouse she'd caught. Almost purring with delight. She even had claws, polished cobalt blue. Was she one of the ruthless partners he'd alluded to? But no, Charlene glimpsed a spark in her eyes that was unmistakably personal. The flame of . . . jealousy.

Rivulets of sweat trickled down from Charlene's hairline. *They're going to kill me.*

The woman spoke. "You want to do it, honey, or should I?"

Charlene's tongue sat like a chunk of heavy, moist meat. She forced it to move. "I don't understand."

"You don't need to understand anything." The woman whispered the next words in her ear. "You messed with my man. You're dead."

Suppressing a chill, Charlene pulled her thoughts together. That sultry voice, that smell . . . She was the woman from the bar, back when she and Max had played pool. Charlene thought she'd been watching him with interest, but it was really her . . .

"Not like I didn't give you enough warnings," the woman hissed.

Warnings? Her mind churned. The flyers, the note, the writing

on her car, the photos, the attack on Ben, the hourglass picture . . .
But it made no sense. Her man, as she called Nails, had come after
her, so why . . .

Charlene swallowed hard, realizing. If the woman didn't want to
blame him, she had to blame Charlene. She was expendable. The
woman's heart . . . not so much.

Charlene's eyes flicked to the ground. The knife still lay on the
grass. If she could only grab it. But the woman's hold was too tight.
Unyielding.

Nails stared at Charlene till she met his eyes, then he lifted his
chin and spread his arms. "Look what you did."

She looked. His face, arms, and hands were ripped with wicked
red slashes, like a huge cat had clawed him. She lifted her own chin.
"I should have done a better job."

"Did you hear that?" the woman shrieked, and shook her. "She's
asking for it."

Charlene braced herself. Nails heaved a breath and his shoulders
rose as he stared silently at her.

The woman adjusted her grip, still waiting for permission. "Just
say the word, honey, and I'll kill her. She deserves it; you know she
does." Her words sounded wet, like she was salivating in
anticipation. "Think of how she hurt you. Everything she did to you,
and how she betrayed you. Taking your money and—"

His head jerked. His focus flashed to the woman. "How do you
know about the money?"

She swallowed.

"Answer me, Raquel." His voice demanded it, his tone dark.
Dangerous.

She huffed. "It was all over the news." Hesitance rippled through
her, the fear of her mistake. Her hold on Charlene tightened
painfully. Sharp fingernails pressed. "Old Perigard got robbed.
They knew it was you."

"No, not that." Shadows pulled out the harsh angles of his face.
"How did you know she took the money from me?"

"I—"

He narrowed his eyes. "I didn't tell you."

"You didn't have to." Her voice rose. "I figured it out. I was
watching you, following you both—"

He grabbed her hand and yanked it near his face, eyes widening
with some kind of realization. He flung her hand from him, reviled
her with a foul name, and balled his fists. "It was you. You took it

and framed her."

"No, honey—"

He bared his teeth and lunged for her. As she threw up her hands to ward him off, Charlene ducked and rolled.

"I was keeping it safe for you." The woman's voice pitched high and piercing. "I only wanted us to be together and—" She gasped.

Turning, Charlene saw he'd rammed her to the ground. The woman's grappling hand tore at the grass and found the knife. The blade flashed up at him, but he seized it, wrested it from her, and tossed it out of reach.

The woman shrieked as he wrestled her.

Charlene wheeled and ran.

―――

Spitting, he cursed the interfering woman. Cursed all women. Nothin' but trouble, with their conniving, double-crossing ways, luring, then striking. He'd realized the truth the instant he saw her fingernails. Bright blue.

In all the time he'd watched the girl, she'd never sported painted nails. She didn't grow them into ugly long claws, either. Unlike Raquel, flashing her talons.

It had been her broken fingernail at the site of his stolen money. She'd planted evidence to convict the girl, but left her own to tell the truth. It enraged him that he hadn't figured it out sooner. She must have swiped the pearls as well. Greedy wench.

He twisted her arms hard, almost breaking them, and felt no remorse. She'd always been too needy. The prison must have been downright desperate when they'd hired this pitiful mess as a CO. Her with her clumpy mascara and plastered on lipstick, tortured straw hair. Beggin' for attention.

He'd seduced her so easily, charming her with everything she wanted to hear, and she was stupid enough to believe him.

Even when the admins got wise and she lost her job, she still wrote to him. He liked getting letters, and she sent money, so he humored her. But if he'd known she'd try to stick to him like a leach once he got out, he'd have sent her death threats.

And stealing his money? She'd crossed the line, no matter her excuse. Keeping it safe for him? Bull. Never believe a woman. Liars, all of them.

His lips curled, despite the painful cuts. He gave her a head-rattling shake.

She gasped for breath. "I helped you! And when you were burning with fever, I took care of you, feeding you, mopping your vomit, making sure you—"

"I never asked for your help. Never needed it." The fact that she'd found him in his trailer infuriated him. It was supposed to be impenetrable.

"All I did was follow you," she said smugly, as if reading his thoughts, "that night you robbed Perigard. I saw you bury the money. In the ground, like a Neanderthal." She sniffed disdainfully. "But that's not when I took it." Her voice trembled. "I thought once I had our baby, you would finally come back to me, that you'd see—"

"I told you we were through. The first time you came to me with your lies."

"They weren't lies, and you know it. I can prove it. The paternity test—"

"You're pathetic."

Anguish flashed in her eyes. "I hate you."

"What'd you expect, hookin' up with a con? Happily-ever-after?"

For once, she appeared speechless.

"You did, didn't you?" He laughed in her face.

Her features mashed together as she struggled in his grasp. "Everything I did for you when you were sick, and I stayed with you all that time until contractions started and I had to leave, and you kept calling out for that other woman. That girl. *Beth.* Charlene Eliza*beth.*" She spat the name out hatefully.

"Shut up." He shook her. "You don't know anything."

"Don't I? I saw you watching her, wanting her. I saw you at her school talking to her. I saw you visit her in her condo in the middle of the night. I lost you both for a little while, but then she came back for her car, and I followed her. I knew it would only be a matter of time till she led me to you again. And she did. She helped you rob her Grandfather. I could have called the cops on you, but I never did." Her raving voice turned desperate. "Doesn't that mean something?"

"Means you're a fool."

Only one thing mattered. He leaned close, smelled her stinkin' perfume. "Where is it, Raquel? My money?"

Her face twitched in the shadows, her eyes shiny black-and-white orbs. "You should have been there. She was so beautiful, our

baby. Perfect. Like a little doll. She even had your nose. But she—"
Raquel choked and sobbed—"she was stillborn. She—"

"Like I care." Tramp that she was, her kid could have been anyone's. "Where's my money?" He shook her again.

Her face hardened, the wet sheen of her eyes icing over, even as she panted pitifully. "You'll never find it."

He swore.

She almost smiled through her agony. "Beg me."

Frustration raged inside him. He clutched her throat and pressed. "Tell me!"

Her eyes rolled. She let out a croak.

A ripple of pleasure ran through him. Here they were again. Like that night in his cell. She'd found the picture of Charlene under his mattress and gone crazy with jealousy. She wouldn't shut up with her wild accusations, so he made her shut up. Till the other COs rescued her.

He'd later told her he was sorry, to get what he wanted from her, but he wasn't.

Here was his chance to finish the job. So much power in his hands. And her neck, so delicate. So easily collapsible.

He lessened the pressure slightly. *Stay in control. Can't kill her yet.*

She wheezed, and her voice came out abrasive. "You would have made a horrible father, anyway. You never had one to show you how to be a real man, you son of a—"

He forced her silent, fingers tightening around her throat. Her bug eyes bulged and he started counting the seconds till she'd be dead.

But the money.

He released his grip.

She sucked in a strangled wisp of air. "You must be just like your mother," she managed in a gravelly voice, "the weakling who killed herself."

He snarled and threw her from him. Harder than he meant. Her head whapped something.

A rock.

Hands quivering, she gurgled weakly, then fell quiet. Blood trickled from her head, staining her pale hair.

"Raquel!" He jumped up and grabbed her head, covered the sticky flow. "Wake up!" he shouted in her face.

―――

Wake up? But why?

She tuned out the unpleasant voice, which was easy to do since it filtered in from so far away, through a haze of pain.

And she was so tired . . . so tired of hurting and struggling. She pictured her child, her peaceful little angel baby with the chubby limbs that wouldn't wiggle and the eyelids that wouldn't open, and she longed for her, with a yearning stronger than any she'd ever felt. Where was she? Where was she?

Not here.

Nothing left for her here. She would go where she was wanted, where she could finally be loved.

If she could only find her way. . .

―――

"Tell me where my money is!"

Her face smoothed. Oblivious. Serene.

"Tell me, Raquel!"

But she didn't.

She couldn't.

No!

He kicked her, the force jarring her limp body, increasing the blood. He paced around her, boiling. She'd escaped after all, taking her secret with her.

He scraped his fingers over his scalp. If he didn't have the money, he had nothing. Nothing. He couldn't live with the emptiness. He had to have something . . . he looked up and saw the girl running, past a dune, into the woods. Free.

He shouldn't have looked. Her spiral curls flashing in the moonlight, taunting and teasing. Tempting. Luring . . .

He licked the corner of his mouth, tasted blood, felt the cut sting. Sharp and flaming, like his tattered hands and arms. She'd cut right through the nail tattoos. Destroyed them. His fingers curled, knuckles crackling.

He had a choice. He could let her go, or he could make her pay.

Really not much of a choice at all.

Consequences.

She needed to taste the consequences.

―――

As Charlene charged off into the woods, she thanked God that Nails's focus had changed, delivering her from his wrath. She tried not to think about the woman, Raquel, and what her fate might be.

Her thoughts returned to Clay, urgency rekindling. She was still too far away. These woods too empty and quiet. She had to believe emergency personnel had found him. That it wasn't too late. If not . . . her mind flashed a picture of him alone, bleeding to death in the black woods, if he wasn't dead already.

Don't let it be too late.

She had to hold onto that shred of hope. The alternative . . . She couldn't face it.

But as she progressed through the trees, she heard no distant wail of police cars, fire trucks, or ambulance. Nothing.

Nothing.

Terrible doubts assaulted her. Had the dispatcher not understood the directions?

"Clay!" she cried into the shaky shadows. "Clay, answer me! Where are you?" She couldn't be close enough, but she called his name anyway, as if she could draw him to her. She pushed aside the scratchy twigs, stumbling as she plowed ahead. Moonlight filtered onto moss and ferns like a weak night light.

Where is he? God, where is he? Lead me to him. Let him be okay.

The restless lake wind whooshed noisily above her in the chattery pine boughs. She rubbed her stinging eyes.

Behind her, a branch snapped, and her hands stilled.

A deep chuckle bounced through the air and coiled her spine.

No. Raw fear jolted her body, seizing her muscles.

"Leave me alone!" she screamed into the darkness. "I already called the cops. For Clay. They'll find you!"

"We're not close enough," came Nails's rough voice. "And you're too late. All they had to do was cart him off in a body bag. They're long gone by now."

No, he's lying.

"There's no one here now but you . . . and me. Sweetie."

Frantic, she flailed forward, shoving branches. Twigs lacerated her hands. But as she fled, the splintering and snapping sticks betrayed her location. "Help!" she screamed. "Help!"

His voice was too clear, too close. "You may not have swiped my money," he paused to pull in air, "but you've still gotta pay for what you did to me. I'll catch you." A branch cracked heavily, almost at her side. "And when I do, I won't shoot you." He heaved another breath. "But you'll want me to."

Her panic exploded. Knowing it was just a matter of time till he reached her, she scrambled for a thick stick, a weapon she could use like a club. There. Perfect. As if it was sent by God. *Dear God, let it be enough.*

How can it be enough? scoffed a despairing inner voice. *Even the knife wasn't enough.*

Still, she clutched the branch and ran, a desperate race for her life as every sinew of her body strained for survival.

She wished Nails would speak again so she'd have a clue how close he was. If she could only find the cops—

She stumbled. The ground suddenly loosened and slid. Arms whirling for balance, she tumbled off the side of a weedy embankment and thudded onto sand.

Heaving herself up, she reclaimed the branch and realized in horror that she'd lost the merciful shelter of foliage. Moonlight illuminated her, spotlighting her on the beach. Her eyes swept up and down the stretch of sand, but there was no rescue in sight.

Nails crashed out of the woods and came for her, his menacing figure growing larger by the second.

Sheer speed would be the only thing keeping her from him now. But her adrenalin waned, begging her to rest. The lakeshore stretched like a race track before her, smooth and endless. Endless as this nightmare. How could she, with her small muscles and low stamina, ever outrun powerful Nails?

But he was knife wounded. Even if it hadn't been fatal, it was something. He'd lost blood. He had to be drained and weakened.

Clay's words rushed at her from the past. *"You survived Abner. You can survive anything this world throws at you."*

Maybe she could, maybe she couldn't.

But she had to try.

She set her teeth and took off, still gripping her stick, though she wondered if she should drop it, if she could run faster without it. Her calves and thighs clenched and burned, strong from so much bike riding. Her feet pounded the beach, but the loose grains tugged at her shoes, slowing her. Kicking up sand, she aimed for the firm wet traction near the water.

She didn't reach it.

As if out of nowhere, Nails leapt in front of her. A bloody cut gleamed clear across his cheek to his chin. His eyes smoldered and his voice came out ragged. "Time to finish what we started back at the cabin."

With all she had left, she drew back and cracked him with her stick. Something dropped in the sand—his gun? She couldn't tell. The blow stunned him.

But it wasn't enough.

Not nearly enough.

"Why you—" He grabbed the stick, wrestled it from her, and downed her with a shocking wallop to her side. Doubling over in pain, her hands and knees plowed into sand. Grains flew up and peppered her eyes.

He flung her to her back, knocking the wind from her. His hands circled her throat and pressed till she gagged. Her fingers clawed at the sand.

The heat of his breath hit her face. "You're dead."

She wheezed for air, sure she was about to pass out, almost welcoming it . . . the stars swam above like ice chips in a midnight sea. Then the vision was blocked by a big, venomous face. Nails. He leaned close, red eyes bulging. "I'll teach you—"

Her hands whipped up, flinging fists of sand into his wild eyeballs.

With a roar, he pulled back to rub at the gritty grains cutting his vision.

It bought her a moment, one precious moment.

She scrambled for the thing that had fallen . . . was it? Could it be? Yes, it was. His gun!

She clutched it and wobbled to her feet, retreating countless stumbling paces back. With a shaking hand, she lifted and aimed.

Already, he was up, lunging toward her, roaring like a bloodthirsty barbarian.

Eyes flinching closed, she fired.

Chapter Thirty-Seven

She missed.

The bullet zinged past him like a playful sprite, shooting up a distant, harmless sand spray.

Charlene ran, gained some precious distance, then turned to see him charging. She had time for only one more shot, if that. Her trembling hands faltered. *I can't do it.*

"Yes, you can." It was as if she heard Clay speaking to her. From the dead.

She choked on a sob.

"Be strong."

She heaved in a shuddering breath.

"Focus, Charlene. Use both hands. Steady." It was like his hands came over hers, calming and guiding. *"You gotta really aim, just like you practiced. That's right. Keep your eye open. Put the pumpkin on the fencepost."*

Ludicrous laughter bubbled.

"Focus, Charlene."

Swallowing hysteria, she planted her feet and braced her stance.

"Ready?"

She lined up her sights and whispered, "Ready."

Both hands firm on the grip, her finger squeezed the trigger.

Her arms and shoulders absorbed the recoil as the bullet burst forth. With a blast of ferocious speed and beautiful precision, the lead bullet buried itself in Nails's chest.

Like a plunging needle from his nightmares, the pain pierced him, then exploded, agony flashing through his body. Tearing out his breath.

He fell to his knees, broken. Rattling. Gasping.

Dying.

He wasn't invincible.

Wasn't tough as nails.

His desperate eyes found her, tried to hold on. She was a vision, wavering moonlight glimmering on curls.

Beth . . .

So sweet and innocent. He tried to reach for her. She could save him.

Her voice was urgent. *"Have you been baptized yet, Lance? It's not too late. It's never too late until—"*

No. It wasn't her. Couldn't be. She held a gun. His chest throbbed. She wouldn't have done this to him. His head dropped to the sand.

He still heard her voice babbling on. *". . . the martyrs' souls were washed clean with baptism of blood."*

Blood? He almost laughed. Plenty of blood here. But he was no martyr. Not even close.

His mouth gaped, but he couldn't breathe. Wheezing, guttural noises clogged his airway, so deep in his throat, choking a silent sob.

Why had he pursued her? Why had he thought it mattered?

His soul was ripping from his body. If he could only hold on . . . but he had nothing. Nothing to hold on to.

No strength. It was gone. What good were muscles when his blood was draining?

He'd never really had anything.

All the vengeful retaliation—it gave him no satisfaction. And all the money, all the accursed money that meant everything to him. Now he knew. With harsh, acute, blinding clarity.

It's nothing.

He couldn't bring it with him. He knew he was going, and it wasn't the money he'd burn with desire for.

The hole in him grew, opening, cavernous . . . a gaping crater that couldn't be filled. Not ever. He'd had his chance.

"Actions have consequences." Mr. Callaghan's stern voice echoed from the past. Curse the man. He'd known. He'd warned him.

Consequences.

He felt it coming.

Judgment.

Fear—that weakness he thought he'd long ago exterminated—returned. Raw and real. Trembling, he tried to swallow, but couldn't. Tried to hide. Couldn't. His eyes squeezed shut.

The hole in him swelled. Black and deep. It ached and throbbed and burned with unquenchable pain. Excruciation. *Excruciation.*

Oh, he could feel, after all.

He could feel. So much. Too much, and too late.

I'm sorry . . .

⸻

His ghastly noises faded. His writhing stilled.

The gun once again trembling in her hands, Charlene grappled with it and backed away from the sight. From the blood. Oozing and spreading, the dark liquid slowly saturated the sand around Nails's body.

He lay, a bulky mound of flesh and bone, blood and muscle. She stared at him for the longest time, thinking nothing, just making sure he wouldn't get back up. He wouldn't fool her again.

He flinched.

She aimed the gun.

His head twitched. Her sweaty hands clutched the gun grip, unable to end the traumatic standoff. Her teeth clamped till her jaw ached.

Her mind recoiled from wrapping around the reality of everything that had happened, and where it left her.

Alive, but alone.

And now that she'd allowed the thought, tears coursed down her face and she dropped to her knees, her delayed relief tempered by pain. An agony of loss.

She had sensed Clay with her so strongly, that now she knew. She had no doubt . . . he had passed on. It was as if God had allowed him to help her, one last time. A final farewell.

The sacrifice of his life, for hers.

Tears slipped hot over her cheeks as pulsations of sorrow wracked her body. Near her, lively waves lapped and surged and retreated. Reliable. Steady. Washing the sand, refining the grains.

She and Clay had come so close . . . but some things were never meant to be.

I'll never see him again.

Not in this life, anyway.

Each beat of her heart was a stabbing pain. Mocking her with vitality. She had her life, but she didn't have him to share it with. *Please, God.*

Sometimes the answer is no.

No.

The moonlight covered her with a silvery shroud of mourning

while the waves continued their constant *shush-shush*, as if to soothe and comfort her.

But she couldn't be comforted. She couldn't. Not now. Perhaps never.

She knew what love was.

She knew it, too late.

A lonely life stretched out ahead of her, bleak and unbearable. How could she go on? How could she possibly—

You're stronger than you realize.

I'm not, I'm not.

You are.

———

At last, Charlene wiped her tears and lifted her chin. Finally convinced that Nails wasn't going anywhere, she picked herself up.

The gun hung heavy in her hand, but she didn't let it go. It was all she had left to hold onto.

So this is how it ends.

Desolate, with dry salty tear trails itching her cheeks, she turned and trudged up the sand, toward the embankment of tall prairie grasses. The stalks sashayed in the cool night breeze, calling to her.

She even heard her name.

"Charlene!"

A silhouetted figure cut through the graceful grasses with an unstable, crazy haste and skidded down the hill to her side. A hand clamped her arm. "Charlene, thank God! Are you okay?"

Her lips trembled as she drank in the sight of him. Living. Breathing.

Clay.

The moonlight in his desperate eyes revealed guarded relief mingled with worry. "Tell me you're okay."

"I am," she breathed. "So much more than okay. Unless I'm dreaming . . ." *Don't let it be a dream. Let it be real.* She almost reached for him, then stopped short at the sight of his left arm tight at his side, strapped securely immobile in a black sling.

"The bullet got me in the shoulder. Thanks to you sending help, they patched me up at the hospital. I'll live."

His stance faltered. She peered closer at his drained face and saw a sheen of sweat. "Shouldn't you still be there? And how did you get here?"

"A cab. I wasn't supposed to leave." It looked like he was trying not to wince. "But I had to . . . find you . . . I saw your car." His eyes looked over her to Nails's inert form and his voice dropped. "You did that?"

She nodded and looked down at the gun, suppressing a shudder. She'd done what she had to. The corner of her lip tugged with emotion. "You taught me well."

He wrapped his right arm around her and pulled her close, speaking into her hair, his voice cracking. "I'm so glad you're all right." There was amazement in his tone, displaced by angry regret when he added, "I should have been here to help you."

"But you did help me. You were with me." She leaned back just enough to place her hand over her heart and whisper, "Right here."

Looking in his eyes, she finally spoke the words that had been trapped, frozen within her for far too long. "I love you, Clay."

A funny look came over his face, as if he was trying to smile, but his eyes went wonky. He started to sway, and she heard him mumble something as he rubbed his head, obviously dizzy.

She shoved her shoulder under him. "Here, lean on me. We've got to get you back to the hospital." She braced herself under his weight as his arm dropped around her. With difficulty, they plodded, staggering, slipping in the sand until they made it up over the grassy rise and on through the trees, past the dunes, and through more foliage.

She drew up short, and Clay stumbled, as her eyes fixed on a sight she didn't want to see. Raquel's lifeless form lay sprawled, mostly hidden in the weeds, but Charlene had known where to look. She shivered. *Lord have mercy.*

Lurching in relief up to the road at last, Clay and Charlene slumped inside the waiting cab. "To the hospital. Hurry!" she ordered the driver. "Hang on, Clay. Just hang on. What were you thinking leaving the hospital like that?"

"They told me—you called me in," he said woozily, his head dropping back against the seat. He inhaled a deep, painful sounding breath. "They—couldn't get ahold of you. To let you know they'd found me." Perspiration beaded his brow. "I knew—you'd come back looking—if you could—"

"Shh," she stopped him from laboring on. "Just rest."

She looked at the cab driver. "I need you to make a call." Hearing her account, he obligingly phoned in the body on the beach, as well as Raquel, while transporting them to the hospital.

Once there, nurses chided Clay for leaving without the doctor's approval. Charlene doubted he registered the scolding, but then he grinned at her before passing out.

Hours later, after police had been in and out of the room countless times with questions and concerns, he awoke groggily, looked around, found her sitting beside him, and rasped, "Say it again."

"What?" She leaned closer.

"Say it again."

Suddenly, she knew. Her lashes lowered shyly. "I love you."

He fell back asleep with an adorable smile on his face.

"You shoulda carried a gun like I told you." Sam burst into the hospital room and scraped a chair to the bedside, directing his words at Clay's slumbering form. "Don't you wish you'd listened to me now?" He leaned forward, studying Clay intently. "You really sleeping, or just ignoring me?" When there was no answer, Sam expelled a breath and shook his head. "He's gonna be the death of me yet."

Charlene listened, half amused and half achingly touched by Sam's concern as he peppered her with questions, his gaze never leaving Clay's face.

At last, he turned and narrowed one eye at her. "You don't look good."

And you have a tendency to point that out. She smiled. "Maybe not, but I feel fine." *More than fine. Clay's alive. He'll be okay.*

She needed nothing more.

They stared at him silently for a long while, both, she believed, relishing the simple sound of his breathing. His messy hair stood out dark against his pale forehead, as did his scattering of freckles. His thick lashes rested stark against his skin.

"I can see Margaret in him." Sam spoke the words so low, she wasn't sure if she was even meant to hear them.

But she whispered, "Me too."

There was a long pause, then Sam surprised her by saying, "I met her in high school." Another pause. His chair creaked. "Three years of classes and studying and exchanging small talk. Wasn't much, but it added up, somehow. I wanted to ask her out, but I was a stupid kid back then." He leaned forward. "I waited too long. When Grant Morrow, the star football player, the guy with the scholarship, moved in on her, I lost my chance. He moved fast. They married right after graduation."

Sam shifted his feet. "I still saw her sometimes. Around town. At church. But I tried not to notice her. Years passed." He halted, and Charlene thought that was the end of his odd reminiscing, but he went on like he hadn't stopped.

"One night I was working in the church basement, fixing the nativity stable, and when I went out to the snowy lot, there was another car. I saw her in there, sleeping. I tapped on her window to ask if she was okay. She looked like she'd been crying. Her car wouldn't start, and she was freezing. I told her to warm up in my car while I gave hers a jump start.

"I should of left it at that, but I got back in my car to tell her hers was ready, and she broke down. Like she just needed someone with an ear to listen. She went on and on about Grant. How an injury killed his football career. How he turned bitter and stopped going to church, turned to drinking. Couldn't hold down a job. Couldn't hold down his temper. I only wanted to comfort her, but . . ." He paused. "That was the night."

He gripped the back of his neck. "After that, she stopped coming to church. I couldn't stand that it was my fault. Her faith was all she'd had left, and I took it."

Charlene frowned. "But she got it back. You know that, right?"

"Thank God for that, but no thanks to me. I went away, joined the army. Traveled more than anyone needs to in one life. Always trying to forget her. I never did. I should of, or I shouldn't have gotten married."

"Married?" She couldn't hide her astonishment. "I didn't know—"

"Why would you? I never told you." Sam eyed the ceiling. "Right after my wedding, I heard Margaret's husband died, and all I could think was, God sure has some timing." He shook his head, gave a short laugh. "If I hadn't married, we could have finally had our chance." His voice went gruff. "Not what I should have been thinking."

He looked at the floor. "My wife deserved more than I had to give her. She stuck with me a long time. Then one day about ten years ago, she left."

Charlene didn't know what to say.

Sam leaned back against his chair and sighed. "I made mistakes. I have regrets." His gaze lifted to the bed. "But Clay will never be one of them."

Charlene sat alone beside Clay when the door opened and a nurse stepped in, one she hadn't seen before. The woman wore green scrubs and her curls were synched in a ponytail. Attractive and slim, she appeared to be in her late thirties. She stopped near Clay's bed and fingered a golden cross necklace while she watched him sleeping.

She turned to Charlene, almost apologetically, and Charlene's heart seized. Surely, there wasn't bad news. Surely—

Charlene braced herself. "Are you one of Clay's nurses?"

"Oh, no. I'm in pediatrics."

Then why are you here?

The nurse blushed. Her gaze fell to her fingers. "I'm sorry." She inhaled and met Charlene's eyes. "They said . . . they told me you were the one who—who shot him. Lance Harding."

Nails? Her spine stiffened. "That's right."

"I'm sure you don't want to talk about it." The nurse moistened her lips. "I'm sorry, but I need to know. Do you think . . . he suffered a lot? Or did he—did he die quick?"

Raquel flashed through her mind, and Charlene wondered if she should be afraid of this woman. She eyed the call button near Clay's bed.

But the woman's face reflected nothing alarming, only gentle concern. Charlene knew she should be repulsed by her question, but even as she thought of Nails's knife wounds, something kept her from mentioning them. She swallowed. "No. No, I don't think he suffered much. He died quick."

A wispy sigh escaped the woman. "Good." Her lips pinched. "I'm sorry. It's just . . . he wasn't always like that." A sad ghost of a smile touched her mouth. Her gaze grew distant. "I knew him once, a long time ago. When he was . . . just a boy."

Her lips moved silently. She touched the cross necklace again, and Charlene had the oddest feeling she was praying. As she turned to leave, Charlene caught sight of her nametag: *Beth.*

Chapter Thirty-Eight

*T*he scent of dirt and freshly cut grass in the sunbaked June day created a warm, heady mixture of new life and hope. An odd thought, in a cemetery. But then again . . . when one believed in resurrection and life everlasting, perhaps it wasn't that odd at all.

"We'll see her again someday," Charlene said softly.

Clay nodded beside her and took her hand. His left arm was still in the sling, but he was healing well, and in another month or so, he'd be free of the restraint.

She knew it had taken a lot for him to work through the pain of the secret his mom had kept from him, but she never doubted he would. He was that kind of person. Understanding. Forgiving. Good.

And today, they were finally planting Margaret's flowers. Clay cupped the roots of the daisies in one palm while dirt sprinkled through his fingers. He set the plant lightly into the trench Charlene had dug in front of the headstone. He took care to hold the stems upright while she mounded dirt over the roots. As she patted the soil in place, she remembered last year, when she had fled to this spot and fallen asleep. Recalling her strange dream, she recounted it to Clay. "And I still can't figure out how I got in the church basement, unless I sleepwalked. Do you think I could have?"

"No."

"Why not?"

"Because I was there. I brought you into the basement."

Her jaw dropped. "You? But how—"

"I came to visit my ma's grave. Never expected to find you here." He scratched the back of his neck, leaving a smear of dirt. "I couldn't stay, but I couldn't leave you here like that. That's when I first broke my promise to stay away from you. And I knew I was in trouble."

She stared, astonished. So her dream had held a grain of reality—as if her heart had sensed him, even as she slept. She paused to brush off her hands, then slipped a card out of her purse and held it carefully by the edges. "And this holy card? On my windshield with a rose?"

The corner of Clay's mouth pulled. "Guilty."

"But why?"

He gave a rueful look, as if she should know. "You were going through a tough time."

She shook her head and laid the card on Margaret's grave, in front of the flowers. Awe, mixed with deep appreciation, swirled within her.

Her hand found his and squeezed. She felt the rough bandage beneath her fingers and brushed the dirt from it, frowning. She'd gotten so used to seeing it, but . . .

He caught her look. "What?"

"You don't need the bandages anymore, you know. You never did."

He frowned grudgingly. "I know." He stared down at his hands for a long moment. Then slowly, he unwound the dirty bandages, revealing the black inked letters that were just that—letters, and nothing more.

Still, he held the cloth strips like he didn't know what to do with them. So she took them and crossed the cemetery, throwing them in the trash. Where they belonged.

Rejoining him, she watered the flowers, then they stepped back to admire the cheery daisies bobbing white and yellow in the breeze.

"Not bad," Clay said.

"Not bad?" She took his hand and smoothed her thumb over the inked skin of his knuckles. "They're beautiful."

And she felt Margaret smiling down on them, agreeing.

"Could you have picked a hotter day to go to the beach?" Charlene wondered aloud on a Tuesday in late August as she helped Clay unload towels, a blanket, and a modest sized cooler from his truck, sweat rolling down her neck. She wasn't complaining, though, and made sure he knew it by her smile. "Look what it does to my hair," she lamented, patting her head. "It's a big puffball."

"But a cute puffball." He gave one of her curls a playful tug. "And those earrings look good on you, by the way." He seized the cooler and heaved it up. Then they walked down through the sandy grass and claimed an isolated stretch of beach as their own.

She peered up and down the strip of endless Lake Michigan

shore. Surrounded by warmth and love and a deep sense of security, her old fears felt long ago and distant, like a fading nightmare displaced by sunny reality.

Nails couldn't steal this day, or any other, from her.

Neither could Raquel—though everything that came to light about the woman had given her a lot to think about. When investigators searched the woman's apartment—in the same building as hers, Charlene had been alarmed to learn—they found pillows stuffed fat with cash. Grandfather's money. In a drawer, they'd found Charlene's pink pearl necklace.

As the investigation proceeded, pieces came together. Apparently, though Raquel had been working as a waitress in a diner, she used to be a CO at the state prison where Nails and Clay had been incarcerated. Clay told her he didn't know the full story—maybe no one but Raquel and Nails did—but he remembered she'd been fired under odd circumstances, right around the time Nails had three years tacked on his sentence. The prison authorities tried to keep it hushed, but something had happened. Some kind of breach of policy.

Clay said rumor on the block had been Raquel and Nails were an item. Until she'd crossed him in some way, and he'd tried to kill her in his cell. If that was true, why she'd gone back to him was a mystery.

But he'd finally gotten her in the end.

And she had no one to care. Charlene thought that was perhaps the saddest part of all.

And the knife . . . it had been sealed in an evidence bag, lying now in an evidence locker. There was no one to claim it. No one to want it. And so eventually, it would be destroyed.

"What are you thinking?" Clay's voice cut into her morbid musing.

She blinked and there was the smile on his face that she'd never tire of seeing. Reminding her this wasn't a day for brooding. Lives had been lost; but by the grace of God, not theirs.

She smiled back at him. Their lives . . . it felt like they were just beginning. "I'm thinking . . . race you to the water!" She took off running.

They splashed each other until they were thoroughly chilled, then sat on a blanket and gazed at the vast lake that seemed to stretch forever. She could have stared at it all afternoon, but Clay lost interest quickly. As he lifted the cooler lid, she laughed. "Hungry already?"

"I'm not getting food." There was a strange tone to his voice.

She watched him lift out something odd, and her forehead puckered. "Is that . . ." She tilted her head and squinted. "Is that a snowball?"

"That's right."

"In *August?*"

"You bet."

"But how? Why?"

"I kept it in my freezer."

She quirked an eyebrow. "There are easier ways to keep food cold. You could just buy ice at the grocery store. You know, like a normal person?"

"That I could. But then, I've never been quite normal." He chuckled, but there was slight apprehension behind the sound. He turned serious, pinning her with steady brown eyes. "This is going to sound crazy, but . . . do you remember this snowball?"

She looked at the icy orb, which was swiftly melting as he held it in his palm. An absurd thought dawned. She dismissed it, only to see him nod as he said, "You left this snowball with me at the beginning of the year. That night I told you I loved you."

"I remember."

Of course she remembered.

He cleared his throat. "You told me when it melted, my feelings for you would be gone. You were wrong." He eased the diminishing snowball into her hands.

Still confused, she nonetheless kept her eyes on the snow melting in her hands, dripping through her fingers, revealing . . .

She gasped. A familiar ring lay wet and shining in her palm. It was the pink pearl one that Clay had caught her admiring back in January.

"The thing is," he said, "my feelings for you are even stronger now, and I need to ask . . ." His husky words paused as he dropped to one knee in the hot sand. "Will you marry me?"

Her eyes riveted to his, genuine love and hope so raw and real in his face. There wasn't a shred of doubt in her mind or heart to give her pause. Her tongue couldn't move fast enough. "I will, Clay. Oh, I will!"

His face broke into a smile. He took her hand in his rough, hard-worked ones and slipped the ring on her finger. Her hand trembled with giddy joy. More than the ring, she loved the fact that he had realized how much it meant to her.

"It's perfect. Still a little chilly," she added with a laugh. "How long was it in that snowball?"

He smiled as if she should know.

"Not—" her heart skipped a beat— "ever since that night?"

"I bought it right after you ran away from me." His voice deepened. "I knew then, impossible as it seemed, that we would end up together, somehow. Someday."

"But . . . how? After everything you said that night, and I didn't even tell you I loved you."

A crooked grin split his face. "But you never said you didn't."

"You believed in us." Her voice caught.

"I did. I always will." He drew her close.

It felt so right. She thought of the thorny path it had taken to get here, and how God had worked their pain and suffering to reach this wondrous and healing moment. "After everything, I can't believe we're finally . . ." Her effervescent rush of words evaporated as Clay touched her face.

His thumb grazed her cheek a moment before his lips claimed hers, strong and tender, and her heart burned with love.

"Now that," he murmured with deep satisfaction, "was definitely no pity kiss."

Epilogue

Eight months later . . .

"*I* knew I should have put my hair up, I just knew it. Why didn't I? Now it's too late." One hand indisposed by a bridal bouquet, Charlene grappled awkwardly with her veil, which whipped and tangled wildly with her curls. She stood outside the doors of Creekside's Catholic Church, waiting for her cue, and her nerves cavorted like the wind wreaking havoc on her carefully tamed and sprayed hairstyle.

"You look fine," Max said beside her, not at all concerned.

"I need to look better than fine." Her voice shrilled unnaturally. "Today, everything has to be perfect—"

"It's time," signaled the coordinator, heaving open the doors.

Max grinned and gave her arm a tug. "Chill, Char."

Her nerves seized. As if in a trance, she ascended the steps, and somehow she didn't trip on her long white gown. Still in turmoil, she entered the church on Max's arm, glad for his steadying grip and even-paced stride. The scent of roses hit her, and organ music ushered her forward. Though the large church was sparsely peopled, every face turned her way.

But suddenly, the only face that mattered was Clay's. There he stood, all the way down past the tulle pew bows at the end of the aisle, waiting for her. Steady. Strong. Confident.

She leveled her gaze and focused on his reassuring smile, and as she glided up the aisle, her nerves smoothed, becoming fluidly serene as the satin of her gown.

Their day was finally here. Her mother's string of pearls draped her throat, the perfect complement to her ring. Clay wore a boutonniere of a single daisy in honor of his mother. Beside him, Sam stood proudly as his best man.

Her walk complete, Max released her with a smile and took his place beside Sam.

Then she and Clay stood before the altar, ready to make their vows before men and God.

"Stop!" boomed a voice.

All heads swung to the aisle. Grandfather stormed up the white runner, his face red and splotchy.

Charlene pulled in a bracing breath. She should have seen this coming. They should have placed guards at the door.

Instinctively, she clutched Clay's arm as she pictured Grandfather yanking her down the aisle in disgrace. At least he hadn't brought Frank.

Too close to her now, his outraged tone shook her like the dark tree branches shuddering behind the stained glass windows. "Move away from him, Charlene."

"No." Maybe it was just her jaded imagination, but she easily envisioned Grandfather yanking out a gun and shooting Clay dead.

She tried to shield Clay, but he moved her aside gently and stepped protectively in front of her. "You're going to have to leave, Mr. Perigard," he said firmly.

"Get away from my granddaughter, you worthless excuse for a life." Grandfather threw a scathing look over his shoulder at the guests. "How dare you all take part in this abomination!"

He fired a gnarled finger at Clay. "He has no business setting foot in a church. He's a criminal, a convict. Worthless. Just read his knuckles," he added spitefully.

Charlene caught a rustle of movement over her shoulder and glanced back to see Father Grady's authoritative figure. A measure of peace descended upon her. The priest's solemn gaze moved past Grandfather to the congregation. He gave a simple, almost imperceptible nod, and two burly men rose, as if understanding his unspoken direction to remove Grandfather immediately.

But Max and Sam were already on it. In their groomsmen tuxedos, they hustled to Grandfather's side. Sam, looking ready to throw a punch, said dangerously, "Watch it, old man. That's my son you're talking about."

"Get off me," Grandfather growled, trying to shrug out of their grasps, but Max and Sam held him securely by his upper arms. The two burly men joined them and, while the guests remained stunned, all four men began forcibly escorting Grandfather down the aisle.

"You're all blind fools," he yelled. "If you had any sense, you'd run that lowlife out of town, just like I ran him out of mine!"

In the pews, little Gabriella started crying in Brook's arms.

"You're the one who needs running out of town," Brook spoke

341

up sharply.

"That's right," agreed another guest. "The nerve! Who do you think you are, crashing in here—"

"So rude," chimed in an old lady.

"I'm Maximillian Perigard," Grandfather roared, "and I forbid this wedding to take place!"

"Get out of here, old man!"

"Clay's a good guy," called out another guest.

"Ten times the man you are, Mr. Perigard."

All the guests began raising their voices in Clay's defense, and their vocal support astonished Charlene as Sam and Max dragged Grandfather out the door.

"Forget him, dear," Fannie, from the fabric store, called to Charlene. She flicked her hand. "Every wedding has some kind of snafu."

"Don't let it ruin your day," added Charlene's stepmother, Joy. Gwen, her stepsister, nodded.

Encouragement rained left and right. Charlene looked out at the faces, not merely guests, but true friends. Regular loyal customers from the woodshop. Church friends. Even Julie from the Woodfield library. Joy and Gwen had both flown in to be bridesmaids. And Charlene was still stunned to see Brook and Gabriella in attendance.

Adjusting their tuxedos, Max and Sam re-entered the church, ready to guard the doors, but the other two men eagerly stepped up to the task so Max and Sam could return to take their places up front.

Clay squeezed Charlene's hand and raised his brows. "Still wanna marry me?" he whispered.

"I should be asking you that." Her shoulders sagged. "You do realize I'm a Perigard, right?"

"Not for long." He grinned. "Any other dark secrets weighing on you?"

"I clean too much."

"Hardly a secret."

"Max says I'm addicted to ChapStick."

"I'll keep you well stocked."

"And . . ." She averted her eyes. "You should know I've been told my heart is ice."

"And I've been called a worthless excuse for a life. I doubt either one's true."

Point taken. She smiled and recaptured his gaze. "I love you."

"Then what are we waiting for?" His thumb traced hers, and a rush of warmth swept through her veins, thrilling her heart.

Father Grady cleared his throat, and she snapped back to her surroundings.

The ceremony proceeded. The incident that had seemed so insurmountable, shrank to a mere glitch and then glided from her thoughts completely as Clay slipped a smooth gold band on her finger. It covered her scar, and she knew in that moment she would never have to see the ugly blemish again, because she would never, ever, take her wedding band off.

———

After the reception dinner, it was time for their dance. Charlene had relented on her old captivity induced resolve not to allow music at her wedding, but had been adamant about putting particular songs on a "do not play" list. She'd asked Clay to choose the song for their dance, so it came as no surprise when she heard the beginnings of a country tune.

As he took her in his arms, she recognized it—the song she'd been singing and dancing to in the woodshop when she thought she was alone.

She tipped her head back and laughed. "Our song."

His eyes twinkled. "Wanna sing our duet?"

"Wanna scare our guests away?"

Smiling broadly, he twirled her. "I'm ready to leave when you are."

"But you're such a good dancer. I could dance all night."

His brows moved roguishly. "Sounds like an invitation to start stepping on your toes."

———

At long last, with her toes unharmed, it was time to depart. They said goodbye to Max, then someone diverted Clay's attention, and Charlene stood alone beside her brother. Remembering their long ago conversation in the bar, she elbowed him. "Still think I'm too young to get married?"

"Huh?" He wrenched his distracted gaze back to her, and she scanned to see where he'd been looking. At Brook?

Registering her question belatedly, he answered, "Nah, you found who you were looking for."

She smiled as Clay returned to her side. "I did."

And while Clay took her arm, she watched Max approach Brook.

A moment later, Charlene glanced back and saw them dancing together.

———

As Clay drove her off into the night, Charlene rested her head on his shoulder. His right shoulder, not his left, as that one still caused him pain, and likely would for the rest of his life. Not that he ever complained about it.

She ran her fingers along his tuxedo sleeve. "Are you going to tell me yet where we're staying tonight?"

He spoke thoughtfully. "There's this great rustic cabin I know about up north, way back in the woods."

Her head whipped up to face him. "You wouldn't."

"Actually, I couldn't. Since I sold it last year." He winked as she shook her head at his terrible joke. He rounded a bend, took a right, and drove down a quiet, tree-lined street. "And I used the money . . . for this."

He pulled into a driveway. "My mistake. Did I say we'd be staying here? I should have said living. Welcome to our new home."

Her fingers tightened on his arm. "Really?"

"Really."

In the glowing halo of the porch light, she could see the house was painted a soft, sunny yellow, complete with white shutters. No fence bound the yard, which flowed freely in pleasant slopes. Bushes and trees dotted the lawn. Tiny flowers lined the sidewalk, and two wooden chairs sat on the front porch.

"I bought the land last year, and Sam—" he paused—"my dad—helped me build. It wasn't easy to keep it from you, let me tell you, but I wanted it to be a surprise. I can't believe I finally get to show you."

He pressed a button on the visor above him. "First, the amazing garage . . ."

The large white door moved upward to reveal new concrete floor and wooden storage shelves. "Very basic, but I'm sure the floor will be oil-stained and the shelves filled with junk soon enough."

Eager to see everything, she reached for the door handle as soon as the truck halted.

"Hold on." He dashed around the back of the truck to her side, then opened the door and scooped her up.

"Clay, your shoulder!"

He gave an exaggerated wince as he pretended to stagger under her weight. "You did eat a lot of wedding cake."

She almost whapped his shoulder. "You don't have to carry me."

"But I want to." Klutzily bundling the train of her gown, he brought her out of the garage to the front door, then right over the threshold and into the house. Faint scents of paint, varnish, and lumber tickled her nose.

When he set her down, her mind whirled with wonder as she surveyed the cream walls and the gleaming wood floors. Nothing like the palatial spaces she'd grown up in, this place was cozier, homier.

Flicking on lights, he led her on a tour through the living room, a well-organized kitchen, a dining room, a basement workshop, then down the hall to two bathrooms and three bedrooms. No less than one piece of handcrafted wood furniture graced each room.

"One last thing," he said, eager as a kid at Christmas as he tugged her down the hall, through the dining room, and out the sliding back door, "and then we can go back in."

He led her across the cool lawn to a large maple tree, under which sat a bench, a simple wooden park bench.

She reached out to touch it. "It's just like the one you carved at the beach," she marveled, "but bigger."

"And I added something. Right here."

Focusing where he pointed, she saw "C&C" carved into the bench back, encircled by a heart. She traced it with her fingertips. "I love it."

Goosebumps rose on her arms. Chill as the evening was, she sat down, and Clay sank beside her. The silence hummed, no words needed. Stars sparked above. Light shone like honey in the windows of the house.

Our house.

Her heart swelled, and she nestled against Clay's side, holding his hand. Somehow, he still smelled of cedar and varnish and sawdust. She imagined he always would.

A happy sigh escaped her lips. After all the running she'd done in her life, fleeing from pain and sorrow and trouble, how lovely it was to simply sit. To soak in the moment.

"So is your dream home everything you hoped it would be?" He sounded suddenly uncertain, like perhaps he had presumed too much. "I know it needs decorating, but I figured—"

"It's perfect."

"Because you know we could sell it and buy a bigger, better

house now that—"

She shushed him with a touch to his lips. He was referring to the money from Grandfather. Timely as it was, the hefty sum had, by no means, been a wedding gift.

As it turned out, the flash drive which she'd given to the police had ended up causing Grandfather a load of trouble. No wonder he had burst into church so angrily today. His top lawyers had recently whittled his case down to a plea bargain in which he got off the hook by paying a large settlement to Clay.

If he wanted to, Clay could use the money to remove his tattoos. Even then, there would be a sizeable sum left over.

Clay was still going on about the house. "You deserve so much more—"

"No," she spoke the realization with a little shiver. "I don't deserve this, not any of it. Not my life. Not you in my life. It's all an amazing gift from God, a blessing, and all I can do is be grateful. For every single moment."

Night insects hummed as she looked heavenward, her soul surging with gratitude—and the hope that there would be many, many moments yet ahead.

"So we keep the house," Clay said.

"We do." Her eyes returned to the comforting structure, tracing its shape fondly. The color, the size, the yard—they were all perfect, but that wasn't what made the place perfect.

She turned to him and said softly, "This will always be my dream home because you made it. For us. And you built it with love."

"True. Though I gotta admit, the lumber and nails were helpful, too." He grinned, encircled her in his arms, and kissed her.

After a long moment, he drew back and she saw something in his eyes that raised a question. The kiss had been tender, deep, but . . . he shifted and she realized he held something in his hands. A dark leather rectangle. His wallet.

As he opened it and thumbed through the contents, she blinked. "Tell me you're not seriously counting your money right now."

He smiled, but instead of answering, slipped out a grayish paper. When he unfolded it, she recognized newsprint and recalled the article. The one about his sentencing. She spotted his solemn courtroom picture.

Her brow creased and her voice lowered. "You were supposed to throw that out."

He gripped the paper tightly. "First, you need to know. The

whole truth. The other reason I kept it." He angled her way, his knees touching hers. "You."

"Me?"

His thumb slid aside, revealing her own black-and-white newsprint picture. Also solemn. Also from five years ago in the courtroom. He stared at it, the muscles of his throat moving. "I thought this picture was all I'd ever have."

His fingers brushed the small grainy photo before he looked up, amazement in his eyes. "And now here you are."

"No." She covered his hand with hers. "Here *we* are."

Together at last.

As they melted into another kiss, the article floated to the ground, forgotten.

Then he took her by the hand and led her out of the cool darkness of the outside world, into the golden light of their home . . . into the warmth and promise of their new life together.

And they knew they were blessed.

Acknowledgements

This story wouldn't have been possible without the contributions and support of so many, and I thank you all with sincerest gratitude:

The readers of *Frozen Footprints* who were eager for a sequel—you truly motivated me. I hope this novel was worth waiting for. (If so, please consider leaving an Amazon review—even just one sentence—it truly makes a difference and I'll be ever so grateful.)

My husband, for reading and critiquing the manuscript. You know which scenes you inspired.

My children, for the times you let me sit at the computer undisturbed. (An amazing feat.) And to my son, who requested inclusion in the story, someday if you read this, you can find your six-year-old self on page 180. Of course, your sisters are there too.

My sisters Monica and Cassandra. What would I do without you? Thank you for believing I could make this book better when I thought I couldn't. Thanks for all the concrete, remarkable ideas and solutions. You've always been my first readers and my first line of defense against laughable (not in a good way!) writing. Even when your advice was hard to hear, you made it fun. I treasure your honest feedback and credit you both with ensuring this story reached its full potential.

My brother-in-law Ray Czech, for invaluable expertise. I'm honored that you took the time to help me with this project.

My late brother Jerome, for crucial input and insight. You were my Max. I can't believe you're gone. When God called you home, part of my heart went with you.

Thanks also to incredible Catholic fiction writer and dear friend Susan Peek for beta reading with such a skillful editor's eye. And thank you for convincing me to participate in a NaNoWriMo April camp, which forced my brain back in gear and threw my procrastination out the window. If not for you, readers would still be waiting for this book.

Last of all, I thank the Good Lord for this story, as well as for the blessings of every moment of every day.

About the Author

*T*herese Heckenkamp was born in Australia but grew up in the United States as a homeschooled student. *After the Thaw* is her third novel and the sequel to her Christian suspense thriller *Frozen Footprints*.

Therese lives in Wisconsin with her husband and three energetic children. As a busy stay-at-home mom, she fits in writing time whenever she can manage (and sometimes when she can't). She dreams up new stories mostly at night when the house is finally quiet.

Her novels *Past Suspicion* and *Frozen Footprints* have both reached #1 Bestseller in various Amazon Kindle categories, including Religious Drama and Religious Mystery.

Therese looks forward to writing many more novels in the future. Visit her online to share feedback and to keep up-to-date on free ebooks, new releases, and more:

Therese's website: www.thereseheckenkamp.com

Facebook: www.facebook.com/therese.heckenkamp

Twitter: www.twitter.com/THeckenkamp

Book website: www.frozen-footprints.com/sequel

CPSIA information can be obtained at www.ICGtesting.com
Printed in the USA
LVOW10s2151260716

497865LV00010B/217/P